CURTAIN CALLS

Joe Ponepinto

Woodward Press

This is a work of fiction. Names, characters, places and incidents are either the product of the author's imagination or are used fictitiously. Any resemblance to actual events or locales or persons, living or dead, is entirely coincidental. Please see the Notes and Acknowledgments on Page 304 for a further explanation of the creation of this book.

Curtain Calls

Copyright © 2015 by Joe Ponepinto

Woodward Press, LLC, a Limited Liability Company
8933 Dexter Ave., Detroit, MI 48206

woodwardpress.com

All rights reserved. No part of this publication may be reproduced or transmitted in any form or by any means, electronic or mechanical, including photocopy, recording, or any information storage and retrieval system, without permission in writing from the publisher.

Cover design by Dora Badger

For information about permission to reproduce selections from this book, contact the Publisher at permissions@woodwardpress.com.

ISBN-13: 978-1-942797-00-5

For Grandpa Gus

CURTAIN CALLS

Chapter 1
Paris, Saturday, July 25, 1914 – Gus

MAX ZAPF promised them fame. He promised Gus and Jack luxury, a grand tour of the great cities of Europe, traveling in first class rail cars and staying in the best rooms the finest hotels had to offer. They'd have the thrill of rubbing elbows with the elite, dining like royalty on the cuisine of famous chefs, on dishes they'd never seen back in the states and that they couldn't even pronounce. "They're just crazy about Americans," the agent said. "Especially cowboys. You'll get the red carpet everywhere you go. And Paris! Bars that never close, and showgirls—showgirls like you can't believe. I've been there! And friendly too, not like the ones who turn up their noses at you on Broadway." He shook his old stogie at them like a finger and grinned. "Anything you want you can find." The price to experience this dream world? Only a show each night and an occasional matinee, in front of hundreds of adoring fans, fifteen minutes of what they would do anyway, singing and playing the tunes of those lonely, rugged heroes they portrayed, never mind the glitter on their vest and chaps, or that they'd grown up in the city and never seen a cow in person, much less roped one. And the encores, of course. Add six minutes for the two extra songs they'd have to perform because the crowd simply wouldn't let them go. "They'll love you kids," Max had said. "This is your big chance."

But as Gus trudged his way to the Theatre du Vaudeville, he cursed the booking agent for tricking him and Jack. Lies. A bigger helping of them than he'd ever dished out before. He'd played them for saps, and they'd agreed, signing that day and even taking less pay than they earned at the houses in the states. No doubt the agent had taken a greater percentage than usual, and lied about that too.

Gus didn't know much about the old world except that it was a place of ancient languages and customs, and crazy politics, with kings and queens instead of a president. He knew the travel would grind on them, more than usual because communicating with the locals would prove nearly impossible. He felt sure Max exaggerated the tales of women and nightlife, despite his denials, because he always did. But Jack wanted it, had let Max coerce him into believing the glamorous life he craved lay just a boat ride away, and in the end they'd overwhelmed Gus's reservations. Now here they were, enduring sparse crowds and a heat wave that had lasted all week, almost broke, with the money they made in each city barely covering daily expenses. Last night the theater manager said the gate had produced less than expected, and they'd have to hold back wages for a few more days, maybe longer. Already Jack had borrowed money to do who knew what in the hours after the evening shows, and in a couple of days neither one might have enough to afford a decent meal.

The Rue de Clichy yawned before him in the evening sun. Parisians took refuge from the glare in their shops and under awnings, but Gus plodded along the sidewalk as though he needed to prove to them the toughness of Americans—or maybe, considering the way he and Jack had been duped, their stupidity. First class compartments had turned into lower berths, gourmet meals became bar fare—

even the voyage across the Atlantic had forced them to share a cabin that barely looked out above the waterline.

The heat that had afflicted the city for the past week smothered the buildings and streets like a layer of dull varnish, turning simple acts like walking and breathing into chores, and it showed no sign of abating. Just a few steps from the Fromentin he'd begun to sweat through his sack coat and high collar, the banjo case on his back rubbing through the worn fabric and forming, he felt sure, a stain in its shape from his neck to his waist. The bag with the rest of his gear dragged on him like an anchor, making it difficult to keep a steady pace.

The waves of air refracting off the street muted the colors of the buildings he'd hoped to see. But that had been Max talking. The scene didn't look so different from his home in the Bowery, just as old and dirty as the place he and Jack had escaped from, a pall of black ash sprinkled on eaves and windowsills, testament to new industries and the cars and trolleys that drove the horses off the roads. A city was a city, after all, filled with crowds and smells and filth.

Damn you, Max. Bad enough they'd fallen for his line, but to fool poor Kera too? She was like Jack, believing in the dazzle of his promises, completely unprepared for the dangers of the road. Vaudeville life could be rough enough at home with cheats and shysters hanging around every backstage; over here every sort of con artist and gigolo would try to take advantage of her. And then in London, Gus had found the newspapers filled with appeals to young men to join the army—the Germans threatened the continent with war, they said, and the nation had to stand ready. Already Russia and Austria and Serbia—he didn't even know where that last one was—had sent troops to fight. Kera and Jack acted like there was nothing to worry about. For sure they'd get themselves in trouble thinking like that, and Gus had kept an eye on her since England. Jack would have to watch out for himself.

Gus walked faster, ignoring the sweat under his clothes and the stares of the Frenchies gawking at the stranger in their midst. The sooner he could get to the theater, to the relative cool of its dark corridors, the sooner he could relax. Max hadn't said *daily* matinees, and Jack hated them because he had to get up by noon, but as long as the Ballo Brothers had to perform, Gus took solace at being where he really wanted to be, up on the stage, immersed in the songs, playing with Jack and yet apart from him, the focus of the crowd but in another place, one that no one else could access, because none of them could ever understand his music the way he could. When he played the sound transcended his senses. It started in his chest, welling inside until to keep it in would cause him to explode. It radiated out from there, his fingers twitching along the frets, his right hand strumming without his thinking about it, the chords in his throat vibrating as if directed from afar. He closed his eyes when he sang, because he didn't want to share the music with anyone.

Steps from the theater shouts came from around a corner, echoing off the Vaudeville's façade. He could feel the anger in the voices even if he couldn't understand the words. Gus stopped to listen and glanced up at the building. In the shadows of the summer sunset it loomed against the pastels of the sky, five stories of arches and friezes, with a row of stone gargoyles along the top edge, looking like a mausoleum of the arts transplanted from a graveyard—an ancient, malicious demeanor daring, rather than enticing patrons inside. The voices grew louder, their disembodied hatred haunting the evening. At the end of the block Gus slowed, and turned onto the adjoining street to investigate. Two groups of men gestured and posed, lobbing insults across the cobblestones. "Traitre!" "Lâche!" He didn't need to translate. There were seven or eight in each group—men of soldiers' ages, and Gus imagined they squabbled over that war. The paper had reported the French were divided over whether the nation should become involved in the affairs of foreigners. Who wanted the war? Who didn't? They would fight about it now. Later they might stand together on a battlefield and die for each other. In London Gus had tried to cable Max, to see if they should sail home before the conflict became serious, but received no reply.

The hair on Gus's forearms shivered in anticipation despite the lingering heat. Passers-by soon gathered to watch and debate the men's arguments, and assess their fighting potential. The French, Gus had learned, judged everything. He could easily avoid the row, just turn back around and continue on to the theater and let the men work it out for themselves. But something else pulled at him. An urge to fight baited Gus, thumbed its nose, dared him to drop the banjo case and raise his fists. An old urge, not quite subdued. His hands reacted first, as they always did. His left reached for the strap that held the case against his back. The right clenched the handle of his garment bag like a club. He had trained his hands to perform, to express, to defeat the impulse to violence. In time they'd made it easy to play his instrument, to focus on the music and shut out the world, and he took that invitation whenever he could. But his past never completely left him, and now his hands clenched in preparation to fight. Maybe his anger at Max had taken him to this precipice, the troubles here in Europe building until he had to lash out. If the men tumbled close enough he might jump in, forget about the show and the fact that most of them stood taller than him, take his frustrations out on these French and let them see how a Yank could handle himself. Fighting had been necessary once, to survive, but that was years ago, an ocean ago.

He caught himself. He should move back to the main road, hurry to the rear entrance and avoid the trouble. The theater, forbidding as it was, offered sanctuary, a brief escape from his concerns. But he could not bring himself to leave, not just yet.

The men ignored the clinging heat, and the two groups began to circle, still taunting, gauging strengths and weaknesses, like prizefighters at the onset of a bout. Gus could smell their sweat as they moved closer. Finally, one could restrain himself no longer and bolted from his pack into the thick of the other, arms windmilling in rage. His enemies welcomed him with kicks and shoves, and had him on the ground in seconds, their anger boiling. The balance of the first group charged and the grand battle disintegrated into a cluster of awkward wrestling holds, men grappling or lunging in a chaos that spilled from the street back onto the sidewalk. Two men tackled an opponent and pinned him like prey to the pavement at Gus's feet. The victim squirmed on the ground as he absorbed their blows. It was not right, not fair. The threesome contorted until one of the pair had his enemy sitting in a chokehold, and the other began kicking at the defenseless face. Cowards! The code of the street demanded Gus act.

A man among the onlookers pointed and shouted. Before he could react something hard hit Gus in the back and he lurched forward. He tripped over someone's foot and landed on the street, scraping the hands he would have raised against these hoodlums. The banjo, pitched from its case, hummed a soft twang, as though in pain. He struggled to free himself from the leather strap that had tangled around his throat. Gus heard the shrill of a police whistle through his embarrassment. The rioters ran off, leaving the injured behind, and several in the crowd came over to attend to them.

Gus sat alone on the sidewalk. Eddies of heat shimmered in the air, turning Samaritans into specters floating over the fallen. The man who had been kicked lay a few feet away. Welts and spatters of blood covered his face. A woman kneeled next to him, shook her head and touched his brow. Was he dead? Gus focused through the thermals rising from the street as though they would reveal the man's spirit as it left the body. He should go to him, like the others, and at least offer his sympathy. But before he could move, music began playing in his head—a ballad—a song he'd played for himself in those desperate times. He had to get to the theater. Tonight's show started in an hour. Jack and Kera would be waiting.

Inside, amid the chatter of the dressing room, Gus rested the banjo against a stretch of shelf and examined it. The peg for the fourth string had loosened, and it wobbled as he tuned. When he plucked, the note wandered a little. The crowd might not notice, but he would. The discord would assault his focus. It would affect every song, every bar.

He stepped back and stared at the instrument. "Damn this place," he said, catching the attention of an actor a few feet away who had been applying his greasepaint and now stopped to look for the source of the vulgar English.

Gus ran his hand along his forehead. He was still sweating. The atmosphere here made it even more difficult to breathe than outside. The management had crammed the entire cast—men and women—into this narrow corridor, this afterthought behind the stage that Gus assumed had once served as a storage room, and now, for whatever reason, was the main changing area.

To either side of him, as well as behind, the players brushed and primped, and adjusted the seams of their costumes, adding to the claustrophobia. Actors in whiteface practiced soliloquies, comedians snapped suspenders as they delivered punchlines. Dancers' feathers tickled their neighbors' ears when they turned their heads. If they weren't vocalizing from their acts, most of the performers gossiped with each other, adding to the din. There were no lights at the changing stations, and no windows, the only illumination coming from a malevolent-looking chandelier with half its bulbs burned out, hanging on a thin cord like the sword of Damocles from the high ceiling, as though waiting for an act to be booed off the stage and into its meager yellow circle before snapping free and putting the hapless entertainer out of his misery. Another danger. The whole city seemed now to pulse with risk.

"Gus! What happened?" Kera squeezed in between him and the actor, forcing the Frenchman to slide over and eliciting another grimace from him. She turned to the actor as if to apologize, and he offered her a leering, hungry gaze, the kind that said she might find him waiting for her outside after the show.

"Your hand… You're bleeding," she said.

"There was some trouble outside…"

"Are you all right?" Kera moved to examine the injury, but Gus pulled his hands away.

"A fight. I got caught in the middle of it," Gus said. "I was thinking of New York, and Max. I should have gone around, but I wanted to watch. Then it got out of hand and I was on the ground. Pretty stupid of me."

"You poor thing. Are you going to be able to play?"

"The banjo's damaged. Look at it."

Kera ran her fingers along its neck and caressed the strings. He knew she couldn't see the injury those hooligans had caused. "How did you get caught in the fight?" she asked. She looked dreamy, as though his involvement made her see him as some kind of hero.

"Not a fight, really," he said. The scrapes on his hands stung, and he'd have to find a way to soothe them before the performances started. "A protest about the war. The French don't know whether to get in or stay out."

Kera blanched, and drew her fingers to the cameo at the hollow of her neck. "War? Oh, Gus! You mean you were serious? Are we in trouble?"

"If you stay in Paris, then yes." It was the actor she had displaced. "All of Europe is arming."

"Gus, why didn't Max tell us? He should have cancelled the trip," Kera said. "We're not scheduled to leave here for another week. What if we're trapped here?"

He'd read the papers in England without fully comprehending. They wrote about alliances and political maneuverings. If one nation came under attack, the others pledged to fight too. It didn't seem much different from the men in the street. Alone, none of them would dare start things.

"We should cable Max," Kera said. "We should find out if there's anything we can do."

Gus started to explain that he'd done that, but the actor interrupted. "Mademoiselle, do not be too concerned."

"What do you mean?"

"If you are leaving the city in a few days you should be safe. France has not yet declared war. But soon, I would think. And then it will spread. The politicians have been pushing us to this for a long time. For a while they came to their senses, and we have had two years of peace. But this time the situation is…what is the word? Not to reverse…"

"Irréversible," she said. "The same as in French."

The actor looked surprised she knew the language, but pleased, and he went on in French for her. Kera reached out to touch Gus's hand as she spoke with him, not wanting him to disengage from the conversation. She'd been that way towards him since the voyage over. A girlish crush. But they came from such different backgrounds, and she was so young. He couldn't…

"It started in Serbia, wherever that is," she reported back. "About a month ago an Austrian duke and his wife were murdered there. The Austrians have started the war to get revenge."

"A trigger," Gus said, and the Frenchman nodded.

"Oui. An excuse to send in the armies," the man said.

Gus slid his hand back to the banjo, running his index finger the length of the strings down to the bridge and holding it there. He felt the frustration of the men in the street, fighting over the policies of their leaders, men who made decisions about whether to risk the lives of others over their disputes. A drop of blood trickled from his finger to the banjo's head, staining it like rust. Gus rubbed at it, but the color wouldn't come off.

"You're still hurt," Kera said. "I'll get Jack."

"No."

"Don't you want him to help?"

"It's not that bad. I wouldn't want him to worry about me."

"Why on earth not?" she asked. "You're partners. Most people think you're really brothers."

"Something's been going on since we got to Paris," he said. "Something strange." He'd blurted it out without thinking.

"Was it something he did?"

"Does," Gus said.

"You can tell me, Gus."

He stayed silent.

Kera straightened. "He's my friend too, you know," she said. "Don't I deserve to hear what he's doing?"

"He goes out at night," Gus said. "After the shows. Doesn't come back to the room until morning." Immediately he regretted telling Kera. Maybe this should just be between him and Jack—they'd spent so many days together since they became a team. They'd had their problems but could always find a way to talk them out. But this was more than a disagreement over lyrics or timing. He turned away from her, to the little mirror, a postcard of glass in a rococo frame against the bricks, and reached for his stage makeup. But Kera wouldn't let it lie.

"Do you have any idea…"

He spoke to his reflection. "I followed him," he said. "A couple of nights ago. He went to a bar."

"He spends all night drinking?"

Why didn't he stop? He wanted Kera and her questions to go away, back into the throng of performers primping for the show. He wanted to run onstage with Jack and perform the way they used to back in the states. But now it was changed. Jack had become a stranger, another of the nameless, suspicious masses who populated the streets and auditoriums of the cities they'd played on the continent. The Jack here in Paris was an impostor, a duplicate snuck in to replace the one he knew.

"Is Jack a drunk, Gus? Is that what it is? Because if he needs our help…"

"No." He turned at last and looked up, into her eyes, as though by doing so she could bring him out of this dilemma. "He met a man there…at the bar. He kissed him."

"On the cheek," Kera said. "Frenchmen do that all the time."

"He kissed him on the mouth. Like a man kisses a woman."

"Oh, you must have misunderstood. Maybe you were too far away to really see. Or it was too dark."

"I don't know. I could barely make them out."

"What else did they do?"

"I didn't stay. The crowd was so thick I didn't want to go further inside. I went back to the hotel."

"Then how can you accuse him? They might have just been good friends. Who knows with all the crazy customs they have over here?"

"Don't you understand what it might mean?"

How could she? All of nineteen, what did she know of such perversions? She should still be in Connecticut, shuttered with her mother, instead of the vaudeville grinder. Because she loved to sing, she said. What was she even doing on this tour with them? He should have never spoken, should have made up some lie—let her think Jack was a lush. People could accept that. If Jack had become—he couldn't bring himself to think the word, much less say it—it meant condemnation, exile. Maybe for him too. They were partners, sometimes roommates—people back home would assume. How could he not have known this about Jack? Or was it that he did, and the real embarrassment lay there? In twelve years there were glances, looks—fleeting at most—looks that meant nothing, that portended everything, dismissed in the familiarity of their years together as awkward, accidental moments. In the close quarters of a hotel room there were bound to be such incidents. He'd thought nothing of them until now.

Kera said, "I'm sure there's an explanation."

"Sure, Kera. Of course." He wouldn't push for her comprehension. He would let the matter lie and she could make whatever sense out of it she wanted.

A man with a handlebar mustache a little way down the rows began warming up on an accordion, playing a tarantella in 6/8 time. Gus tracked the notes that poured from the bellows: quarters and eighths, sharps, flats—as though transcribing them as he listened—and they took him out of the conversation. Kera continued to speak, asking more questions, but he was elsewhere, the mathematics of the silly tune transfixing him so that her words were lost because they were not music. The practice session stopped as abruptly as it started, and Gus returned to find Kera staring.

"You're not even listening to me."

"I am," Gus said, "But this thing with Jack has me worried."

She turned and walked away to dress for the show. Gus's eyes followed her as she shifted down the cramped aisle and ducked behind a blue cloth embroidered with birds of paradise where she could change. He'd tried not to return her longing glances, and dismissed her attraction to him, waiting for it to pass. He made excuses: she was less than half his age, too naïve, of a different class…something to deny any feeling for her. Still, he found it hard to dismiss her friendliness, the feeling that he could talk to her at any time and about any subject—almost. She was nothing like the French girls in the dance numbers—flirty and insincere, not at all the way Max had described them, teasing even the slightest movement into a seduction. Or the women he'd known, the women on the circuit—older than him, experienced, aggressive, desperate, often tougher than the men. Perhaps if he found her prettier, he might feel differently, and he sometimes chastised himself for his shallowness—he was no catch himself. Nature had given Kera an angel's voice, but had placed it in a stout, farm girl's body that he found unappealing. He would have to be careful what he said, how he acted, to be sure he didn't hurt her feelings. Kera needed his protection, his guidance. But she wanted his love.

Like Jack—with a man. But that type of desire was wrong. There were morals and laws to say so.

Gus turned to his mirror, and leaned in to inspect his face, tired and drawn from the evening's events. He maneuvered to study the confusion of his hair. It always looked uncombed, unkempt, no matter what he did to it, different from other men's, a rebellion against conventions of style. The fight and the heat had made it wilder tonight, like fire, and he didn't know if it was worth trying to smooth it. The Stetson would cover it well enough.

His hand had stopped bleeding, although it remained a little raw, but not enough, even with the slight damage to the banjo, for the audience to notice any difference in his performance. They needn't know what had happened. They should never know anything except what the performer chose to let them see. He slid the makeup kit in front of him and dabbed a cloth into the grease. He would cover his troubles in a veneer of white. But when the makeup touched his skin he stopped. He envisioned Jack's face in the reflection, its symmetry demure, almost like a woman's, peering out at him, into him, with an expression that was not quite empathy, not quite concupiscence. When his own visage returned he forced himself to trace the furrows lining his mouth, the puffiness under his eyes. His life was supposed to be so glamorous, but in more than a decade in the business all he had to show for it was this tired face, an empty wallet and the fear that all his decisions—to team up with Jack, to ignore poor Kera, to put his music ahead of everything and everyone—were mistakes. He would change everything now, if he could.

"Oh, Gus!" Kera called to him and he turned back to her. "Would you help me with the clasp?" She'd reappeared from behind the screen, her nightly transformation under way. Gone was the unremarkable ellipse of her body, replaced by pillows of curves in pink, augmented, no doubt, by a suffocatingly tight corset. Her dress accentuated her bosom with an empire waist, below which fell a cascade of silky fabric that cinched at the knee before plummeting to the floor. The French actor stared. She walked back to her space, the excess of her hem swishing against the chairs and ankles of the other performers, and pirouetted, offering him a slope of perfect, unblemished skin at the base of her neck. In her heels she stood taller than him, not a great achievement considering his diminutive stature, but still, another excuse. He moved his right hand up to secure the clasp. His left hand, for a moment hanging at his side, had no reason to tremble, yet it did.

She went back to her station and finished her makeup with rouge and a ruby-colored lipstick, and hung a string of imitation pearls around her neck. Next, a towering wig of blond curls and feathers pulled from the bag at her feet. She fitted it to her head, adjusting the wire frame underneath until properly shaped for a woman of worldly experience. Finally, white gloves and a pink parasol, and Kera McGuin had retired for the evening; in her place, the Parisienne Nightingale. She did a half turn towards him. How could this plain girl have been so quickly, so completely changed into something this tempting? As before each show on the tour, he knew she presented a mirage, but there must be some part of the finished product contained within that austere, pre-show package. How well she hid her beauty, revealing it only for paying customers. Perhaps if they met in a venue besides the stage... He'd passed a café each day on the way to the theater. They would share a table in the cool of the morning. Kera would stir her coffee lazily while he talked about his music.

The Nightingale batted her eyelashes at him in mock flirtation, while Kera, underneath, smiled with sincerity. Gus smiled back, trying to remember what she looked like without the costume.

The stage manager, LaRoche, a pencil-thin man in a snug black coat and gray pants, slipped in from offstage, clapping his hands and imploring the performers in French to make themselves ready, as the show would begin in a few minutes. Kera fluffed her wig, then took out her sheet music. She had to coordinate with the piano player, she said. Last night's performance had not gone well.

Gus and Jack went on immediately following her. Gus pulled a leather gunbelt brimming with bullets from his bag and strapped it low around his hips, then slid a silver-colored, cast iron six-shooter into its holster. If only it were real! He could have a chat with the cashier and make sure everyone was paid tonight. He took his frayed Stetson out and smoothed it with his hand, then tapped a small dent into the side to add support and make sure the old thing didn't collapse in the middle of a song. He wrestled it into the proper angle on his head, covering the distraction of his hair, and began to look for Jack.

Gus stood at the edge of the stage curtain, just out of view of the audience, his fingers grazing the canvas that felt more like a tarpaulin than a drape. He looked out at a half-empty theater. The red velour of vacant seats shone more vibrantly than the dull wardrobe of the sparse audience. The balconies were deserted, save for some boys who'd probably snuck in. These represented the descendants of the culture that had created vaudeville. How would the art survive if even they refused to support it?

Three Gypsies—or so they called themselves, although everyone in the show knew they were Frenchmen with painted mustaches and embroidered vests—scratched out folk tunes on old fiddles. They perpetrated a sham for the audience's benefit, not that different than the hoax he and Jack imposed on the crowds. Cowboy troubadours they told the newspapers, sons of a rancher exiled from his land by a crooked trust and a complicit government, telling their story in song to a public weaned on sentiment. What was really unfair was how they had to hide the truth—no one would listen to two boys from the Bowery crooning western ballads. But the papers back home would print anything, as long as free tickets to the evening show were on the table, so the story, and the act, worked. Gus wondered if all this news of war comprised a deception too, made up to give the people something to obsess about so their government could raise taxes or conscript young men.

But politics faded as Gus let the music take him. He watched Kera, just a few feet away, waiting to go on next, primping and posing, taking deep breaths in preparation, and thought she might be trying to make them suggestive in his presence. The fingers of his right hand twitched as if he were picking the notes of the melody on the banjo, a fraction of a second behind the players onstage. Then he had the tune, and anticipated the swells and valleys of the song. He let his mind drift from the stage, and turned inward, to that place only he and the music could share. But an atonal ringing interrupted the dream. The musicians wore no bells, no finger cymbals, so it did not come from the stage. Where then? He felt a presence next to him. Gus broke from his trance to see Jack, his spurs still jingling, a hand sliding up to embrace his shoulder. Gus took a step away, as if the hand carried a disease. "What do you want?" he asked.

Jack raised his chin, as if Gus's retreat had offended him. "I want to get paid," he said. His makeup was too heavy; it buried his face. With the dome of pomade clamped down on his head Jack looked ghoulish, like he was ready to go back to the shadows as soon as the show was over.

"We all do," Gus said.

"Can you give me something? To tide me over?"

"There's nothing to give. I'm as bad off as you are."

The fiddlers dashed offstage. Questions and conversation would have to wait. The emcee directed the placard be changed as he introduced Kera. He affixed a French pronunciation to her name and elongated the syllables, turning two names into three and dubbing her "Kera Mack-Guin, le Rossignol Parisien." She seemed confused, not ready to perform. Gus watched as she walked out amid a smattering of applause, all the small crowd could generate.

The piano player started, then stopped. Kera froze. She had always greeted crowds like an opera diva, with a smile and outstretched arms before launching into her first song. Tonight, however, she acted as though there were a barrier between performer and audience—perhaps the tiny crowd had surprised her, perhaps their talk about Jack had done it. She began tentatively, the piano player came in too fast, and they struggled to synchronize. Her first number was "Listen to the Mockingbird," and during the refrain she slowed again, tripping the pianist and causing him to stamp the floor in irritation. For once a song didn't take Gus into his world of notes and symbols. Kera sang so poorly he could focus only on her predicament. She'd been nervous since they talked. He glanced at Jack, who looked as concerned as he.

Kera stumbled through two more stanzas, varying the tempo as she warbled, forcing the accompanist to shift his timing as they hunted for the right pace. The little birdcalls she appended to each line of the refrain were barely audible. At the close, she spun the parasol in front of her face to hide from the audience, but Gus could see the embarrassment in her expression. They rewarded her effort with little more than polite applause. But she had one more song in order to fulfill her slot on the bill. Kera replaced the parasol to her shoulder, waved apologetically at the pianist, nodded to him, and began a rendition of "I Wonder Why I Love You So."

She had sung this song two or three times a day, nearly every day since they'd landed on the continent, yet tonight she infused it with an emotion that hadn't come through before. The piano player, by now ready for any deviation, picked up on her vocal cues and stayed in time through her improvisations. Within two bars Gus found himself elsewhere—he and Kera stood alone in the great hall, and her voice echoed from the stalls to the back balcony, creating a sound that to Gus transcended mere notes. And this time he heard the words as well:

> *I wonder why I love to have you near*
> *And tell me things I long to know,*
> *When we're far apart my own sweetheart,*
> *I wonder, wonder why I love you so.*

She finished with a flourish, holding the final note for several extra seconds, until she stopped and bowed to the audience. They applauded with more enthusiasm than they had shown the French acts. It took Gus a moment to shake himself back to the present, to see Jack clapping furiously along with the crowd. As Kera walked offstage his partner ran to embrace her. Gus heard the words he might have said himself if he'd had the chance—magnificent, wondrous—but would he have uttered them? He didn't know, and was glad Jack had gotten to her first. But as he started for the stage Jack had more to say—a plea for Kera's help. "I'm desperate," he said. "Just a few sou. I know you haven't been paid either, but I thought maybe you had a little to spare..."

Gus felt his stomach tighten. Had he changed so much that he would take advantage of the girl like this? Oh, Jack. What had gotten hold of him? But he had to go onstage. The audience waited and Gus could sense their restlessness. Kera had brought them to life and they craved more of the Americans' entertainment.

Kera told Jack to see her after the performance. He was welcome to share whatever she had. Gus said, "No!" but she didn't hear, and the emcee, a man more concerned with punctuality than sentiment, had the sign changed. With Jack still behind the curtain he announced, "Mesdames et Messieurs, les cowboys Américains, les Frères Ballo!"

Gus went out alone and waited in the spotlight, banjo in hand. He stared at the crowd, unwilling to start without his partner, and the crowd stared back, finding the scene increasingly funny, which made him even more anxious for the music to begin. He could not face them without playing, and began to think of running backstage, not stopping until he made it to the street, where the men had battled over politics. He would look for the beaten man, to apologize for being unable to help. But that man was gone now. Gus looked back behind the curtains, to where Jack continued to perform for Kera, showering praise for her singing, pleading his poverty. Come on, Jack! Gus brought the banjo to his hip. He could at least strum, mark time until Jack came out, to placate the crowd and LaRoche, who surely watched everything from some hiding place.

At last his partner ran onstage, smiling broadly and launching into "Every Little Movement" before Gus had a chance to react. Gus joined in with his trademark flourish, having forgotten the scrapes on his hands and having to endure the feeling of his raw fingers against the steel strings. And the damage to the banjo was worse than he thought. Every riff sounded slightly off. Jack noticed and shot him a puzzled look, as though his playing caused it. The crowd must have heard it too. Their faces were blank. No one smiled. They might begin whistling at any moment.

Gus focused on the banjo. He gripped the neck tighter to offset the wandering chords. But his voice started to waver—he had to sacrifice his vocals to keep the banjo's sound from becoming sour. He shot a panicked look at Jack. His partner was the better singer anyway. Jack raised the volume of his voice, automatically, the result of so many performances together, so many contingencies and adjustments. If they could get through this first song Gus would try to explain what happened in the seconds between the numbers.

They hit the refrain. *Ev'ry little movement has a meaning all its own.* What relevance those words had tonight. Gus closed his eyes through the final stanza, and made his troubles part of the performance. He'd restrained himself from fighting outside the theater, but he was fighting now, to make it to the end of the song, to keep the act going. He began to play faster, almost as though possessed, challenging Jack to keep up, until, at last, he found himself in the music, riveted to the score. He closed his eyes. Jack no longer stood at his side; the crowd dissipated. He imagined the scene outside the theater walls; what it would be like to float among the clouds that had presided over the violence outside.

The audience gave the Ballos as enthusiastic an ovation as it had bestowed on Kera. Jack took a step back to assess his partner. "I'm okay now," Gus said, but Jack didn't comprehend. Never mind. He nodded, the same nod he'd given Jack in the middle of every show on the tour.

Jack bowed like a courtly troubadour, arms sweeping to his sides and his guitar dangling from his left hand, while Gus tipped the brim of his Stetson, as much of an acknowledgment as he ever offered to the crowd. They looked at each other. Jack's perfect face eased into a half smile, his usual tease for the audience—or was it for him this time? Gus tapped the toe of his boot on the hardwood and they segued into "Red Wing," a mindless ditty about a lovesick Indian maiden—but always a favorite with crowds back home. Without trying, their voices, for the first time in weeks, sang in unison, and the harmony it produced caught Gus by surprise. This time he stayed onstage with Jack and didn't let his mind travel to some far off refuge. Why couldn't it be like this every time they played? It had happened without practice, without reason. The audience drank it in. Gus saw Kera, still in costume, just offstage, holding on to the curtain where she could observe. Even LaRoche had stopped his goading and watched them perform.

The crowd clapped in rhythm, and the sound interlaced with their music and made Gus quiver. He turned towards Jack and watched him playing to the crowd. His partner rocked his head and moved his shoulders to the beat, imploring the audience to make noise—he was as connected to them as Gus was to the music. Then Jack turned to him and they stared at each other, frozen in the space between the notes, ripping away the masks of animosity they'd worn since arriving in Paris, becoming Gus and Jackie again, two young crooners who'd met by chance in a bar on the lower east side.

They stood together under the spotlights as the echoes of music faded. Gus wiped sweat from his forehead with his sleeve. He turned to go backstage. But the crowd wanted more. Jack waved to the audience and shook his guitar in excitement. He wanted more too. The crowd roared its approval. To a passerby on the street the sounds coming from the half-filled house would have made it seem at capacity, as cheering and cries of "Encore!" pierced the sullen evening air.

Jack mouthed "Santa Fe." Why that one? They hadn't performed it in months. But it was what the French wanted to hear, a tune about a lonesome cowboy on a deserted trail. Gus closed his eyes for a moment as he strummed. The song always filled him with melancholy, and though he'd never been near New Mexico it took him back to the darkest days of his life, alone and on the streets, the days he'd tried so hard to forget but never could. When he looked out at the audience they had changed again—no one smiled at his memories.

When the song ended he heard more applause, from somewhere. Jack bowed, then ran offstage. But Gus could not move. He was transfixed, staring at the crowd, at the threatening faces. The emcee walked to the center of the stage, directed the placard be changed, and waved at Gus to move.

The ovation stopped, but Gus remained in the spotlight. Someone in the stalls shouted at him. LaRoche loomed just off the stage, looking like he might drag Gus away. Kera ran out in front of him, geisha steps in her vase-shaped dress, and took Gus's hand to lead him away. The emcee jabbered at them while the next act, a team of jugglers, ran on and went into their routine, tossing colored pins to each other across the stage, and Kera kept her hand on Gus's head, holding it down as though they were ducking artillery until they were out of the way.

Backstage she helped him out of his gunbelt and vest. Gus struggled to find a way to explain it to her.

"You don't have to," she said. "Whatever it was has passed."

Jack came up from the other end of the dressing room and spoke to her. He ignored Gus. "It doesn't have to be too much," Jack said. "Just enough to buy food for a couple of days."

Gus stared at him. Had he chosen the song because he knew the effect it would have on him?

Kera fished in her purse for some coins, and dropped a few into Jack's palm. He kept the hand out until she added two more.

"You're so wonderful, Kera," Jack said. "You're a beautiful princess. An angel, come from heaven to rescue me." He shoved the coins into his pocket and took her hands in his. "I'll repay you, you know. As soon as we get paid."

Gus waited until his partner was out of earshot. "Why did you give him that money? He won't use it for food."

"I know," she said.

"Then why?"

"He's in trouble, Gus. Everyone gets into trouble sometimes. I guess I just wanted to help him." She went back behind the screen to change out of her dress.

Gus looked down the aisle and saw Jack hurrying, wiping the greasepaint from his face with a towel and shedding his costume. In a minute he had changed back into street clothes and packed his gear into his bag.

Kera came back to her station still wearing the corset and the jewelry, but in the dress she'd worn before the show. The mismatch made Gus stare for a few moments, and Kera hid a smile with her hand.

Jack had made it to the dressing room exit. Gus said, "I'm going to follow him. I'll see you back at the Fromentin."

"I'm going with you," she said.

"You can't."

"And why not? You can't tell me I'm not old enough. Not here."

"You're not finished changing. You can't go out like that."

"Then help me."

Helping her dress earlier had made him nervous. The feeling had surprised him, and now he hesitated to get close. But she took his hand in hers and stroked the skin where he'd injured it in the street. The touch calmed him, and he slipped behind her to undo the clasp of her necklace. The last time he'd done something like this… He had to think. No, the last time it had been the wife of a magician in a show in Richmond. She came to his hotel room after midnight. There'd been no time for romance.

"We'd better hurry," Kera said. She pulled off her bracelets and threw them into her bag. "Can we leave our things here?"

"We'll have to," Gus said. "We'll stash everything under the shelf and cover it with a blanket or something." That meant his banjo too. He'd never left it unattended. It rested at an angle against the ledge, like a man waiting for a drink. Apropos. The instrument belonged in the barroom, in places like the ones where he and Jack learned how to perform. It was entertainment for the common man, never seen in an orchestra. A misfit of the music world. Born of the streets, like him, and throughout his tenure in show business it had been the perfect compliment to his existence—fast and bright to thrill the crowds; forlorn in the lonely hours away from the stage. How could he leave it here unguarded?

Kera threw a shawl around her shoulders and ran to the door. She looked back at him. "Gus!"

He put the banjo in its case and stashed it behind the bags.

Outside the sun had finally set, but there was no moon, no stars—the clouds clamped down like the lid on a skillet, holding the heat of the day against the city.

Chapter 2
Saturday night – Kera

THEY TAILED Jack through the alleys of Paris, as he ignored the city's main streets and its tourist grandeur for his clandestine purpose. Kera and Gus kept their distance, waiting for Jack to turn the next corner, then running to catch up, hoping they could still see him before he changed course again. They worried that the hard soles of Kera's shoes would alert him to their presence, but Gus's partner paid no attention to ambient sounds, not that he could have discerned who made them. Even here, far from better-known entertainments, people congregated by the dozens in seedy clubs that were little more than tenements with open doors, bistros drowned in wine and laced with the scents of cigar smoke and the rotting garbage strewn outside. These people hadn't been at the theater, but they still enjoyed the Paris nightlife. They were oblivious to the hour and the talk of war Gus had mentioned—something about their carrying on said they simply didn't care—bring on the soldiers and the guns, we will not change the way we live. What attractions could such places hold for them? Kera was curious to know.

She felt anxious at first, racing through these dark corridors alone with Gus. But when he slowed and intimated she could give up the chase after another turn or two, she ignored him. This marked the first night in their three weeks on the continent that she had an opportunity to explore a city away from traditional sights, and the idea excited her. She would not abandon this chance to finally have some fun—she'd love to have it with Gus, but if he decided to go back to the hotel, maybe she would go on without him.

Jack led them back to the street, past a club where a large crowd was packed in so tight, patrons' buttocks flattened against the windows at the front. As they went by the open doors, she stopped to look inside. A man in an evening coat bargained with the maître d' for a table, while his companion, a woman wearing a flowered hat as wide as serving tray, flirted with a waiter. She wanted to stay, investigate the fun, but Gus pulled her past. Jack didn't pause for this invitation, so apparently, neither would he.

"Why don't we let Jack go? We can follow him tomorrow," Kera said. "We could go inside for a while."

"That's not why we came out tonight," Gus said.

He could speak for himself. She'd begun to have doubts about Gus in the week since they'd arrived in Paris and he hadn't accepted any of her invitations to step out, or recognized her flirtations, now matter how obvious she made them. She'd always swooned over brooding artists, and ever since the voyage from New York, she'd tried to find ways to make him notice. She'd felt the attraction when they met briefly at Max's to sign the contracts, but didn't think anything of it until she encountered him aboard ship. Gus was leaning over the railing at the stern, his hair standing in the wind as though electrically charged, staring down into the steamer's wake as though thinking about jumping. The forlorn pose reminded her of her father—how alone he always seemed to be, even among friends or family.

"Don't do it," she said, trying to make a joke.

Gus didn't play along. "It's the best place to be on a ship. One of the few places where a person can think or dream."

For the rest of the passage Kera tried to be near him, but he cloistered himself when the other passengers sunned on deck or played at games. At meals Kera saved a seat for him. But when he didn't show for two days she gave up on this plan. During the first days of the tour, in Edinburgh, she loitered in their hotel lobby, hoping he might come down for a meal or a newspaper. If he did, she planned to act as though their meeting had been serendipitous, and invite him for a walk among the shops nearby. A simple walk was all. They could take their time—talk about their careers or their lives back home. She wouldn't push him for details, though, and he might appreciate that. But again he refused to cooperate. Eventually she became too embarrassed sitting there alone, and left, looking at the clock as though an appointment had been broken, and walked out to visit the stores on her own.

Occasionally she could hear him practicing on the banjo through thin hotel walls, playing somber tunes that weren't part of his act. Those were the hardest times. The poor, lonely man. How she'd wanted to go to his room and rush inside to console him, to rest his head on her bosom and put her arms around his shoulders. Once, walking through the hallway, she stopped at his door and listened to the squeaks of his fingers as they slid along the strings, and the little taps of the pick as he strummed. She pressed her ear to the door and heard his breathing. She closed her eyes and coiled her hand to knock, but then withdrew it, too afraid to disturb his solitude.

Jack had slowed and looked around, as though trying to remember exactly where the evening's rendezvous would take place, but then went around a corner and into another alleyway, out of their sight. Gus left her behind to follow him. When she caught up, he stood, head down and hands on hips.

"We've lost him," he said. He began to walk down the alley, but there was no sign or sound of anything resembling a cabaret. Whatever club Jack had ducked into didn't advertise like the rest.

"Let's wait a moment," Kera said. "If there's a place near here other people may go inside too. Then we'll know where he went." They stood near the brick façade of an old building slick with soot and condensation from the night air, and strained to peer through the black of the moonless evening. The only light by which to see came from the flickering lamps of the main streets, filtering around corners, barely enough to make out the shapes of people moving in the distance. Kera moved closer until she leaned against Gus's shoulder. They lingered like that for a moment, their bodies touching, until he turned and she saw his eyes looking into the night, past her, they way they did when they spoke in the dressing area. She pulled away from him, as though she had bumped into a stranger.

Finally, two shadows disappeared into the middle of the alley. Gus began walking. "Maybe there," he said. "Must be." Kera ran to stay with him, the soles of her shoes rapping against the cobblestones like Morse code. The sound echoed off the bricks, and before they could find the doorway a group of three men, each several inches taller than Gus, moved into their path. Kera recoiled and stood behind Gus, who refused to give ground to these interlopers. The men wore tattered, dark coats that were too heavy for the July weather. The one in the middle leaned his face into theirs, the poor light illuminating him like one of the carved grotesqueries that ringed the theater. Kera smelled the rest—the odor of grease embedded in the fibers of his coat, a whiff of raw onion on his breath. He spoke to Gus in French and then laughed.

"He wants to know what we're doing here," Kera said. "He says we look like we're lost."

"Touristes," the man said, and he nodded at his friends, who began to surround the couple.

Gus took Kera's hand and pulled her closer behind him.

One of the ruffians made a grab for her and snatched the shawl from around her shoulders. She held on to Gus and he twisted away from her, as if knowing he would have to fight, and not wanting to be constrained before it started. But as he brought his hands up to defend himself, someone called from a doorway in the building.

Kera heard the speaker shout in French, "Andre! I thought I had seen the last of your ugly face." The leader of the group looked over and the voice spoke again. "Don't you remember what happened the last time you pestered my customers?" The men began to back away. As soon as they left an opening, Gus grabbed Kera's hand again and pulled her towards the door. They ran inside, past whomever had saved them.

They stood in the foyer of what could have been a block of flats. The light here was only a little better, but a concoction of voice and piano wafting from the far end of the hallway indicated they'd found the club Jack had sought. A crude handbill hung crookedly next to a stairwell leading down. "Le Secret" it read, fitting for this darkened doorway. They waited for their benefactor to come back inside.

Kera caught her breath. She stood behind Gus and reassessed him. He would have fought for her! Never mind the odds, he had pulled her from those men and placed himself in the way, daring them to go through him to get to her. And he did it spontaneously, without considering the outcome. Maybe it was more than just chivalry.

A gaunt man, with oily hair to his shoulders and a black coat hanging like a cape, ducked through the doorway. He threw the butt of a cigarette on the floor and pulled another from his coat pocket, slipping it between his lips. He spoke to them in heavily accented English while lighting it. "You are Americans, yes?"

"Yes," Gus said. "Did you call to those men?"

The man took a long drag before answering. "I must apologize for Andre and his friends. They do not like to work for a living. They look for simple people, like yourselves, from which to steal."

"Well, you came along in the nick of time," Kera said.

"There was nothing 'nick' about it, as you say. I must always be watching for Andre. He is bad for my business."

"This club, you mean?"

"Oui. I am the owner." He bobbed his head as if a formal bow entailed too much effort. "Renoult."

"Gus…Gustav Amato." He put out his hand but the Frenchman did not take it.

Renoult turned towards Kera and made another gesture. He stared at her face, at the blouse the thief had uncovered, at the allure molded by the corset she hadn't time to remove. "And do you have a name?" he asked.

Kera's voice caught for a moment at the question. She managed to whisper her name.

Renoult turned back to Gus. "Monsieur, do you not know how dangerous it is to walk in these streets at night? And to bring a woman of obvious culture to this cesspool…" He spoke to him like a teacher lecturing a slow student, but Gus didn't respond. Kera thought it strange the man would disparage his own club. He leaned down to look at Gus more closely. "Why are you here, monsieur?"

"We're looking for someone," Gus answered, still peering into the stairwell. "He may be here already."

Renoult gazed down at the two of them—a condescending look, she thought, perhaps reserved for outsiders. Considering how he had referred to his cabaret, it could be he looked down on everything. He exhaled his next puff of smoke in their direction and said, "Of course. Everyone is looking for someone. Follow me then." In a moment he ran down the stairs and out of sight. Kera heard his shoes against the bare boards for the first few steps as he descended. As they followed the sound of the revels from below became louder, the air warm and acrid.

They stood one step from the bottom, peering into a

basement ringed by small tables designed for two, but accommodating as many as six people, some of whom sat on crates, while others stood or squatted. A piano player banged a harsh tune from the keys. The lighting here, provided by a few bare bulbs strung overhead, was minimized by a cloud of tobacco smoke hanging two feet thick from the ceiling. Everyone leaned in to watch a man and woman in a small clearing on the wooden floor, who appeared to wrestle in time to the rhythm. The male dancer, dressed in a loose shirt that billowed as he moved, slapped the woman, and the crowd cheered in astonishment and then approval. He threw her to the floor and they applauded. The woman rubbed her face as she rose, smearing lipstick across her makeup. Kera had heard of the Apache dance, but even seeing it in person she could still scarcely believe it was an act. She looked at Gus and saw his hands tensing.

The woman threw a roundhouse punch at the man, but he caught her arm, twirled her around and pushed her into the audience. Two men caught her, turned her back around and giddily shoved her towards her tormentor. Gus began to push against the bodies in front of him, as though searching for an opening through which he might affect a rescue. After the scene outside Kera sensed Gus was still ready to fight. But when she started to speak, to assure him the violence was only a dance, she saw a look more like curiosity than anger. Did he only want to get closer? Or to run out to the dance floor and become part of the act?

As he started to wedge himself past the other patrons, the woman dancer took the advantage in the fight. She stalked her partner across the floor, her tattered blouse waving and her hair bobbing in time to her movements, and pulled her fist back to throw a punch. But the move was a fake, and instead she kicked him to the side of the knee, like a footballer, sending him into a half sitting, half kneeling position. He held his leg and she struck—a hard slap to the face, and then another with her backhand. Kera crossed her arms around her bosom. Maybe she shouldn't be enjoying this spectacle, but she was. With every blow, she held herself tighter. Perhaps the energy of the crowd had affected her, or the fact that Gus found it all so interesting. Kera stood on her toes to get a better view.

The man caught the woman's hand on her next swing. He pulled her down to the floor as he jumped up, and raised the heel of his half boot until he held it inches from her defiant jaw. She clutched the boot for a moment before pushing it slowly to the floor, and then wrapped her arms around the man's leg and rested her head against his thigh, submitting at last. He reached down and took a handful of her hair, and jerked her head back until she was obliged to look at his sneer. The music crashed to a stop and the crowd exploded in an ovation.

Kera shivered. She cheered along with them for a few seconds, and then caught herself. Everyone would see. Gus would see. She tried to pretend the scene had no effect, that she was above the vagrants who performed these shows, as her parents had taught her. But a stranger standing next to her screamed, "Remarquable!" Her body became caught in the celebration; patrons bumped against her, their shoulders rubbing hers, their hands touching her hips.

Let him see.

She turned to the man and shouted, "Oui! C'était merveilleux!"

The man smiled, his raised mustache revealing a row of gapped and crooked teeth, and he reached to put his arm around her shoulder. Kera twisted away and pushed towards Gus.

Once the applause quieted and the dancers made their way offstage, the crowd began to thin, as though this marked the last performance of the evening. Light conversation and piano music made an odd counterpoint to the cacophony of a few minutes before, and enough patrons made their way up the stairs to allow Kera to take in the cabaret. It encompassed the entire basement of the building above. The walls consisted of unadorned, scarred bricks, criss-crossed with water and sewage pipes running to and from the upper floors. Kera felt sure Renoult operated the bistro on a shoestring, spending the income to cater to the clientele's lusts, rather than redecorating. She assessed him, despite his airs, as a struggling businessman, doing what he had to do to keep the door open.

The bar sat against the near wall, adjacent to a passage to some back rooms. A few dozen bottles sat on shelves in front of a mirror. The layout was small enough to be operated by one man, who at the moment bent down below the counter. She'd seen much larger and more fashionable places back on the east coast, but for tonight this would do nicely. A single waitress scurried among the tables, taking orders.

Once the bulk of customers had cleared out, Gus and Kera made their way to the bar. "Finally," Kera said. "I've endured enough pushing about this evening."

Renoult idled at the counter, and when they arrived he leaned in towards the now towering bartender, a man big and broad enough to have doubled as the bouncer.

"These two," Renoult said in French, raising his eyebrows in their direction. "Americans. They wish for a night of fun among the peasants. Be sure they are well entertained." He paused a moment, then added, "And be sure they are well overcharged."

Kera dropped her jaw at his remark and Renoult, not realizing until then that Kera understood, smiled, lingered for a few moments on the unbuttoned portion of her blouse, and at last headed for a corner of the club.

Kera finished her drink in a few sips and ordered another. She turned to face the dance floor, offering Gus her corset-enhanced profile. That, and her makeup remained in place from the show, and now, she hoped, they would work to her advantage. She'd noticed how Gus's look changed whenever she went into costume, and now she leaned back until her elbows rested on the counter, pressing her bosom out until it was unavoidable.

Two men at the end of the bar watched her and nudged each other—perhaps giving themselves encouragement to walk over—and she looked away. Gus though, had a different focus, as usual off in the distance somewhere. He scanned the crowd for Jack. This was too much. Kera stood right next to him, looking as suggestive as she could, almost wanton, making blatant the message she'd sent him for weeks. Perhaps she made it too easy. She looked back at the two men. If she could attract one of them to come over and talk to her, then Gus would surely notice. If he had any feelings at all, seeing her flirt with someone else would have to arouse them.

They looked rough—like every other man in the club—unshaven and wearing threadbare jackets. They murmured to each other, nodding their heads as they spoke obviously and unabashedly about Kera. She waved at them shyly. One of them pointed to himself, but as he was the more menacing of the two, she shook her head until the other noticed. Then she nodded yes. The man made his way around the bar, walking in front of Gus to get to her. He gazed down into her cleavage, and presented a pale, thin, but not unfriendly face.

"You wish to speak with me, mademoiselle?" he said in French.

"Buy me a drink, monsieur."

"Of course." He held two fingers up for the bartender.

As he laid his free hand on the bar, Kera slid hers over until her fingers grazed against his. Her hand trembled—she had never been so bold—but she forced herself to maintain the contact, and began to stroke his skin.

The man looked surprised and pulled the hand away. "Are you sure you know what you are doing?"

"I think so…I mean, of course I do."

"I think of course not," he said. "You see, I am with the young man." He pointed back to the one Kera had thought too frightening for flirtation, who smiled at them. He was missing a tooth. But this man with her seemed so nice, perhaps the other was a gentleman as well.

"Would he like to join us?"

"Yes, yes. I'm sure he would." He waved at his friend, who began slipping around the patrons at the bar.

"Good. Then you can both flirt with me."

"Ah, mademoiselle, still you do not understand."

"What is to understand? Do you not find me attractive?"

"Yes, but... We are together, he and I. As in..." he paused, as though searching for a polite term..."boyfriends."

Had she not been leaning with her back to the bar, Kera would surely have retreated a few steps. Gus had warned her, but the idea of men with men hadn't become real until she saw these two look into each other's eyes and clasp hands. And Gus now, still at his post, searching the crowd like a hungry dog. Had he come here to expose his singing partner, or was the truth something else? She had expected his indignation over the Apache dancers, but saw him enthralled; now the anger she assumed prodded him to follow Jack was in fact, what...envy? She noticed her new friends weren't the only "boyfriends" in the place. Men flirted with men and women with women at many of the tables. Everyone held hands or hugged, with which gender it seemed not to matter. The red-haired waitress sat on a customer's lap. And as she tried to make sense of her surroundings, she saw two women standing in a gray corner put their hands to each other's faces and kiss. Now what would her family think? They'd ridiculed the people in her vaudeville domain as vagrants and worse, but if they saw what she viewed this evening they might faint. By the values of that pompous and proper world she'd left, God himself might come down and destroy this Sodom at any moment, but before He did Kera would keep looking. She could not stop. The butterflies she felt watching the dancers returned. This was how these people lived—did they feel like this all the time?

She turned to the first man. "Monsieur, what place is this?"

"This place?" He smiled, as though reading her thoughts. "This is Paris. In Paris, no one minds."

She fanned herself with her hand and the men laughed. What an evening. She'd wanted excitement, and now she had more in an hour than she had experienced in three weeks.

The barman slid the drinks up to Kera and the men. Somehow he'd known to pour a third. She reached for hers, and without waiting for them to offer a toast, or ask what it was, took a sip. A ripple of heat rose from her throat to her temples. They had captured the afternoon sun and put it in a bottle.

But she began to relax. The men clicked their glasses together and drank. When they finished, she said, "Monsieur, explain something, please. You and your friend…you were looking at me. I thought…"

"Yes, of course we were looking," he said. "We saw you at your show last night. We were wondering if it was really you."

"Oh, my. I'm so sorry."

"Do not apologize. We very much enjoyed your singing. And we would like to have another drink with you."

"I would like that. And perhaps you could also do me a small favor." The bartender placed three more tumblers of whiskey in front of them. The movement caught Gus's eye, and he turned briefly to see to whom Kera was talking before continuing his surveillance.

She would give Gus one more chance. "This man," she said, nodding at him. "I am trying to make him jealous."

The Frenchman took a moment to inspect Gus, turning back with his nose wrinkled as though he'd been asked to sample bad cheese. "And so he should be. We would be delighted to help the great Parisienne Nightingale." He held his glass up and she tapped hers into it. They paused for a second, as Gus, hearing the sound, turned to watch them sip the whiskey and laugh.

"I am Charles, by the way, and my friend is Nicholas. And I take it the gentleman speaks no French?"

"Not a word. We could talk about the moon for all he knows."

"Excellent! This will be fun!"

Kera put her hand up to cover her laugh.

"Oh, do not hide it, mademoiselle," Nicholas said. "Let him see you are having fun."

Standing at the bar with these strangers, with whom she could never have the kind of relationship she wanted with Gus, Kera realized she was drinking and laughing as though they had been friends for years. It was fun. Still, all she wanted was for Gus to see it. Finally, he did.

"Who is this?" Gus asked.

She looked at Charles, whose smile encouraged her. "They saw the show. They thought I was good."

Charles raised his glass and his eyebrows for Gus, and introduced himself with a slight bow.

Gus asked, "What do you want?"

Charles shrugged, and Kera translated for him. "Ah," he said. "Tell him that I want what I always want—to enjoy myself." He slid his arm around Kera's shoulders. Nicholas moved in close enough to touch his hip to hers.

"Oh, I couldn't tell him that," Kera said. "He might get the wrong idea."

"But, my dear, the wrong idea is exactly what you wish him to have, no?"

She turned and told it to Gus, as the men grinned at him.

Gus only stared, as if considering another comment entirely. His gaze hovered for a moment on each of them, and Kera felt anxious about her plan, and about the idea of pursuing Gus at all. How could she ever reach him?

"I think I may have made a mistake," she said to the men.

"Not at all," Nicholas replied. "Already I can see he is interested."

"I think I should tell him the truth."

"Believe me, my dear," Charles said. "That would be the worst thing you could do. You have no choice now but to continue with the ruse. Trust me, I see the spark of desire in him."

"Do you really…?"

"I know this look when I see it. He is fighting himself." Charles signaled to the bartender for three more drinks. He leaned in close to whisper in her ear. "If you giggle now I think that may do the trick."

She began to laugh—a forced laugh at first, but then more girlish. She turned to see Gus still looking at them, his face puzzled. He put his hand on Charles's shoulder, and Charles instinctively pulled back, spilling a few drops of his drink.

Gus motioned towards a darker corner of the cabaret. "Look there," he said to Kera. "Do you see him?"

Kera didn't understand at first, so Gus pointed across the dance floor. Two men stood at a small table. Although their faces were in shadow, Kera could tell clearly that one of them was Jack. The other was a scarecrow of a man, whose limbs hung from his body as though they had been merely tied into place. The way he stood, though, leaning against the wall, leering into Jack, gave the impression he possessed some power over him.

Gus said, "Now you see what I was talking about?"

She added the evidence quickly—this place, the secrecy with which Jack had come here, the fact that he stood so very close to this dangerous looking fellow. She'd known Jack for the entire trip. He was outgoing, but not flamboyant. She didn't remember him ever looking at men. The alcohol she'd drunk exaggerated her confusion. "But what are they doing? Just talking?"

Gus looked at Charles. "That man," he said. "By the wall. Who is he?" He turned back to Kera. "Ask him who that man is with Jack."

"Him?" Charles said when she translated. "I have seen him. His name is Raoul. Tell your friend he is bad news."

"Bad news?"

"Your friend should avoid this one," Charles said. "I have heard things."

"What things?"

"Not the kind of things one tells a lady."

She suspected Gus had already surmised this answer, so didn't bother to translate. She expected too that he would look satisfied, as though he had proven his case. But Gus's stare said he wanted to see more. Tailing Jack to this place was not enough. What did he want—to follow Jack into this Raoul's bedroom? "Gus, I think we should go back to the hotel now," she said.

But Gus did not hear, remaining fixed on the two men in the corner. She watched him in profile as he watched Jack. The complexity of Gus's face, the deep lines and peering eyes, contrasted with the simplicity of Jack's. Some of the women in the show had mentioned how exquisite they found him, but Kera thought of him as a statue in a museum—nice to look at, but not much more. In comparing the two of them she felt a small injustice that the man she desired had not the face, but the heart of stone.

Kera watched as Jack placed his hand on Raoul's chest, then leaned closer and whispered something into his ear. Raoul took two fingers of the hand and bent them backwards until Jack grimaced and pulled away. But when Jack turned to leave, Raoul held him by the wrist and pulled him back, closer, like a mantis retrieving its prey. They clinched like the brutal dancers, and after a few moments of watching Kera noticed Jack's grimace turn into a look of satisfaction. Somehow he took pleasure from the pain.

She finished her drink and looked again at Gus. The

alcohol and smoke made it difficult to concentrate. One more drink and she might have the courage to take hold of him as Raoul had Jack. She slid her hand along the bar, closer to where he stood, as he watched Jack's exhibition.

She closed her eyes and felt her consciousness spinning. She saw Jack and that man with their arms around each other, kissing like lovers, the way she wanted to kiss Gus. In another moment the scene changed—now Gus and Jack embraced. They stopped to acknowledge her before returning to their lust. Then someone touched her shoulder. Gus? She opened her eyes and turned to see Charles behind her.

"Perhaps the lady no longer requires our services?" he asked.

"Oh. I'm so sorry. It's just that our friend there… It's such a surprise."

"I understand," Charles said. "It is always a shock to learn of someone's, shall I say, preferences."

"Yes," she said. "This has been quite an evening."

"I will return to my…preference," he said, motioning to Nicholas. "But I have enjoyed our meeting. I do hope we shall see each other again while you are in Paris." He took the hand that had edged its way towards Gus and brought it to his lips.

Kera wondered what this could have meant, finally deciding that in this place, the answer could be anything. She refused to give it further thought. "Thank you for the drinks," she said as Charles and Nicholas negotiated a path back around the bar.

When she looked back towards the corner, Jack and Raoul were gone. Gus looked up at the stairwell, where apparently they had made an exit.

"I wonder if he'll even bother to come back this time," he said.

"Of course he will, Gus. The act is important to him." She wished she believed that herself. "Poor Jack," she said.

"Why do you say that?"

"I just feel sorry for him," she said. "It was almost like he wanted to have that Raoul hurt him."

Kera assumed that having tracked down Jack, Gus would want to go back to the theater to pick up their things. Instead he turned towards the bartender and ordered, with hand gestures, two beers. "Oh, I've already had enough to drink, Gus. I really couldn't have anything else."

"I thought I should thank our host." He nodded in the direction of Renoult, who sat hunched over a table with three other men at the far end of the room. "He helped us out. I should show my gratitude."

He hadn't even bothered to ask if she wanted something. Gus had brought her here to change her mind about Jack, but all her opinions were shifting now.

Rather than be left alone at the bar, Kera followed him to Renoult's table. The three men with their host didn't look anything like the other patrons in the cabaret. They were older and dressed in dark suits, and looked as though they would go back to a business office after their meeting here. All had varying amounts of gray in their hair and two had full beards. Had they been younger they still wouldn't have fit in—it was obvious none of them had come to indulge their cravings.

Kera strained to listen in on their conversation as she and Gus approached. She heard one of the men say, "He must act. Jaurès must call for the workers to strike!" To which Renoult slapped his hand on the table and responded, "For what purpose? The generals have their minds made up, and the sheep will follow them."

Gus held the two glasses out like a waitress in a beer garden. "Mr. Renoult?" he said.

Kera realized that since there were four men at the table he should have brought drinks for all of them.

Renoult looked up with displeasure at the interruption. "Yes, monsieur? How can I help you?" He seemed to have forgotten who Gus was.

"I just want to thank you…"

Renoult turned to the men at the table and said, in French, "With this? Does he expect me to drink beer like a pig farmer?" The men laughed. Kera saw Gus tense.

Renoult draped an arm over the back of his chair and spoke to Gus in English this time. "Monsieur, I do not care for beer. It is the drink of, how do you say, the commoner."

Gus lowered the glasses to his side.

Kera feared he might fling their contents at Renoult. She stepped up behind him and whispered, "Talk to him and I'll be right back."

Gus put the beers on an empty table nearby and began to mumble something about how dark and dangerous it had been in the alley, and Kera went back to the bar as quickly as she could. She turned her purse upside down on the counter and slid the coins that came out to the bartender. "A bottle!" she said. "Something that Monsieur Renoult would like. And glasses! Five… no, six of them. Hurry!" The bartender took the coins—every last sou—and pulled a bottle of cognac from under the bar. Kera gathered the glasses into her bag—the only place she could think to carry them—grabbed the bottle and raced to the other side of the room, just in time to hear Renoult admonish Gus once more.

"I thank you for your trouble, but we are very busy here. Why don't you go back to the bar and have your fun there?" he said.

Kera slipped past Gus and set the bottle in the middle of the little table. As she pulled the glasses out of her purse and placed one in front of each of the men, she said in French, "What the gentleman meant to say, messieurs, was how much we appreciate your intervention earlier this evening. He simply was not sure of the best way to thank you."

Renoult raised an eyebrow as he looked at Kera. He uncorked the bottle and poured for the men at the table.

Kera produced the final two glasses and gave one to Gus. Renoult stared at them for a moment, as if fighting an urge to accept these unwelcome guests. Finally he grinned and held the bottle up to pour for them. The group toasted to France and Renoult added an extra benediction. "I do not know who you are my friends, but you are welcome for your sentiment." He offered them chairs, and when two of the other men complained about having to stop their discussion, he looked at them harshly as if to question their sense of hospitality.

Renoult did not introduce the others at the table, and Kera became uncomfortable that they had interrupted something of importance. But he *had* invited them to sit—it would be rude for them to leave now. Renoult poured another round, and the men drank while she nursed her first glass. He began to make small talk with them, asking what parts of Paris they had enjoyed since they'd arrived.

Gus told him instead about their performances at the Theatre du Vaudeville, which seemed to transform Renoult from disinterested host to a man calculating how he could use these singers in his own club. But while Gus spoke, Kera had difficulty following the conversation clearly. She'd had four—this would be five—drinks. She looked across the table and thought one of the men with Renoult was leering at her. This one, though, wasn't as shabby as the two she had enticed earlier—he wore a gold ring, perhaps a wedding ring, and another, more decorative band with a large ruby. His clothes spoke of a man of considerable means. But he had to be at least sixty. She wondered how she looked, with her blouse still undone, her makeup and hair messed from the evening of excitement. Could he think her a prostitute? She made a grab at her open collar and tried to button it with one unsteady hand, but failed, and hoped that her action did not somehow encourage him. She leaned in to listen to Gus and Renoult and tried to ignore him.

Renoult grilled him about their arrangement with the

theater. Gus told him about their acts, their troubles getting paid, and that he hoped to resolve that issue before they had to leave. "Too bad you are going so soon," Renoult said. "I might have had use for you here." He poured another round and emptied the bottle.

Gus said, "Well, maybe we could extend our stay a little." Kera thought she was too drunk to have heard that. Why on earth would he want to stay to work in this place? She began to ask Gus about it, but the man with the rings still looked at her, and he had worked up the courage to speak.

"It is unusual," he said, "to find a woman of such beauty and grace in Monsieur Renoult's chamber of horrors." He lifted his glass between the fingers of his cupped hand in tribute to her. The man sitting between him and Kera rolled his eyes, as if he'd seen his associate's advances before.

She felt her eyelids flutter.

He took a sip of his cognac to reaffirm his toast, and introduced himself as Maurice Bertré, an editor for a Paris newspaper. The man between them whispered something to Bertré, which the older man waved off, his heavy ring like a pendulum swinging above the table. Bertré leaned in front of his friend to be closer to Kera, and the other pulled back from the table to let him.

For a few seconds she wondered why this new suitor didn't assume she was with Gus, but the answer was clear— since sitting at the table Gus had talked with Renoult and hadn't looked at her once. Everything she'd tried had failed. Gus had been more interested in Jack, and now in Renoult. She could not reach him after all. She downed the last of her drink and leaned towards Bertré. Why not talk to this old, possibly married man? He looked important. He was interesting and articulate. *He* was paying attention to her. And if she engaged in something illicit with him, well, as Charles had said, no one would mind.

Before she realized it Kera had told Bertré about her

singing, and had given him the name of the hotel. He suggested dinner the next day, Sunday, providing she didn't have a show to perform. He would arrange it all and have a car come by to take her to the restaurant. "Why not? I only have a matinee tomorrow," Kera heard herself say. "I've been here for nearly a week and haven't seen much of the sights." She glanced at Gus as she said this.

"A shortcoming we shall have to rectify," Bertré said, with the confidence of a man who had an entire city behind him, as though Paris existed to advance the amorous intentions of its male population.

He said also that he would try to attend her performance if he could finish some business first. "I anticipate that I will hear the lovely song of a rare and beautiful bird," he said.

The last man, the one sitting to Renoult's left, finally tired of waiting for him to get back to their original discussion and implored him, "Renoult! Can you rid us of these two tramps at last? We have much left to discuss, and I must still go to back to *L'Humanite* afterwards."

"Idiot!" Renoult replied. "Were you not listening? Have you not yet deduced that the lady speaks French?" He turned to Kera and spoke in French, since Gus had not caught the insult. "I must apologize again," he said. "My associate is tired and anxious—and he is a fool on top of that."

"It is all right, monsieur. I'm just glad that my friend did not hear."

Renoult thanked her. "But it is true," he said, switching back to English so they both could understand. "We must return to our business. These times are very troubled for us. We have much work to do."

"Is this about that war?" Gus asked.

"I am afraid so, monsieur."

"Are we in danger?" Kera said.

"Not so far. But the governments of Europe have been itching to fight each other for a long time. There are many hatreds at play. When it begins it will move quickly."

"But isn't it a long way from Paris?" Kera asked.

"What fighting there is, is distant," Renoult said. "But the flames are ready to ignite everywhere."

Gus said, "I've seen fighting in the streets."

"The people are confused," Renoult said. "They are being lied to." The man between Kera and Bertré raised his palm as if to warn Renoult not to say too much.

Gus asked, "Which side…?"

"We are for peace, monsieur. It is always the most difficult way."

Gus stood up. "Then we'll wish you good luck," he said.

Kera rose and looked at Bertré, who smiled at her. A war is starting and he is more concerned with a seduction. Strange, these Frenchmen. Even this man—so respectable—even he acts like the rest of the crowd—pleasure comes before self-preservation.

She took a few steps and stumbled sideways, bumping into Gus. She tried to put her arm on his shoulder for support, but he had already started for the stairwell, forcing her to walk a twisting, unsure path behind him. Before she could get to the stairs, the giant barman brushed past her and bounded up the steps. One more shove in an evening of continuous jostling. She took the stairs with caution. If Gus had to wait, so what? But what if he didn't wait? What if he was drunk himself, or so angry at how she'd flirted with those men he decided to walk back without her? They had almost been assaulted coming here, and Renoult wouldn't be outside this time to stifle the threat.

It took her what seemed like several minutes to get to the foyer, and she saw that indeed Gus had gone. She couldn't stay here. She had to get back to the Fromentin. The thought of walking the many blocks in the black night alone frightened her, and she was hardly sure of the way. She drew a deep breath to steady herself and prepare for the ordeal, took off her shoes and put them in her bag—at least she wouldn't attract attention that way. Kera took a quick look around the doorway to the alley, although in the dark she could see nothing. Then someone ran towards her—she couldn't even tell from which direction. She jumped back inside just as the huge man arrived, and fell against the wall in fear.

"Please, please!" the barman said in a baritone. "Do not be alarmed. Monsieur Bertré sent me to help you…to find a taxi to take you back to your hotel." Kera remained against the wall. "He was afraid it would be too dangerous for you to walk."

She relaxed a little. "Come," the man said. "The taxi is waiting just outside the alley. Your friend is already in it."

She went with him around the corner, leaning on his arm for balance. Gus sat behind the driver and watched her get in. He extended his hand to guide her to the seat as the barman held the door open. A touch of chivalry at last. He must be drunk, she decided.

The barman pulled a calling card from his pocket and handed it to her. The tiny block letters read, "M. Bertré."

Kera slipped the card into the sleeve of her blouse.

Gus said the name of the hotel. He still held her hand.

She began to speak to him, but stopped to close her eyes for a moment. She slept until the taxi jerked to a stop in front of the hotel.

Chapter 3
Sunday morning, July 26 – Jack

JACK HADN'T bathed since before Le Secret. Raoul's apartment had no running water, only the toilet and sink down the hall, and by morning the unrelenting heat had turned him into a sweaty mass. Scant ventilation came from a tiny window that overlooked an alley strewn with puddles of grease and rotting garbage, and was best left closed to diminish the stench. Even so, it made him nauseous.

He touched his forearm—the skin felt raw and chafed, the stubble of his hair irritating, itching, and made worse when he scratched. He had paid the price for the spectacular arousal he'd experienced at Raoul's hand, the deft manager of the straight razor that had glided over his skin; the cool steel slipping through lather so smartly the bubbles made a sizzling sound as they popped. Raoul's suggestion had disgusted him at first, and then scared him. But once he acquiesced, Jack felt the hairs on his body give themselves over to that irresistible blade, one by one, each pull and slice releasing a tiny exclamation of joy that collectively became a chorus of ecstasy rising from his body. His freshly bared skin pulsated in the air, as though plunged into ice, despite the blanket of heat smothering the room. He lay there, eyes closed, while Raoul performed this subtle, dangerous massage, and allowed himself to float on the sensation. Finally, an hour later, when he had been shaved completely clean from his neck to his toes, he gave himself over to his barber, in the process abandoning whatever reservations he had of partaking of what he felt sure Gus—and even Kera— would call depraved and disgraceful. But to hell with Gus. To hell with the act. For the moment he would rather yield himself to this severe, knife-like passion, and worry about the cost later.

Jack had never expected such pure pleasure from one as admittedly ragged-looking as Raoul. He had gone to Le Secret on the advice of a man he met the night before, who assured him the clientele were of exquisite proportions. Like a customer led on by an exaggerated advertisement, Jack discovered the boast debatable. Certainly the man who followed him around the bar, the one haunting him from the shadows, was not of the class of men he hoped to meet. He resembled something of a scarecrow, wearing a jacket much too large and pitifully old, and making the ensemble worse by sporting a yellow tie secured crookedly around his neck. Jack tried to avoid him at first, hoping to strike up a conversation, or at least a visual encounter, with someone else, to preempt the gargoyle's advances, but no one else there spoke English, and Jack was left to sit alone at the bar. When Raoul came over, he resigned himself that it would be the best he could do that night.

He could barely understand Raoul's words. "I drink for you," he'd said, and Jack didn't know if that meant a toast or a gift. It didn't matter though, since he had only the few coins Kera had given him and he was reluctant to spend them. Let this creature buy him a drink, and if he turned out to be as strange as he seemed, Jack would make an excuse and leave. It might surprise Gus if he got back to the hotel room before dawn.

But Jack discovered a magnetism to Raoul that drew

him in. Raoul ordered the drinks for both of them, claiming he would appreciate a fine brandy. And when the bartender filled the order too slowly to suit him, Raoul slapped the bar in impatience and commanded the man to hurry. As he gestured, Raoul's thick, greasy mane bounced about his neck. Jack felt himself mesmerized by its movement—he had always been attracted to men who lived free of society's dictates, and now he began to look past the rough façade into a defiant, aloof spectre of the mystery he'd sought since arriving in the city.

Within two drinks they had transformed into a magician and his subject. Whenever Raoul spoke he shook his head and looked off into the corners of the club, as though searching for someone better. This only made Jack work harder to keep his attention. He put the palm of his hand in the middle of Raoul's chest. "What are you looking for?" he asked. "Everything you want is right in front of you." Raoul had nearly broken Jack's fingers when he took the hand in his and twisted it away. Despite the pain Jack maintained contact. Raoul's domination made Jack's muscles tighten. Raoul then shook him off, stood abruptly away from the bar and walked to a table in the dark. Jack followed, now entranced. Dancers took the floor and the rest of the clientele crowded around them, but Jack preferred to stay in the corner. While everyone else watched the Apache, he fixated on Raoul. The man from last night had been right— it had simply taken some time to see it. The rest of the evening now stretched open before him, and he became eager to get it under way.

Jack was about to suggest they leave when he saw familiar figures coming down the stairs, pausing before they reached the bottom in order to see over the crowd. He knew Gus must suspect his evening activities—after the week here even that simpleton should be able to put it together—but he never thought Kera would find out. Gus must have dragged her along. Jack thought for a moment that if Gus wanted entertainment, he just might give him some—but then Kera would see it too. She was still his friend. Damn him for bringing her. He turned to Raoul and said, "Now. Where is your apartment?"

The shave had been as close as Jack had come to washing in nearly two days. But lather made a poor substitute for soap. He moved his fingers to his shoulder, touching skin slick with a mixture of sweat and oil. He ran his palm over his head. The pomade he used in his hair had broken down and saturated his scalp, and the hair itself had hardened into matted ringlets that clung to him like glue. He rolled over on the bare mattress and tried to rub some of the filth from his body.

It hadn't mattered much until now, so hypnotized was he by Raoul. They'd lain together for hours, until Raoul rose abruptly, dressed and left, declining to say where he was going, or when he would return, leaving Jack in the dark without a sense of the time. Jack knew he would never find his way back to the hotel and decided to stay. He might miss the matinee at the Vaudeville, but what of it? Why give them another free performance? In the morning he found a length of stale bread and some cheese, and that and a half bottle of warm beer became breakfast. He dressed in the sweaty clothes from the night before. But Raoul came back—drunk, with a near empty bottle in his hand—and sat on the bare floor next to Jack. He reached up along the mattress until his hand encompassed Jack's knee. Jack felt the pressure of the embrace, a cold, restricting sleeve against movement, against his will. Raoul clamped down harder and began to twist, rotating Jack's lower leg from this fulcrum like the limb of a marionette, forcing his heel to touch the inner thigh of his opposite leg, then further until it reached his crotch—painful now with the stretch of his tendons to the point of tearing. Raoul's elongated, bony fingers appeared incapable of damage—suitable, perhaps, for holding a glass of wine or a flower. But on contact they became the coils of a python, wrapping ever more tightly, the hold deepening with any attempt at struggle, and Jack could not pull them away. He felt Raoul's hand press into the stubbly skin along his calf, down to the ankle, pausing to tweak his toes before preparing to pounce across into his groin.

"Not now," Jack said. It was the first time he had objected.

Raoul stopped his hand and swung his body up onto his knees. Jack raised his head from the bed.

"I need…to bathe. Please. I am disgusting. Can you get some water?"

Raoul recoiled and whipped the back of his hand across Jack's mouth like the python's tongue. "Pig!" he said, in a voice that sounded to Jack like the wind rushing between buildings. He rose, put on his pants and took a swig from a bottle on the little table by the window. Wordless, he went out into the hallway, leaving the door open behind him. Jack struggled up and poked around the doorjamb to watch Raoul go shoeless towards the sink at the end of the hall. Jack moved the door so no one could see him from outside, but left it open, and sat back down on the bed. He started sweating again. He could feel his pulse pounding behind his ears. The rest of his body became numb—waiting, anticipating. He took short, quick breaths. Raoul's unpredictability held him fast now, and kept him from running like a crazy man from this dank prison, down the stairs and into the street.

Jack's legs began to shake. The pain in his knee made him wince as he walked to the table and snuck a drink from the bottle—a harsh rye whiskey. He realized that Raoul would smell the alcohol on his breath, and so stumbled back to the bed and began licking the far side of the mattress to try to reduce the odor.

Raoul pushed the door open. He had a pitcher and a small basin, and put them on the floor by the bed. "You are disgust," he said in his halting English. "Wash."

Jack swung around, careful not to let his breath escape. He sat on the floor, next to the basin, poured the water in and dipped his fingers tentatively before running wet hands along his face and neck, and down the front of his chest to his abdomen. Raoul stood and watched, transfixed. Jack looked up at him. He wanted to ask for soap, but was unsure how the request would be received. Raoul seemed to interpret this and grunted. He took the jug and went back out into the hall.

Jack kept applying drips of water to his body, not wanting to waste what he had. It was barely enough to wet above his waist, but he managed to save some to pour over his head. The drops trickled down his shoulders and onto the floor, disappearing into the cracks in the floorboards. Jack wondered if it would drip into the apartment below and alert the tenant to their night of debauchery.

He reveled in the wetness. He still was far from being clean, but it felt wonderful even to rinse some of the sweat off his irritated skin. Raoul came in again, with another jug of water and a small cake of soap, and handed them to Jack. He had a towel too, and stood by like a guard, waiting for him to finish.

"Merci," Jack said, and began to indulge himself, like a man who hadn't eaten for days. He rubbed the soap on top of his head until his hair filled with suds, then left his hands in the bubbles, massaging his temples and scalp, closing his eyes and imagining himself back in the hotel room, bathing in the tub while Gus sat on the bed, picking morosely at his banjo. He'd splash the water occasionally, trying to get Gus to turn around, but it was useless. Jack would start to sing, and Gus would get up and leave the room.

Raoul snapped him out of the fantasy. "Wash everything," he said, nodding towards the lower half of Jack's union suit, which was still around his hips. Jack soaped his legs and feet. He slid the cake between his toes, taking more time, now that he had ample water to do the job. He heard

Raoul exhale deeply, and say, "everything" again, in that ominous tone. Jack wriggled and slid the suit off, placing it on the mattress, and started to lather. He looked at Raoul, who was unbuttoning his pants.

"Give me the towel," Jack said. But Raoul instead flipped it onto the table and sat on the edge of the bed. He put his hands on Jack's shoulders and slid them along the wet skin. In a moment those fingers slipped around Jack's biceps, gripping, almost penetrating the flesh, surely leaving marks, and pulling Jack up and onto the mattress. He dared not fight him or the pain would become worse, and so allowed his body to become limp with acquiescence. But what had been indescribable pleasure just hours ago yielded to fear and guilt over what he had left behind—his commitments to the act and to Kera's friendship. Did they miss him? Were they trying to find him? And when they left for home in a few days would they care if he was with them? Jack closed his eyes and tried to substitute erotic delight for the self-loathing that began to overtake him.

When Jack awoke later he was dry, except for his hair, and the towel spread across his loins. He leaned on an elbow to look at Raoul, who sat in a chair by the table, naked, reading a book under a bare electric bulb, and smiling. Jack had not seen him smile before, and the sight was something of a shock—it didn't seem that someone with the temperament of Raoul would ever smile. Raoul murmured in French and then laughed and said, "Oui. Oh, oui." Jack watched for a while, laying his head back down to the mattress and half closing his eyes, so Raoul might think him still asleep. His lover kept changing positions in the chair, trying in vain to make himself more comfortable, but his flat, bony backside made it impossible. Jack couldn't understand how one so thin, emaciated in fact, could possess the strength he had displayed. Or did Raoul possess another kind of power over him? Until this afternoon he had been alternately angry or withdrawn, but here was another mood, one he had hoped to encounter sooner. Jack sat up and asked, "What are you reading?"

Raoul held up the book, but Jack couldn't read the cover and leaned over the edge of the bed, squinting.

"L'Oiseau Bleu," Raoul said. "Blue Bird. By Maeterlinck." He went back to reading.

"Maeter . . ? I don't know…"

"A Belgian."

"Is it a comedy?"

"No."

"You were laughing."

Raoul turned and now seemed on the verge of tears. "Such truth in a play of children. Wondrous! Maeterlinck—he speaks to me."

"Tell me," Jack said, sympathetic to the point of nearly crying himself. "Read to me." This seemed to please Raoul, and Jack sat up on the bed like a boy about to hear a fairy tale.

Raoul stared down at the book, apparently collecting his thoughts, preparing to translate the text into his fractured English. "This is the scene in a forest," he said. "The children, they come to steal the Blue Bird. The trees speak to them." He read deliberately, in bursts of recognition followed by near incomprehension: "Your father…he has done us much harm…He has put to murder…six hundred!" He stopped.

"What does it mean?"

"It is message. Maeterlinck masks the words. But I know. The killers—Jaurès and his kind—they make the deaths. They make death of the nation. Maeterlinck, he understands."

Jack failed to see how a Belgian could comprehend what was killing France. "How can they murder the country?"

"They keep us out of war."

"I don't understand."

Raoul placed the book on the table. "When it is war,

France will once again be great. But if we do not fight, we are weak and puny. Our enemies destroy us." He picked up the book again and ran his finger, like a pencil, along the page until he located the sentence he sought. "See? He says, 'Your father. Your father he has done us the harm.' He speaks of Jaurès. He is their father."

Jack tried to appear sympathetic, but he feared it looked like confusion, and the joy Raoul displayed when he read the passage the first time vanished. He struggled in his chair, like a man trying to free himself from shackles. He turned the page. "Listen!" he said, and read again. "We…the trees…we must not assume…responsabilité…for severe measures… The day when man hears what we are about to do…there will be…dreadful vengeance."

Jack didn't dare speak for fear of saying the wrong thing, but then, perhaps not speaking would infuriate him. Finally he said, "Yes. It is excellent."

"No!" Raoul said. "We are the trees. We patriots."

Jack thought he had a glimmer of meaning. "The patriots wish for France to be strong," he said.

Raoul clapped his hands together. "Yes! You see! And Jaurès and his weaklings, they make France into weaklings."

Jack felt his shoulders relax as the elation of having pleased Raoul eased his anxiety, even if he still had no idea about the hidden meaning in the play. He spoke again, hoping to make a deeper connection. "I admit he sounds like a terrible fellow," he said. "Who is this Jaurès?"

"My enemy. The enemy of all France."

"But why?"

"He wishes France not to fight."

"Fight against…who?"

Raoul slapped his forehead in frustration. "L'Allemagne! Who else can it be?"

Jack didn't know what nation or people Raoul meant, but he played along. "I am stupid, I know. Please…tell me

Raoul…I don't know the history. What did these people do to France?"

Jack's patronizing calmed Raoul's anger towards him at least, if not towards those Allemagnes. He pictured his lover at the head of an army, sword raised, wrapped in a flag, like an image he had once seen of Liberty.

Raoul dug the point of his forefinger into the wooden table and stared at it, as if a map lay in front of him. "They steal our land," he said. "Our honor. France is weak many years. Weaklings give Alsace and Lorraine to les Allemands. Forty years France is shamed." He pounded a fist into the table, verifying the shame as personal as well.

Jack remembered Gus saying something about a war on the way. "But now France will fight again? To win back the land?"

"We must fight. To rescue our brothers from slavery."

"Then France will be great again!"

"No."

"But you said…"

"First, we must rid of Jaurès. He fills France like cowards."

"How? What does he say?"

"He cries too many die… Of course men die! How else does France make glory?"

Jack tried to show his support for Raoul by changing his tone, "Why do they listen to him?"

"No more!" Raoul said. "I am tired. I must think how to defeat Jaurès. Then the people will come to the cause." He reclined as much as possible in the chair and crossed a leg over his knee, a professor of warfare pondering strategy for the struggle ahead. The picture suddenly seemed ridiculous to Jack. Try as he might to envision him in thoughtful repose, he saw only Raoul's raw, nude form entwined in the hard chair, more suited to animal passions than to anything intellectual.

Jack threw the towel aside and reached for his union

suit. He had some thinking of his own to do, and unlike Raoul, preferred to do it dressed. He began to slip into the garment, but stopped. It smelled as rancid as he had been, and putting it on would defeat the progress he'd made towards cleanliness. Some water remained in the basin, and some soap too, and Jack sat on the floor in with his legs scissored under him, dipped the fabric and began scrubbing.

Raoul's argument hadn't made much sense, but he assumed it was because he didn't know French history, and had to rely on Raoul's weak translations of the Maeter...whatever it was...for the logic. But the fragments of Raoul's assertions simply didn't fit together. They were more like random thoughts plucked from the ether of his mind to support a conclusion he had already decided was fact. He looked over at Raoul, who now mumbled to himself in French and pointing fingers at the air in front of him. Although Jack couldn't understand the comments, the gestures indicated Raoul was formulating a plan. It scared him. His itching skin and painful knee reminded him of what Raoul might do to satisfy his appetite for pleasure; how far might he go to quench a thirst for revenge, even if against only a perceived threat?

Despite the heat of the evening, Jack felt an unpleasant chill of recognition. How far had *he* gone to strike at Gus? Was this affair a way of lashing out at the person he'd shared the vaudeville road with for the last twelve years? He thought about that long time together—longer than most acts, longer than many of the marriages among his show biz acquaintances. Each of them was sixteen and ready to wade into the world. Even then Jack felt the attraction, and he felt sure Gus did too.

Maybe they should never have gotten together in the first place. Everyone told him that. Even Max Zapf sat him down in his office one day and said he could headline on his own if he worked hard enough. Gus, Max said, could play, but his singing fell far short of Jack's, and being saddled with a partner who didn't have the same level of talent would eventually become a burden. Jack didn't care. It was about more than talent. Jack wanted him around, so he proposed the idea of the lonesome cowboys, banjo and guitar, harmony from the old west. Acting the lonesome bit seemed better than living it, but when Gus refused to come around, his opinion changed. Performing on the road with Gus became a daily reminder that his partner would never feel the same way about him. And they had grown into completely different types of people. Gus only wanted to practice and perform. He seemed to have forgotten a world existed outside the theater.

As much as Jack enjoyed interacting with audiences, he looked forward more to the after hours. Once in London, and now in Paris, he dallied, unfettered by the Puritan opinions he encountered back home. It was so much easier to play on the continent. It only took the right questions, asked properly, to the right people. Amazingly, no one seemed to mind, and his post-show explorations became the highlights of his days. He found it funny, after the dozen years, that such affairs would lead to the disintegration of his and Gus's "marriage." Like an unhappy couple they had begun to quarrel over even minor differences. After their latest spat Jack looked for a new excuse to spite his partner. Then Raoul came along.

Raoul was asleep, his torso sprawled across the little table as though he had fallen unconscious in mid-thought, his head cocked awkwardly towards the closed window, and he snored lightly, the sound of a man completely unburdened by the consequences of his plans and hatreds. The book of the play lay next to his outstretched hand, teetering on the edge of the table as though seeking freedom from those brutal, crushing fingers. Jack could see the muscles of Raoul's shoulders and back just beneath the skin, taut and ready to spring, even in sleep, ready to snatch "The Blue Bird" back from its flight like some strange and savage carnivore. He saw, in Raoul's slumber, what he had not perceived while he was awake—an evil that would hurt or kill without remorse—and Jack felt fear rising inside him. He had to escape from here.

He felt caged, desperate to get out. He wanted to run out of the flat and into the street, back to the hotel, back to the frustrating security of the Ballo Brothers. Jack reached for his underwear, but it was still damp from the washing and he left it. He stood up slowly, feeling with the balls of his feet before putting his entire weight on the floor so as not to cause the boards to creak, and then slid over to the corner where his pants and shirt had lain in a heap—they would be relatively clean. He sat on the floor and put the pants on with excruciating care, working them inch by inch over his ankles and knees, sliding them painfully up his ravaged thighs, watching Raoul every second for any sign of movement. The shirt would be easier—he could do it standing up. Jack couldn't remember what had happened to his shoes, but that was fine—the shoes clomping down the hallway would surely wake Raoul. He buttoned one button—enough for now. Just a few steps to the door. Jack visualized opening it with enough care to keep the hinges from sounding an alarm. If he had to take an hour to do it, he would.

Raoul flicked a dreamless finger into the book, moving it a fraction of an inch, but enough to invoke the whole of the earth's gravity against Jack's escape. Almost before the thump of the book against the floor reached his ears, Raoul grasped Jack's wrist like a manacle. "You do not leave," he said.

Raoul dragged him back to the bed and plucked the shirt button open with his free hand. He pulled the shirt off quickly, in a single motion. Jack stood motionless, trying to detach himself from the situation. Raoul seemed to sense this—he brought him back to the moment by biting down hard on his nipple. The pain was unbearable, but Jack knew that if he screamed out Raoul would find a way to make it worse. He felt himself being pushed down onto the mattress. Raoul hovered over him, a drop of blood at the corner of his mouth. He wiped it away, then undid Jack's pants and yanked them off with such force that the friction burned his hips. Raoul rose from the bed and walked to a small cabinet on the far side of the apartment where the razor lay.

Jack knew what Raoul had in mind. He tried as hard and as quickly as he could to refocus his mind somewhere else. Onstage with Gus. They were walking out and Kera was coming back towards them. She had been wonderful. The crowd was ecstatic. They took their places and waited for the emcee to make the announcement. Gus tapped his toe on the hardwood floor. They would sing "Western Rose" once again. They looked at each other and smiled, and together began to strum.

Raoul took Jack's wrists in his hand and peeled his belt from his pants. He looped the strict leather around Jack's forearms and tightened it, then secured the other end to the bed frame. "It is better for you to not move," he said. He flicked open the straight razor in his hand. He had a towel but no shaving cream—not even soap to soothe the burning. There would be no ecstasy for Jack this time—no shared arousal, only Raoul's. "Lie flat," he said. Jack did as he was told. "You are bad boy, yes?"

"Yes, I am," Jack said.

"We start on the leg this time," Raoul said. He touched the blade to Jack's thigh, let it sit on the skin, cool and menacing. Like a surgeon Raoul examined the leg, as though looking for the best place for an incision. Jack held his breath. Finally Raoul began to slide the metal across the chafed surface. It stung, but was bearable. Raoul then stopped, pressed the edge into the skin just until it split, and traced a shallow path above the knee. They both watched as blood filled the line in red. Raoul exhaled and ran his finger along the cut.

Curtain Calls

Jack whispered, "No."
"Quiet!"
Jack closed his eyes, went back to the stage, and was already into the second stanza.

Chapter 4

Sunday morning – Kera

KERA AWOKE to a tempest within. Her mind roiled and forced her from sleep before her body was ready. Six a.m. She shook and perspired, even in the morning cool. Although she'd had less than five hours to recover, she knew she wouldn't be able to get back to sleep. While the rest of the Paris bar crowd, Gus included, would likely sleep off their drunken revels until noon, she rose earlier than usual, her hangover intensified by the contradictions the Parisians had presented to her, as well as the guilt she felt over her attraction to their indulgences. They were vulgar; they drank to excess—and their attitude intrigued her. They faced an oncoming war with almost complete indifference.

Their opinion of the war—or lack of one—did not seem the safest course, but then, they had Renoult and his group to care about it for them, leaving them free to drink and chase each other. Let the old men worry about the nation; what can we do about it? Life became more thrilling that way.

She remembered the Apache dancers. Kera, sitting up, reached behind her head and took a handful of her bobbed hair. She pulled, gently at first, then harder, like a man, like a lover who refused to be denied, until her lips moved higher and parted for his kiss, and she was looking at the ceiling. Her eyes remained open, fixed on the intricate patterns she imagined in the plaster, as though she watched clouds floating overhead. She forced herself to stop.

The hotel dining room wouldn't open for an hour, since it was Sunday, and Kera drew a hot bath with which she might steam away the throbbing in her head and the confusion she harbored over the sexual habits of this place—and of Jack, and even of Gus. As she rose she saw the calling card she'd placed on her nightstand. Monsieur Bertré had shown her the interest she hoped to get from Gus. He had fixated on her while the others talked about the theater and politics. But how could she take him seriously? He was at least sixty, although a handsome sixty, with the steel blue eyes of a virile, younger man, his gray hair and beard conservatively trimmed in the manner of a gentleman, who despite whatever other matters might demand his attention, never missed an appointment with the barber. Even his fingernails were immaculate—translucent, cultivated pearls, filed to an elegant smoothness and embedded neatly within manicured cuticles. They were so unlike Gus's fingers, callused and raw from the labor of the banjo. But the attraction to Bertré diminished just past his fingertips, for a few inches above them shone that gold ring, which precluded anything more than flirtation. At least, that was the way Kera remembered it. She might have been mistaken, for how could Bertré have been so audacious as to invite her to dinner in front of his friends, who would surely know if he were married? It could have been a different kind of ring, and in the smoky light of the cabaret and her own mental state she could have missed some aspect of it that would have made that clear. Then again, as Charles had said, this was Paris. Perhaps Bertré and his companions just didn't care about convention.

She had accepted his offer, that much she recalled. But

Bertré hadn't set a time. Perhaps in Paris a woman of culture knew instinctively when to be ready for dinner. Kera would have to prepare early—by six thirty she thought, to be safe—and wait for the car he said he would send. She sat at the vanity and brushed her hair as the water in the tub rose. She removed her nightshirt, unable to recall having put it on before she went to bed, and looked in the mirror. What did Bertré see that Gus didn't? She was not a spectacular beauty, and didn't consider herself such even in the guise of the Nightingale. The wig and makeup made her feel pretentious and gaudy, a plaything for the audience. Apart from some promotional photos Max had insisted on, she'd never allowed herself to pose for pictures in costume—what would her mother think?

She assessed her body, her shoulders and hips filling the reflection before her. There were plenty of suitors who liked her that way. But her face was her best feature, pure like a child's; as pretty, she believed, without makeup as with it. She debated for a few minutes about meeting Bertré without the powder and rouge she'd worn last night, but decided to present herself the way he'd been attracted. She would squeeze into the corset as well. Let him see her as he wanted. If Gus really wasn't interested perhaps she could get to know Bertré. He'd promised to show her the city. She would regret it as soon as she left if she didn't take him up on the opportunity. And if the French weren't afraid of this war, she would try not to fear it as well.

Kera went downstairs after seven. The plain white blouse and black skirt would do for the daytime. She was the first breakfast guest in the dining room. And thank goodness the hotel had a dining room. After Max had booked them into steerage on the ship coming over, she feared their hotel would be of similar quality, but the agent had surprised her. The Royal Fromentin wasn't the Waldorf, but it was comfortable, and within walking distance from the theater, saving the performers the trouble of deciphering the Paris trolley system or springing for taxi fare. And since Kera didn't have to double up as Gus and Jack had, she enjoyed the added benefit of a private room—clearly a mistake in planning by the usually spendthrift Max. The dining room faced the sunrise, and the cloudless morning was already bright, perhaps too bright for Kera's day-after sensitivities. She sat in a corner, away from the windows, at a table for two with immaculate linen and silver. The scent of the fresh tablecloth was the first sign that she was returning to her usual self, and she began to relax.

Kera had the waiter pour her a cup of coffee, and then went to the buffet and chose a croissant and peach. Some newspapers lay draped over a rack near the display of food, and she rummaged through them. The London Times was two weeks old. She had seen *Le Figaro* previously—occasionally one of the local performers left the French daily in the theater dressing room. Next to it was another French language publication, *L'Humanité*. Both had yesterday's date, and since she saw nothing more recent Kera took them back to her table. She scanned the stories for information about the fighting in the east. Perhaps she should take more of an interest in events, as Gus had suggested.

There was little in *Le Figaro* that made the situation any clearer to her—merely reports of communications between governments, but nothing regarding the sources of the conflict, and nothing about what might happen next. *L'Humanité* was different. The paper ran articles on the debate within the French government over whether to seek neutrality in the conflict. Opinion columns debated the pros and cons of whether French workers should declare a general strike and shut down the country to keep it out of the war. Although the tabloid seemed to have much more news about these events than its competitor, the causes of the trouble still confused her. She didn't see how what happened a thousand miles to the east could have such an effect on France. She could ask Gus to explain it. But it was still too early to disturb him. And Kera wasn't so sure she wanted to see him now, after last night. Instead, she would ask Bertré when she went to dinner. He had said he was a newspaperman. He would tell her what it all meant and if she should be concerned.

After breakfast Kera decided to make use of what little temperate portion of the day remained before the reigning heat wave overtook the city, and she walked out to the streets of Montmartre to peruse the shops. There was nothing open on the Rue Fromentin, this being Sunday, save for a small streetside café that had no customers under its red and white umbrellas. Kera contented herself looking into the windows of the clothing stores, which daubed flashes of color among the apartments and offices. She lingered by the generous displays of dresses and accessories behind the large panes. In the states she rarely had an opportunity to browse such fashions—she was usually performing or traveling, and even if she had the time to shop, she was as likely as not to be bivouacked in some dreary frontier city where the fashions trailed at least a decade behind the times. In Paris, it seemed, culture and style lay nearly anywhere one cared to look. She imagined making the leisurely walk on the arm of Gus, but quickly changed it to a picture of Bertré. They would walk slowly, in perfect step. As she reached the end of the street, Kera looked over the tops of the apartments across from her. The upper half of the Eiffel Tower was painted against the cloudless morning sky. She leaned her head as if in search of her man's shoulder, the romanticism of the moment overpowering her sense of aloneness for a second. It was, even from over a mile away, as beautiful as she had seen in postcards, and she made it a point to visit the site close up before she left the city—with an escort, of course.

What would it be like to live here all the time? She saw it in colors, like a synesthete. Instead of the grim gray of street, clouds and clothing she experienced on her tours of

American theaters, bright reds and yellows, and blues like this sky, would greet her each day. The thought of such an exciting city becoming her home made her anxious, as though, with luck, it might somehow come true.

Kera turned the corner to the Rue Duperré and stopped in front of a milliner's named Madame Plumé. The bloom of a persimmon-colored hat caught her eye. It was a simple yet spectacular affair—a straw brim and crown in red-orange, adorned with three silk flowers in an even livelier orange hue, just bleeding color. She bent down a little—the sun was behind her and the shop window reflective, and she positioned herself to approximate what it might look like if the hat rested on her head.

"Lovely. Yes!" said a man in overalls coming down the sidewalk. "Were I a wealthy man I would buy it for you."

Kera hadn't seen him and straightened when he spoke. Normally she would apologize, or turn away. But a new mood struck her. "And were you a wealthy man," she said, "I would let you." And she smiled at him as he tipped an imaginary hat of his own.

By design standards the hat in the window was plain compared to the one she wore, and to most of the hats she saw back in America, but no hat this color would dare be more complex without making a spectacle of itself. As it was, she thought it perfect, and she had to have it. She wanted to buy it before her dinner with Bertré tonight, but the shop wouldn't open until Monday. She would have to find time to purchase it during the week. Kera made a note of the address and walked on, buoyant on the wave of her impending purchase. Her morning malaise had passed.

At noon Kera came back down to the dining room, before she had to leave for the matinee at the theater. The temperature had climbed again to nearly one hundred degrees and the stuffiness of the poorly ventilated room dictated she make it a light lunch. Two couples entered just after her, and a middle-aged man and woman sat at a table a few feet away. She sensed they were spending their last day here—they displayed the touch of apprehension that accompanies having to catch a train soon. She imagined them as typical tourists, having come from a provincial town to see the sights of the great city. The couple spoke almost in whispers, but in the quiet dining room Kera could translate every word.

"I don't want to leave either," the husband said, "but after all, it's only two days. And we can come back again when it's safe. We'll have another holiday then."

"Are you sure we have to leave now?" the wife asked.

"I don't know. But why take a chance? If we stay they may draft me. The army is drafting everyone right now."

"You are serious?"

"Who knows?" the husband said. "If the generals get their way they may even draft you."

The wife chuckled and patted her husband's hand.

Kera wanted to know more, but then she'd have to admit to eavesdropping, so she made up her mind to find a newspaper. Perhaps some new report would explain the couple's unease. Something had happened, somewhere, and it was significant enough to frighten people out of Paris. Had the war come to France overnight?

She took a last bite of her lunch and rushed out of the dining room. She found no newspapers in the hotel lobby, and began to presume that the news was indeed bad and the staff was hiding the facts from the guests. Although she anticipated his response, she went up to the chausseur.

"Have you received the newspapers today?" she asked.

He was young, not much older than she, and he smiled broadly at her. "No madame. There seems to be some trouble with the delivery."

"Then I suppose it makes no sense to ask you what is happening with this war everyone is talking about."

"War? There is no war, madame."

"I just heard some of the other guests. They said they were leaving early because of it."

"That must be the couple from Lyons," he said. "They are departing today, but not on account of any war. It is another matter. You must have misunderstood."

"I'm quite sure of what I heard," she said. The clerk shrugged his shoulders. This was fruitless. "When the newspapers get here will you please have someone bring one to my room?" she asked.

"Certainly, madame. As soon as they arrive."

He would likely ignore her request, and felt sure the papers had already arrived and been removed from the lobby. The couple in the dining room must have seen the report before the staff got to it.

Kera went back to her room and gathered her things for the matinee. She realized as she did that she had spent almost all her money last night at Le Secret. There were just a few francs left, her emergency money, hidden under her lingerie in the dresser, along with the ticket for passage back to the states. She took two francs, leaving just three, not even enough for the train to Le Havre to catch the ship. She would check with Gus to see if he'd made any progress with the management about their pay. If he hadn't, she might have to approach them herself. Perhaps she would do it in costume—men seemed to respond more obligingly to her that way.

She went downstairs and through the lobby to the street. The sun beat down from a still cloudless sky, making it even hotter on the sidewalk than in the hotel. The heat became unbearable in just a few dozen yards. As she turned the corner onto the Boulevard de Clichy, she stopped, took out a franc note and looked at it. By the time she walked to the theater she would be exhausted, and it might affect her performance. Kera was already short of what she needed to get to the seaport, so what would be the difference if she spent some of this? She hailed a taxi.

The drive took only a few minutes but was worth it. As

the car pulled up to the theater's side door, Kera saw Gus squinting in the sun as he came down the avenue. He looked haggard, as though he hadn't slept well either, his gaze fixed down at the cobblestones as he walked. It was too late to offer him a ride, but too far away to wait for in the heat. Kera paid the driver and went inside.

As she usually did, Kera peeked from behind the curtain to gauge the crowd, and this time she looked to see if Bertré had kept his word about attending the revue. She didn't see him—in fact, she saw hardly anyone in a house three quarters empty. Matinees were often less well attended than evening shows, and this one, affected as well by the news and the stifling temperature of the afternoon, was sure to be a loss for the promoters, and in turn, the performers. She decided not to tell Gus. He would find out when he and Jack walked onstage.

Miraculously, someone had placed a few tiny, noisy electric fans on the counter in the dressing area, affording some slight relief in the otherwise stagnant atmosphere. Kera expected to see Gus cloistered at the end of the room, brooding until stage time as usual, oblivious to the people around him, including her, as he prepared himself for the show. She would talk to him anyway.

Instead Gus was waiting for her when she came in. "He never came back to the room last night," he said. "He always comes in by sunrise, but this time he's gone."

"Jack?"

"I didn't even see him go. It was like he vanished."

"I hope he's all right."

"I should have known this was going to happen. After last night…" His voice became almost a whisper. "I'll have to go on by myself."

"I'm so sorry, Gus," she said. "I wish there were some way I could help."

"There is. Will you tell LaRoche that it's just going to be me?"

"Of course."

"Tell him it's Gustav Ballo."

"What will you sing?"

"I'm not really sure," he said. "A couple songs might work without the harmony."

Kera sensed a change in his voice. He seemed almost contemplative, aware of his predicament, for once trying to reason his way out of a dilemma instead of closing himself off, but it was odd to see him this way—without the wall he erected to keep the world at bay. If only this change were permanent.

Kera thought for a moment about offering to sing the harmony with him, but she'd have to have the sheet music onstage, and that wouldn't look good to the audience. Without a chance to rehearse they would probably have difficulty staying in sync. She didn't know what else to do, and started looking for LaRoche.

The manager refused to stand for the variation. "Unacceptable," he said. "Tell him we are paying for two cowboys, and we will have two cowboys."

"You aren't paying for anything!" Kera surprised herself with the tone she used. "None of us has been paid for more than a week."

LaRoche jerked his head back, as though he hadn't known about the lack of pay. He stuck two fingers into his collar to loosen its grip on his throat. "That is not my concern."

"Well, if you don't let Gus go on by himself, then I won't go on either." She felt an excitement at her words, knowing LaRoche would have to give in or lose both American acts.

"What do I care?" He waved his hand and turned away from her. "I have more important business to attend to. Just make sure he doesn't fall asleep on the stage this time."

"Gustav Ballo," Kera called as LaRoche walked away. "Introduce him as Gustav Ballo."

Her request, of course, was ignored, and after Kera

performed the emcee introduced Gus as the Ballo Brothers. She watched from the side as he walked slowly to center stage, his Stetson pulled down lower than usual, almost covering his eyes. Gus brought the banjo up to play, but paused, raising his index finger. "Un Ballo," he explained to the sparse crowd, using perhaps the only French word he'd picked up in three weeks in the country. A few people laughed. Someone called out, "Où est votre frère?" Gus shrugged, knowing neither what the person said, nor where his "brother" was. He tapped his toe as he would if Jack were there, but instead of the usual furious burst from their instruments, Gus merely strummed, laying down a simple melody as background. He held the banjo at a strange angle. His singing sounded flat, as though he didn't care.

She went back out and watched from behind the curtain. Since Gus never made eye contact with the audience Kera had always found it difficult to tell how detached he was from any show, but this afternoon she felt sure he performed in the Theatre du Vaudeville in body only. His mind seemed far away, perhaps searching the alleys and cabarets of Paris trying to find Jack. She watched the faces in the audience—most of them did not enjoy the spectacle. Many were talking as he sang. Someone in the crowd whistled. Gus acted as though he hadn't heard, but Kera feared if he went on much longer the whistling would spread, wake him from his dream and force him from the stage. She didn't want to be there when that happened, and went backstage to change out of her costume.

As she started for the dressing room, LaRoche stopped her and pointed a finger in her face. "Your boyfriend," he said. "Tell him if he doesn't have his partner with him tomorrow, he is out." He gestured towards the exit. "I don't care if you go with him or no!"

Kera had her wig off and was removing her gloves and jewelry when Gus came backstage. She hoped he would continue to confide in her, and even moved another performer's things from the station next to hers to make space for him, but the old Gus had returned. He stopped a dozen feet away, in a corner of the room, and laid his banjo gently against the wall. But then he took off his hat and flung it to the ground. He ripped the gun belt from his hips and flipped it onto the counter, nearly hitting the mirror, and landing hard enough on the shelf to startle several of the performers still preparing for the show.

"I'm sorry, Gus. I guess it didn't go very well," she said over the two French comedians between them.

"I don't know what I'm doing out there."

"Jack will come back. There must be a reason he didn't make it to the theater today."

"I don't need him," Gus said without turning to face her. "I just need a little more practice is all."

"Maybe there's something we can do..." She started to say the word "together," but stopped.

"No, I have to figure this out myself." He slid his belongings off the counter and into his bag. He didn't bother to change back into street clothes, but put the banjo in its case, picked up his things, and walked out the rear door and into the street.

Kera knew it wouldn't help to go out after him, and started to take off the rest of her costume. She looked around the dressing room, memorizing the scene, then picked up her bags and walked out into the heat of the mid afternoon to hail another taxi.

A loud knocking at her door awakened Kera, who had fallen asleep already dressed for dinner. She had put on her best gown—the only one presentable at the kind of dinner Bertré would surely provide—white cotton, high waisted and nicely cinched at the midriff thanks to the corset. She hoped it was worth the half hour it had taken to put it on. The neckline was cut low and square, the sleeves elbow length and lacy, and embroidered with white roses. As she scrambled to answer, she saw that the dress had wrinkled while she slept. It had been uncomfortably warm when she finished getting ready, and she lay back on the bed for just a moment to rest. An hour later the driver stood in the hallway, and she had no time to smooth out the fabric, or to fix her makeup and hair again. She was groggy from the short sleep as well. Her body had finally allowed her to achieve the deep slumber she needed to recover from the night before, and having been shocked out of it she had trouble getting her bearings. She reached for a veiled hat—as much to hide her face as shade it from the sun—and tied it under her chin. Taking her purse she stumbled towards the door. She would try to fix everything on the way downstairs.

But it was no driver, it was Bertré. "Oh, monsieur," she said. "My apologies. The room was very hot and I was waiting…"

"You look magnificent," Bertré said. "If only our French women took such care with their appearance."

She felt glad she'd worn the dress and corset. Anything less and she would have been embarrassed beside Bertré, who wore a tailored, charcoal colored suit. A gold watch chain hung from the pocket of his vest. She wondered if he had taken as long to prepare as she. He was a picture.

She took his arm and he led them to the stairs, while he described the restaurant he had selected for their dinner. "A quaint little place, but wonderful cuisine, and an atmosphere perfect for two people to get to know one another," he said. "I know the owner personally."

But as they walked past the front desk, she saw Gus. In all the times she had sat in hotel lobbies, hoping to catch him in passing, she'd never been able to time her mission well enough. Now, when she least wanted to run into him, he was there on a divan, wearing a black coat frayed at the seams, picking at his banjo and looking slightly sunburned. He looked like an itinerant street performer, like the ones who played outside theaters in America, looking to sop up a few pennies from those in the audience who hadn't had quite enough entertainment for the day. She was sure Bertré would see him as the same, or worse, and hoped they could pass without his noticing. He held a French newspaper in his hand, and he got up as they approached. She loosened her grip on Bertré's arm.

"Oh, Gus. You remember Monsieur Bertré?" she said. "We met him in the cabaret. He was with the owner."

"Of course," Gus said. "How's tricks?"

Bertré nodded slightly and looked down at the shorter man. "How is magic?"

"Tricks. It's like, how are you?"

"Then I am well." Bertré looked at Kera. "And who is this...homunculus?"

Gus answered for her. "You don't remember?"

"There was only one event worth remembering from last evening," Bertré said, "and that was making the acquaintance of this fabulous creature."

Gus took a step back, as if repulsed by Bertré's hyperbole, or by Kera's gullibility.

"Are you waiting for someone, Gus?" she asked.

"I was," he said, staring at her.

"Good," Kera said. "Good for you. This is our only evening in Paris without a show. You should get out and enjoy the city." As she said this, however, she noticed how intently Gus focused on her. His eyes studied her dress, her face—they seemed to plead for her to look back. Why couldn't he have said something last night, when she was trying so hard to get him to notice? Why not even at the matinee? But, no. She had concluded that Gus wasn't interested, and she would live with that. She promised Bertré this date, and she would go on it.

Gus said, "I hope you have a fine time tonight." He sat back down and looked out the front window.

"And you, too. Wherever you're going."

Bertré took her by the elbow and led her to the waiting

taxi outside. Kera took a glance over her shoulder at Gus. He remained motionless, not watching them leave. As Bertré held the car door for her, he said, "An odd one, that little fellow, isn't he?"

"He is lonely, monsieur. We are all lonely, are we not?"

The taxi wound its way through the Paris streets, out of Montmartre and within sight of the Seine. They motored past a variety of shops, most of them shuttered for the Sabbath. Kera was immediately disoriented. She began to imagine walking along the river in the twilight, her arm entwined with Gus's, instead of Bertré's.

Bertré shook her out of the dream. "Have I mentioned the owner of our restaurant is a personal friend of mine?" he said.

Only been a few minutes had passed and he needed to point that out again.

"It is a small place, but the food is wondrous. Everything first rate—the way a meal in Paris should be."

"Monsieur Bertré," Kera said. "I hope you have not gone to too much trouble for me."

"When one entertains a beautiful woman, the word 'trouble' does not exist. Every effort becomes a pleasure in such delightful company," he said. "And I must insist you call me Maurice. Monsieur Bertré is for the waiter."

"I am flattered."

"I see that you are not used to being treated as a lady should be. Tonight, all that will change."

Perhaps this was another insult directed at Gus, but she knew Bertré would never admit to it.

"I looked for you at the matinee today," she said.

He smiled. "I so wished to have been there. But with Jaurès away, much of the management of the newspaper falls on me."

"Yes, you said you were a journalist. Which newspaper is it?"

"*L'Humanite.*"

"Oh! I was reading it this morning in the hotel."

"I am surprised," Bertré said. "Some hotels will not permit us to leave copies."

"And they did not have today's edition. They made up some lie about a delivery problem."

"That," Bertré said, checking the condition of his fingernails, "does not surprise me. Those who do not agree with what we have to say wish to silence us."

"Monsieur…Maurice. What is happening? Is there a war? I have a thousand questions for you."

"In time, my dear. I will answer your questions. But for the moment, let us enjoy our evening. You will find that life in Paris is all about enjoyment."

Kera was puzzled. Was Bertré no different than the hotel staff—so occupied with an ulterior motive that he too chose to keep the truth from her? If anyone knew the weight of current events, he did. Kera decided she would not give him the satisfaction of her "delightful company" until he shared what he knew.

The taxi driver maneuvered into a narrow side street, where the low evening sun cast deep shadows. Paint hung off old buildings in strips like worn wallpaper. Here night had already arrived. They stopped in front of Le Paon—The Peacock—and having watched Bertré examine his nails a minute ago, Kera thought it a fitting location for their dinner. The restaurant was not streetside, but through a hallway on the ground floor of an austere apartment building. At the end of the corridor sat a room with a half dozen bare tables and a doorway into the kitchen. Beyond that she saw a small courtyard filled with ferns and violets, and another six tables set for dinner. Low brick walls overflowing with ivy partitioned the outside of the restaurant from its neighbors on either side, and the apartment building effectively blocked any connection with the rest of Paris, creating an island within the city. For light, a series of gas torches lined the sides and the center. A bald man with a moustache as big as the bristles on her hairbrush, the ends waxed and curled into spirals, came out from the kitchen. His lips held the stub of a cigarette and Kera thought that in a minute the embers might ignite the hair on his face. Bertré embraced the man by the shoulders and said it was good to see him after such a long while, and introduced him as Dominic. He then walked her to the outside area. Kera did not see any other diners. All this secrecy confirmed to her that Bertré was married. Why else would he go to such an out-of-the-way location except to ensure they would not be seen?

"Jaurès," she said as they were seated. "Who is he? One of your friends mentioned him at the cabaret last night as well." Kera wasn't about to allow Bertré to steer the conversation away from current events yet.

Bertré, however, busied himself by ordering a Pouilly-Fuisse. "This is one of the few places where one can get a decent bottle of wine these days."

"These days?" Kera pressed him. "What makes these days so different? Maurice, you must tell me what is happening. I will not allow myself to enjoy our dinner until you do."

Bertré smiled. "Very well. But I assure you there is no need to be alarmed."

"Everyone is saying that! I'll decide whether I should be alarmed or not. Now tell me!"

"It is true," he started, "that there is trouble in the east. In the Balkans, to be exact." He chuckled and added, "But when is there not trouble in the Balkans?"

She'd never heard of such a place before, and wished she had paid more attention to world events. But she couldn't let Bertré in on her ignorance. "Isn't it more serious this time?"

"To be sure. The Austrians have moved against the Serbs. But they are fifteen hundred kilometers away."

"Why then is the theater deserted? Why did I hear a couple in my hotel this afternoon talking about leaving Paris before the husband was drafted? I know there is more than you are telling me, Maurice."

He stared at her for a few seconds before answering. Finally he said, "Do you really wish to spoil our evening together with talk of politics?"

She clutched her serviette in frustration as though preparing to throw it onto the table. "Not ten minutes ago you said there were people who wished to silence you and your newspaper. Now that I want to hear, you are being silent of your own accord."

The waiter brought the wine, and they both waited while he poured and Bertré tasted. When their glasses were filled Bertré began again. This time he was more serious, and spoke in whispers, even though they were the only ones in the courtyard. "Were it merely the Austrians and the Serbs, there would be no need to worry," he said. "But the Russians will fight to protect the Serbs, and the Germans will fight on the side of the Austrians. And if those nations go to war as well, there are many in France who wish us to become involved for Russia and against Germany."

"But why? What do the French care about this?"

"It is insanity, I know. But it is the way of Europe. Our nations have been bound together in hatred for more than a thousand years."

"But surely in these modern times you have leaders who see there is no reason to go to war."

"There are some. Even now we wait for Jaurès to return to Paris. If anyone can put a stop to this madness, he can."

"Again Jaurès. Who is this Jaurès?"

"You have not heard of him?"

She felt ignorant, apologetic. "I have not, I'm afraid."

Bertré paused, as though trying to understand how Jaurès's fame had not spread to America. He said, "He is the voice of those who resist the war mongers. He is the voice of reason in an unreasonable age. Only two years ago Jaurès alone prevented war in Europe. This time, however, I am not so sure. The generals may have their way."

"I don't understand. How can one man stop a war?"

"With his words, my dear. Jaurès makes men see themselves as brothers, not as enemies."

"You make him sound quite remarkable."

"I assure you, he is not like you and me."

"Is he a god?" She smiled to show him it was a jest, but Bertré's face remained impassive.

"No. He is a man. But he thinks like a god."

"Then he shall be successful," she said. "After all, if he holds such sway over millions…"

"Too much has changed in Europe, and in France. Everyone seems ready to fight this time. Those of us who understand that peace is the future are an even smaller minority."

"If he isn't successful…" Kera said. "If there is war, what happens to Paris? Will it be safe? Gus and Jack and I must be here for another week."

Bertré pondered again. "You should be fine." But he hesitated, apparently thinking it over. "One never knows, however. If the ministers and generals are such fools as to lead us into this conflict, who can say if they are even capable of protecting us?"

"Should we leave then?"

"Perhaps not," Bertré said. "There may be something I can do to help you."

"Really? What could you do?"

Before he could answer the waiter returned to take their order. Bertré didn't need a menu. He ordered appetizers for both of them, then entrees accompanied by a red Bourgogne. Kera considered the risks of partaking of more than two glasses of sherry for a second night. When he was done he launched into another topic, neglecting Kera's question about how he could guarantee the Americans' safety. This time she didn't try to bring him back.

He lifted his glass and waited for her to do the same. "To the Parisienne Nightingale. As beautiful in person as she is on the stage."

This talk was far more pleasurable to Kera than that of politics, and also rare. The men she knew in the states were slow to compliment, preferring to discuss themselves or their careers, as though the choice of pursuing romance were entirely up to them. As the wine flowed, she began to forget the conversation about war and let herself float along with Bertré's flattery. His voice was as smooth and polished as his fingernails, and she trusted him. But each time she inquired about his business or his background, he delved further into *her* life—her singing, her tour of England and the continent, even her family in America. She knew she was talking a great deal—probably more than she had in the weeks on tour with Gus and Jack, more than she'd ever been encouraged to by her mother and stuffy relatives in Connecticut—and she reveled in being able to speak so openly and without criticism. She knew also that she was drinking as much as last night. But each time she looked at her wine glass, it was full, as though she hadn't been drinking at all.

When they rose at the end of dinner Kera felt herself wobbling. But instead of Gus's retreat, Bertré met her with a waiting, welcoming arm, offering her balance and security against embarrassment in the eyes of the other diners. Although…there still were no other diners. Had Bertré reserved the entire restaurant to preclude the possibility of them being seen together? It couldn't be. He was such a gentleman—it was merely a coincidence. Still, she resolved to ask him about his marital status as soon as he dropped her back at the hotel.

The owner, no doubt at Bertré's bidding, had already retained a taxi for the return trip. Bertré handed a slip of paper to the driver, presumably with the hotel address, before getting in and continuing his praise of her appearance and talents. Since Kera hadn't recognized any of the streets while coming, she didn't expect to remember them on the way back, so she was startled when the taxi stopped in front of a well-maintained apartment house instead of the Royal Fromentin.

Although her head spun from the wine, she kept her guard. "Maurice I am shocked. Surely you know I am a woman of more virtue than this!"

Bertré patted her hand. "More respect for you I could not have," he said. "But allow me to explain."

"This is your home?"

"No, no. Not at all."

"Then what?"

"I was thinking about our talk earlier—about the possibility of war and how it might affect life in Paris. I remembered you were so concerned about your safety, as am I. And I know the neighborhood of your hotel. It is not always the best place to be. I realized; I have this apartment. I am not using it. It is safe. This is a wonderful neighborhood. The apartment is lovely. And if you wish, it is yours, for as long as you desire to remain in Paris."

"But I couldn't stay here."

"And why not?"

"I could never afford to pay you."

"I would not accept payment if you could," Bertré said.

"But still…"

"Why don't you come upstairs and take a look? If it does not meet with your approval, I will take you back to the hotel immediately. Here," he said, handing the taxi driver some coins, "I will have the driver wait while we go up."

She couldn't fight his logic and his assurances, and agreed to go up for a quick look. By the time they reached the front steps Kera believed she might be convinced to stay. A red-jacketed portier greeted them, calling Bertré by name, and ran ahead to summon the elevator. The bright foyer's décor was lush—a hand-woven runner graced the marble tile floors, and the walls featured intricate flowered wallpaper above, paneled wainscoting below. Compared to this the foyer of the Fromentin resembled the interior of a barn.

Bertré's apartment was on the top floor of the four-story building and was as lavishly decorated. The three rooms had a museum quality, reminding her of her father's study back home. The living room was lined with French pastorals and busts of ancient Greek poets and statesmen, whose presence helped confirm Bertré's air of superiority. Antique furniture graced the carpets. She stopped just past the doorway.

"You said you were a journalist. This does not look like the apartment of a journalist."

"My family has money," Bertré said. "And someone has to help keep the newspaper alive. *L'Humanite* is not always the most popular of journals, but I believe in what we do. If that costs me a few francs, it is well worth it." He walked towards the balcony, stopping at a cabinet. "Please, come inside. There is much more to see." He pulled out a crystal decanter and two glasses.

Kera hesitated. "Maurice, you know I have had enough to drink. I cannot…"

He put one glass down. "Then you won't mind if I have a taste. This is an excellent Pomerol."

"If this is not your home, what is it?" Kera asked. "Don't you have a home to go to?"

"Yes, of course. That is why I am able to offer this apartment to you."

"But why? You've only known me for a day—less than a day. How can I trust you? How can you trust me?"

Bertré put his glass down and moved close to Kera. He took her by the hand, leading her into the cocoon of his family's wealth. "Perhaps once in a life a man meets a woman who transcends every notion of beauty he has ever known. A woman, he knows instantly, who is his destiny. And to the possession of her he will dedicate himself. Last night, I met such a woman."

His tone indicated he had more to say, but he stopped.

Kera felt his arms slipping around her. She took his hands in hers and removed them from her hips. As she did so, he grabbed her wrists and pulled her towards him. Kera broke free and pushed him away. "Maurice! I told you I wasn't that kind of girl!"

"You are a girl? Let me show you how much of a woman you are," he said, and lunged forward to grab her. He braced himself and pulled her in slowly with both hands. Why did love always have to be in the hands of the man? If Kera let him dictate the situation, Bertré would impose his will. He would ruin her reputation. She squirmed and freed an arm, wound up and slapped him hard just above that perfectly trimmed beard.

He stopped and breathed heavily, and looked ready to give up the attempt. But Kera felt strange inside. She should have been scared. She should have run for the door while she had the chance and screamed for the portier to come and rescue her. But she wasn't afraid now. The same feeling—the one she'd had at the club while watching the Apache dancers—came over her. It started in the pit of her stomach—a confused undulation of anxiety and pleasure— and it spread out from there. It moved upwards to her chest, and she took a deep breath so that it might speed the feeling on to her head. And it went down, embracing her hips, sliding along her thighs and back up again, like smooth hands slipping between her legs. It could be Maurice's hands—those perfect fingers caressing her. The core of her body began to vibrate.

She slapped him again.

She stood back and let a little smile come to her lips. It was all Bertré needed to see.

He slapped her cheek, but without force.

"Harder," she said. "Like this." Kera hit him hard enough to turn his head around.

This time he seized her by the waistband of her dress and pulled her in, his arousal like rage, until she pressed against him. He bent her backwards as he kissed her, and she grasped the hair at his temples and pulled. They fell against the wall, skewing one of his paintings. After a minute they released, panting, gathering energy for more. Bertré took her hand and she relaxed, closed her eyes and fell into his kiss. And in that kiss she gave up her resolve to find out if he was married.

He placed his hand in the small of her back and began to nudge her towards the bedroom. While she walked, her mind swimming with wine and romance, Kera closed her eyes, and for a moment the image of Gus appeared—sitting on the divan in the lobby of the Fromentin, dressed shabbily, but dressed for her, waiting for her, after all the times she had waited for him. He had a newspaper. Now she understood. He had wanted her to translate—they would sit together and she would read and learn what was going on about this war, and he would teach her what the stories meant. Dear Gus.

She pictured him staring forlornly out into the street as they had left. But when she opened her eyes it was Bertré in front of her—so attentive, and so eager and willing to show her how he felt. Kera felt ready to explore these new sensations—the emotions that the French dancers had revealed to her. Gus could never help her reach their depths. She could not imagine him partaking in anything where he would have to lose control of himself. No, it was Bertré who would go with her tonight to that new place. She looked at him—his jacket, vest and tie were already on the floor.

And she would stay in his apartment. If Gus found out, how would she explain it to him? But then, why should she? It was all so confusing, and she didn't want to be confused now. She let her reservations drain away. Tonight, she would abandon the anxieties of the past few weeks and give herself to Bertré.

Chapter 5
Monday midday, July 27 – Gus

NOTHING BUT trouble now, ever since they arrived in Paris. Gus dressed quickly before he changed his mind, before he examined his options too closely and determined the one he'd chosen was not as promising as it seemed. He'd missed the breakfast service, and would go to the theater hungry, the better to keep his resolve sharp. They'd been pushing him into a fight—the whole city had—and now he would take them up on it. They'd learn that he knew how to stand up for himself. He would demand the back pay from the management today, and he wouldn't quit until he had it, even if it didn't prompt Jack's return, or keep Kera out of the clutches of that Frenchman.

He'd stayed up late the night before, fingering the steel of his banjo but keeping the strings from resonating, mouthing the lyrics as he ran through the songs from the act in his head, trying to imagine how his voice should sound during the next performance if Jack still hadn't returned. A little practice and the crowd pleaser from when he crooned in bars along the Bowery, before he met Jack, would come back; it would be the voice he had projected the other night when the two of them created that pitch-perfect harmony.

But even in the ideal acoustics of his mind he couldn't do it. The voice he heard echoed from the matinee; it sounded hollow and detached, as though he no longer cared about the music. Instead of an audience in front of him he'd visualized the chaos of Le Secret—the mass of bodies pressed against each other on the dance floor, his partner like a fly in the grasp of a spider, and Kera flirting with those men. Each time he heard a door or a footstep in the hotel hallway he paused his imagining. Was it Jack? Kera? Was Bertré with her? How naïve of her to trust that gigolo. Gus had looked into the arrogance of the Frenchman's eyes and knew his motive was seduction. His airs, his insults were part of the deception. How could she not see it? And just when Gus had felt ready to accept her, to seek her company, she abandoned him; she stood by while Bertré ridiculed him. She'd dressed up for the Frenchman too. She hadn't worn that outfit on the tour before.

He would have to forget all that now. He needed her to translate at the theater. LaRoche did not speak English, and neither did any of the management as far as he knew. Having Kera with him would keep them from making excuses that he couldn't understand.

Gus stopped by her room and knocked…he waited and knocked again. She must have gone out for a stroll. At the front desk, he asked the clerk if he could leave a message.

"Ah monsieur, I am afraid the lady is already gone."

"This is for when she returns."

"You don't understand, monsieur. Miss McGuin has checked out. She left this morning."

Gus's shoulders slumped. "This morning? Where did she go?"

"She did not say, monsieur. She had the boy bring her things down and put them in the taxi. A gentleman was with her."

"An old man? The one with the beard?"

"Yes, monsieur."

Gus turned and looked out the front door, as though they could still be seen walking to the car. "How long?" he asked.

The clerk checked a clock over his shoulder. "Perhaps two hours."

Gus shuffled towards the lobby entrance, touching things along the way—the back of a chair, a lamp, the leaves of a fern—things of substance. The deskman and the bellboy and the other hotel guests no longer existed for him, precluded from this empty reality.

"Monsieur, is there anything I can do?"

Gus headed into the street without acknowledging the clerk. The late morning had already heated up—there would be no break from the weather today. The bricks of Montmartre's buildings and streets worked like an oven, reflecting thick waves of heat off stone walls and cobbles. Gus wiped sweat from his forehead.

The sounds of the boulevard unnerved him, and reawakened him to his surroundings. In the sunlight he could see how filthy everything was, covered with the soot and grime of the city. Paris was old, older by far than New York, and crumbling in places. Perhaps the war would come and reduce it to dust. He walked past open shops and offices arranged randomly among cramped apartment buildings, each absorbing its share of the heat, save one lone store whose proprietor had the good sense to install an awning. Three pedestrians had gathered underneath for a respite. Everyone else sweltered. As he walked it was not so hard to imagine he was still on the Bowery, enduring a steamy Manhattan day.

A man with stained overalls plodded out from a butcher shop and sloshed a bucket of waste into the gutter, missing Gus's shoes by a few inches. He watched the blood from the pail trickle along the curb, as though someone had been shot. He was alert now to the sounds of the boulevard—cars, trolleys and horses made a sort of march with their cadences, and Gus picked up the beat, matching his footfalls to the rhythm of the tune that played in his head. But his fervor of a few minutes ago had dissipated, and he had to refocus on his task, to assure himself that he could do it, and that he should.

When Gus reached the theater he went around to the performers' entrance in the back. But the black door was locked, and no one came to open it when he knocked. Someone should have heard—there had always been access for performers who wanted to get in a little extra practice time. He tried another of the side entrances with no success.

The front door shouldn't have been open at this time of day, but since the usual passages were locked, maybe it was. He had to walk the length of the block to get there, ducking under an awning that shaded a little café at the theater's perimeter. The sidewalk here was crowded, and Gus weaved his way around groups of people who walked leisurely, sharing none of his anxiety over the impending war. How was it that he, a foreigner, knew the danger that threatened, but they did not? When he had to stop to allow a group of women to pass in the opposite direction, he raised his hand as if to warn them, but what could he say that they would understand? A waiter, seeing him loiter, offered to seat him at a small table. He ignored the man.

At the front entry the dirty windows of the theater's second floor management offices made the Vaudeville look more malevolent than before. The doors were shut, and a hand-lettered flyer hung somewhat crookedly from the middle of the five portals, as if whomever placed it had been in a hurry. There was a large line of text at the top, and some smaller handwriting beneath, but Gus understood none of it. He tugged on two of the doors to make sure they wouldn't open, then kicked one, more to attract attention than to cause damage. Perhaps the staff had all gone somewhere together for a meal. Or ran off to enlist.

Gus went to the edge of the street and waved at the first

person he saw on the sidewalk. An old woman ran into the road to get away when she saw him coming, barely avoiding a motorcar barreling along. A heavy fellow dressed in overalls and carrying a sack of what looked like flour over his shoulder came from the other direction.

"You there! Sir!" Gus said, quickly changing to "Monsieur" when the man ignored him. "English," he said. "Do you speak English?"

Nothing.

As Gus turned to look for another pedestrian, another man addressed him from behind. "Perhaps I can help you, monsieur. You are looking for something?"

"You speak English? Yes, you do."

The old man was well dressed, in a gray suit and vest, and a cravat around his neck despite the heat. He seemed content with the temperature, smiling under a bushy mustache that curled around his jaw and connected up with his sideburns. As he spoke he leaned on a cane, and Gus noticed him grimace as he shifted.

"Could you translate that sign? On the door." Gus pointed.

The man strained to read it. "It means, closed until further notice."

"Closed? It can't be closed."

The Frenchman moved closer to the theater, supporting himself on his walking stick as he went. "Perhaps there is an explanation in the small print," he said. "Let's have a look, yes?" Gus's saw he was effectively crippled—his right leg appeared to be almost useless, dragging along like an anchor after the rest of his body.

"Bear with me, monsieur." There was a carefree quality to the man's voice, something that implied he enjoyed helping Gus despite his handicap. "I am not as quick as I once was. It's an old war injury—the Prussians, you know." Gus could only wait until the man shuffled his way to the door.

"And now, let us see what the trouble is about." He leaned, and then stopped and straightened.

"What is it?" Gus asked.

The man pulled a pair of spectacles from the pocket of his coat and breathed on them. "Ah, sometimes I forget I need these." Then, with a flourish, a handkerchief from another pocket. Gus crossed his arms while the man cleaned, meticulously, inspecting the lenses against the sky and pulling them back to clean again. Perhaps he wanted to prolong the experience, as the old like to do.

At last the man fixed his glasses and translated: "Dear ladies and gentlemen, due to unforeseen circumstances the management has been forced to close the Theatre du Vaudeville. All performances are cancelled for an indefinite period. Our apologies." He turned to Gus. "Is it because you have a ticket, monsieur?"

Gus said, "No. I have nothing here now."

"I don't understand."

Gus began to walk back to the hotel, but the old man called out. "Monsieur, you should not let your troubles make you so downhearted. Why not come around the corner with me? There is a little place where we can talk and have a coffee."

"There's something else I need to do right now." The man wished him well, and Gus started walking again towards the Fromentin. First Jack, then Kera, now this. At least the management recognized the danger to come. But then their decision was no doubt mercenary—LaRoche and the staff would keep the doors open through an invasion if the crowds kept coming. And if money motivated them, closing the theater without warning was their best course—now no tickets need be refunded, none of the performers need be paid, and the cash would stay in the promoters' pockets.

If the theater stayed closed for more than a few days Gus would run out of money well before it was time to go back to the states. With Jack and Kera gone he was alone, and would have to hunker in his hotel room, coming down only for meals until it was time to catch the ship. But even then he had no way to pay for the train to Le Havre. He had the steamer passage still, but by that time he wouldn't be able to get to it. What a mistake this trip had been. Max was back in New York, in that swanky office of his. But how could he have known what would happen? Or maybe he had known, and let them come here anyway.

When he reached the hotel, Gus had sweated through his shirt. He began up the stairs, thinking he would take a bath and retire for a while to ponder the situation. Two steps up he stopped, turned around and went to the front desk.

"Yes, monsieur?"

"In a half hour I would like a taxi, please. I will be checking out."

"As you wish."

He washed in cold water from the sink. After dressing Gus threw a handful of clothes into his canvas bag. The rest, including the cowboy costume and accoutrements, would prove too much to carry. They would weigh him down. He put them in the drawers of the wardrobe for the next guest to find—a gift from the states—and went downstairs. The banjo case knocked against the banister as he stepped onto the landing, and a man in a suit looked up from his newspaper, displeased at the interruption.

"I have to leave," Gus said as he laid the room key on the counter. "It's an emergency."

"We are sorry to hear that, monsieur. We hope you have enjoyed your time with us."

The clerk scratched something into the register with a fountain pen. He asked if Gus needed help with his bags, and when Gus said no, went back to his duties. Gus waited, but the clerk appeared done with him.

"Don't I get some of the money back?"

"What money, monsieur?"

"The reservation," Gus said. "It was paid in advance. There's still a week left, so the difference should be refunded."

"Impossible, monsieur." The clerk backed up a step. "You must understand, when you reserve a room, the payment is...there is no refunding. It is the policy."

"That doesn't seem very fair..."

"What can be done?" the clerk said. He went back to his ledger.

But Gus couldn't leave. He'd lived without money before, endured cheap promoters who reneged on promises, let Max Zapf wheedle him for more than his ten percent. Having a bankroll or getting the upper hand in a transaction never seemed important compared to performing. But this was different. In New York, yes, he had ways of getting by, places he could go for a night's flop or find some food, but here he could barely communicate. Who would help him? The man with the newspaper had shown him what to expect from the French—ignorance and indifference. He had to have the cash.

Gus sat on the divan across from the guest, who pretended not to notice, and ran through his diminishing options. He nodded to himself and popped open the banjo case. That Klare Kummer song, "Cheating," would do. They'd never know the title, of course, but he'd get some satisfaction, whether it worked or not. He ripped the first chord as loud as he could. He played what had been written as a quiet tune like a march, thrashing the steel harder, until he was sure the sound carried to the upper floors. The clerk ran over to confront him.

"What is this you are doing?"

Gus smiled but kept strumming. "Playing for my supper."

"This must stop immediately!"

"Well, you know what to do then..."

The clerk hesitated. He said, "I will speak to the

manager." He ran to meet his supervisor, who had come to investigate.

The manager adjusted his tie and folded his hands on the counter. "Monsieur?" Gus stopped playing and joined him, just ahead of a man arriving to register.

"I don't want to make a scene," Gus said.

"Monsieur, we cannot do this. You did not pay for the room. The money was sent from America. It is not yours. We cannot give it to you."

"But it's not yours either. That money was part of *my* contract." Gus lifted the banjo and began to strum lightly.

"Then I suppose I shall have to call for la police," the manager said.

Gus went into the melody and turned to face the new guest. The man had several suitcases and looked exhausted, as though he had traveled for hours to get there. "You know what this one's called?" he said to the man. "It's 'Bandits' March.'"

The guest repeated, "Bandits?"

"That's right. Like crooks. Criminals."

The manager pounded the counter. "Criminel? Comment vous oser! Monsieur, you must leave this hotel immediately!"

"That's what I'm trying to do. Just give me my money and I'll be gone."

The Frenchmen huddled together for a few seconds, apparently debating the logic of continuing to argue with Gus while keeping their new guest waiting. The manager reached into the cash box and pulled out a small stack of francs, counting out the balance for the remainder of the reservation. "Very well monsieur—twenty francs. Now, please, leave this place."

"That was my intention from the start," Gus said. He took the money, having no idea if the amount was correct or if indeed they were criminals, and walked to the waiting taxi. "Train station," he told the driver.

As the taxi wound through crowded streets Gus considered the possibility he had stolen the money from the hotel. The room was in his contract, but its value wasn't anything he would have received. The hotel shouldn't get it—that room would be rented again, probably to the man who had just arrived. Had he cheated Max? He got his usual percentage. The promoters? They hadn't paid him in full and the money in his pocket didn't cover what he'd been shorted. And what about Jack and Kera? Some of this was Jack's, and Kera probably hadn't asked for a refund. It couldn't be made into any kind of sense. For once he would have to be selfish. He closed his eyes. He'd seen enough of Paris in the last day.

It was only a few minutes to the trains, but the driver had to shake Gus by the shoulder to rouse him when they arrived. He held out his hand for the fare and said something Gus didn't understand. Gus pulled out the francs and peeled one from the stack. The driver snatched it and jumped back into the taxi, then gunned the car away from the curb.

A swarm of travelers idled in front of the station, and inside hundreds more moved in every direction, put there, it seemed, to be negotiated before Gus could escape from the city. He stopped to catch his breath, and reached into his coat pocket for a wrinkled piece of paper—the reservation for his passage back home. He read it over and put it back. The sun glared through from above, and he looked to assess the layout of the building. A soaring glass ceiling curved three stories high, illuminating the station and passengers below, tinting them blue through a mosaic of panes. He stood, fascinated by the spectacle of light and air. He had never seen such spaciousness before, and he wished to be up there, away from the jostling on the ground. Space meant freedom, it meant distance—it was what he dreamed of onstage, flying over the hundreds of pairs of eyes that judged him. Jack played because he loved the crowd. To Gus the people were something to be endured. Who had created this architecture? What genius could imagine a building where every square inch wasn't destined to be filled with plaster or brick, every space partitioned into a cell? Silently, he thanked whoever had designed it. That person was an artist, a musician, in a way.

But he couldn't loiter. Gus walked through the multitudes crisscrossing their way about the station. He made it to a ticket window and waited in line until it was his turn, and then slipped the ship's passage in front of the cashier and pointed to "Le Havre."

"Oui. Aller-retour?"

Retour sounded enough like return to Gus that he instinctively answered no, and the cashier produced a single ticket.

Gus pulled out the francs and held them in front of the man, who took a few bills and offered some change. At least this time he wasn't being cheated, as he now suspected had happened at the hotel and with the taxi. Gus looked to the schedule board for Le Havre, and found it listed next to "Qaui 14." He understood that. This was becoming easier. Alone, without Kera or anyone to help, he was finding his way. Soon he would locate the track, and then he would be on his way out of France—just as he was beginning to make some sense of the place.

Maybe the country wasn't so terrible. Once the train passed out of the city and its suburbs, the view became one of wheat fields and pastures in gold and green, quaint farm towns and rustic stations for the hour-plus ride to Rouen. He had a bench seat to himself, and pulled the banjo case a little closer, for security as he examined the faces of the other passengers in the car. They looked like the guest in the hotel lobby, harsh and distrustful, intolerant of the stranger in their midst. He could not relax around them.

Despite the soothing cadence of the wheels against the rails, it was always best to stay alert—the boxcars in the states had taught him that. A man who said he was your friend might put a shiv in your ribs while you slept if he thought you had something worth stealing. Gus never trusted other travelers in those days; kept his back to the wall and stayed close to the door to keep from being cornered. He'd fought sometimes and jumped more than once, in the middle of the line, when the faces and the stares became too much to bear. He'd taken the punishment of the fall to protect the banjo, landing miles from the nearest town or city and having to hike the rest of the way. Once there he wandered, knowing no one, but knowing that someone always wanted music. He'd follow the town's rough men to the bars, anxious over whether they'd give a stranger a break, hoping they'd lead him to a tavern with a sympathetic owner, who would trade a meal for happy customers, and where the patrons would pay a few pennies to hear a tune. But sometimes they'd ask his name, and sometimes he'd forget to change it. And the nasty ones would call him the "little wop." The taverns could be as violent as the rails.

The train pulled into Rouen and he saw a café where he could have bought a sandwich and a coffee, but he stayed in his seat and fed off his hunger and his yearning for escape. No telling if he'd need the francs for something else before he could board the ship. He was still glad he'd left. If only the train would go faster on this next leg to the port.

It was another hour of farmland on the way into Le Havre, and the pastels of the fields faded into the gray of industry, too morose in their war preparations to permit color. The train went all the way to the ships, with the end of the line grayer still, and Gus stayed aboard until he was the last passenger at the last stop, until the conductor rousted him from the bench.

Being outside again, in the briny air of the docks, helped rejuvenate him. But he had no idea how to find the correct steamship, and the port was endless, vast berths in a line to the horizon. A taxi idled a hundred yards away, and he walked to the car. The driver didn't react. Gus took out his passage and showed it to the man, pointing this time to the name of the ship, the Rochambeau, hoping he would understand.

The driver turned with a concerned look. He began rattling something off in French—it sounded like questions—and then paused as if waiting for answers. But Gus could only shrug. The driver reached back and opened the rear door.

The cabbie talked and gestured all the way to the ship's landing, despite Gus's incomprehension. Something about the request was bothering him. And when he stopped the car next to some small buildings at the foot of a vacant dock, the problem became clear—there was no ship. The sight elicited more jabber from the man. He held out his hand. This time Gus took a moment to check the fare on the meter on top of the hood, as though he knew what it meant, gave the driver a franc and waited for change.

What had made him think this ship would be in port just because he needed it? That it would leave today instead of at its scheduled departure? The stupidity of his plan sunk in as the taxi clattered away. The driver was probably laughing at him still. The buildings looked abandoned—they were processing centers for passengers and cargo when the ship was in port, but empty now. But there must be someone inside, if only to log goods to be transported and watch over the gloom. Maybe he could trade his fare for another that was leaving today. The main doors were closed, but like the theater, there might be another entrance further back.

He let his bag fall just inside the door, its thump echoing in the cavernous interior. This was a depressing place, nothing like the Paris station that had captivated his imagination, except that it could also accommodate hundreds of people at a time. But now it was barren, save for a lighted doorway towards the back. Gus walked to it, exhausted, his shoes scraping. There was a powdery, gritty smell of worn concrete from the floor. He poked his head around the doorjamb. Two men sat at desks, making entries into ledgers.

"Excuse me, monsieur," Gus said, and the one closest to the front of the room looked up.

"Oui?"

"I don't suppose you speak English."

"Anglais?"

But the second man paused from his work and walked over. "What is it that I may help you with?" he asked.

He handed over the paper. "Can I exchange this reservation? I need a ship back to the United States."

The agent moved his glasses further down his nose to examine the document. After a few moments he said, "The Rochambeau—it is not due here for several days. You can see that," and he pointed to the departure date.

"Yes, I know. I would like to exchange…"

"Exchange?" He pushed his glasses back up and went over to his coworker, slipping the paper under the man's gaze. The two spoke in French for a minute. Gus understood but one word: "Ha!" said the man at the desk as he slid the form back to the other.

The agent walked back, shaking his head. "Impossible," he said.

"All I want is to be put on a ship back to the states," Gus said. "Exchange. For another ship."

"Listen. There are no other ships. Most of them have been commandeered by the navy to carry troops. You will be lucky to get passage on the Rochambeau when it arrives."

"But I need to leave now. I can't stay in France."

Again the workers huddled. The agent returned and said, "There is nothing we can do for you. But you may still be in luck. There is an American ship. Perhaps they can help you."

"And where…"

"Berth vingt deux…twenty two."

"How do I get there? I don't imagine there is a way to get a taxi from here."

"True, monsieur. You must walk. The number twenty two is three kilometers or so."

"And how far is that?"

"Kilometers? In English—a mile perhaps."

He went out through the side door again. A mile to the American ship, and then what? A wind came through the passageway between the structures, hard enough to force him to catch his balance. Gus felt a cold, biting gust of air, much colder than the hot day should have allowed, but that was typical of narrow spaces where the wind funneled. Still, they were the best places to hide from the crowds and the thieves—even from those who might wish to help. One could sleep, or meditate, and no one could approach without giving himself away. Gus knew from experience the wind would not subside, it would continue singing around corners. The sun had passed beyond the alley hours ago, and in this elongated, detached world night had fallen. The American staff would probably turn him away too. Kera had turned him away. In his own way Jack had done so as well. Or had it been his doing? Had he given them no choice? Been so distant from the people he knew that they thought him hostile, unwilling to accept them as friends? The past overcame Gus there, in that alley. It embraced him in its icy wind.

He came to a stairwell leading down to a padlocked door and stopped walking, lowered himself and the banjo into it, and pulled the lapels of his coat together. No one would notice him here, and a week was nothing out of a life, nothing compared to a year on the streets. In a week the Rochambeau would come, and he would be here to meet it. He settled into the hard place and felt its confinement, but that was the attraction. It was safe. He was hungry, but it would pass. It always did, much quicker than disappointment. He would not play the banjo here—never in the stairwells and alleys because it might attract the wrong kind of attention. He always waited until morning when he could find a spot on the sidewalk among the crowds before he dared take the instrument out. He was lonely too, but that was another feeling that could be ignored and overcome, with some effort. The worst of each day on the streets was the sameness, the circular journey of a place like this, huddled with the banjo, enduring the elements, between chapters of his life, waiting for it to begin again. Yet how quickly he returned to the narrow spaces when he had the chance.

The port was silent, save for the wind. He had hardly seen anyone since he departed the train—no passengers, no burly stevedores, and no ships for them to unload, only a few empty hulls that floated like jetsam on the water. If it were possible to sleep through the days until his ship docked he would gladly do it.

Something—stronger than the wind—shook Gus by the shoulder. "Monsieur." A voice he recognized. "Monsieur, are you all right?"

Then some French, to a second person. The clerks from the steamship line.

"Do you need a doctor?"

"A doctor?"

"Are you injured?"

Gus ran his fingers along the concrete of the stairwell. "No, I'm all right. Just waiting."

"Waiting? What is it you are waiting for?"

"My ship."

The man who spoke English translated and the other smiled.

"You cannot stay here."

Gus looked up at him.

"You should go into the city and find a room if you wish to wait. It will be several days." He reached out a hand to help with the bag. "Please. If you stay we will be forced to call the police."

Outside the passageway the evening sun still shone on the roadways. Walking through the heat reflected from their surfaces felt like swimming. Gus did not recall how far it was to the train station. He did not want to find a room—he would not be able to afford one for that long, not on the pittance the Fromentin staff had given him. He did not want to wait, did not want to go back to Paris, but what else could he do? It was good that the walk was long. He would walk and he would think, until he decided what to do next. The air still felt cold to him.

He ascended to the platform, and the other passengers watched the stranger who had bundled up in the infernal heat. Gus sat near the tracks, took out the banjo and played songs until the train pulled in.

The sun had not quite set when the train made Paris, although it was nearing nine o'clock. Expenses had reduced Gus to just a few francs. There wasn't nearly enough to go back to the Fromentin—they would likely throw him out anyway—or probably any other hotel in the area. He hadn't eaten all day, and in passing the sidewalk cafés his hunger magnified. He kicked at the sidewalk in frustration. To be returned to this again—a vagabond roaming the streets, always famished, hopeless, broken. Sleeping with one eye open. The goal of each new day being just to get it over with. Going from bar to bar with the banjo, a song for a meal, mister, if you can spare it. The smells from one of the cafés were too much to resist, and shaking fingers pulled another note from his pocket. He had spent almost everything with which he'd left the hotel. "Anything," he said to a waiter. "Whatever this will buy." A baguette and cheese, but when the waiter tried to show him to a table, Gus took the food and walked until he was alone, under the awning of a dress shop. He ate with a need he did not want anyone to see.

A few more blocks of aimless wandering and he found himself at the Theatre du Vaudeville. Of course he would come here. Nothing had changed since this morning. The note remained as well, although someone had splattered it with what looked like a tomato—perhaps another jilted performer.

He went round to the rear door, where he and Kera had taken up their pursuit of Jack two nights ago. If he could retrace his steps from there to Le Secret, perhaps the owner would help him. But could he remember how to get there? It had been pitch black, and it was getting dark again. He would have to try. A right turn at the end of the street, a left and another right. It seemed correct, but he couldn't be sure. He remembered seeing some large clubs and later a few smaller ones, but he hadn't taken note of the names, or of the streets they had traveled down behind Jack. Apart from that there hadn't been any landmarks he could remember, just dull brick buildings that all looked the same in the night. There had been that group of ruffians he and Kera ran into. Maybe running into them again wouldn't be so bad—at least he'd know he was near the place.

He stood at an intersection for a moment. Traffic was light, only people on bicycles and a few cars and taxis on this night. He put down his bag and reached into his pocket to count his remaining cash. If this didn't work he would be broke again, but when had that mattered? He waved his hand. In a minute, a taxi pulled to the curb. Gus leaned in and said, "Le Secret?"

The driver shrugged, then put his finger to his lips, as if Gus had asked for his confidence.

"No, no," Gus said. "Le Secret," and he began to mime a bar patron in the act of downing a drink. The driver was amused, but said nothing. Finally, Gus had it. "Cabaret. Le Secret cabaret," he said.

"Ah...vous? Le Secret?" The driver seemed surprised, but he waved Gus in. As Gus threw his things in the back and climbed in the driver kept staring, shaking his head, but eventually put the cab in gear.

The trip was brief. Gus had only been a few blocks away. He got out and looked around, not finding it. The club had been off an alley, where the cab wouldn't fit, and he walked into the space between two buildings. Now it was nearly as dark as the first time he had been there, and he proceeded slowly, until he found the entrance. The noise from the basement was nothing like it had been Saturday—only the hint of a few people chatting and the occasional ting of a glass. But he found the little sign near the stairway and went down.

There were perhaps a dozen customers, and no entertainment. Gus looked around for the owner, and not seeing him, went to the bar. "Monsieur…ah, Remy?" he asked, unable to think of the man's name. The bartender had no idea. He tried to ask the waitress, but when she saw a short, disheveled man, she ignored him and went to take orders from some customers before he could speak.

Gus walked to an empty table in a corner. He slid his bag underneath and pulled his banjo around in front, and started fingering the strings. They needed tuning from the jostling of the day, and he set to twisting the pegs and listening to the notes as he plucked. When he was ready he walked to the middle of the room, to the space for the floorshow. He borrowed a chair, placed it in the open area and sat down. Then he began to play. Softly at first, just strumming the banjo, waiting to see what the reaction from the sparse crowd would be.

There wasn't any. Any other time this indifference might have caused Gus to stop, but tonight it served as encouragement —they wouldn't kick him out. He played a little louder. Still none of the patrons looked up. Emboldened, he began to sing. He tried "Ragtime Cowboy Joe," but slowly, matching his mood. His singing was still off, but now people were paying attention, even the waitress who had snubbed him, whom Gus saw run into a back room.

A minute later the owner, as intimidating as the first time they had met, stood a few feet away, his arms crossed and a sour look that seemed to curl the cigarette hanging from his lips. A few of the patrons in the club applauded lightly. The owner waited for a moment, then spread his hands and asked, in English, "What is this?"

"Singing," Gus said. "Only singing. Do you remember me, Monsieur Remy?"

"Remy? What is Remy?"

Gus looked at the floor. "I'm sorry. I can't remember…"

"My name is Renoult." He sucked on his smoke and studied Gus. "Ah yes. The man with the beer."

Gus pursed his lips and nodded.

"And what is the purpose?" Renoult asked, hands now on hips.

"For your customers. Entertainment. You have no show tonight."

"On Monday night? I may as well throw my money in the toilet than to have a show for these wretches." He motioned towards the groups huddled around the tables. "I hope you don't expect me to pay for this singing business."

"No monsieur, I don't."

"Then what do you wish?"

Renoult loomed over Gus like a tree about to fall, and made him feel the folly of this appeal. Why should the Frenchman let him perform here, or give him a place to stay? They had no attachment. In fact, the club owner barely remembered him. They had spoken for perhaps five minutes, and for half that time Gus had acted the fool. It was lunacy to ask for this favor, but it would be worse not to, for if Renoult wouldn't let him stay here he would be on the streets. No more. He had been on the streets for the last time. Anything would be better than to be in that prison again. Gus let the banjo slide from his grip until it rested on the floor. Finally he looked up and said, "Your help, sir. I need your help."

The cabaret owner looked down at Gus as though assessing his story and comparing it to those of other unfortunates who no doubt passed his way. He seemed also to be considering some possibilities. He grabbed another chair and slid it in front of Gus, and sat down. He crossed his legs and placed his elbow on his thigh, his chin in his hand. "Tell me," he said, "what has happened to you?"

Gus wavered. How to tell it? The embarrassment of what he'd done today weighed on him, and he tried to frame the events in some kind of positive way. But his day had been a comedy, a farce. He believed the Frenchman would see him again as a fool, but told the story anyway, stressing that had it not been for the closing of the Vaudeville, none of it would have happened.

To Gus's surprise, Renoult withheld condescension, and showed interest in the affair between Kera and his associate, Bertré. He was willing to let him stay in one of the backrooms at Le Secret in return for nightly performances and a few other menial tasks. It was all Gus had asked for, yet he felt empty. Was it truly better than the streets? He was a dog that had wandered in and was allowed to stay. He would have to answer to Renoult, and how many others? The bartender, that conceited waitress. And for how long? There likely wouldn't be much tip money from the crowd that frequented Le Secret. He might be trapped here, three thousand miles from New York, indefinitely. And what if the war came to the city? Perhaps then it would be best to have a roof, even this one, over his head.

Renoult let him put his things in the room. It was no more than a storage area. He would have to find some bedding to place on the floor, and he'd have to bathe in the sink in the men's room—a men's room that smelled as though it hadn't been cleaned in weeks. But for now he went back out to the bar and reclaimed his chair, and began to play again—the banjo alone, without vocals.

Renoult went to a table in the corner and the waitress

brought him a cognac. Gus noticed one of the men he'd seen talking with him Saturday night come down the stairs with a companion. Both men joined Renoult, and they launched into another heated conversation. He listened, trying to pick up a word or two, but it was useless. The tone of their discussion became anxious, and Gus began again to wonder how he would ever get away from here. He counted coins in his head as he played, and decided he had enough to cable Max in the morning and beg for money.

Chapter 6
Wednesday morning, July 29 – Kera

SO, THE oddest looking man was the most important. Kera sat alone in a stiff-backed seat, spying across the aisle as he hunched over a leather notebook. Bertré was up, parading about the railroad car, making conversation with whomever would listen, and that left her to observe Jean Jaurès work on the speech he was to give later in the day in Brussels. He filled most of a bench designed for two. He did not look as she had imagined, given as she was to inventing heroes in the guise of dark and handsome athletes, leading men of the theater who parsed dilemmas and saved the day through a combination of physical prowess and sagacity. Jaurès had the pale complexion of a man who rarely stepped outside—he was short, rotund, and waddled a bit when he walked, using a cane for balance. Kera smiled at her misconception. Bertré had made him sound like the nation's champion—how then could he not look the part?

  She watched as he stroked the gray moustache that arched across the span of his face like a bridge, and pulled on his wiry beard, thick and chopped abruptly at the end. It was nothing like Bertré's perfect adornment, resembling instead a worn shaving brush. When she had been introduced to Jaurès at the train platform, he was jovial, welcoming her to his party of friends and journalists like a man hosting a dinner party. As he spoke to each person he often broke into laughter. But now, as he concentrated on his text, he was oblivious to the commotion around him. He engulfed his papers with his girth, his narrowed eyes focused, his wedge of a nose pointing straight at the speech Bertré had told her would forestall the war that threatened France—the war most thought inevitable. Jaurès looked up occasionally, as though entertaining a profound thought, and once looked directly at her. Kera smiled back, but when he didn't respond, she looked again at those eyes. He was not looking *at* something, but *into* something—an idea, or a vision of the future. Were it not for his eyes he would look rather ordinary, but with them he radiated an intimidating kind of intelligence, one that dared others to challenge him. She imagined Jaurès never spoke or acted without making a careful study of all the options available, calculating the outcomes of each possibility far ahead. How unlike most men. What would Gus say when faced with a man like this? He had trouble enough talking to Renoult at the bar. He would no doubt be speechless. It was good for her to have left Paris, and Gus, for these few days—she must get him out of her mind. Jaurès continued to stare, and she became embarrassed and looked away, out the window, until she felt his gaze had returned to his work.

The express trundled through the French countryside. The rhythm of the wheels clicking against the rails and the sway of the car combined to settle her and soothe the pain the unforgiving seat infused into her lower spine. This trip was not what Kera had anticipated when Bertré insisted she accompany him, but she consoled herself that the two days in Belgium would be interesting nonetheless. When he mentioned Brussels she had assumed a relaxing time enjoying fine restaurants, shops and museums, but it was now clear that the group's purpose was solely to support

Jaurès. She wondered why he didn't tell her, why he felt he had to cover the truth to get her to attend. Even if she had known she would have come. Although she could have stayed in Bertré's flat in Paris for the two days, she would have felt quite guilty to refuse her new lover, who had lavished her with the attentions and zeal of a much younger man, whether in public or private—her mind still swirled over his appetite in the bedroom. She'd noticed, too, that the questionable gold ring he'd worn at Le Secret and at dinner was gone from his finger, and with it her curiosity about his marital status.

She fidgeted again in the seat. She found it odd that they forced themselves to sit on these hard benches when Bertré had offered to pay for compartments that would have accommodated the eight members of the group in comfort. But Jaurès had been adamant they disdain the trappings that the workers they represented couldn't afford. "You can take the first-class car if you wish, Maurice," he'd said, "but it is important for me not to appear frivolous and self-important. We speak for the workers; we must travel like the workers, not like the elites who are promoting the war."

"Yes, of course, you're right," Bertré said. And at that they all decided to remain with him in second class.

Finally Bertré returned to the seat, moving in close to her, but not quite touching. Kera adjusted the brilliant hat from Madame Plume's, the only article of color among the blacks and grays of the delegation's clothing. She hoped that he might finally comment on it, but he said nothing, just as he had when she wore it back to the apartment. Instead he concentrated on what was outside the car, and pointed out a few small towns in the distance as the train passed them. He noted the fields of crops, and began a recitation of facts about the region's agriculture. It made her feel awkward, as though she were a schoolgirl among adults. Since she'd arrived at the Gare Saint Lazare, she'd felt out of place among these people. Jaurès had been pleasant, but she suspected the others, a Monsieur Sembat and his wife, and three other men from *L'Humanite*, distrusted her as an outsider. They were civil enough, but of their business they kept to themselves, and it was clear they all knew a great deal about the political situation that Jaurès would address in Brussels. They had been involved with the man and his cause for some time, and seemed to regard him with a reverence typically reserved for a holy man. Perhaps to them he was. If a man could stop a war with a speech... Kera saw that they made sure Jaurès had what he needed and was where he needed to be, and was not unnecessarily bothered, leaving him the opportunity to work on his arguments.

It was fascinating. The entourage treated Jaurès the way she'd seen sycophants fawning over Broadway stars. He seemed far less assuming than those actors, but she supposed he could be like that. Bertré admired him the way a boy makes an icon of a soldier. During dinner last evening he had told her that Europe had been on the brink of war two years before, and Jaurès's speech had so motivated the delegates at the convention that they returned to their home capitals and forced the governments to cooperate instead of fight. The armies, coiled along each other's borders like snakes in ambush, were withdrawn, and negotiations begun. Maybe Jaurès deserved their adulation. His theater, she thought, was merely on a different stage.

She interrupted Bertré's geography lesson. "Maurice, the country is beautiful, but you are ignoring what is important. I want to know more about our trip. Everyone seems so concerned about the outcome of the speech."

"But there is no reason for you to be."

"Yes, there is. What if Monsieur Jaurès cannot stop the war?"

"I have every faith in him. He has the ability to make men see the truth."

Another in the party, Jean Longuet, who stood nearby, overheard him and put his hand on Bertré's shoulder. "It's going to be impossible this time, Maurice," he said. "The Austrians have officially declared war on Serbia. The Russians are sticking their noses in to protect the Serbs."

"When did this happen?"

"We received word just before we left for the station." Longuet was young and trim, clean-shaven, with a still boyish face, and while he spoke he looked not at them, but out the window of the train, as though thinking about something else. A young Jaurès in training.

Bertré shook his head. "He knows?"

"Yes. But somehow he still believes peace is possible."

"Good…good," Bertré said. "When Jaurès speaks today, he might yet convince the Russians…"

"Who have already begun mobilizing," Longuet said, his voice tensing. "There's no stopping it this time."

Kera tried again to make sense of it. "I still don't understand how this brings war to France. Why can't you simply let them fight their own war?" she asked.

Longuet ran a hand through his curls and looked at her as if she were stupid. "Of course it is the ridiculous treaty with Russia," he said. "If they choose to fight, we're honor bound to fight alongside them… Honor!" he said with disgust. "Our politicians have the honor of pickpockets."

Bertré admonished him with a wave of his hand. "You forget, my friend, Jaurès is a politician, as well as our editor."

"Of course I didn't mean him," Longuet said. "He's the exception."

Kera had to know. "How can he be both?" she asked.

"The man never rests," Longuet explained. "He spends half his day at the Chamber and half at *L'Humanite*, and all of it dedicated to the people. He's always working, thinking…even at home with his wife and daughter."

"Married as well? How does his wife stand it?"

"She understands," Bertré said, "as we do, how important Jaurès is to France."

"She must be a remarkable woman."

"She knows her place in his life," Bertré said.

His comment bothered Kera. It had the ring of her family's antique philosophy, and sounded as though he expected all women to subordinate themselves to their men, to give up their dreams in lieu of their master's. Were his attentions these past few days just a ruse to make her dependent on him, to put her in that same position in their relationship?

Bertré surprised her further. "Too bad Jaurès can't control the Chamber the way he controls his own home," he said.

Kera began to debate him, but Longuet interrupted, "The treaties will be the destruction of France. I think we would be far better off without them. As far as I'm concerned, we should break them and be done with it."

"Why do you even need these agreements?"

Bertré took a breath, like a parent about to give a lengthy answer. "When we fought the Prussians forty years ago our country was devastated. We lost a good deal of land to them. To make sure it would never happen again, we aligned ourselves with the English and the Russians. If one country were attacked, all would respond against the attacker. It seemed logical…"

Longuet cut him off. "The reality is, it doesn't work. Instead of protecting nations, it merely means that if two countries decide to fight, everyone must be involved. Share the carnage, so to speak."

"It's true," Bertré said. "The Germans have a similar treaty with the Austrians, and they are itching to exercise it. Do they really care about Austria's interests, or is it an excuse to steal more land?"

"We all know the answer to that," Longuet said.

"But we have to help the Russians because if we break the alliance we may never be trusted again."

"So…you will all fight because it says so on a piece of paper?"

"It's more than that," Longuet said. "France will fight because the men in power are fools. They see land and glory too, and they'll take any opportunity to grab at them. They don't care about the cost in men's lives. That's what this is really about. The common man's life doesn't matter. That's what Jaurès is fighting for—to convince the ministers and the generals that even the life of a single man has value." He folded his arms as he spoke, as if angry that the world did not understand. "The paper is simply the justification. When we protest, they wave it under our noses like the Tricolor and say, 'What can we do? We must honor our commitments.'"

"But if enough of the delegates support us, and get their followers to comply," Bertré said, "we can make those in power see that war is not feasible. The men will refuse to fight, not just in France, but all across the continent."

"They will fight," Longuet said. "When they feel the point of a soldier's bayonet in their sides, they will fight. When they feel the holes in their stomachs because all the food has gone to the army, they'll have no choice."

"No." Bertré was adamant. "The people will strike. France will be the example. We will shut the nation down and they will be unable to make war. All Jaurès has to do is ask them."

"I pray you're right and I'm wrong," Longuet said, "but I fear the worst. There's more than simply adhering to treaties in this arrangement. As soon as Russia declares war the Germans will have an excuse to arm. They'll say they're fighting the Russians, but you and I know their eyes will be on France. What they didn't take forty years ago they will try to annex this time. And when they march across our borders, what do we do then? I tell you it's already too late to stop this."

They all looked over at Jaurès, still working away at his speech. "I fear this time his efforts will come to nothing," Longuet said. The young man turned to Kera. "And you, madame. You should leave this country and go back where you will be safe."

She grasped Bertré's arm and held it tightly. He patted her hand. "No harm will come to her," he said to Longuet. "Don't be such an alarmist. You always see the worst possible outcome."

"Perhaps. But at least I have my eyes open."

Kera relaxed as best she could in the seat, and rested her head on the now silent Bertré's shoulder. This thinking was strange to her. The French acted as though wars happened among the nations all the time. She had known nothing like it in America. Yes, the country had its wars, but they were all fought for good reasons and in faraway places. Even the Civil War seemed a time and a world away from her Connecticut home. And whatever happened you could still go about your business. The closest anyone she knew experienced such fighting was by reading about it in the newspapers, where it seemed more like a tale, a story for children. Here, it lurked around every corner, like plague, always ready to infest. And yet these people accepted the fact. War was simply part of their lives. Why were there not more men like Jaurès working to change it?

She had so many more questions, but was embarrassed to ask should the others in the party witness her ignorance. What of Paris? Would there be fighting in the city? Would Gus try to leave without her? And Jack—had he come back? She thought of Gus sitting alone in his hotel room, strumming the banjo while the sounds of men marching served as backdrop. How could she be so insensitive about his welfare? He may not have loved her, but she still cared about him, and yet when Bertré came along she abandoned him without hesitation. She resolved that when the group returned to Paris she would find him—and Jack—and would make Bertré provide for their safety as well.

When the train pulled into Brussels the party was met by a delegation from the convention—the *Second Internationale,* Bertré had informed her proudly—a massive assemblage of party representatives from across the continent. They divided into several taxis for the drive to the city's largest meeting hall, the Maison du Peuple. Kera squeezed in with Bertré, Jaurès and a man named Vaillant. She remained quiet while Jaurès alternately practiced his lines and listened to the response from the others—Bertré applauding and Vaillant correcting—until they reached the building. It was a monstrous structure, four stories high and lined with row after row of windows, conforming to the curve of the boulevard and devouring an entire city block— a slab of concrete that dwarfed the other structures around it and darkened them with its enormous shadow.

A tall man embraced Jaurès the moment he stepped from the cab. "Excellent," Bertré said. "A very good sign."

Kera tugged on his sleeve. "Who is it?"

"Hugo Haase, head of the German Socialists. If he is with Jaurès there is hope."

She wanted to ask him to explain what he meant, but Bertré moved forward to stand next to Jaurès and shake the German's hand, and Kera melted into the background, again feeling ill-placed. She didn't want to be a burden to him—it was obvious he knew his way among these people—but neither did she wish to be alone in the crowd, unable to converse in the language of European politics, a mute among the throng speaking animatedly about current affairs. She would stay close to Bertré but not interfere, and hoped he would not forget about her in the excitement of the moment.

Apparently the Internationale had been under way for several days, and many of the delegates had given their speeches prior to the group's arrival. Today, she understood, was the last day of the event, and Jaurès would be the final speaker, just as he had been two years before.

Jaurès and Haase walked together towards the entrance, Bertré at their heels, and as they moved, the mass of assistants, journalists and spectators filled in behind like a wave washing over a beach, separating Kera from them. She tried to squeeze through the crowd, but they were pushing as well to get closer to the politicians, and she made no headway. She watched from the curb as the men went into the building, and then waited while the dozens of bodies fought their way in. She had no choice now except to follow the group from afar. Once inside, she noticed that those not directly involved with the politicians were barred from the front of the hall where they were to speak, and she saw an opportunity to catch up to her party. With one hand on her hat and the other clutching her bag, she ran down the middle aisle, past row after row of clamorous delegates, all straining to see Jaurès walk by and surprised to see a woman in an orange hat running after them.

A few seats had been reserved for Jaurès's group between a pair of ornate columns off to the side. As Kera reached them, she discovered they were not enough—only six chairs had been left open for the eight people, and she feared she would have to walk all the way back to the rear in embarrassment if Bertré didn't insist she remain. To her horror, he hesitated, as though realizing a mistake in bringing her along from Paris. He looked around in confusion. Perhaps she did not belong at the front of this assembly, but if she had to sit elsewhere she expected at least that he would join her, rather than leave her in the crowd. But two men nearby recognized Jaurès and volunteered to stand, offering their seats to the group. Kera wound up sitting a few chairs away from Bertré, and for the time being it was fine with her.

Another delegate spoke first, delivering a halting, unfocused rant about workers' rights and the glorious struggle against the bourgeois. Kera had no idea who this man was, and since she sat too far away from Bertré, she couldn't ask. The man spoke of histories and philosophies, of theory against theory, and a struggle of ideologies in a changing world. Maybe Kera didn't know much about politics, but she knew when a man had lost his audience. The speaker droned on for what seemed like a half hour, eventually yielding the stage more from the indifference of the crowd rather than because the speech was finished.

A recess was called. The delegates began to cluster in small groups to talk, or wander away from the proceedings altogether. By the time the speaker introduced Jaurès, the hall had filled with noise and confusion, and Kera feared they would continue to ignore him. The president pounded his gavel on the podium, but still the delegates carried on as if the program had ended.

Jaurès walked heavily to the stage. Kera saw in his gait the burden these people had placed upon him, and how seriously he took it. She saw too, exhaustion brought on by the heat, which was as oppressive as what they had hoped to leave in Paris, compounded by his fight against the forces of war. Jaurès had sweated through both his shirt and his coat, and a dark stain traversed the back of his jacket, from his neck to his waist. His hair was matted and damp, and wisps of it hung down in front of his forehead. He labored just to breathe.

But as Jaurès prepared to speak, he became energized. He took a wide stance and leaned forward, planting himself like a colossus through which the massed armies of Europe would have to pass if they wished to initiate this war. He stood quiet for a moment, looking down at his text, his chest heaving with every breath. Then he raised his head slowly and faced the audience. Jaurès focused over the top of the crowd, his gaze penetrating the smoke and the clouds of doubt that had filled the air. He placed one hand on the podium.

"Citizens!" he cried. The chatter of the hall succumbed. Kera felt a rush of electricity fire through her. "I stand before you today, as I did two years ago, to protest against the immoral acts by the governments of Europe against the people."

The delegates were not disappointed. They interrupted Jaurès repeatedly with applause as he assailed the leaders of the continent's governments, accusing them of ignoring the will of the people in their vain quests for national glory. He stressed, over and over, the desire for peace among the nations, and promised that the common man would not acquiesce to the whims of power. Kera cheered when the crowd cheered, stood when they stood. Despite being a woman who was scarcely concerned about the state of affairs in her own country, she was overwhelmed. She had never experienced the defiance of such a speech—she could not fully understand its meaning, but she recognized how committed these people were to stopping the war. How terrible it must be, she thought, to live with an eternal threat of conflict, but she could not imagine for herself how terrible. Jaurès, as though aware of her ignorance, supplied the details. He talked of the death of men, women and children wrought by madmen flaunting new military technologies. And the coming war would be more than guns and bombs, he said. It would, like the wars before it, bring death through disease—as many dead from pestilence as by the blows of the enemy—but millions this time, he predicted.

Jaurès swayed as he spoke, filled with a resolve that was more than his stout body could contain. From where she sat, Kera could see beads of sweat forming on his brow and dripping on the papers on the podium. But he never stopped to daub his forehead or to compose himself. He had the crowd, and would not give them a second to reconsider.

Then Jaurès spoke in words that taxed Kera's comprehension. He said, "When typhus finishes the work begun by bullets, disillusioned men will turn on their rulers, whether German, French, Russian or Italian, and demand their explanation for all those corpses. And then, the unchained revolution will cry out to them: 'Begone! And ask pardon of God and men!'" Was he telling them to revolt, to overthrow their governments? She couldn't envision such a thing happening in America. For all their apparent culture and sophistication, the Europeans seemed completely confused about how to maintain themselves as nations. They seemed more like tribes of ill-bred children. By now, though, the crowd was frenzied—war or not she felt the mob would go about the business of revolution as soon as the proceedings finished. Jaurès ended with a call for peace and justice, but Kera sensed that if the delegates had their way, justice would be what they alone decided.

When he was done, Jaurès rolled his speech and thrust it into his coat pocket, and then came down from the platform. His party and dozens of spectators surrounded him. Bertré was in among them. Kera couldn't see him, so she waited for the group to break up. But they remained in orbit around their sun as he walked off the stage, again leaving her alone. She ran after them, but couldn't get closer. Once more she could do nothing but flit about the fringes of the mass trying to follow Jaurès. The group herded through a doorway, taking several minutes to accomplish the task. Kera had to maneuver past delegates who continued to mill around the stage, and by the time she reached the hallway the party had gone, probably already on their way to a restaurant. She didn't even know the name of the hotel where they were staying—Bertré had said he would take care of everything, as usual.

This was the reverse of what he'd done just a few nights before. Then he had thought only of her. Now that she was with him, relying on him, he had forgotten about her. But it couldn't be. He must have been unable to get out of the crowd, and the tide of bodies simply swept him away. Yes, that must be it. Still, she felt helpless.

Kera walked tentatively into the crowded passageway, looking for a familiar, or least a friendly face. Strangers, all looking for something themselves, brushed her aside, and she moved close to the wall to avoid them. Then a hand reached out and grabbed her arm. She turned, expecting to see

Bertré, but it was Longuet. "I noticed you were missing from the fun. I thought I'd better wait for you," he said.

"Oh, thank goodness. Everyone moved so quickly. I thought I would never find the group again."

"Everyone wants his two minutes with Jaurès," he said.

"Yes. I had no idea how important he was."

"Come. You and I can walk to the hotel from here. It's only a few blocks. Bertré will see you've been left in good hands."

Longuet led her to a side entrance, and they ducked out onto the sidewalk. Kera opened her parasol to block the sun, and offered a bit of shade to the young man, who leaned sideways to accept it, taking care not to touch her while they made their way.

"Where did they all go?" she asked.

"Jaurès is meeting with the senior delegates. They're planning strategy—they will demand their governments desist from military action."

"Then he was successful."

"Hardly," Longuet said. "They're fooling themselves. Jaurès too, for once. This war will not be stopped. It's too long coming."

"I'm surprised. I thought everyone in the group took Jaurès's every word as law."

"Some do. I assure you, though, I'm a realist about these things."

"So you've given up?"

Longuet stopped to look at her. He seemed insulted.

"I'm sorry," she said. "I didn't mean to put it that way."

"In a sense you're correct." He started to walk again, but looked out at the street instead of at Kera. "I will always struggle for peace and the freedom of the common man, but I know this time we're doomed to failure. My hope now is to at least keep France out of the war, but frankly, I don't see that happening either."

"And what of Jaurès?"

"He's quite the optimist. He thinks it's still possible to keep the conflict restricted to the Balkans. Somehow he thinks we can come to terms with the Germans."

"That's not possible?"

"There are too many who are burning for war, despite what they say in public. As much as the Germans desire to invade France, there are many here who wish to return the favor. They believe we have a score to settle with Berlin—a wound that's been festering since they defeated us."

"Then Maurice was right. It has been going on forever."

"You don't understand," Longuet said. "Your country is too young to comprehend what these petty hatreds mean to our people. You don't have the history we do. To some in government, fighting the Germans is their reason for living. Even in the party there are those who allow their nationalist pride to overshadow their pledge to represent all men."

Kera was quiet for a minute, thinking about what Longuet had said. As they approached the hotel lobby, she stopped him. "Tell me, monsieur," she said. "If everything you say is true, if all this today is just a show and the war will come anyway, why do you and Jaurès continue to speak out?"

Longuet smiled. "You might say we are men of the future. We hope that by working today, the common man…and woman…of tomorrow will have a say in their own destinies."

What a rare idea. She smiled at the difference between his attitude and Bertré's old-fashioned values. She walked with him to the front desk, and he made sure she was properly checked in and had her bags.

He said, "It's been a pleasure, but now I must run and join the others to watch Jaurès."

She touched his forearm to thank him, and then watched as he walked away. "Wait!" she said. "Could I go with you?"

Longuet stopped. "It's just a roomful of old men,

arguing. Why would you want to do that? If I didn't have to be there I might not go myself."

"You're just saying that to keep me away."

Longuet smiled. "Are you certain? I promise it won't be very entertaining."

"I'll just sit there. I won't make a sound."

He motioned her to join him. "I don't understand why you're interested."

"Monsieur Longuet," Kera said, adopting a tone of mock indignation. "I've come all the way from Paris for the convention. Of course I'm interested. I find Monsieur Jaurès quite remarkable."

Longuet held his arm extended and she took it, and they went back out onto the street. "It's Jean, by the way," he said. "And we'll have to walk quickly."

The door to the room in which Jaurès met with the lead delegates was nearly ten feet tall and heavy as a drawbridge, and impossible for anyone to move without its groan alerting everyone in the room. When Longuet heaved it open, he stepped aside and let Kera precede him. She walked in to the gaze of ten men at the main table, Jaurès among them, who stopped their negotiations to see who had disturbed the proceedings. This time Jaurès stared at her *and* saw her. He raised an eyebrow. An audience of dozens more encircling the bargaining area noticed her too, and Kera went from the proud saunter with which she entered to a stooping, embarrassed slide into a seat next to Bertré, who looked at her with reproach. She looked back to see Longuet sneaking into a seat as though he hadn't been with her.

She didn't want to interrupt the meeting again, but her desire to speak to Bertré proved greater than her ability to control herself. She whispered into his ear, "Darling, why did you leave me there alone in the hall? I was lost. Thank goodness Longuet stayed behind to help me."

"My dear," he said in a tone reserved for an annoying

stranger. "Do you not understand the importance of what is happening here? Jaurès is speaking. You must be quiet."

Kera sat back in shock. Last night in the apartment Bertré had told her he was in love with her—only two days into their relationship—but it was clear now that he loved this part of his life even more. Her man was a sycophant, a toady to this politician. It was as though he admired being a part of the statesman's circle so much that he couldn't be his own man in Jaurès's presence. The realizations came quickly. Her life had changed drastically in just a couple of days, but now she felt she would have to reevaluate her feelings. She'd been foolish to believe him and even more of a fool to agree to take his apartment. It seemed the right choice, abandoning Gus and opting for the security and love Bertré offered, but she had only jumped from one difficult situation to another. These things were not supposed to happen so quickly. She would think about them tonight. But for now she had no choice but to listen to the debate.

Jaurès suggested that a mass strike by workers throughout Europe was the only way to stop the conflict from spreading to other countries now that Austria had declared war. "We must shut down the businesses and the governments. We must make them see that workers will not support the conflict."

But the response he received now, after the speeches and euphoria of the general assembly, was markedly changed. One by one, the leaders of the parties in Germany, Russia and Austria said such a measure wouldn't be possible in their countries. "Events have moved too quickly this time," the German, Haase, said. "We will implore our government to search for ways to hold the peace, but a strike now would be impossible. I'm not even sure it would be effective."

Bertré sat forward in his chair. He spoke quietly, to no one, "He doesn't want to stop it. He wants war too."

Jaurès continued to pressure the delegates for a commitment. "What then, do you suggest?" he asked Haase.

"We must have a strategy, a weapon with which to make the governments capitulate."

"There is nothing," Haase said, slapping the tabletop. "The armies are deploying. Tell me that the French are not already sending troops to our border."

Jaurés looked surprised at this, as though unaware of French troops mobilizing. "Do we not have the right to protect ourselves?" he said. Now Kera could see the truth of Longuet's argument—nationalism had crept into the deliberations, pulling the coalition apart.

Jaurés caught himself, however. He said, "But as long as hostilities have not begun we can still make the case for peace. I will personally meet with the leaders of our government. Will you do the same?"

Haase and the others grumbled and began making excuses. Kera knew the outcome of this meeting wouldn't change the inevitability of war. Longuet had been correct. Why was it that pessimists always seemed to be right? She became anxious that the party return to France as quickly as possible, even sooner than their planned departure of tomorrow afternoon. She wanted to get back to the states. She wanted to find Gus and Jack and leave Europe, and go back to the life she'd known before. But it was no longer that simple. She was at the mercy of Bertré, who apparently wouldn't make a move without Jaurés's approval. She would have to wait and hope she still enough time to get out safely. In the interim she thought about what she could do while she waited.

Kera rose, and as distractingly as she had made her entrance, navigated the crowd and exited. She knew the way back to the hotel by now, and walked there directly, ignoring the hot afternoon as best she could. When she got to the front desk she informed the staff that there had been a mistake, and that Monsieur Bertré had inadvertently booked them into the same suite. The gentleman was to be moved to a separate room, at his expense. Then she asked the clerk to have a telegram sent back to the United States, to Max Zapf. She begged Max to change the passage to Friday, or the next soonest day. The three of them were in great danger. The boy didn't speak English, so she wrote it out and instructed him to have it sent it letter by letter, never mind what it meant. If he did it correctly the message should make enough sense to Max. She billed that to Bertré as well.

    By seven o'clock Bertré and the rest of the party still hadn't returned from the meeting. Just as well. Kera telephoned room service and ordered dinner to be brought up—coq au vin and a glass of Bordeaux, and petit fours with coffee, why not? She went upstairs, locked the door and tried to relax. Hours later Bertré's pounding on her door awakened her. She sat silently, and hoped he would think she'd gone elsewhere. She needed time before she would be ready to talk with him again.

Chapter 7
Thursday afternoon, July 30 – Gus

RENOULT LEANED back in his chair, anticipating gratitude, but Gus displayed none. The small salary the owner offered would make no difference in three days time. When the Rochambeau made port Gus would be here still, a rag in his hands, pushing dust out of the owner's way so he could convince himself of the quality of his establishment. The dust and dirt described this place—a pall of soot from the alleys above sifting through floorboards and joists to settle on every surface in the club. Le Secret's gloom matched Gus's demeanor. He felt trapped. Because the basement had no windows, he rarely saw the sun. He cleaned, he straightened, he polished; when enough customers came in he pulled out the banjo and played. When the crowds left he helped the staff put up chairs and glasses, turned off the new fangled electric lights—bare bulbs that turned night into dusk—and candle in hand, shuffled back to his space in the storage room. He lay between boxes thick with mold, where he kept the threadbare blankets that served as mattress and sheets.

When the others went home it meant sleep. In the crypt-like aura of the flame he laid his banjo into the cradle of its case, taking care to make it secure in the velour lining, a more comfortable bed than he had on the flannel heaped over the concrete floor. He was content to work hard each day in the club, the only way he could fatigue himself enough to sleep on the cruel surface. By morning, though, the cement petrified his joints with pain, and he faced each new day already sapped of energy.

A few times a day Gus went up to the alley, where he dumped the trash left by Le Secret's patrons. The first two days he walked out to the street where he could gauge the arc of the sun and estimate the time. By the third he didn't care enough even to do that. What would be the point? Whether it was nine or eleven or three, he had nothing to look forward to but another round of cleaning and strumming, and the hardness of night in that little room. Some sympathetic customers had thrown a few coins at his feet while he played, but they didn't add up to enough to afford a good meal outside the club, or a trip to the barber, let alone get him to Le Havre again in time to meet the ship home. Later he would walk to the telegraph office to see if Max had deemed it important enough to answer his cable.

Renoult ran his hand across the top of the table, examined his fingers and rubbed them together like a man demanding payment. "I know the vermin who come in to drown their livers don't care if it's clean, but I do, "he said. "And when Jaurès's friends come by they shouldn't have to dirty their trousers just to have a drink."

He had come in early, even before the barman, Albert, and the waitress, Aimée, to inspect, to see if Gus had cleaned to his satisfaction. He weaved among the tables and toured the bar, checking under edges and along the counter. Gus watched him while continuing to sweep out corners. How could Renoult complain? Everything was bound to be in better shape, since he doubted anyone had cleaned the place before. Gus even scoured the toilet and sink each day, since that offered the only place to wash and clean his clothes, and the thought of touching those surfaces after Le Secret's drunks had finished using them sickened him.

Renoult got up and continued checking tables and edges. Gus propped the broom against the wall. "Some of this wasn't cleaned for months," he said. "Maybe longer."

Renoult looked amused. "Perhaps never," he said. He snapped his fingers at Albert and gestured for a cigarette. "But then, you have the time, no? And difficult work, as they say, is good for the soul."

The barman smiled at this, but Gus refused to see the humor. "I didn't think you would find it funny," Renoult said. "But no matter. I like you anyway."

Still no reaction from Gus. He could not simply shift into a good mood. He muttered a thank you.

Renoult paused for a moment and looked around his club as if planning improvements. He took a drag on his smoke and snuffed it out on the tabletop, leaving the butt for Gus to remove, then clomped up the stairs to whatever he did in the club's off hours. A man like him might indulge himself at the local houses before coming back to drink his own liquor. He was the owner, after all, and like the theater owners Gus had met back in the states he'd probably developed a variety of appetites that swallowed up most of what he made from his business, and kept him from paying employees and performers what they were worth. Most of the American owners had been fat and arrogant, as well as cheap. At least Renoult seemed civilized. Another man would have continued to let him rot in this dungeon without ever offering a salary.

Gus grabbed the broom and took a few more swipes at the floor, then stopped. He stared at the bartender, who was arranging bottles on the shelves behind his counter. How did he know to smile at Renoult's joke, since he'd spoken in English?

"Albert." Gus said. He spit the "t" like a true American, mispronouncing the French. The muscular young man turned around. Two buttons of his white shirt lay open at the neck, revealing a surge of chest hair, and his sleeves were rolled up, all to expose as much of his physique as might be permitted in public. Although his eyes suggested he was too young to be working here, he had a full handlebar mustache that reached to the edges of his face, like a middle-aged man, and a nose that approximated a French Alp, in size as well as shape. Gus bellied up to the bar and leaned in with his hands splayed on the counter. "Why didn't you tell me you spoke English?"

Albert was half again Gus's size. He took a step until he too pressed against the bar, and loomed over Gus. "My name," he breathed in a baritone, "is Albere…"

"All right," Gus said, "'Albere. Why didn't you say something before?"

"We didn't know if you would last for more than a few days in this place," Albert said. "We thought perhaps it wouldn't be worth the effort. So many come and go, you know." It took Gus a second to connect Albert's voice to someone who couldn't be more than twenty-five.

"Renoult thinks I'm worth something."

"Yes, now. But you looked like you didn't want to be bothered with any of us."

The comment wasn't an insult. Gus had heard, and felt it, before—from hotel staff, train conductors, stagehands, performers…occasionally from Jack. People assumed his detachment meant annoyance, his indifference a scowl, warning them off. So many times he abstained from contact, as though assuming a role or performing onstage—the aloof musician too focused on his art to be concerned with the trivialities of others. This time, however, the words carried a different meaning. Maybe he had finally heard them often enough, or that coming from a man who had no reason to be afraid of him they made more sense. Maybe it was Le Secret—this place, his situation, his despair. But now they rang true—he *had* wanted people to leave him alone. If only he could tell Albert—tell everyone—that his remoteness meant not anger but anxiety, that he was as wary of them. It rarely mattered if he wasn't friendly with the other performers in a show, if he never suggested a meal or drinks, because in a few days he would move on and leave the problem behind. The music *was* more important back then. But now, entombed here for who knew how long, these acquaintances had begun to matter. If his coworkers thought him too arrogant to interact with them, this purgatory would descend into hell. It had become too easy to feign disinterest. He found it simple to keep his distance, to seek places where he could stuff himself into a wall and pretend it was a fortress, immerse himself in sound and dreams, disconnect from the world and his own conscience. He had done it in New York, dwelling in the narrow spaces until he became partners with Jack. And again a few days ago in Le Havre. A relapse, he'd thought—understandable because of the frustrations he'd experienced. But now he knew he had been doing it all along, mentally if not physically—running away without running, without even moving, removing himself to another world in which he was the sole inhabitant—a realm of solipsism, of denial and stupidity.

Gus pushed away from the bar and began to go back to cleaning. He stopped and turned. "I didn't mean it," he said.

Albert smiled back. "Let me pour you something." He reached behind him for a bottle of whiskey, his enormous hand nearly covering the circumference of the glass. "One of the benefits of working in this place."

"Doesn't Renoult mind?"

"How can he mind what he does not know? Besides, we don't take advantage. And I doubt the monsieur would care."

"Why not?" Gus asked.

"Because for all his hardness, he has a heart."

"Him?"

"Oui."

Gus took a swallow. He'd been surrounded by alcohol for half a week and it had never occurred to him to sneak back into the bar after everyone had left and partake of the inventory. The elixir burned a little going down, and Gus felt its warmth rising into his head. Albert topped off the glass and Gus drank again. Through the whiskey's haze Le Secret and its staff took on new dimensions. He had misjudged Renoult and Albert. And how many others?

Albert brought the bottle over, but Gus waved him away. "I have to finish sweeping," he said. "You never know when people will start to come in."

"You will see," Albert said. "After a while here things begin to improve."

"What do you mean?"

He nodded towards an area off the bar, where Aimée was slicing bread. "Do you know her?"

Noticed, yes. Constantly. He'd snuck glances while he played and she waited tables. She was little, like him. Her red hair looked like wildfire falling to her shoulders, one of which was often bared by a loose sweater. He stared as she allowed patrons to grab her by the hips and pull her onto their laps. Gus had never seen a woman so uninhibited. If she were in the mood she would let whoever had reeled her in to kiss her as well. He sat a few feet away, playing the banjo, watching the real show at Le Secret each night. To be as free as the French…

"We haven't spoken," Gus said.

Albert laughed. "I am not surprised. You speak no French and she speaks no English."

"What about her then?"

"She was living in the street with her baby. Selling herself to men for food. Somebody—the pimp—he beat her up and left her to rot. Then Renoult finds her and brings her in. He gives her work. He buys food for the baby. Soon she has a flat of her own. I hear he was poor once himself."

"So then Renoult and her…"

"Oh no. Still she is unattached. The mother comes to live with her and watches the baby when she is here."

Gus threw back the last of his whiskey. "What about the way she fools around with the customers?"

"Is good for the tips, no? And if she finds a man attractive, why shouldn't she enjoy herself?"

"You mean she still sells herself?"

Albert looked surprised that this lifestyle offended Gus. "I'm sure that it helps provide for the baby," he said. After a pause he added, "And then sometimes it is just for the fun. She can be quite the wild one."

Gus perused the specimen in front of him. Nose and all, he was handsome. Nothing in this man suggested marriage or home or any kind of future, yet Gus could see he had no trouble obtaining the women he wanted—perhaps more than just women—since his first visit here he'd been replaying the images of Jack and that man. Albert obliged the examination by flexing beneath the open shirt, and Gus finally parsed the innuendo. "You've been with her?"

"Of course." And though he didn't need to explain further, Albert held up a lecturing finger and added, "And not for money, mind you."

Gus had wanted to think of Aimée as a woman who didn't belong in the city, but had no choice. He imagined her coming from one of the farms he'd seen on the train to Le Havre, a victim of some drought or pestilence, forced to leave her family so she could make money to send back to them. The permissiveness of her hair and clothes he explained to himself as her rural naïveté; her manner with the customers as forced upon her by circumstances. Inside she would be like him, thrust into a world of selfishness, aching for an opportunity to escape. But every notion about what motivated people that he'd brought to Paris had been challenged. She enjoyed her life in the cabaret as much as the customers.

Albert raised his eyebrows, guessing Gus's thoughts. "You are interested?"

How could he be? But he was. He looked up at the bartender. "I doubt she'd be interested in me."

"And why do you say that? I've seen her looking at you."

"You're making that up."

"If that is what you wish to believe…"

Gus took the broom and started walking towards the center of the room. After two steps he stopped. "Can you teach me what to say to her in French?"

Albert erupted in laughter. "We'll turn you into a Frenchman yet!"

Gus laughed too, the first time, he recalled, since arriving in Paris. But the emotion didn't last long. "No," he said. "I don't think that will happen."

"And why not?"

"I have to leave in a few days. To go back to the states."

"A shame," Albert said. "You should have more of a chance to appreciate Paris."

Gus continued his thought, "That's if I can get to the ship."

"Why can you not?"

"I haven't been too smart about things lately." Gus considered his own understatement.

Aimée dropped her bread knife and it shivered on the floor. Gus and Albert looked over as she picked it up and wiped the blade under the arm of her blouse. When she realized they stared at her, she pushed the hair out of her face and smiled. Gus noticed one of her teeth was crooked. She was not perfect and that was all right with him. He smiled back.

"See," Albert said, "she likes you already." He put the whiskey away and picked up his bar towel.

When Aimée went back to her chore Gus reached for the broom again. "How is it," he asked Albert, "that you speak English in a place like this?"

Albert smiled. "In London," he said. "A woman. Wealthy and most generous. We gave each other what we had."

Within an hour the first of Le Secret's customers made their way down the stairs. Gus wouldn't have to perform for them—the two men had only liquid entertainment in mind and they draped themselves over the bar in an oblivious resolution to pursue it. Albert watched them as he worked, making sure they didn't reach for anything they hadn't purchased. They, in turn, watched him, perhaps looking for an opportunity. Gus let the little drama unfold, but in a minute his attention was diverted by the sound of heavy shoes coming down the steps. Renoult and some of the men who been with him that first night trooped to a table on the far side of the club and sat down deliberately, like officers preparing a battle plan. Renoult wagged four fingers and called to Albert, "Cognac. Chabasse," and the barman hurried over with bottle and glasses.

An afternoon get-together. Gus ran into the back room for his banjo. Surely they'd appreciate some music as they ruminated over drinks. He felt good about Le Secret and the fact that he worked here. They would pay him, and the people seemed to like him. He would give these gentlemen a good show, never mind his other problems.

When he came back out Gus slid into a chair near their table. The men jabbered away in French—the three visitors all seeming to speak at once, and Renoult listening as though gathering the details of a report. Gus ripped the pick across the strings. But before he could play another note, Renoult had turned in his chair and raised a palm like a traffic cop.

"What is this? No one asked for banjo."

"I thought they might like…"

Renoult opened his mouth as if to berate, but changed his tone. "Of course you wouldn't know," he said. "But this is very important and we need silence. Go back to cleaning, please. Better yet…" He reached into his wallet and pulled out a franc note. "You are cooped up in here too long. Here is your first pay. Why not go around the corner and have a coffee?"

Gus took the bill, went back and put his instrument in its case, but when he came out he went behind the bar where Albert was arranging shot glasses. The big man looked surprised. "Another tumbler, my friend?"

Gus picked up a towel and a glass, and although it was dry, began to wipe the inside. He leaned in to whisper. "Can you tell me what they're saying—without Renoult seeing?"

"You wish to eavesdrop?"

"They may know what happened to a woman I know."

"Aha!" Albert said. "I should have known you were the ladies man after all."

Since Albert had finished preparing the bar for business, the pair had to pretend to clean and straighten. Gus signaled to him that they shouldn't look at each other.

"They are talking about the man, Jaurès," Albert said. Gus didn't recognize the name, but kept watching the group so as not to let on. "The thin one says he would be a fool to believe the premier. Now Renoult says *he* is the fool to doubt Jaurès. The first one says he knows the army is massing outside Paris, and they are just waiting for an order to march to the German border. He says Jaurès would be blind not to see the significance."

"Then it's about the war. It sounds like it's almost here."

"We will see."

"You're not worried?"

"I never trouble myself with these things. Renoult, he and his friends are always in here talking. For two years I have worked while they have been talking, and as you see, we are all still here. What has changed?"

"But they said the army is moving. They're ready to march."

"Two years ago I hear the same talk, and is there a war? La guerre, she is a fickle one. She flies in and all the men chase after her. But they haven't caught her yet."

"La what?"

"La guerre. It means the war."

"And it's a bird…that men try to catch."

"Something like that," Albert said. "Perhaps this time there may be more than talking. Perhaps, for once, I should be concerned. I hear the army is drafting everyone they can find."

"Do you think you'll be drafted?"

"My friend, they will have to locate me first. If I have to, I will hide with my relatives in the country. I am a lover, of course. A soldier? Hardly."

"La gare," Gus tried. He took a glance at the barman, who must have been a general's dream—what a fighter he could be if he had the heart. The sight of an army of Alberts would send the enemy running back to their barracks. Instead he would rather hide under the skirts of his girlfriends and relatives. He hadn't had to fight to survive and now he would not, even if his safety or his country depended on it. Perhaps, being so big, no one had dared take him on. Gus inched closer to his new friend. He barely came to Albert's shoulder. He had never had a choice about fighting.

"La guerre," Albert corrected. He kept cleaning as though the conversation had been about nothing. "If I were you," he said. "I would be concerned. If you stay here you may find yourself in the army."

"But I don't even speak French."

"The army needs men. Why should they care what language when they are only going to be shot…"

Gus turned and looked at the barman, who was fighting a smile. Albert said, "A sense of humor sometimes helps in a crisis." He gave Gus a light punch in the shoulder.

"Come on," Gus said. "Listen. Are they still talking about politics? Have they said anything about the woman?"

"So you were serious?"

"Yes."

Albert turned his focus back to the men. "Still more gibberish. They are arguing over whether they should have all the workers in France walk off their jobs. As if they could do it! They say it will stop the war. They say Jaurès claims it is their last weapon."

"Now they say they will urge Jaurès to declare the strike tomorrow, before the government can stop it." Albert paused.

Renoult looked towards the bar and waved for another round of drinks. Albert picked up the bottle, but Gus put his hand on his arm. "Let me take that to them," he said.

Renoult looked surprised that it was Gus, not Albert, with the bottle, and he watched closely as he poured, as if expecting him to spill. When Gus was done, and since he could not speak to them in French, he bowed to the group. They laughed, and Renoult said, "Please, God forbid, we are not royalty. Get up."

"Monsieur Renoult, would you do me a favor?"

"What is that?"

"Would you ask your friends if any of them have seen Kera McGuin? She's the woman who was here with me when we came in. She was talking to the other man…the one with the beard."

"Very well," Renoult said.

One man had already looked up when Gus mentioned her name. "Kera?" he said. "Oui. J'ai vu Kera."

Renoult laughed. "It seems there is much to tell. I will have Landrieu enlighten us all." The man gave his version of the affair, of how Bertré had seduced her with dinners and gifts, and how she had moved in with him after only one night—outrageous, he said, even for Paris.

"Ask him where she is," he demanded of Renoult.

"Landrieu says she is staying at his apartment near the Seine."

"How do I find this Bertré?"

Renoult rose from the table and escorted Gus back to the bar. "That is enough, Gustav. Landrieu has told you what he knows and that is all there is to it. You are keeping us from our business, and you are trying my patience."

"But it's important…"

"It's more important what we do. You must forget this for now."

Renoult's look said one more question might find Gus out of the storage room and in the street. He looked for things to clean or straighten, all the while keeping watch over the discussion at the table.

In another half hour a few more patrons had found their way downstairs. Aimée hurried among them, flirting and taking orders, and Albert poured shots and beers. Gus knew it was time to break out the banjo, but the men at the table might be finished with their talk any minute, and he hoped to have a chance to catch this Landrieu fellow before he left. He would know where to find the man with the beard, and Gus would figure a way to communicate with him. An address, a street name—that was all he wanted. He would work out the details later.

Finally, the men stood up. They shook hands, and one of them hugged Renoult. They headed for the stairs. Gus began to make his way towards them, but Renoult was watching, and shook his head slowly with a countenance that said they were not to be bothered. What was the use? Kera had made her decision a few days ago, and she would have to live with it. He would as well. He was trapped—in this basement and this arrangement. If he defied Renoult he might lose the beggar's existence he had left to him—as if that were worth protecting. Yet without it… He didn't trust himself outside. Even the storage room was better. The men went up the stairs and Gus listened to their footsteps diminish.

He approached Renoult, who was sliding some coins from the bar into his pocket.

"Why don't any of you want to fight…in the war, I mean?" Gus asked.

Renoult turned to Gus. "Albert tells you this, yes?"

Gus nodded. "I didn't mean to hear it. He translated for me."

Renoult looked out at the far corner of the cabaret as he spoke. "What is the purpose of fighting?"

"To defend yourselves?"

"Defend, yes. We are not cowards, if that is what you think. But this war is not about defense."

"Then what?"

"You ask many questions, Gustav," Renoult said. "You wish to leave and go back home, so why do you want to know?"

"I've had to fight."

"I see," Renoult said. "And what was gained?"

Gus thought for a few moments. Now he looked away, out towards the tables, where Aimée stood with one foot propped on a chair, revealing her ankle and calf from under her skirt, talking to a customer. "Another day," he said.

"You could not have done otherwise," Renoult said. "I understand it. But for France another day comes if we do not fight this war. You see, everything we have—our loved ones, our land, our way of life—would be lost in a war."

Gus held onto the edge of the bar. "I had only myself," he said. He felt Renoult's hand on his shoulder.

"Take a few minutes," Renoult said, "to relax before the mob takes over. I have the dancers coming in later and I expect a big business tonight." Gus pulled the franc from his pocket and inspected it. "Put it away," Renoult said. "If you want a drink from the bar, you do not have to pay."

"I was thinking I should see if there's a telegram from my agent. I thought I might walk over there."

Renoult nodded that it was all right. Gus swung the banjo onto his back. Yes, it would only be a few minutes, and he could trust Albert to look after it, but the place was becoming busy, and all it would take would be a moment of distraction for an accident. Gus ran his hand up and down the smooth neck. He loved the way the instrument felt in his hands—despite the damage it still felt solid, dependable. This was the only tie he had left to his life in the states, and he wanted it with him. He walked towards the stairs, through the thickening cigarette smoke and the hard laughter of people who had come to lose themselves for a few hours. When he went outside he was surprised to find the harsh light of the day still glaring, peering into every nook and corner of the street.

Chapter 8
Thursday afternoon – Kera

IN PARIS she would soften, she had it planned. He would pay a price for his inattention, for his abandoning her in the mob of followers, for embarrassing her in the meeting of old men. By morning he might begin to understand why she'd locked him out of her bedroom, but she demanded penance as well. Not until the train neared Paris would she converse again. He would wait even longer before he could touch her.

Kera skipped breakfast and left the hotel to avoid seeing Bertré, preferring instead to tour the streets of Brussels until it was time to board the train. She would sit close to the rest of the group, perhaps with Longuet, and he wouldn't dare talk of their personal business in front of the others.

The hotel was located in an expensive part of the city, and at first, Kera decided to window shop at the boutiques and dress shops that lined the boulevard. It only depressed her. She was nearly out of her own money and Bertré's insistence on paying for everything meant she had none of his, so if she found something that caught her eye, she wouldn't be able to purchase it. Even buying breakfast was out of the question, as she had to save most of her coins for a taxi to the station. What could she do for a few hours that would keep her away from him? Down the avenue she saw a banner hanging from a stern-looking building with marble columns in front, advertising a new art exhibit. She'd never had time for an indulgence like this on the road in the states. And she could certainly make this last all morning. A line of toga-clad statues of women perched on the parapet atop the columns, welcoming her to a show of Flemish paintings of the Northern Renaissance. Obscure, but intriguing. She began to feel good about this decision.

She could just afford admission to the Royal Museum of Art. The fact it was Thursday morning meant smaller crowds, and Kera walked at leisure among the galleries of van Eyck, Coustens, and their contemporaries. As she exited a room filled with the art of Bruegel the Elder, she noticed a short, heavy man in a black coat, holding a cane and bowler at his side, far down the long hallway, walking in the other direction. She took a few steps towards him, and then stopped to be sure. When he turned and she saw the thick beard angling from his jaw, she knew it was Jaurès. He seemed to be alone. No Vaillant, no Sembat or Longuet, and thank God, no Bertré. Could it be he too wanted to get away from everyone for a few hours? Kera had just begun to understand the pressures on him—traveling throughout Europe, making speeches, fighting his own government over the war, keeping the morale of the others high. Everywhere he went a crowd followed, sometimes his own people, sometimes admirers, all wanting to see him, talk to him, and take up more of his valuable, diminishing time. If he'd had enough of that by now and decided to quit and take his wife on an extended vacation, she wouldn't be surprised. But he wasn't that kind of man. She sensed Jaurès would see the crisis through, until the moment the armies opened fire on each other, and even then continue his efforts in the cause of shortening the conflict.

Kera followed from a distance for a few minutes, observing him as he perused the paintings, feeling for a moment like one of the voyeurs who loitered backstage when she performed in New York. He turned into a room of Quentin Massys and she waited just outside, pretending to appreciate a display of artist's brushes and palettes while she watched him stand before a painting of a man and wife—he counting money, she turning the pages of a Bible but with her gaze on her husband's tally instead of the Scripture. Greed trumps righteousness, Kera decided. She saw Jaurès's shoulders sag, as if to convey he too understood the artist's point in the same way. No wonder. He faced that attitude every day in politics, and here it was again in art. Like the artist, Jaurès knew what drove men to act. Her empathy for him welled in her chest. She breathed deeply and clutched her purse tighter. She wanted so much to converse with him, to tell him how wonderful his speech had been yesterday, and to give him the kind of encouragement he had imparted to the others. She imagined he had risen early at the hotel, perhaps unable to sleep with all that must be on his mind. He'd tip-toed through the halls and out to the street, so as not to be noticed by anyone who might inform his entourage, and then sauntered off to some discreet sidewalk café, away from the main streets, where he quietly sipped a coffee in blessed anonymity and waited until the museum opened. Well, she wouldn't spoil his adventure for him. But she would watch him…for just a few more minutes.

Kera loitered in the hall before deciding to go her own way. She stood against the wall and saw Jaurès come out, and made sure he was walking in the opposite direction before heading towards the second floor exhibits. In the large museum she felt sure she'd be able to avoid Jaurès for the remainder of the morning. But in whatever room she happened to find herself she couldn't forget the image of him standing before the Massys, shoulders weighted, surrendering to the inevitability of people's self-interest, and the near impossibility of altering human nature. Kera suspected he knew, like Longuet, that the war could not be stopped now—and worse, that his life, dedicated as it was to the common people, might be as futile as his efforts at the Internationale had been. Most of the workers he spoke for, she believed, were no different than the couple in the painting—making a show of piety for the public, but in truth obsessed with material gain, caring little about the man who devoted himself to their cause.

Kera thought about Gus. What a contrast he was to Jaurès. Where Jaurès dutifully took the weight of the world's problems upon his shoulders, Gus had managed to live a life, as far as she knew, almost completely without responsibility. Perhaps that was why he hadn't been interested in her. It would have made him responsible—for her safety, for her happiness. How could she have made him understand that just by being with her those responsibilities would have been fulfilled?

At one Kera boarded the express back to Paris. She'd managed to avoid Bertré by skipping lunch, subsisting on a baguette from a local bakery. It had not been nearly enough and now she was ravenous. She had checked out of the hotel without running into any of the others and used her last few coins to take a taxi to the station and have her bags carried. She was apprehensive about meeting expenses once she got back to the city, especially if Bertré did not apologize to her by then.

She settled into a seat facing the rear of the train, so she could see him board, and sat in the middle of the bench, daring him to sit next to her.

Bertré stepped on, predictably, just behind Jaurès, with the rest of the group, except for Longuet, following. They headed for the empty seats nearby.

As they came close, Jaurès stopped and took off his bowler to address her. He offered her a courteous, but weary smile. "Madamoiselle McGuin," he said, "I was wondering if perhaps you were familiar with the works of Massys."

Kera started and put her hand on the cameo clasped to her collar. Had he seen her at the museum? How? She was sure she'd stayed out of sight.

"I happened to visit an exhibition of Flemish masters this morning. Magnificent works of art. I thought you might have appreciated them." Then he winked and she knew.

"Why yes," Kera said, "His paintings are so full of meaning. I'm so glad you had a chance to get away from your busy schedule and enjoy them."

"Thank you. It was wonderful to have some time to relax."

To her surprise Jaurès slid into the seat across from her, his large frame filling the bench, and leaving no room for anyone else. "I hope you don't mind if I join you for a while," he said. "I'm so tired I don't think I could walk another two meters."

"Oh, my, of course not."

Bertré stood at the side of the seat and stared at them. Kera looked towards the rear of the train, trying to ignore him, but she could sense every aspect of him—the rhythm of his breathing, the sweet cologne on his neck, the pressure of his hand upon the seat back. Finally she turned towards him and he spoke: "Will you let me in?"

Without words, she slid towards the window. He sat next to her, just brushing the fabric of her dress. They both looked past Jaurès to see Longuet bound up the steps into the car, and take a seat across from the Sembats. Bertré exhaled as though he were upset with the young man's lack of punctuality.

Jaurès ignored him. "Well my dear," he said, "I hope you enjoyed your day in Brussels. It's quite a lovely city." The train lurched forward and began to leave the station. It rocked as it crossed the track switches, forcing Kera and Bertré to rub shoulders until it was out of the rail yard and onto a segment of track where it could pick up speed. Each time they touched she made it a point not to look in his direction.

"I wish there had been more time to sightsee, but I didn't want to miss your speech. It was very inspiring," Kera said. "I even saw some of the deliberations afterwards."

"I know," Jaurès said.

"Oh, I'm sorry," Kera said, recalling how she had interrupted the proceedings. "I must have made a nuisance of myself."

"Not at all. Those old men were glad to see an attractive woman in their presence for once. And I must say it makes it easier to negotiate with them when they're so distracted."

Kera put her hand over her mouth to hide a smile, and thanked him.

"Now Maurice," Jaurès said with his hand raised like a parent, "What did you purchase for the lady during our stay?" He stifled a yawn, and then sat back in his seat to await a report of fine jewelry or fashion.

Kera held her breath. She became afraid he would retaliate for her avoidance by blurting out something like, "A separate room!" But Bertré shook his head and muttered that there hadn't been time.

"What's that?" Jaurès asked. "You purchased nothing? Maurice, I am shocked. You must make time for a beautiful woman, especially when the affair is new."

Bertré seemed at a loss as to how to respond. Kera sensed this sort of teasing was something new in his relationship with Jaurès.

"Well," Jaurès said, "You must promise that as soon as we get back to Paris you'll purchase the lady something to make up for your neglect."

"Yes, yes," Bertré said. "Just as soon as we reach the city."

Surely Jaurès had more important matters on his mind. Why was he concerned? Did he know the trouble they were having? Had Bertré spoken to him?

Before she could continue the conversation, Vaillant came up and put a hand on Jaurès's shoulder. "We need to discuss what you will say to the premier when we return tonight," he said.

Jaurès groaned. "Yes, if he will see us. Was there an answer to our cable before we left?"

"No."

"Well, we'll get in. He'll have to see us."

Jaurès turned back to Kera and Bertré. "You will have to excuse me," he said. "It seems the work never stops." He rose to go with Vaillant. Bertré got up as well and looked as if he would accompany Jaurès. "No, no," Jaurès said. "You stay here and pay some attention to the lovely lady. We'll be fine." With that he walked towards the rear of the car with his aide.

Kera could see how the last few days had worn him down. As Jaurès passed each seat he placed a hand on its back for support, like a much older man. By the time he reached the rear seats he virtually fell in, and Vaillant had to help straighten him.

That left Kera and Bertré alone and she became anxious that with no one else to hear he would begin to berate her for locking him out last night. He was not so aggressive as to start right in on that, however, and his delay answered Kera's prayer. Longuet jumped up and walked through the aisle to them, sliding into the opposite seat like a child on holiday. He nodded his respects to Bertré.

"Oh, Jean, how good to see you again," Kera said.

He smiled, and turned to Bertré. "Maurice, this is one time you should have insisted on paying for first class. You can see how exhausted Jaurès is. I'm afraid for his health."

"He never lets me pay for that. You've heard him."

"This time, I think, he would have agreed. Or at least been so tired he couldn't fight it."

"Perhaps you are right," Bertré said, "but what can we do about it now?"

"When we get back to Paris we need to make sure he goes home to rest. No matter what else he has planned. I've already spoken to the Sembats and they agree. He'll kill himself at this pace."

"I will do what I can, but I know he's trying to get in to see the premier as soon as he reaches the city. You know how difficult it is to get him to change his mind."

"We won't give him the opportunity," Longuet said. "Help me get him into a cab and I'll personally see he gets home."

"You're a good man, Jean," Kera said, "to care for him so much."

"Yes," Longuet said, looking as though he appreciated the compliment. "He means everything to us. I don't know what France would do without him." He turned to watch Jaurès for a few seconds, then turned back. "Look at him. He knows the fight is just about over. It's all over his face, yet he keeps on looking for one more opportunity, one more argument to make to the government. He's not willing to admit that this time we've lost."

"As long as there is a breath in him, he'll keep trying," Bertré said.

"He'll keep trying, but look at the eyes," Longuet said. "He sees the war is just a few days away, and he sees what it will do to our people."

Kera recalled how she had seen Jaurès peering intently into the air on the trip from Paris. She reached out and patted Longuet's hand. He pulled her fingers to his lips, kissed them and rose. He walked up to the front of the car and stood at the door, looking out the windows, watching the Belgian countryside. For Bertré the silence between himself and Kera had apparently reached its limit, and he switched to the bench opposite her. It was fine with Kera. She too, turned towards the window.

An hour or so into the trip Vaillant and Jaurès completed their business, and the assistant moved up a few rows to join Guesde, leaving the master alone in the back of the car. Jaurès almost immediately dropped his head to his chest. It was not the normal rest of a man who had been working too hard. He didn't try to lie down on the bench or maneuver himself into a more comfortable position. He didn't lean his head back to relax or place an arm along the back of the seat. Instead he simply lost consciousness. Active one second, immobile the next. He didn't snore, in fact, from where Kera sat he seemed not to breathe. He slouched, head down, mouth slightly open, arms at his sides, as though suspended in time.

She watched him and assumed he slept, but couldn't help noticing his unnatural position, and considered asking one of the others to help her lay him down on the bench. But Longuet came back from the front of the car. He had noticed the odd way Jaurès was sitting as well. Kera asked, "Is he all right?"

"Is who all right?" Bertré asked.

"It's Jaurès," Longuet said. "I think he's sleeping, but he looks…strange."

Bertré got up and turned around to see. "I never saw anyone sleep like that."

"It's troubling," Longuet said.

Kera and Longuet gasped simultaneously, and she knew he had conceived of the same horrible possibility—that Jaurès was not asleep, that the weight of his responsibilities and the crushing pressures of politics had conspired, in the few seconds he was left alone, to stop his heart. Longuet had been right—he knew the battle was over and that the war would soon start, and in the great man's grudging acknowledgment of defeat he had surrendered not only his fight against the insanity of the conflict, but also his will to go on. And in dropping his resolve he left open a door through which death, unannounced, had found a way to take him.

Longuet whispered, "It can't be."

Kera held her breath. She looked at Longuet and saw his

eyes begin to tear as he moved to the rear of the car. These people, this cause would be lost without Jaurès. She put her hand on Bertré's shoulder as they continued to stare at him—still unmoving except for the jostling of the train as it went around a curve.

"I refuse," Bertré said. "I refuse to believe it."

Kera touched her lover. "Go to him," she said.

They joined Longuet. Vaillant, Guesde and the Sembats, when they saw the distress on the faces of their associates, suspected a problem, and they too rose and went back. All seven of them crowded around the body, each one too afraid to confirm their suspicions. "Can you tell if he's breathing?" Vaillant asked.

Bertré was closest, and finally he leaned in to check. He put his hand near Jaurès's open mouth. "Thank God," he said. "He is still with us."

Kera exhaled. She thought of having seen Jaurès at the museum earlier, and how he had managed to slip away from the rest of them for a morning's respite. He had nearly done so again, but this time, instead of a refreshing few hours away from the impositions on his time and judgment, he would have left them rudderless—at sea in a storm only he seemed to be able to navigate.

Longuet shook his head and laughed softly, as though amused that someone had played a trick on him. The others began to return to their seats, muttering about the stupidity of people who couldn't tell a sleeping man from a dead one.

As Bertré drew back to the aisle, Jaurès opened his eyes. Kera, Bertré and Longuet stood there, looking at him the way the devout gaze upon an icon in a church. "What is it?" Jaurès asked. "Is there something you need?"

"No, sir. Nothing. We were just checking to see if you were comfortable," Bertré said. "Go back to sleep."

The three of them, still stunned by their own imaginations, shuffled back to their benches. Longuet sat across from Kera and Bertré, and stared at a point in the front of the car, appearing not to focus. Bertré spoke first. "We can't tell him what we thought," he said.

Longuet said, "No. He would think us fools."

"I hope the others don't tell him either."

"They won't," Kera said. "I saw their faces. They thought the same thing."

Longuet lit a cigarette. "The thing is," he said, murmuring, "when I thought he was dead, my only thought was for myself and the rest of us—whether we would be able to go on without him." He exhaled a cloud of smoke into the air above his head. "I thought about how we would have to start all over. The party would be in ruins, of course. All the factions he held together would leave and try to go on their own. And then we would have to find someone who knew as much as he, and could speak as eloquently to try to put things back together."

"I don't think that would happen very easily," Bertré said.

"No. And I am ashamed for thinking it."

"Why?" Kera asked.

"Because it's obvious that I should care more for this man who has given his life for France. But he appears to die and all I think about is how it affects the living."

"But that's what death is, Jean," Kera said. "It shows how important and loved a man like Jaurès is by the emotion his passing brings."

"I would like to believe that," Longuet said. "Thank you for saying it." He rose and went to the front of the car again, and sat by himself for the remainder of the trip back to Paris.

Bertré turned to Kera when he was gone. "Did you really think Jaurès was dead?"

"For a moment, yes. It's silly, I know."

"No. Not at all. I thought so too—for a moment." He looked to the rear of the car as he spoke to her. "I had no idea you and he got along so famously."

Kera smiled. "He is actually very easy to get to know."

Bertré began to speak again, but Kera shushed him with a finger to his lips. She took his hand in hers and placed it on her lap, and held it there until the train pulled into the Gare Saint Lazare.

*

A messenger from *L'Humanite* was waiting for Jaurès when the train pulled in and handed him a note. "The premier has betrayed us," Jaurès said as he read. "He has sent word to the Russians that France will honor its treaty. Troops are heading towards the border with Germany. The police have been ordered to break up demonstrations against the government, and to arrest those who refuse to disperse." He stopped and crumpled the paper in his hand. "Come," he said to Vaillant. "We must go see Viviani at once."

Vaillant told Jaurès he would hail a taxi and began running through the station towards the street. Jaurès pulled Longuet and Guesde aside. "Come with us to the chamber and get as many of our supporters together as you can," he said. "As soon as we're able, I will make a motion to declare France neutral in the hostilities between Russia and Germany."

Longuet said, "Yes, of course," but he looked at Kera and shook his head as if to lament his plan to see that Jaurès went home to rest. His expression said he believed this new task faced failure as well. He nodded a quick goodbye and took off with Guesde.

Jaurès checked his pocket watch and moved closer to Bertré and Kera. "Maurice, I want you to go back to *L'Humanite*," he said. "Compose an editorial denouncing the government and setting the terms for a general strike among the workers. I'll review it when I return and we should be in time for tomorrow's paper."

Finally, always the gentleman, Jaurès turned to Kera. He took her hand and said, "My dear, I'm sorry, but I need Maurice to do this for me now. But tomorrow, he promises *two* expensive gifts for you! Isn't that right?"

Bertré only smiled. How could he argue?

When the main group left, Bertré paid the messenger several francs to see that the other men's bags were delivered to the newspaper office, where they could pick them up later. Kera then followed him as he rushed to a taxi and barked the address to the driver. "Maurice, what does it all mean?" she asked.

"It is what we feared—worse than what we feared. The premier has placed France in the middle of this war, and he is so afraid of what the people will think he is trying to cut off discussion. But we will not stand for it. When our editorial appears tomorrow, Viviani will feel our strength. We will shut down the country if need be. Then we'll see what kind of war he can fight without us."

"So Longuet was right all along. He said the war couldn't be stopped."

"He's not right yet. We still have a chance. The people will listen to Jaurès."

Bertré began to compose his editorial during the ride to *L'Humanite*. "I don't suppose you have paper and pencil in your bag, my darling," he said. When Kera answered no, he continued as though she would memorize his every word. "First, we must make the government's treachery public knowledge. Then we describe what the war will do to France, and to the millions of people who will lose their loved ones and their security…"

But Kera wasn't listening. She was swept up in a wave of pride. He was no longer merely Jaurès's lackey. He was a leader, fighting for millions of the oppressed, who unlike him, had little means to influence the decisions that governed their lives. He was rambling now, talking about how each worker must walk away from his job when Jaurès gave the order. It didn't matter if she remembered any of it—she knew he would recreate the arguments once he got to the office.

When the cab pulled up outside *L'Humanite*, Bertré

bolted from the car and through the door of the newspaper, leaving Kera to pay the driver. Since she had no money left, she had to apologize and go inside for the fare. But Bertré was already sitting at a typewriter, explaining the situation to two younger reporters, and feeding paper into the carriage. Kera squeezed in between the two and leaned over Bertré's shoulder. "Maurice…"

"My dear, this is a very bad time," he said. "You know how important it is for me to write this."

"But Maurice…"

"I have to ask you to wait over there." He gestured with his head towards the far end of the office.

"Maurice, don't ignore me! This is what you did to me in Brussels, and I won't have it again!"

Bertré stopped typing and looked up. "What did I do?"

"This! I am important to you only when Jaurès is not around, or when you are not doing his bidding."

"What are you talking about?"

"I need money to pay the taxi. I have none and the man is waiting."

The two reporters laughed. Bertré looked embarrassed. "I am sorry," he said. "Yes, I am dedicated to his cause, and yes, I will do whatever I can to help him…"

"I understand," Kera said, "but the money…"

Bertré looked at one of the young men. "Landrieu, would you mind taking care of that? I'll reimburse you later—I'll buy you a drink at dinner."

The reporter snickered and his friend pushed him on the shoulder as they reacted to their superior's comeuppance. Landrieu dug into his pockets to make sure he had enough and ran out the door. Bertré, still sitting, took Kera's hand in his. He stared at the other reporter until the man realized he should leave. Then Bertré said, "I know what you must think of me, darling. But please, bear with me. This is so important to the nation. I'll be done soon and we can have a nice dinner someplace."

Kera felt her face redden. Of course he was right. The entire time they had spent with Jaurès she thought only of herself. She chastised Bertré for not being his own man and punished him for not lavishing his attention on her as he had done in Paris, all the while ignoring the crisis that stalked France. He was as much a patriot as Jaurès, only his role was different. If that meant drafting an editorial for him, or keeping him on schedule, or even carrying his bags, it was still important to the effort, and she shouldn't think him less of a man for doing it. She knew now that to be with him was to be with two men—the private one, the lover who saw to her every need and made her feel like royalty; and the public man, devoted to a cause in which he truly believed and who would do whatever was asked of him to see it succeed. It did not embarrass him to perform menial tasks for Jaurès, so why should she be embarrassed for him? She stood a few paces behind and watched him work to save his country. He was not a fast typist, but he tapped away without pause, as though the editorial was completely written in his mind and he had only to transfer it to the paper. When he finished each page he pulled it and its carbon copy out of the carriage and handed them to one of the younger reporters for proofreading, who, in turn, handed it to another. Each of them occasionally noted a misspelling or grammatical error and brought it to his attention while he composed the rest. Since most of the newspaper had already been prepared for the next day, the few other staff members still at the office gathered around the scene to watch.

Ten people crowded around the desk where Bertré worked, packed together like a line of agate type. Kera moved a few steps back—everything here looked as cramped as the group surrounding her lover. A dozen little desks pressed up against each other. All sorts of papers, blotters and books blanketed them. They were arranged so there were only two aisles through which to walk, and those reporters (the newest ones, she assumed) whose desks were farthest from the door had to parade past everyone else before they could sit down. Only one desk sat off by itself in a corner of the room, facing towards the center. It had to be Jaurès's. The walls of the office were almost as cluttered as the desks, with papers and bulletins and drawings tacked up on the plaster. She wondered what Bertré thought of this place and this type of work, considering how different it was from what he could afford in his personal life. The sheer chaos of such a place must have played havoc with his usually immaculate sensibilities. His dedication to Jaurès had to be absolute for him to put up with these working conditions.

Bertré finished the editorial, and once the changes and corrections were penciled in, he decided to have the typesetter begin preparing the page for the next day's paper. It was too close to press time to delay if this would appear in the next edition. Once the original was messengered to the production house, Bertré stood in the middle of the office, reading from the carbon copy to whomever would listen. "The people know this war will visit death and pestilence upon our nation, even if the leaders of the government have duped themselves into believing otherwise," he read. "It is time for us to remind them of their duty to the country, rather than to their own perverted dreams of so-called glorious victory." Several of the staff stopped him with exclamations of approval.

He was working towards a crescendo when Jaurès and the others returned from the Chamber of Deputies. "Maurice," Jaurès said, "where is the editorial? We are going to have to change it." He was in such a rush that he still had his bowler on his head.

"What do you mean?" Bertré asked. "Have you changed your mind about calling for a strike?"

"The information we received at the station was premature. The premier assures us that the troop movements are only a precaution, and that the army will go no closer than ten kilometers from the border. It is only a defensive maneuver—the Germans won't look on it as a provocation."

"And the report about the police crackdown on demonstrations?" Landrieu asked.

"He says that is false, and I believe him," Jaurès said. "He says there will be increased patrols and a heightened awareness because of the present situation, but that no one group will be singled out for harassment."

Kera looked at Longuet, who stood behind Jaurès, arms folded in front of him, shoulders hunched, his lips pursed tight with dissatisfaction. He pushed through the assembled staff and stormed to his desk, where he pulled out the chair, thumping the back legs noisily against the floor.

"As expected, our friend Longuet doesn't believe it." Jaurès said, finally removing his hat.

"Viviani is a good liar," Longuet responded without turning back to look at the crowd.

"He wouldn't dare lie at this point," Jaurès said. "He knows what we're capable of doing if we find he is duplicitous."

Longuet turned and said, "It only makes sense for him to lie to you now. In a few days he can order the troops to the border and it will be too late for us to respond. Once the fighting starts we will lose what little momentum we have to stop it. The workers won't strike at that point."

Jaurès pulled at his beard. "You may be right, Jean," he said. "But if I call the premier a liar in print now we'll lose support anyway. The best we can do is act as if we believe him and put all his pronouncements in the paper. If he goes back on his word then it is he who calls himself a liar."

"Then no matter what we do, we fail." Longuet went back to the papers on his desk.

"If you mean we stop trying to keep the war from occurring, or if it does, to shorten it, then you are mistaken, my friend," Jaurès said.

Bertré got up and moved between Longuet and Jaurès. Kera had sensed the animosity growing between them since they'd left for Brussels yesterday. "Why don't you keep quiet for once," he said to the younger man. "Every decision we make you argue. Every move we plan you predict will fail."

"Someone has to see the other side of things," Longuet said, holding his ground even as Bertré moved until they were within inches.

"That is for the opposition," Bertré said. "You should support us. We don't need backbiters in times like this."

"I'm only trying to add a dash of reality to the deliberations."

"It's not reality," Bertré said, "It's negativism. Why don't you take your ideas over to the Nationalists? We don't need them."

"We?" Longuet came back. "What is this, we? Jaurès makes the decisions, not you. You think by nipping at his heels all day you become one of the party's leaders?"

Bertré grabbed Longuet by the lapels of his jacket. "Perhaps you don't need to go to the Nationalists. We know someone is tipping our plans to them—maybe it's you."

Longuet, in turn, grabbed Bertré's coat. "You doubt my loyalty? I am the only one who cares enough to speak the truth! But then, how would you know what truth is? You're nothing but Jaurès's puppy!"

"I'm a puppy, eh?"

Everyone else in the newsroom looked to Jaurès to say something. He seemed too surprised, or too tired to speak.

Now nose to nose with Bertré, Longuet said, "Yes. A whimpering little dog who follows his master around all day, waiting to be told what to do and when to do it. Don't think we all didn't see the spectacle in Brussels when you abandoned poor Kera to trot after Jaurès."

Finally, Jaurès said, "Enough you two."

But Longuet didn't stop. "Master, may I eat now? May I take a piss now?"

Bertré began pushing Longuet backwards. "And what is

your interest in Kera?" he demanded. "You seemed to spend a great deal of your time with her in Brussels."

"Only because you didn't! Does that make you jealous?"

"Ha! The last thing I have to worry about is Kera becoming interested in a boy."

"Instead of a dried-up old man? Perhaps you should think again."

Bertré pushed him hard into the wall, but Longuet turned and broke from the older man's grip. He pulled back and threw a punch that glanced off the top of Bertré's ducking head. Bertré responded with a blow of his own that landed on Longuet's ear. Longuet took another swing that caught Bertré on the chin and sent him backwards two steps. Bertré tried a kick that missed, and then lunged for his opponent. They began to grapple and wrestled each other into a desk before breaking. Before either could strike again, the other staffers were on them, pulling them to a safer distance. Kera ran to Bertré and put her hands on his shoulders. He was breathing hard, but began to speak. Jaurès cut him off. "I see we have a pair of children on our hands. No one is running to the Nationalists. I trust you both and I need both of you if we are to be successful. Now clean yourselves up and get back to work."

Then Jaurès began to laugh.

"What's so funny?" Longuet asked.

"You two are quite a sight," Jaurès said. "If everyone in the French army fought like you two, the government would never consider going to war." The rest of the room erupted. Longuet managed a smile. Kera tried hard not to laugh, but couldn't keep a grin from her lips. She had to duck behind the still angry Bertré to keep him from seeing it.

"All right," Jaurès said. "Let them go. They're a threat only to themselves. Now let's get back to this newspaper before we miss the deadline."

Bertré went to his desk. Longuet looked as though he wanted to shake the man's hand, but Bertré refused to make eye contact, and the younger man walked by without extending his palm. Just then, one of the younger staff members took off running, through the door and into the street. Jaurès watched him. "Now what is that about?" he asked.

"Damn it. I've already sent the editorial to be typeset," Bertré said between breaths. "He must have gone to stop it."

Jaurès sat down next to Bertré's desk. He exhaled a long breath, and loosened his tie. He patted Bertré on the back. "Let me see the carbon," he said. "Perhaps we can use some of what you've written. Instead of saying what we'll do tomorrow, we can say what we'll do if the premier fails to live up to his word."

The two men worked at the rewrite for another half hour, with the same assembly line of assistants handling the proofreading and corrections. Kera now sat, entranced by the process, in a chair next to one of the reporters' desks. Just as they finished, the messenger and the reporter who went to catch him returned. The messenger waved the original editorial in the air as he entered. Several of the staff members applauded their efforts. "You must have run quite fast," one said.

Bertré offered his hand to the reporter. "Well done. You must come and join us for dinner." Then he turned to the messenger. "How fast did he have to run to catch you?"

"He came up on me like a race horse," the messenger said.

Bertré handed him the revised article. "Here," he said. "You must go even faster than that to the printer if we are to get this into tomorrow's edition."

The man's knees buckled on receiving this news. Jaurès looked at him and said, "I know you can do it. We're counting on you."

The messenger saluted Jaurès and started for the door.

Jaurès called after him, "Tell Marcel we'll be by to check the galleys after dinner, and then he can start the presses."

He waited until the messenger was out of sight and walked over to Kera. "That is all we can do tonight," he said. "Now it is time to relax a little. Would you care to accompany me to dinner?" He shot a glance at Bertré over his shoulder, and then smiled at her, as though he knew he was annoying her boyfriend with this gesture.

Kera couldn't believe how quickly he was able to change his roles. "Monsieur, you amaze me," she said. "You go from politician one minute to editor the next, then referee. And when that is done you are ready to become the bon vivant."

Bertré came over. "If you think you are going to steal her away from me, you are quite mistaken." He and Jaurès laughed. "Come. Let's you and I go have a drink at Renoult's place and tell him what's happened. Then we'll all go to Coq d'Or. I know the chef and I'll have him prepare something special for us." As they started to leave he shot a look over his shoulder at Longuet.

Chapter 9
Thursday evening – Gus

THERE WAS no applause; no coins fell at his feet while he played. Gus could have pantomimed his music and no one in the crowd would have known the difference. He could not compete with the dancers, not even before they arrived. The customers waited for them, saving their attention and their tips for the Apache, and while Gus picked at the banjo they ignored him, boisterous over the impending floor show, carrying on like children, arguing, speaking louder and louder to be heard over the increasing din, forgetting the courtesies due his performance.

He would play, then, for himself. But not songs from the act—nothing, in fact, that might remind him of Jack or Kera. He strummed aimlessly as he searched for a melody that would take him away from the cabaret and the back room and all these people who refused to acknowledge him. It wasn't just the French. Max hadn't answered his cable, not even to say there was nothing he could do to help. Gus sleepwalked from the telegraph office, took the wrong turn and found himself in yet another alley with yet another club, as though so many French went to the cabarets there needed to be one on every corner to accommodate the population.

By the time he found his way back to Le Secret, the crowd had doubled and he knew he'd better make music before Renoult noticed.

He reached back to a day long before the tour, before meeting his partner, to a time as desperate as this. Another war raged, but this one was an export, an adventure, and the whole country was in favor of it. No one debated the potential cost in lives or material; instead people reveled in the intoxication of pride and gain. The melody came as easily now as when he traded it for table scraps and beer. The chords played automatically. Still, the crowd remained uninterested. Their own war meant nothing to them, so why should this alien tune matter? Gus began to sing.

Most of the time he'd been staying at Le Secret he hadn't sung, discarding lyrics over the memory of his last performance at the theater. He knew hardly anyone would understand his words, but he belted them out.

> *Crossed the straits to avenge the Maine*
> *And now I'm comin' home again.*
> *We were there for Teddy's rough ride*
> *Up San Juan Hill, right by his side.*

The club became noticeably quieter. A few heads turned towards him as though trying to make out the meaning. He kept on:

> *Forward, upward, as comrades fell*
> *Bullets flying, a living hell*
> *We fought to see our foe's despair*
> *Victors in this bloody…la guerre.*

That word. Albert's word. It was supposed to have been "hero's war." The bad rhyme had bothered him even then, and now he'd fixed it, unconsciously, and given the patrons something to understand. Aimée, tray of drinks in her hands, looked at him with her head cocked. A few of the crowd noticed the phrase as well. Renoult, who meditated over a cognac, came over. He stopped in front of Gus, folded his arms and waited for him to finish the song. Gus, startled at the attention he received, looked at the floor as he continued.

He plucked the final notes and let the banjo rest on his knee. Renoult began to clap, and the rest of the crowd mimicked his approval, although Gus suspected most of them had no idea what they were applauding. "Where did you learn that one?" Renoult asked.

"My grandfather taught me."

"And la guerre?"

"Albert."

"So now you make commentary on our politics, yes?"

"It just came into my head."

Renoult looked around. Customers were still buzzing over the possible sense of Gus's crooning. "As you can see, the vermin want more of it," he said. "Continue, then. Why don't you play a song for Paris?"

"That was all the French I know," Gus said.

"Go on in English. But we will have to teach you more of le Français."

"Maybe Albert has some time."

Renoult laughed. "I was thinking you might enjoy it more if the little one was your teacher." He gestured towards Aimée. "She could teach you a few things more than words."

Gus looked away, and Renoult, still chuckling, went to the bar. The owner pulled Albert aside and the two of them conversed with their backs to Gus as he probed the past for another song. If the French wanted to ignore the possibility they might be attacked any day, he would spare them another martial ditty. There was a dance he played in the Bowery—light and fast, and the bar crowd always loved it. "A Little Kiss of Love." That was it. He was only a few bars in when a man stood up and shouted something. Whatever it was the rest of the crowd agreed. Two women came out from the tables and began to dance in front of him, their long skirts sweeping the floor as they twirled in each other's arms, totally out of time with the music, but as long as they were enjoying… The women dipped close by, maybe to tease him, and he almost lost the tempo. A few of the others turned their chairs to watch the show. Two young men, one in a suit too tight even for his slender build, the other in clothes that fit like the rags of a beggar, came out, thrust themselves between the women, and after a harmless slap to the face of the vagabond, moved off with them in couples that looked more like wrestlers than dancers—the beggar made a snack of his partner's neck, and her head snapped back until her hair brushed the face of a sitting customer. The other woman bared a thigh and wrapped it around the thin man's hip, and they stood at the corner of the dance floor scowling, daring each other to go further until they broke into convulsive laughter. Albert had begun to circulate through the crowd, stopping at every table—he was holding some kind of satchel and nearly everyone he spoke to reached inside. More of the customers got up to dance. They pressed closer to the music, almost touching him, throwing what remained of the rhythm out of time, encroaching now on the private world of his art.

This was Jack's element. Jack would get up and waltz through the cabaret like a minstrel, stopping at tables, sitting for a while as he played, drinking in the adulation like wine. If he could only be like that! For Gus the audience was a price to pay to be able to perform. But this time the smiles and laughter, the applause weren't teasing. Gus finished and they cheered. Albert came up to him with a bag full of coins and placed it at his feet.

"What is that?"

"Renoult told me to do it."

Gus left the banjo behind to speak to the owner at the bar. "I don't understand."

"So you do know some French. You were fooling with me."

"But I don't…"

"Un petit baiser d'amour! A little kiss of love. It's a French song."

"I didn't know."

Renoult began to sing it for him, far off key: "Un petit baiser d'amour, c'est le bonheur suprême…"

Albert tried to translate in time to his boss, even farther from the pitch. "A little kiss of love, is the supreme happiness…"

"That's the song," Gus said.

"A little kiss once a day, is so good when you are in love!"

Renoult poured for all of them and they and the crowd toasted too. Aimeé stopped her waitressing and applauded, and Gus watched her.

"Well done, Gustav," Renoult said. "A little bit more playing and then the dancers will be here."

"Wait," Gus said. "And that?" He pointed to the bag of coins.

"Now you can pay for your train, when the time comes."

The cash was enough to accommodate Kera and Jack as well, if they somehow showed up in time. He could use some to get himself and his clothes cleaned up. Money had always been the problem; now maybe it was the solution. He should hide the bag in the back room among his blankets and the moldy boxes. But no. It would be all right here. He left it on the floor as he played. A few other patrons came out to dance, and two of them added handfuls of coins to the bag.

Halfway through, two men in suits came down the stairs. The first was heavy, all in black, and he used a cane to help him walk. He removed a bowler from his head as he entered the room. His beard was rough, scattered, like Gus's hair. He looked like he belonged with the group that had spoken with Renoult earlier, but Gus felt sure he hadn't seen him before. The second one came down a few steps behind.

It was Bertré. There was no mistaking the perfection of his manner, the details of his grooming. So smug he'd be loathsome even if he'd never met Kera. Renoult rushed to meet them at the entrance and placed his hands on Bertré's shoulders. The two men embraced. Bertré leaned to whisper something into Renoult's ear, and gave him an envelope. Renoult threw up his hands as if protesting, but tucked the letter into a pocket. Then he backed away and allowed himself to be formally introduced to the other man. He seemed—hard as it was to believe—intimidated. Renoult, who could conjure an insult for anyone, acted like a boy meeting a favorite athlete. He leaned down to be at the shorter man's level and seemed to be making excuses about something, all the while with a smile—something else Gus hadn't seen before—stretched across his face. But Renoult's pleasure turned immediately to a grimace, however, as he had trouble leading the men through the crowd. The customers were as interested as he in this new man, and some tried to stop him and talk, but Renoult would have none of it. He brought them to the farthest corner of the club, and forced another group to abandon their table to make room. He began to raise his hand, but Albert was already on the way with a bottle.

Gus stopped his song and followed them. Renoult watched, his eyes warning him to go back, but Gus didn't stop until he was pressing his legs on the back of Bertré's chair.

"Gustav," Renoult said. "Go back to the singing."

"He knows where Kera is."

"I will ask when we have a chance. Right now we have business to discuss."

"I know he speaks English." Bertré turned his chair away from Gus and twisted around. Gus stood as tall as he could manage. "Is she all right?"

Renoult signaled to Bertré that he didn't have to answer, then rose and faced his employee. "Do you have any idea who we are sitting with? This man is too important to be bothered by your antics. Now, go away and leave us."

Whoever it was, he had the power to turn Renoult into a schoolboy. Then Renoult addressed his guest as "Monsieur Jaurès," and he understood. He looked at the rotund man in black, who had used the pause in the conversation to take a sip of his drink. His hand engulfed the little glass. He seemed more interested in the liquor than in what was happening in front of him. Gus had expected a man more like Bertré, tall and commanding.

Jaurès asked something of Renoult in French. He began to rap his knuckles on the table to get his host's attention.

Renoult said, "Gustav, if you do not go back to your job immediately, I will have Albert return the money to the customers. Monsieur Jaurès is the most important man in our city, and you interrupt his conversation to inquire about a woman. If you don't stop, I will throw you back into the alley, where you belong."

"So I see the homunculus has surfaced," Bertré said. "I believe I met you at the Royal Fromentin. What have you been doing with yourself?"

Gus looked into Bertrè's eyes. The man's gaze looked sincere, but his tone was clearly taunting. How he must have deceived Kera. "Can you tell me where she is?"

"She is safe, and that is all you need to be concerned about."

"I don't trust you."

Renoult took hold of Gus by the shoulder and began dragging him away.

Bertré said, "But she does not wish to see *you*." Then he addressed Renoult in French.

Renoult answered in English, perhaps so Gus could hear, perhaps lost in the confusion of the moment. "Must I do even more dirty work for you?"

Bertré glanced at Jaurès, then back at Renoult, and put a finger to his lips. Jaurès, though, had had enough of the interruptions. He called to Bertré and began lecturing him. Gus didn't understand a word, but he enjoyed the timbre of it, even as Renoult had turned him around and was escorting him away. He saw Bertré wilting under the severity of the remarks. Jaurès's voice sang Gus's vindication. He told the dandy off like a troublesome child. Bertré tried to make his case, but Jaurès cut him off, all the while wagging a finger at him. Gus had been dragged a few feet when Bertré called to him. "Monsieur!"

Renoult let him go.

Bertré had the empty look of someone humiliated, forced into an unpleasant task. "I apologize," he said. "I know you are her friend. Kera is staying in an apartment I own in a safer part of the city." His voice was a monotone. "I will give you the address should you wish to see her." He began to write on the back of a calling card.

Gus lifted his hand in thanks—this had come from Jaurès. It was a small gesture, yet a great favor. Who belittles a friend to help a stranger? The Frenchman acknowledged him, then rapped the table again to summon the others back. Gus took the card and said to Bertré, "Tell her you saw me."

Albert was waiting for him at the bar. He had stored the banjo and the coins. "You are too trusting," he said, nodding towards the crowd. "These thieves will steal the money they have just given you. They will steal the shoes off your feet if you stand still long enough."

Gus maneuvered so he could see the men at the table while he played, especially this Jaurès, who was shaking his head over something Renoult told him. He didn't know him, hadn't really met him, but he felt a kinship—sympathy perhaps, for no other reason than having to put up with that scoundrel Bertré. He wasn't the only one watching. All over the cabaret people turned towards Jaurès as though waiting for him to address the crowd. Gus knew enough to let the men carry on their conversation without interruption. If he sang again it might excite the customers, so he sat and only brushed the strings—a small gesture in return.

The three men talked and drank for a few minutes more. Jaurès put on his hat, offered thanks to Renoult and made his way to the stairs, with Bertré in tow. Gus wasn't sure, but he thought Jaurès tipped the brim of his bowler to him as he walked by, but it might have been to a woman at a table behind. The card Bertré had given him pushed against his pocket and he was struck with an impulse to see Kera immediately, to guarantee her safety, and to lecture her about that boor. And she could tell him more about the strange Frenchman, Jaurès. But the club was nearly full. Albert would need help. He would have to wait until tomorrow.

Renoult gave Bertré's envelope to Albert and put his hand on the bartender's arm, giving him instructions. Albert bounded up the steps. Renoult signaled for Gus. "Put the banjo aside for a while. I need you to help me at the bar," he said.

"Sure. Is Albert okay?"

"I have sent him on an errand. It is the worst time for him to go, but I am the servant of Jaurès, what can I do?"

Renoult handed Gus an apron and donned one himself. They set up a few glasses and began to take orders from the men at the rail and from Aimée, who worked the tables. As requests came in, Renoult filled a few, but mostly he spoke with patrons and directed Gus to retrieve bottles and pour drinks. How the man enjoyed the notoriety that came with owning the bar. Renoult was friends with nearly every customer, including the two drunks who had been hanging over the counter since before anyone else arrived. He shook hands with people as they came up, waved to those at tables, and made jokes and conversation with others who wanted to spend a few moments. When the procession subsided, he turned and spoke to Gus. "It is too bad you wish to go back to America so soon," Renoult said. "If we could teach you some French, you could take over for Albert sometimes."

Aimée marched towards the bar with two full glasses in her hands. She slammed the drinks onto the counter, spilling their contents. "Stupide!" she said to Gus, following it with a stream of what sounded to him like insults. She turned to Renoult and complained to him as well.

"She says it is the wrong drink and now she has lost her tip because of it," Renoult explained. "Get the vodka from the shelf. Apparently you gave them gin last time."

The correct bottle found, he brought it to the bar, all the while trying to make eye contact with Aimée. "I'm sorry," he said, but she didn't comprehend.

Or did she? Her scowl had vanished. The white blouse slid from her shoulder. Her eyes still peered hard at him, but the anger seemed replaced with curiosity. She ran her hand through her hair—wilder it seemed than even a minute ago—and parted her lips. He had been ambivalent at first, but now he wanted her. This was how it should feel, what he never felt for Kera. He stared at Aimée, unabashed, the reticence he presented to the rest of the crowd for the moment subdued.

"Je suis désolé," Renoult whispered to him. "Tell her."

Gus finished the pour and said, "Zay swee…zee swee…Oh, I'm just sorry."

Aimée laughed, almost spilling the new drinks as she lifted them. She put one back down, patted Gus's hand and said something else in French before heading out to the customers. She swayed her hips a little more deliberately as she walked away.

"She says you are a silly thing," Renoult said. "That means, I think, she likes you."

Without clocks, Gus couldn't tell how long Albert had been gone, only that Le Secret was packed and Renoult had stopped helping, opting to join a man and two young women at one of the tables. The heat of the late afternoon was making its way into the cellar, aggravated by the closeness of bodies.

He was still unsure of where to locate the various liquors behind the bar. Patrons placed orders not knowing he spoke only English, and if they didn't ask for something he recognized from his brief stint with Renoult, he had to pantomime for them to point to it, which brought muttered, likely belittling comments. At least Aimée sympathized—instead of merely shouting out orders she helped him find the proper bottles. If the customer wanted a mixed drink, she came behind the bar and made it herself, carefully explaining the creation to Gus, albeit in French. He nodded his understanding as she spoke, despite not catching a word. As she worked he watched from behind, staring at a curve of her lightly freckled bare shoulder. Again he was reminded of the strangeness of this place—nowhere back in the states could he experience such sights. He brought his hand up to touch her—but how could he? They hadn't truly spoken to each other—had only communicated through awkward gestures. But Albert would have touched her now—maybe she was trying to get him to do the same. He moved his hand closer to that bare skin—but by the time he'd made up his mind to go ahead, she was done mixing drinks and off to her tables, where one of the patrons grabbed her hand and pulled her onto his lap, and she threw her arms around the man's neck, kissed him on the mouth and then slapped him to make him let go. How could he be attracted to someone like that?

Albert wedged through the throng, breathless, his shirt soaked through, as though he'd been running. "It's about time," Gus said. "Where did he send you?"

"I cannot tell," Albert replied, donning an apron and rushing to quell the surge at the bar. He put his hands up to let the angrier customers know competence had returned.

Gus looked out at Aimée as she patted another man on his cheek. "So many mysteries."

Albert poured a brandy for an impatient man who was tapping the counter with his knuckles. "I promised Renoult," he said. "He said no one must know."

"Was it for Jaurès?" Gus said.

"An emergency, they said. But the envelope was sealed. I cannot be sure." Albert pointed to a bottle on the top shelf. "The green one please," he said. "I am curious, though, myself, what was so important that I must run through the streets in the steam bath outside."

Gus retrieved an absinthe, and stared at the green elixir glowing in the basement's dim light.

"He sent me to the Chamber. To the draft office," Albert said. "What do you think of it?"

"The draft office? Could be they wanted to get a good look at you, in case they decide to call you up."

Albert laughed and nudged Gus's shoulder. "That's good, my friend. You are learning."

They quieted when Renoult came over to the bar. "Albert can handle things now. You have done well."

As Apache time neared, people rumbled into the club in all manner of dress and drunkenness, filling it to capacity until the stairwell was backed up almost to the top. Customers moved tables and chairs closer to the dance floor, and the crowd's noise overwhelmed his banjo. He stopped playing and made his way to the bar, intending to ask Albert if he needed help with the rush, and the moment he stood up someone grabbed the seat he'd been using. Two men pushed the upright piano in the corner through the mob to the center, and a man in a vest started playing with a fervor that reminded Gus of battle—there was hostility, retribution in the music. Two dancers ran into the little clearing ringed by the customers. When had they arrived? He remembered the woman. The man was different this time—a Negro, of all things. It might have been the original dancer from the other night, only for some reason in blackface, but no, this was a black man. Back home this would not be allowed, yet here the man was the star of the proceedings. Gus studied him as he prepared for the show, looking at the eyes, the countenance, trying to understand how he viewed his environment, whether he really wanted to be here or thought himself a misfit, fighting because he had to, because there was nothing else he was permitted to do. The dancer saw him looking and grinned, but Gus could not tell from this how he felt. It was a show business smile, painted on for the audience.

The woman bowed to the gathering before the act began, and was promptly kicked in her behind by her partner, sending her sprawling. The mob went wild. Someone yelled above the din, "Encore!" The word didn't make sense. The dancers wrestled their way around the floor. Everyone was screaming, applauding, their faces twisted in desire as they drank in the violence. The act was a show, but the emotions of the crowd were real. Gus watched them. They don't want war, but they do want this. Was there that much difference between the two?

The crowd pushed closer to catch a glimpse of the action, occasionally knocking one of their own into the clearing and interfering with the timing of the Apache. Albert became a madman behind the bar, moving faster than possible for a man his size, and with a coordination to match—when a drunk tried to lean over and steal a whiskey, Albert grabbed him by the shirt and pushed him backwards to the floor, all while continuing to pour with his other hand. Here was Gus's soldier, in service to the bar. But the big man kept his wits. While bystanders pulled the lush back into the throng, he leaned over to Gus. "Best to get these things out of here," he said, kicking at the banjo and the coins. "I can't fight them off all night."

He had to take them to the back room. But how to get there through the crush? Gus stood, banjo in one hand, satchel in the other, at the edge of the floor as the dancers escalated their gyrations. He worked between bodies, moving as the crowd moved, searching for eddies that might carry him through. Now he was part of the act, or so it must have seemed to the people who pushed him into the path of the Apache couple. The woman dancer backed into him and, apparently thinking she had come up against the crowd, threw an elbow that caught Gus in the ribs. He stepped back and someone took hold of his wrist.

He dropped the bag, and watched as it emptied onto the floorboards. Half a dozen patrons lurched for the money, spilling across the dance floor and stopping the show. Albert pushed his way in as the cabaret became silent except for the sound of people, on their knees, scraping the cash into their pockets. He lifted one man by the collar and swatted the money from his hands. "Voleurs!" Renoult was beside him. The rest of the scroungers scurried back into the crowd rather than face him.

"We are sorry," Renoult said. "We give it to you and then we take it away. I saw the faces. They are not welcome at Le Secret from now on."

Gus stood over the pile of silver, but did not move to pick it up. "Tell them thank you, but I don't really need it."

"But it is yours," Albert said. "It's your ticket home. You deserve it."

Aimeé kicked a man behind his knee, and when he buckled out of her way she walked into the clearing. She picked up the bag and gave it to Gus, then pulled him down until they were both kneeling on the floor. As he held it open, she scooped in handfuls of sou. A few from the crowd joined them. Gus recognized one of the women who had danced to his music earlier. The Apache dancers collected stray coins and brought them to him.

But when they were done collecting the money the show was over. The energy of the mob had dissipated, too weak now to encourage the dancers back onto the floor. They did not seem disappointed, and instead of leaving sat at a table with a few of their fans. The piano was moved back to the corner. Renoult kept most of the customers by offering a free round. Gus took his money and his instrument to the storage room. This time the crowd parted to let him pass.

With the mass of drunks pressing in for their libations Albert must have needed more help, but Gus stayed in the back, in the dark. He had no candles with him, and no way to light them, and sat on the floor in the oblivion of the room. A glimmer from the club, diffused around corners, served as his only light. The chatter of the crowd ricocheted off the bricks, disassociated, distorted into the echoes of a nightmare. She had wanted him to have the money. Her hands had been light, like the wings of a bird. He'd been ready to leave it on the floor—the more of it he had the more trouble it caused. Gus ran his hand the along the bag, discerned the edges of the coins through the canvas, felt its heft pressing down on the concrete. He could leave tonight, after everyone went home—throw his things into the satchel, take handfuls of coins for food and passage to Le Havre, and leave the rest behind, a gift for whoever cared to look for him. The banjo would provide for a few days once there if necessary—all he'd have to do is find the men who would lead him to the bars. He closed his eyes and waited.

He opened them later, how much later he did not know. Someone stood at the entrance to the storage room, a silhouette barely visible against the shadows. A man called his name and struggled with English: "Albert, he say come." Albert was probably drowning in orders, and Renoult, sitting in his corner, sipping a cognac, would be unwilling to lend a hand.

He brushed along the wall, twisted his head around the corner. The cabaret was still dense with patrons, and the cloud from their cigarettes hung from the ceiling almost to the tabletops. Gus could barely see Albert over the customers surrounding him. Aimée pushed her way from table to table without giving the patrons pause for talk or grope. Renoult sat in a corner with his glass and a woman in a stiff-looking red dress who had loosened the bottom of her skirts enough for her to drape her leg over his. Her petticoat spilled to the side and Gus was embarrassed for her, even if she was not.

When Albert saw him, the big man set down the glasses he was holding, clasped his hands together like a plow and forged a path through the throng to let Gus in. For the next few hours they worked without a break, Albert and Aimée shouting orders above the chatter, Gus retrieving bottles from the shelves and sneaking looks at her.

During a lull, Gus asked, "Is Renoult mad at me?"

"He is making much money tonight. It softens the anger."

"He looked mad."

"Oh, yes. Quite angry that you stopped the Apache."

"What did you say to him?"

"Just to remind him you would be gone in a few days. I think he may miss you a little bit then. Perhaps I will too."

What to do with the idea of being missed? In twelve years on the road, there'd been no chums to pat him on the back and wish him well, no women to pine over his memory. Promoters and managers never asked when he and Jack would return. Perhaps his mother had said it years before, but now, he couldn't remember.

By the time the last customers left, shooed from Le Secret by Renoult's verbal abuse, it had to have been well past midnight. The evening had been successful for the cabaret, but the work was not done—they still had tables and floors to clean, and chairs to straighten. He might as well get to it.

Renoult had been asleep at his table for hours and the young woman had managed to escape. But awake now he came over. "Leave it, Gustav," he said. "I don't want to be accused of being a slave driver. Get some rest. We can do the cleaning later. We will open later tomorrow…or tonight, I mean."

As soon as he was offered the respite, Gus realized how exhausted he was. "Thank you, monsieur," he said, and without waiting to offer goodnights to the others, trudged back to his room. Again he forgot to take the candle. This time it didn't matter. He felt his way in until he kicked against the blankets on the floor, and all he had to do was lie down.

He found the bedding, sat down and pulled off his shoes, pants and shirt, and lay back. The cool concrete offered a perfect feeling this time. The cabaret was quiet, and outside, in the alley, the last whoops and shouts of drunken customers echoed off buildings and faded into the night. He heard footsteps as the others went up the stairs, and relaxed. But there was one more set of feet still in the place, and instead of leaving, they seemed to be coming closer. It could be Renoult, come to give him some task that needed to be done first thing when he awoke. But the steps seemed lighter, smaller. The person carried a candle to negotiate the dark passage.

He saw the flame first as Aimée turned the corner and came into the room. "Gustav," she said, and then something in French. She was tired, it was in her voice, but still it had a sweetness attached, a remedy to the poison of loud noises—the shouts and stamping feet, harsh music and laughter over the Apache dancers—that soothed. When she spoke, the ends of her sentences lilted upwards, as though taking off into the air. He sat up, propped on his elbows to watch her.

She put the candle on a crate nearby and knelt in front of him. The light was not kind. Her hair looked more undone than usual. He reached for her hand and brought it to his lips. She spoke again and brushed the other hand against his cheek, and it grated over the day's stubble. Gus wished to say something that would make her smile, but he only knew the word for war. "Beautiful. You are beautiful," he said. Aimée put her hands on his shoulders and pushed him back onto the blankets. Her voice floated above him and he reached for it. She moved forward, sat down beside him, and let him remove her things.

Chapter 10
Thursday evening – Jack

JACK FOUNDERED in a sea of humidity on the floor of Raoul's flat, bathed in sweat. The heat wave that afflicted Paris bore down through the atmosphere all day, and by evening nearly any activity had become a chore. It wafted into the crevice between Raoul's flat and the adjacent building, cooking the garbage in the alley, sending rotten thermals upwards through the window to infiltrate Jack's prison. He was still nearly paralyzed from the sting of his skin, raw from where Raoul's blade had stripped him of his dignity, slicing hair and epidermis away without thought to emollient or the pain he would experience later. Or was it sickness that made him perspire so vehemently? Had the torture weakened him, left him open to diseases living within the filth of Raoul's room? He was too disoriented to know. Oozes and trickles of blood had coated him as the butcher worked, and since then had dried like rust in patches on his arms, legs and chest. After a few minutes of the ordeal Jack had stopped fighting, tried to relax his body and endure, but the scrape of the steel, excoriating him inch by agonizing inch, became too much to bear. He reacted to every slice, until Raoul beat him to make him lie still. Jack closed his eyes to accept his end, but no, Raoul was saving him for other tortures—his host had brought him only close enough to death to experience its vulgarity, its humiliation. Once Jack's body was stripped down to a glowing, aching rawness, Raoul went mad with arousal, and Jack was too weak from the brutality he'd already been through to remain conscious for what came next.

Now Jack, not quite asleep, lay limp against the side of the bed, the top of his union suit down around his waist, his legs splayed across the floorboards, his right arm crooked, up and over the top of the mattress, lashed into place for the past day with a leather strap secured to the bedpost. It was just a length of belt, doubled and tied around the buckle—it should have been a simple thing to remove, but Jack couldn't muster the strength even to right himself and face the task, let alone undo the knot. He hung there by his wrist, like the victim of an execution gone awry, swaying in the breeze long after the crowd had gone, and waiting for whatever punishments Raoul could dream up next. Would he even appreciate them in this state of mind? He tried, in his flickering awareness, to consider options. If he couldn't move, could he at least scream for help? If it came, what would the rescuer think, seeing him almost naked, blood-soaked and bound? Would the horror of the sight, the sheer disgust of it turn others away or worse, entice them to sadism, to prolong the attack on his body for having been forced to view so revolting a scene? It was useless, though. When Jack opened his mouth only a peep, like a bird's came out, followed by a gurgle. He'd had nothing to drink all day, despite drowning in this nightmare. He sensed infections advancing into his wounds, sapping his fading strength. Unable to act he had no options, and could only wait for Raoul to return and decide whether and when he wished to finish the job. Jack hoped it would come soon. The anxiety he'd felt when he realized what a monster he'd fallen in with had left him. Hope had gone with it as well. All thoughts of a future—returning to Gus and Kera and the act; sailing back to the states—dissipated at Raoul's hands, and there was now just present and past, and in the vague awareness Jack possessed of his surroundings, he could not help but slip into a swirling mix of consciousness and dreams.

Ravaged by thirst and starvation, twisted by the pain of the injuries, his mind played music. Echoes of his guitar in disjointed measures, atonal, muddled by the sound of a hundred people talking at once. His father's bar in the Bowery. The hollow strum of a banjo, and standing behind him, murmuring about a chance to play for something to eat, a boy, small and lost—kicking at the ground and shaking his head, his hair rising like Pentecostal fire. He played and the crowd became a horde, their surging noise engulfing the boy's music, threatening to drive him from the stage, until Jack interceded. Then they are alone, he and the boy, naked in silence and near darkness, tremors of desire coursing through Jack's body.

Jack cried, remembering Gus. His father had taken one look at the skinny teen and gave him the twenty-three skidoo, told him his kind wasn't welcome, and Jack lied—said he knew him, would vouch for him, that he could play a mean banjo. Gus's music was fury. When the song was over and the newcomer had his fill of table scraps, Jack urged him to stay. They could share his room, he said; rest up before leaving in the morning. He'd rustle up some breakfast to give him strength for the day ahead, if he'd like. There was no place else to go, Jack told him, not at this hour. They could talk about music.

The boy said yes and Jack sat on the floor of his room in the back of the bar, looking up at Gus as his new friend fingered the banjo. You can have my bed since it's only one night, and I'll get some blankets and stay down here.

And then he watched him.

He watched the callused fingers rake the pick across the strings, watched a leg dangle from the edge of the mattress.

He watched the uncombed hair sway as it bobbed to the music. He looked into Gus's eyes while he played—eyes focused somewhere far away, past the wall of the room and peering into who knew where. And he thought if he pretended to be unable to find blankets the boy might suggest they share the bed. But it didn't happen. Instead Gus turned away to strip for bed, and in the flickers of candle flame Jack saw rows of scars on the backs of his legs, arranged like slats, as though he'd sat on a burning park bench.

"How did you get those?"

No answer.

"They look like they hurt."

"Not anymore."

Then Gus lay on the bed, curled into the wall, and pulled the blanket over him as though he were freezing.

In the morning, stiff from the rough sleep, Jack sat on the end of the bed, nestling his hip against the bump of Gus's feet and serenaded him with a subdued guitar. He waited for him to wake. We could try a tune together maybe, he said. I sing a little bit too. In between the songs, questions: where are you going; how did you get here; where have you been living? Jack said, "I bet I can talk the old man into giving you a job, like me, if you want. You bus the tables and play once an hour."

"He would do that for me, your father?" Gus said.

"He'd do it for me."

Why Gus had to think about it for so long Jack could not figure. It had to be better than how he'd been living. But the boy just stared out the door, into the bar, looking at the empty tables. He blinked his eyes and Jack thought he saw them moisten, and then he knew the scars had come from Gus's father. "Why did he do it?" he asked.

Again Gus was silent.

"Stay here. It'll be easy."

Gus said nothing was supposed to be easy, but that it sounded okay.

*

Heavy shoes clomped outside the door of the flat. Everything about Raoul belied his scarecrow's appearance—his strength, his passions, his evil, and now his shoes—all monstrous. He pushed into the room and threw newspapers and a small bag on the table. Angry at something, as before. Jack watched as he took off his jacket, soiled and smelling of sweat, and turned towards him. But his face turned calm. "You awake at last, my puppet," he said. "Look. I have brought you for eating." He pulled out a baguette and tossed it to Jack. It slid across the floor and into his bare leg. Jack didn't care what dirt it might pick up on its way. He took the bread in his free hand and bit—the baguette was stale, and he didn't have the strength to break the surface, so he sucked on it until it was soft enough to chew. Jack made a drinking motion with the bread. "Oui," Raoul said, and placed a bottle of warm beer in front of him. It wouldn't have mattered if it had been a bowl of bath water—Jack drank it down in a single gulp. Raoul took another baguette and a few inches of salami out of the bag and placed them on the table. He bit off half the meat and chewed with part of it hanging from his lips. The other half he flipped to Jack. It landed at the edge of his reach and Jack had to stretch for a few seconds to get at it. Hunger gave him the strength he needed, and he felt an imperceptible movement of the bed frame as he touched his fingertips to the salami and pulled it closer. Jack jammed the entire piece into his mouth, chewing and sucking greedily until it was doughy enough to slide down his throat. In a few seconds his stomach began to reject the combination, but he held on for fear of what Raoul might do if he vomited in his presence.

Raoul sat in the chair, across from him. "I not mean to hurt you too much. I cannot help," he said.

Jack lifted his head to face him, but because of the strap had to keep it at an angle. If he looked Christ-like, bare and bloodied, as though he'd just been taken from the cross, it might draw sympathy. Raoul came over and began to stroke his sopping hair. "You see," he said. "Now I care for you. I get water and wash."

Whatever had turned Raoul's mind, Jack was grateful for it. He struggled to clear his throat—if there was a time to ask for favors, this was it. "May I…may I put some clothes back on?" he asked.

"Oui. After wash."

Jack tried to force a smile. It was important that Raoul think he was still devoted to him. He spoke again. "Then, would you undo the binding?"

"Oh, no," Raoul said. "I must not."

"But, why?"

"You will make for escape. I have you here."

"I promise," Jack said. "I promise I will stay."

Raoul shook his head, the moist hair shaggy around his neck like a dog in the rain. He reached over to the strap and took the loose end in his hand, and pulled hard to tighten it. The force of the tug clamped the leather down, like a tourniquet on Jack's wrist, and he felt his fingers going numb. "No," Raoul said. "You stay." His voice was calm despite the violence he practiced. Then he went into the hallway with the washbowl.

Despite the nausea the beer and stale bread churned up inside him, the food had begun to give him some strength. While Raoul was gone Jack worked to wrench his body into a sitting position. It was still uncomfortable with his arm stretched across the bed, but it was better than lying on the floor. Sitting he was better able to breathe through the humid air. His skin still burned, but the room was clearing, and he looked around the tiny apartment. Raoul had strewn the newspapers over the table, and one headline was partially visible: Chambre Débats la Guerre…meaningless.

When Raoul came back to the room he tried to ask about the latest events, but his jailer ignored him, instead tending to his wounds, dabbing the sores and dried blood with a soapy cloth. The cuts that hadn't fully scabbed over sang with misery from the soap and Jack felt the need to collapse back to the floor. But Raoul held him steady. He maneuvered himself between Jack and the bed and rested Jack's body against his chest for support. "Not so much soap," Jack said. "It burns. Just the water."

"As you wish." Raoul rinsed out the rag and began dabbing again. He held him like that for nearly an hour, as far as Jack could tell, until Raoul squirmed free of their embrace and lay him back against the side of the mattress. He walked over to the table and began reading the newspapers.

Jack closed his eyes. He only wanted to rest, but that would be impossible with his arm still tied down. He spoke again—if he could convince Raoul of his interest in current affairs, of his sincerity about not trying to escape, he might yet get him to undo the bind. "It must be important news," he said, "that you have so many journals with you today."

Raoul looked up from the papers, but instead of answering he stared at the window. The day's light had begun to fade. He picked up a candle and its holder from the floor and examined them like an artist studies his work for flaws. He turned the holder slowly in his hands, rotating it completely before putting it in the center of the table. But he made no effort to light it.

"What's wrong?" Jack asked.

Again no answer. Finally, Raoul took a deep breath and said something in French. It sounded to Jack like an incantation, as though he were asking the candle for guidance. Maybe this was his way of praying. He couldn't see Raoul sitting quietly in a church, confessing his sins and waiting to be absolved. He must believe he is speaking to God; getting advice directly from Him.

Jack had been going about it all wrong. Instead of pleading with Raoul to unbind and feed him, instead of being helpless, he had to reverse the roles. He had to find a way to make Raoul open himself, to make a connection that eventually might lead to trust, and then freedom. It would not be easy in his depleted state, but he had to try, or else he would be ignored again until Raoul's next whim. He could starve to death by then. The mysticism Raoul seemed to attach to the candle gave him a thought. He sat himself as straight as he could against the bed and lowered his gaze. The binding around his wrist tightened, and he lost circulation in his fingers. His skin still screamed from the soap in his wounds, and he fought against the pain to put on a good show. He closed his eyes again, taking himself back onstage in the Theatre du Vaudeville, ready to play for the audience, delivering himself to them, letting them show their appreciation in return. Their eyes on him—their pleasure at his music always energized him. It had kept him going all these years, even after the friendship with Gus faded. Now, if he played it right, if he stayed in control of the act, it might save his life. He banished the pain from his face, and let his voice rasp from his still burning thirst. In the eddies of heat and dreams it was not hard to do. "How can I help you, Raoul?"

Raoul looked over. "You wish…?"

"To help you. I see you are troubled."

Raoul stared at him, then up at the ceiling, as though the voice had come from there. "How? How you can help?"

"Tell me what it is that you desire. I will advise you."

"Advise?"

"I can tell you what you must do to achieve your wish."

"No. You cannot." Raoul went back to his newspapers.

Jack held his breath for a moment. He could just try to wait him out—to wait until he left again and he had more of his strength back. He had moved the bed. In another hour or so he would be capable of freeing himself. But what if Raoul didn't leave? What if he had another change of mind instead and decided to add more restraints or go back to his butchering ways? Jack had to keep probing his captor's mind. "Yes, Raoul. I can help. I want to help you. And if we work together you will be successful."

"No. This I must decide."

"It would be easier if we decide together. Then you would have the strength of two. Come. What is the problem? Has the war you spoke of begun?"

"No. Everywhere is fighting. But in France is making peace. Like women." He pushed the newspapers away from him. "A nation who is cowards."

"You are not a coward."

"No. But there are many."

"You are a hero. You, and the others who believe as you do—you are the heroes."

"Then why this?" Raoul held up one of the papers to show Jack the front page.

Jack couldn't read it, but knew it must have reported some effort at peace. "You must ignore such things," he said. "You must be strong, and others will follow you. You must be the leader and show the way. Don't let the cowards stand in your way."

Raoul took a swig from his bottle of beer and wiped it with his sleeve. He flipped the last of the hard salami into his mouth and slurred, "It is right. They are the barrier to France of greatness."

"Then you must knock them down. Smash them."

"Oui. Oui. You speak truth. I know now."

"Good," said Jack. "Excellent. I wish to help you." He felt strength returning to his arms and legs, excitement over the possibility that he had reached Raoul and become an ally in his silly fantasy. He had Raoul excited too, and in that state he would surely accept the offer of help and release him. Once he was free of the bindings and back outside he would find some moment—when a crowd was near perhaps—to take himself away from this madman. "Of course you must undo the strap so that I can accompany you…"

Raoul pivoted in the chair and faced Jack. "For you too dangerous. You stay…in safety. I see to it."

"No! I can help. I am not afraid…"

"Look—how you are weak. You rest."

"But if you release me I will be strong again."

Raoul came over and knelt beside Jack. He put one hand on his shoulder and one on his knee, and Jack recoiled. The care he had taken to cover his fear was exposed in an instant. The charade was over and he cowered as Raoul moved closer.

"You see," Raoul said. "You are of them—the cowards. You not fight. You are fear." Raoul held Jack's face in the fingers of one hand and squeezed. Jack felt the muscles under the skin compress, the bones of his cheeks begin to move inwards. He grabbed at Raoul's forearm with his free hand but it was like trying to pull a strong limb from a tree. Jack tried to talk—to say that he wasn't a coward—but he couldn't move his mouth. Raoul twisted Jack's face to the side and let him go. Then he stood up and went to his closet.

He pulled out a loose-fitting jacket and slipped it on. The dark fabric was so worn it reflected the last rays of light coming through the window. And it was heavy, like a winter garment. It would be much too warm for the hot summer night. "I did not know the way. But you show me. Your weakness is my strength." Raoul lifted the razor from the inside pocket, inspected it and put it back. "Tonight, I kill Jaurès. I show all France I am hero. People follow me in glory."

Jack slumped back against the bed. Raoul sat on the mattress and untied the belt from around the bedpost. But before Jack could begin to experience the sensation of freedom, Raoul wrapped the leather around both his wrists and pulled him harshly back into bondage. He retied the strap to the bed, this time with a force that burned against Jack's chafed skin. "You wait," Raoul said as he rose. "I come back. We make victory." He pulled a handkerchief from the pocket of his pants and tied it around Jack's mouth. "No noise from you," he said. With that he left. Jack could hear the heavy shoes throbbing against the floor as he went down the hallway.

He hadn't been able to keep the pretense up for more

than a minute before giving in to his fear. As soon as Raoul had come over to him…It was the same force that had originally attracted him, now channeled towards violence, and it was more powerful than before. Raoul's passion fed off Jack's desire. His evil grew from Jack's fear, and was revitalized to go back out into the world. It was Jack's own wish to be controlled that had brought him to this misery. He had allowed Raoul to abuse him with passion—allowed him to turn it into something else, something wicked, and he had followed it, served it like a slave, never asking anything for himself except to be allowed to be near it.

It had been the same all these years with Gus. The whole idea of them as a duo—banjo and guitar playing the songs of the prairie—had been Jack's. That first night at the bar should have been a warning—the Irish patrons wanted nothing to do with an Italian kid, and they were as merciless to Gus each night afterwards, whether he was on stage or bussing tables. Gus tried to assert himself, but the toughs, luckily for him, refused to take him seriously. It only took two days for Jack's father to change his mind about taking the newcomer in. When Jack saw him packing his clothes, it took him a while to realize Gus was leaving, since the boy gave no indication of sadness or loss at having to go. He acted as though this had been just another stop on a road going to some unknown place, and that eviction was always expected. He lifted the straps of his banjo and bag onto his shoulders—didn't speak, didn't look back. He was down the block when Jack, guitar and bag in his hands, caught up. "We're a team," he said. "Can't kick you out and expect me to stay too." Gus was indifferent, like he didn't care whether Jack tagged along or not. "Do you have any idea where we're going?" Jack asked.

"Next place that looks like food and drink for a song," Gus said.

"Right. Of course. Best way to get by," Jack said. "But maybe we should charge them too."

"They won't let you play if you try to get money out of them."

"How do you know?"

"There's too many wants to play as it is."

Jack was having trouble keeping Gus's pace with all his belongings swinging free. But his brain was moving fast. "If we charge them a dollar, then they know we're good. Only a beginner plays for free."

"A dollar? No one will pay that."

"Look," Jack said. "I got a dollar saved up in my pockets. We stop someplace and they don't want to pay it, I'll give it to you." Gus couldn't argue. Jack had set their course. He had an in with this boy. When Gus stopped at a corner and put his hand to block the sun from his eyes, Jack imagined Michelangelo's David under the ragged clothes. He had made the right choice. He'd continue to come up with ideas to keep them together, would make them successful, this team. He was already imagining what they might call the act. They'd be big. They'd last for years. And somewhere in that time the change in Gus he'd waited for would come. Until then he'd play the game he had invented for himself—watching, waiting, taking every chance to be near and compliment.

But what had his ideas done for him in all that time? Gus had no use for him now, and he hated Gus. The act was doomed to die, and he would probably be dead himself in another day or so. Good. At least there would be an end to the pain. And when he was dead and roaming whatever underworld he was sentenced to, he would find that man—the one Raoul hunted—and apologize to him for causing his death as well, and then he would set off for the permanent hell he deserved.

Jack leaned forward as far as he could and tried to pull his arms over the top of his head. The bed didn't move this time. He contorted his body by rolling onto his side, until finally he was sitting up, facing the bed with his legs underneath it. The pain was excruciating, but necessary. In this position he could get more leverage. But breathing was almost impossible. He couldn't get nearly enough air through his nose alone and had to rest for a minute before each attempt. Jack leaned back and pulled. A small scrape of metal against wood. The bed had moved perhaps a quarter inch. He tried again and achieved another fraction. How could he be so weak? At this rate it would take a full day to drag the bed just to the door. One more pull—a bit more distance this time. He continued to work at the cloth with his mouth, but it was as tight as the leather strap.

He needed rest. But he couldn't. Raoul would come back and see that the bed had been moved. Jack had to pull it all the way until he could get to the door. Then what? How could he open it while bound up? He could kick the door until someone heard. He could turn the latch with his feet. Perhaps with his efforts, something would loosen—the gag or the belt—and he could make enough noise to be noticed. He'd driven the pain away by thinking about music, and he conjured once more a wonderful night on stage as a Ballo. Jack tapped his foot on the ground to start the song, as Gus had done thousands of times over the years, and pulled with everything he had.

Chapter 11
Thursday night – Kera

COQ D'OR was packed, even at this late hour. The day's heat had persisted into the evening, forcing residents out of their stifling homes, and many looked for restaurants with sidewalk accommodations, like this one, where they could relax, maybe catch a breeze, and let someone else deal with the steam bath of the kitchen. Here, extra tables had been brought out and the service area extended to the street.

When the journalists arrived they found another group waiting ahead of them. Bertré played his usual card—his influence would get them seated quickly, he said, and he went inside to find the manager. Longuet and the others looked to Jaurès—typically his sense of fairness wouldn't allow him to push others aside to gain advantage. But he was so exhausted after the flood of events that he condoned Bertré's act without protest. Kera feared Longuet might take up the cause of the party to be displaced and start another row with her lover, but even he said nothing—they were all too drained to debate. Instead, he asked Jaurès to let him find a taxi to take him home. "You're too tired to be standing here like this. You need a good night's rest," he said.

Kera agreed. She started to tell him how haggard he

looked. But it might be insulting. Instead she said, "Perhaps, monsieur, you are working too hard."

Jaurès shifted his feet as though having trouble supporting his weight, even with the cane. "I'm fine," he said. "And after such a day who could deny me a few moments of relaxation?"

Out alone, on the town. Traveling to Brussels and back. Working all day at his government post and then rushing off to the newspaper. Kera wondered what Jaurès's wife thought of all this. He rarely spoke of her, and never to lament how much he missed her during these hectic days. It couldn't be that she wasn't allowed to join the group—after all, Sembat had brought his wife to Brussels, and here she was with Bertré. Kera would have loved to meet her, if only to have another woman along from time to time with whom she could talk of things besides politics. Jaurès was such a wonderful man, she felt sure his wife would be as friendly and articulate. Perhaps she understood his importance, and didn't mind the separation. In return, Jaurès might deliberately avoid speaking of her to keep her from the limelight—the world in which Jaurès operated placed enough of a burden on him, why make his wife endure it as well? There was another possibility, of course. She couldn't help remembering what Bertré had said. But she couldn't believe Jaurès was married to a little hausfrau, who was too embarrassing to the man to be let loose in public.

Maybe they didn't get along well. Was Jaurès as coldhearted to her as he was warm to everyone else? At last she might have found a flaw in the great man's personality. This was foolish, of course. She knew nothing about Jaurès's private life and since neither he, nor any of the others spoke of it, she wouldn't allow herself to assume anything about the relationship. But if she found the right moment, she would ask Maurice, and demand the truth.

They went inside to wait for Bertré. Waiters moved in slow motion among crowded tables; diners hovered over their food. The talk among the customers made up for their languor, however. The chatter was festive, belying the temperature and the dark political news. Kera heard snippets about painting and literature—even a conversation on horse racing, as if these people remained unaware of the military situation. The din seemed to make Jaurès uncomfortable, as though he couldn't think with the racket—and she knew he was always thinking.

Bertré came out with the owner, a balding gentleman with a pencil mustache who was sweating from working at the stove, and they stopped near the kitchen's swinging doors. This man waved towards the back, and two of the staff emerged with a table, plopping it down in what had been the wait staff's path to the kitchen. One of them snapped a tablecloth into place. Then they gathered up vacant chairs and brought them over until they had six, enough for the party. Kera and the others snaked their way towards the setup, but Jaurès hesitated before sidestepping carefully between the rows of diners.

Each of them would have a few square inches in which to set their dinner and drinks. Longuet and Landrieu volunteered to sit back so the others would have more room, but it was still ridiculously cramped, and Kera rubbed thighs with both Bertré and Nueve, the messenger, who was being rewarded for his quick feet. She sat directly across from Jaurès and watched as he endured the jostling of waiters going to and from the kitchen. He was not pleased.

"I'm afraid this is the best they could do," Bertré said. "On another night, it wouldn't have been a problem, but on such a warm evening…" Kera noticed that for once her lover's connections hadn't helped. He tried to conduct himself as though he had plenty of room—unfurling his serviette with his usual flair and placing it on his lap—but he knocked against her arm in the process and she had to lean far into Nueve to give him space to complete the maneuver. "It may be a bit tight, but I assure you, Martine has promised to prepare something special in your honor," he said to Jaurès. "A meal fit for a statesman."

"No!" Jaurès said. "I've had enough. I am not a sardine. I cannot take this treatment any longer." He pushed his chair back into the path of yet another waiter, and stood up. "If you wish to join me, I'll be at Café du Croissant."

Landrieu and Nueve stood. Kera looked at Bertré, who seemed non-plussed. "But Jean, our chef will be quite insulted," he said.

"That is too bad," Jaurès said. "But if good food can't be accompanied by decent arrangements, it's not worth it."

Longuet pushed up from the table, and Kera watched him. He turned to look away, but couldn't hide the look of satisfaction at seeing his rival embarrassed.

Kera rose as well and took Bertré's hand in hers. "It's all right," she told him. "You did what you could. But we're all tired and hungry. It's best we go someplace not so crowded."

Bertré went into the back to apologize to the owner while the rest of the party renegotiated the winding path to the sidewalk. Jaurès began walking away before Bertré returned. "He can catch up to us," he said, setting his bowler onto his head and taking off at a brisk pace.

Kera thought about waiting for Bertré, but she didn't want to stand alone on the street in the night, and stayed with the group. She remembered what it had felt like when Bertré followed Jaurès in Brussels and left her in the crowd. Would he notice that she'd abandoned him? She looked for him as she kept pace with the others. But instead of her lover she saw a thin man in a loose, dark jacket—a spectre in the gloom of the street lights—walking towards them. She recalled the ruffian who accosted her and Gus that first night at Le Secret and remembered the onion on his breath. Bertré was several yards behind him. She didn't dare call out—who knew what the man might think if he turned and saw Bertré in his finery—an easy mark, maybe. The rings and watch chain he wore tonight might be magnets to a desperate criminal, and she only stared as the figure approached.

Perhaps he suspected they watched him, because he turned the corner and ducked into an alley. Another alley. So many in Paris. So convenient for a city that sometimes wished to hide the darker side of its character. A sharp turn between the bricks and one was free to become dangerous, or at least appear so. To her Paris had become the world on the other side of the looking glass—decadent morals cherished as much as decent ones. In the past few days the boundary had become easy for her to traverse.

Bertré caught up to her. "Martine is very angry with me. He says we made a spectacle back there. I'll be lucky if he gives me a decent table from now on."

"Oh, come Maurice, it can't be that bad."

"You have no idea. His ego…when he thinks he has been insulted he remembers in perpetuity."

They walked quickly to stay with the others. "You men and your reputations," Kera said. "And you think women are easily insulted!"

"And he says Jaurès will never be welcome in his restaurant."

"Ah, well. Then we should say goodbye to Coq d'Or." As she said it, Kera turned to take one last look at the customers overflowing from the bistro. Was that the ragged man again, loitering at the corner?

At Café du Croissant, a few blocks away, the scene was far different. Only a few tables were occupied and the group had their choice of seats. Jaurès preferred to sit on the sidewalk, to catch what little breeze the evening offered. It was far quieter as well, with the handful of customers producing only a murmur of conversation above the clinking of glasses and utensils. They pulled two tables together and set chairs far enough apart so each one could relax. Jaurès fell hard into his chair—Kera thought he might break it with his girth—and ordered sherry for all. "We've earned this," he said.

But Bertré was dissatisfied with the accommodations. "I can only imagine the kind of food that is served here. To be honest, this place seems quite pedestrian."

Jaurès ignored him, but Kera recognized he was trying to save face—to regain his stature as the group's sophisticate. "I'm sure everything will be all right, Maurice," she said. "It was just an unfortunate incident."

Jaurès held up his glass, but not as a toast. "I apologize to all of you for my display at Coq d'Or. I should have kept in control of myself. Perhaps Longuet was right and I should have gone home. But it's too late for that. And since we're here, let's enjoy ourselves. No more bickering, if you please."

Heavy shoes slapped against the pavement. Someone was running, coming closer. Kera was startled, and looked for the dark man, but it was another of the younger staffers from *L'Humanite*, carrying a telegram. He gave it to Longuet, explaining that it had come to the newspaper office and he had been following their trail ever since. "And I have news for you as well, monsieur," he said to Jaurès. "Something has happened which was just reported to us."

The two men looked at each other, as if wondering who should go first. "Let me, sir," Longuet said. "In light of the government's recent decisions, I can only assume yours is bad news, and will put a damper on the evening. Mine, we do not know. So let's save the bad for the last."

"Reasonable," Jaurès said. "Please go ahead."

Longuet unfolded the paper with the nonchalance of a man opening a note from a good friend. But in an instant his face went pale. "My God," he said. "I've been drafted!" Jaurès reached over and clasped his shoulder. "I don't understand how this could happen," Longuet went on.

"Terrible news," Bertré said. "Simply terrible. But after all, you are the correct age, and the army is desperately in need of men."

"Jean, leave this to me," Jaurès said, "I will see what I can do. Perhaps we can get this deferred. At the least we can get you assigned to a non-combat unit."

Longuet slumped in his chair, speechless in his disbelief. Kera wanted to console him as well, but thought better of it with Bertré sitting there, still smarting from the punches his enemy had landed earlier. But Longuet had been so kind to her in Brussels. He was intelligent and thoughtful, so much his own man. What if his enormous passion for the cause, and for life, was wasted on some battlefield as though he were a common soldier? She had to say something. "Trust Monsieur Jaurès," she said. "If anyone can help you, he can."

"It seems odd they would send it to the office," Jaurès said. "Shouldn't it have been sent to your home?"

"You're right," Landrieu said. "My cousin received his notice a few days ago, and it was sent to his home."

"It could be they tried," Bertré said, "but didn't find you there. It seems like an obvious thing to do—your name is in the newspaper almost every day."

"But still," Jaurès said. "Are you saying that a clerk took it upon himself to send the notice to *L'Humanite*?"

"Someone is playing games with you, Longuet," Landrieu said.

"Do you think?" Longuet looked hopeful for the first time since opening the telegram.

Jaurès picked up the paper and studied it. "This certainly looks official. I recognize the seal. It says you have three days to report. That means we have that long to figure this out and contest it." He put the slip in his pocket. "Let me take it with me. I have friends at the Chamber who may be able to help."

Kera suspected Bertré was reveling in this turn of events. His comments hadn't contained much sympathy—in fact, he seemed to take the army's side. And now, looking at him, she thought she saw the trace of a smile. The government, supposedly their common opponent in this political fight, had vanquished his foe for him. She asked, "Maurice, you have friends in the government too. Is there anyone you know who can help?"

"No one who's involved in draft matters. It seems the government has outsmarted our friend Longuet." He turned away from the others and winked at her. What did that mean? Could he be so shallow as to not care what happened to Longuet? Yes, they had disagreed back at *L'Humanite*, but a mature man puts such childishness behind him.

Longuet ordered another drink, and when it came, he toasted the group. "To the finest journalists I will ever have the privilege of working with," he said, and then threw back the sherry in a single swallow. "This will be a good night to get drunk."

The messenger stood beside the table, waiting for Jaurès to give him permission to speak. Bertré looked at Jaurès and said, "Well, at least we know *you* won't be drafted, eh?" He laughed, but no one joined him in the joke.

Now Kera was more than upset with him. It was one thing to wish bad luck on a rival, but now he exhibited bad taste. When he tried to put his arm around her shoulder, she shook him off.

Jaurès turned to the young man. "What is your news?"

The messenger stood at attention. "We have just heard… The police arrested a group of people protesting against the war near the Arc de Triomphe. Among them is your associate, Monsieur Sembat…"

"Sembat? How is that possible?" Jaurès slapped the table, gaining the notice of the other diners in the café.

"He and his wife were strolling after dinner and they happened to pass the rally. He stopped to wish them well and thank them for being good citizens, and that is when the police came."

"This is Viviani's doing, you know," Longuet said, still slack in his chair.

"What of Sembat's wife?" Jaurès asked.

"She was released after being questioned."

"I can't believe the premier would do it. After he promised…"

Kera looked to Longuet. He had said the premier would lie to Jaurès. But he barely moved except to finish a third drink and wave weakly for another. This was no time to gloat. She knew he didn't want to be right about this, but his pragmatism had forced him to say it. He would be right about everything—and the reward for his prescience would be induction into the army.

Jaurès started to get up. "I must go. I must bail Sembat out of jail."

The messenger interrupted. "Vaillant is already on his way there, sir. He is the one who told me to find you and give you the news."

"Good man…both of you," Jaurès patted the messenger's shoulder. "Then please go back to *L'Humanite* and wait for them. When Sembat is freed, tell them all to join us here at the café—his wife too. They know the place."

The messenger took off running down the sidewalk as Jaurès sat back down. He leaned forward and let his hands hang between his knees. His shoulders drooped and his stomach sagged, and Kera could see he was not only physically exhausted, but also dejected by these new problems. He looked up and stared into the night sky, but it was not the clear, piercing stare Kera had seen on the train to Brussels. She saw no determination in his eyes this time. He was not conjuring a new idea, but searching, pleading, hoping to stumble onto a strategy that he hadn't yet tried. His posture said surrender, although she knew he would never admit it, and he looked as though he might be wishing for an end to the conflict against the warmongers, whatever the outcome. A momentary lapse—understandable, no doubt—because a few seconds later he righted himself and addressed the table.

"A difficult evening," he said, tapping the rim of his glass. "But our struggle has been filled with difficult times.

We shall get through these crises as well." He looked at Longuet as he continued. "All of us. The premier has gone back on his word and we're almost without options, but we cannot rest. The future of France—indeed of all Europe—depends on our efforts." Everyone touched glasses as Jaurès began to laugh. "And we still have to get to the printer to check the newspaper," he said.

"Let me do that for you, monsieur," Longuet said. "You should go home and be with your wife, even if it's for just a few hours."

Jaurès nodded at him. "And do you not have troubles of your own? It may be this draft notice is legitimate and that you'll be gone in a few days. Do you wish to spend them staring at sheets of newsprint? Don't worry. My wife understands."

Kera knew it. He couldn't be cruel to his wife. Her imagination annoyed her sometimes. Still, if the opportunity arose, she would ask Bertré what he knew about the man's life.

A waiter placed another sherry in front of Longuet and asked to take their orders. As he made his way around the table, Kera noticed a figure standing in the shadows at the street corner. It seemed to be the one who had followed them from Coq d'Or.

Bertré bickered with the waiter about wine. He was dissatisfied with the vintages listed on the hand-written menu, and insisted there had to be something better in the back. "You can't tell me the owner drinks this rot," he said to the server, flicking his finger against the page. "What does he save for himself?"

"Maurice," she said. "Do you see that man there?"

"Please, my dear, I am trying to find us something decent to go with dinner." He turned to make sure the waiter could hear, and said, "I'm sure we'll need it to wash down the food."

The waiter, apparently as obstinate as Bertré, answered.

"I assure you monsieur, these vintages are all of excellent quality, and any of them would be a perfect match to your selection for dinner."

Kera nudged Bertré, but he went on. "Are you serious? It would be better to gargle with some of these wines than to drink them."

"Maurice, must you be so arrogant about everything?" Kera asked. "Sometimes it's like being with a child." The others at the table sat up at her pronouncement. Bertré raised his eyebrows. Longuet, nearly drunk, put his glass down and applauded. "At last someone with the courage to speak the truth to this snob," he said.

She'd surprised herself by saying it. And it wasn't due only to the pressures they were under. He *was* arrogant and demanding, and she had never liked that aspect of him. But she had chosen the wrong time. In private, perhaps, he might have understood her intentions, but in front of the others—especially Jaurès—he would never forgive her.

Bertré stared at Kera, but addressed the waiter. "Very well," he said. "Just bring us whatever wine you please. It hardly matters which one. There are some at this table who wouldn't know the difference if they were served a glass of vinegar." Then he rose and walked a few yards down the sidewalk to light a cigarette.

Kera started to go after him, but Jaurès motioned her to stay. "Best to leave him for a while. He does not like to have his sensibilities questioned. And this evening we're both guilty of that transgression."

Longuet raised yet another glass in a swaying hand. "All three of us," he said. "But in my case it was a pleasure to speak. If only he would learn the lesson." Jaurès chuckled, turning away so Bertré wouldn't be able to see.

As Bertré kept walking, Kera noticed the stranger again in the other direction. He had come even closer than before. "Jean," she said to Longuet. "That man loitering over there. Do you know him?"

"Know him?" He raised his glass to signal the waiter. "I can't even see him at this point."

Jaurès turned to look. "He appears to be a beggar or some other unfortunate. What about him?"

"He's been following us since Coq d'Or."

"Well if he wants money, he'll have to come back another time," Jaurès said. "For once I am too tired to deal with every supplicant."

Landrieu nudged Nueve. "Let's go talk to him," he said. "We'll give him the business, eh?"

"Better to send him to Bertré," Longuet said. "He's got the money to deal with it."

"Ha! A good idea," Nueve said. "Might be worth another laugh. Let's go."

They pushed their chairs back and stood up, flexing themselves like athletes. Kera imagined they had been waiting all night for something like this, some moment when they could prove themselves in front of Jaurès—especially Landrieu—at least Nueve had distinguished himself as a runner. But this would be different. Like young men in every occupation, they'd sat with the group, listening to the conversation, too afraid to speak and be exposed for the idiots they knew they were in their superior's eyes. Their virility would finally prove valuable. They began to go towards the stranger, but Kera had a glint of recognition and stopped them. "No. Don't."

"It's all right," Landrieu said. "Your boyfriend can handle it."

"It's not that. I think I may have seen this man before."

"This bum?" Landrieu said. "You know him? He looks like bad news."

Longuet piped up again. "Ah, what other strange secrets is our Kera hiding?"

As he crept closer the details of the stranger had begun to register in Kera's memory. The hard face and Medusa hair. The leering posture that seemed so menacing. When

Landrieu said "bad news" it clicked. This was the man she had seen with Jack in Le Secret—the one he left with. What was he doing here, following them? It didn't matter. He might know where Jack was and why he had never come back to the theater or the hotel. "Come with me," she said to the two young men. "I have to talk with him. He may know about a friend of mine whom I haven't seen for several days. I'm very concerned about him."

The three went towards the ragged man, who leaned against the bricks of an apartment building. "You there!" Landrieu called. "The lady wishes to speak with you." But when he saw them coming he turned and ran.

"Wait, monsieur! I need to know about Jack. I saw you with him." The men gave chase, but the stranger galloped into an alley and was gone by the time they turned the corner. They came back to Kera, arms wide in apology. "It's all right," she said. "You didn't know he would run away."

They trudged back to the table just as Bertré had returned. He ignored everyone and sat looking out into the street, his glass of sherry on the table between his fingers, his manicured nails reflecting the moonlight. Kera thought they shone more than the pearls she wore—and on which he hadn't commented. She could apologize now, but why do it in front of everyone and degrade herself? He'd had it coming. If she hadn't said it, Longuet or one of the others—maybe even Jaurès—would have said something. She wasn't sorry. He could be most pretentious at times. When they were back at the apartment she would reconsider.

The waiter offered the wine to Bertré for inspection, but he only waved his hand for the man to open it. Instead of tasting, he directed the waiter to pour. This time no one made a toast, and they sat in the warm evening without speaking. So much had occurred in the last forty-eight hours, and in the last thirty minutes, that it seemed to Kera senseless to discuss anything. Longuet was nearly asleep. Jaurès squirmed in his seat as though ready to leave, but since he had given instructions for the Sembats and Vaillant to join them, he had to stay. The young men, Landrieu and Nueve, were still afraid to initiate conversation and sat like schoolboys, waiting to be spoken to.

When dinner came they all—except for the lethargic Longuet—ate quietly. Bertré made a show of chewing everything with a pained expression, as if to reinforce his prediction about the food. When he took a sip of wine he sloshed it around his palate and puckered his lips as if its taste offended him, and made little sucking noises as though preparing to spit it out. Kera wanted to throw hers in his face—he simply wouldn't stop. He couldn't relax his conceit no matter what the situation. She wanted to scream at him to stop acting like a pompous fool and accept that he wasn't going to receive his usual cuisine and service in a sidewalk café. One more noise and she *was* going to do it, even if it meant offending him again.

As if he could know what she thought, Jaurès opened a new line of discussion. "My dear Kera," he said, "what adventures did you have this afternoon when we left you to continue our business? I hope you didn't sit up in your apartment in this heat."

"Thank you, monsieur. In fact I did go out for a while." Bertré appeared to perk up at this news. "There is so much of this city I don't know, so I took a walk. I found myself along the river, and sat for a while under the trees."

"Good, good," Jaurès said. "No need for you to be cooped up. Now tell me, has Maurice delivered on his promise? Has he purchased you the two gifts we negotiated on the train back from Brussels?"

Kera blushed. "Oh, sir. You know he hasn't had time. You put him right to work on our return." She looked at Bertré, who did his best to ignore the proceedings. This might be an opportunity to assuage his damaged ego without offering an apology. "You know how important he is to your efforts." As she said it she wondered if Jaurès had known that simply starting a conversation would lead to the beginning of reconciliation.

"Yes," Jaurès said. "No one works harder for us." He looked over to Longuet, perhaps afraid his statement would rile him, but the future soldier snored softly in his chair behind his untouched meal. Kera looked too. How young he was, and what potential he emanated, even in sleep. Although unconscious he had his jaw set as if about to speak—no doubt to question the latest plan or the government's motives. He turned sideways in his chair, pulled up a leg like a child, and a forelock fell across his eye. He brushed it away without waking. Jaurès continued to observe him, a patriarch watching his scion, and she knew—this was the man Jaurès had in mind to lead the party in the future, not Bertré. His intellectual vigor grated at times, but it was the sign of a mind that wouldn't accept conditions at face value. Perhaps he wasn't ready yet, but soon, with Jaurès's guidance, he would be. And when that time came, Bertré would either leave the inner circle or be cast aside. Jaurès must have known this too, but he couldn't allow friendships to interfere in matters of the party. He had to keep the balance between the two men, as well as solve this crisis of war. Kera sighed. How could the government do this to Longuet? She looked at Landrieu and Nueve—would they be next? Would draft notices await them back at the newspaper office? And what of Jaurès—after learning of the latest events tonight, he had looked, for the first time since she had met him, ready to accept defeat. How much farther was he willing to stretch himself for this cause?

"Tell me," she said. "Did you go back to the Chamber of Deputies after you finished the newspaper's editorial?"

"Actually, no. We had business with another of our supporters, a Monsieur Renoult."

"Renoult? Do you mean the cabaret owner? I know him as well."

"Yes, that's the one," Jaurès said. "But how does someone

so cultured and refined make the acquaintance of a man who runs a basement nightclub?"

"I should ask you the same question!" Ah, she might begin to enjoy herself again. If Bertré wouldn't talk, she could still have an engaging conversation with Jaurès, and do it right in front of her lover while he pouted.

Jaurès laughed. "Very good. You have turned the tables on me. In fact, though, Renoult is a friend and adviser. He knows many people in this city. And he's always willing to help. Despite the appearance of his business he has the interests of France at heart. He is a patriot."

"I see," Kera said. She lifted her glass to her lips, reticent to offer the story of her own encounter with Renoult. She didn't want to talk about Gus in front of Bertré.

Jaurès wouldn't let her get away with it. "Come. How is it *you* came to know him?"

She couldn't be rude to Jaurès. "A friend of mine took me there—I had no idea what to expect. Believe me, I was quite surprised." Kera felt again the warmth of the evening, and she dabbed at her moist neck with her napkin. "It's a very… I'm not sure how to describe it."

"A very tolerant place, would you say?" Jaurès said.

"Yes, that's it. And Renoult tolerates many types of activity." She stifled a giggle remembering it.

Bertré dropped his knife and fork onto his plate, letting them clank loudly against the porcelain. He lifted his glass and spoke while still chewing—something Kera had never seen him do—without looking at either of them. "You might be surprised as well to know who else Monsieur Jaurès and I ran into at Le Secret today." Kera turned to face his profile. "Your little friend from the theater."

"You mean Gus?"

"I don't recall his name. I believe he is now working there as some kind of janitor."

"Maurice, I think you exaggerate. Was he not also performing for the crowd?" Jaurès said.

211

"How did he look? Was he all right?"

Bertré puffed his chest out. "He was as well as can be expected for a man who was sweeping floors and washing glasses. The work seemed to suit him, if you ask me."

"That's very hard to believe. It doesn't sound at all like him."

"Perhaps when the theater closed he didn't have the good fortune to seduce a benefactor, and was afflicted with hard times."

Kera burned at the insult, but she had to ignore it to find out more. "Did you talk to him?"

"Indeed. I had no choice. Your friend is quite the violent little fellow. He nearly assaulted me."

Jaurès cut in again. "Your friend's zeal was in your cause, my dear. He suspected Maurice knew where you could be found, and simply let his emotions get out of control."

"You mean he was asking about me?"

"And he should be finding you soon. He was given the address of Maurice's apartment."

"Over my objection, I might add," Bertré said. "I think you can only come to grief by associating with this character. My advice would be to have the portier send him away when he arrives."

"Maurice, the country prepares to bleed and yet you find the time to carry on like a jealous suitor," Jaurès said. "I was afraid you would start a fistfight with that banjo player. I see you're still resentful of him."

"Of that one? Hardly. I am only concerned about the lady's safety."

"As you say. In that case why not escort our dear Kera home after dinner? I'll have Landrieu and Nueve revive Longuet and get him safely home as well. After Vaillant and the Sembats arrive I'll go to the printer's and look over the proofs."

"Are you sure? I've always gone with you."

"For once I will do the job myself. I can take Vaillant with me if I need another pair of eyes."

"But, I'm sure Kera doesn't mind coming along," Bertré said.

"She is tired. We're all tired. Please do this for her...and for me. With all that's happening I need some time alone to think of how we will respond."

Bertré stared at Jaurès. Kera knew he'd been at the leader's side for years, and that his money had kept the newspaper in business through the lean times. But Jaurès was finally telling him that the money, not his insights, had kept him privy to the group's decisions, and that this time, with the stakes so great, he would make the decisions without his counsel, perhaps waiting for Longuet to sober, or for Vaillant to arrive to talk them over. She could see in her lover's face that he understood, and that it couldn't have been delivered at a moment that would hurt him more. He would need her tonight to get over the sting of Jaurès's rebuke, and despite their argument she would be there for him.

Why then was she thinking of Gus? As soon as Bertré mentioned him she felt that old pang of desire—which had never been returned, but which had never been completely abandoned. Now she knew where he was, and that he had been through something terrible if he was working as Bertré described. How much he must have changed. She would stay with Maurice tonight. She would do what she could—what she had to—to get him through the pit of his depression. She owed him that much. But in the morning she would make some excuse to go out, and she would find Gus.

Bertré rose and went out to the curb to look for a taxi. He made no effort to pay for the dinner, as he did on almost every other occasion. He would let Jaurès take care of it for once. He signaled to her. "Let's go." She gathered her purse and stepped quickly to be with him. The Sembats and Vaillant were coming up the walk, but Bertré ignored them to wave at an approaching cab. She looked back at Jaurès and the three young men, and saw them stand and greet the new arrivals.

[handwritten annotation: yet another simile!]

Chapter 12
Friday morning, July 31 – Gus

GUS TWISTED himself like a contortionist, propping his foot over the edge of the sink in the washroom, clinging with one hand to the porcelain, itself clinging lopsidedly to the old brickwork, and with the other hand he scrubbed, chasing a cake of soap between his toes like a fish that had jumped out of its tank. Since Gus had camped at Le Secret he'd had to bathe standing up, maneuvering his head and limbs under the spigot, trying to fit everything in the closet-sized lav. There was no hot water, but he no longer minded the cold. It had been a shock after the luxury of the Fromentin's piping baths, but since the heat wave had yet to subside, he'd grown to appreciate the cool splash, especially in the middle of the day. The washroom had no mirror, so he did everything, including shaving, by feel—the hygienics of a blind man—and occasionally Gus would have to go back in for a few more strokes after checking the results in the glass behind the bottles in the bar. Today he'd risen early and gone up to the alley for a few deep, smoke-free breaths, expecting to be assaulted by a ferocious morning sun, another day in the week-long Parisian steamer that started with first light and hung on until after midnight. He couldn't remember the last time the back of his neck felt dry. But as he climbed he felt the air still relatively cool, and when he reached the entrance to the building he saw a saturnine sky of purple and gray—the sun, preparing for another day of soul-charring heat, hadn't quite burned away the nighttime clouds. Gus inhaled, drawing air tinged with grease and rotting produce to replace the nicotine vapors that filled his lungs downstairs. Although the pall of cigarette smoke had become bearable, there were nights, like last night, when the mob turned Le Secret into a gas chamber. By closing time he had been red-eyed and hoarse from the sting of the fumes.

The alley's foul aroma was, at least, a change, and to Gus it was almost a pleasure. He took it in by the gallon, like a tenor preparing to sing. He stood erect, stretched his arms over his head and considered the night's accomplishments as the sun broke through the cover to cast a spotlight on his face, and he visualized taking the bow he never took on stage.

Aimée had long gone. She'd stayed with him for an hour, perhaps two. Their sensual probing had swelled to a shared, raging lust, and when they were spent they lay on the rocky floor, her body across his, touching fingers, lips and loins, as many places as possible, a delirium of convergence. His back and shoulders ached from the cement, but the lushness of her skin pressing against him more than offset the discomfort. He lost himself in the sumptuousness of it, and even found sleep after a time, only to be jolted awake by her bouncing off him and crying, "Mon bébé!" She threw her blouse and skirt back on and ran out, thumping the walls in the darkness, slapping her bare soles against the wooden steps as she ascended. At first Gus started to get up—she shouldn't have to go out in the middle of the night alone like that. But she was so far ahead—and she must know the way. She went home by herself like that every night and knew how to keep safe. He let her go and lay back down to relish the experience.

Curtain Calls

He thought of her again as he stropped his razor against the leather Renoult had loaned. When she'd leaned over him, the cascade of her hair covered his face like a waterfall, screening the light from the candle. In that dim haze she looked perfect, and he felt perfect as well. What flaws he'd perceived in her before were lost behind the partition she draped between them and the criticizing world.

She would come in soon, and Gus became anxious about seeing her. What would he say? He couldn't say anything; they couldn't even talk to each other. Last night had been a chorus of sounds—whispers and panting, little gasps of surprise—the thrum of synchronous love that needed no explanation, no exchange of words. Afterwards, she cooed and sang in French, and he hummed his contentment in time with her until he drifted to sleep. But what would happen when she came in today? Was he supposed to ask Albert to be their translator? What if she had changed her mind—was only interested in the one night? He felt carefully along the edge of his sideburn until the blade nestled against it, then pulled gently downward—the cold steel and cold water, with only a thin layer of soap to protect his face, were the bracing reminder he needed to deal with this possibility. What if he hadn't been good enough? He knew from the others how experienced she was. Had she expected more of him? He would have to act aloof. If she still wanted him, let her come to him again. Or should he take the risk? He felt the razor scrape his skin as though chastising him for being too careless with his feelings.

It would be best if Albert showed up first today. He could cover for him when he left to look for Kera—tell Aimée that he had gone on an errand for Renoult. After last night the urge to see her again had calmed, but it might still be good to find her. She would want to see him. He would only be gone for an hour or two, and when he returned, then he would be ready to face Aimée.

Gus pulled on his trousers and went out to the bar to

examine his reflection through bottles of gin and whiskey. When he finished he reached for a fifth of Scotch. He'd need a little fortitude to find some words to say to Kera, especially if that Frenchman were there when he went to call. Aside from recounting his time at Le Secret there wouldn't be much else he'd want to say—the trip to Le Havre…no, too much the embarrassment, and he surely couldn't tell her about Aimée. Perhaps she would still want to go with him back to the states. It would be satisfying to watch her leave Bertré behind.

But she might not want to see him—he hadn't considered that. Of course she wouldn't go with him. She'd made her choice when she checked out of the hotel. She would stay here, in Paris, and he would sail back to New York without her, without Jack, and that would be the end of it. At least he could boast to Max Zapf about last night. He'd probably love to hear the story. Then he would forget about all of them and go back to the music. He would purge Aimée from the record of his life and assign the sweet memory to his private thoughts, to be visited only in the most solitary times. He took a swig from the bottle and wiped his mouth on the bar towel.

He'd be just in time for the autumn season at the east coast theaters. The best plan would be to get back on the circuit right away so he didn't have to dwell on what had happened here. Max could set him up as a solo act—truly a lonesome cowboy this time. Gus surveyed the empty tables and chairs, and raised the bottle to toast the cabaret. In a week he would be back on schedule, as though this detour had never occurred.

He had a few hours before anyone else came in for work. Since Renoult had sent everyone home, Albert hadn't done a very good job of closing the bar. There were streaks on the counter and glasses had been left out, with the remains of the liquors they'd held glued to the insides. Gus took up the towel again and rubbed out the marks. He washed the glasses and placed them on shelves under the bar. He straightened chairs and cleared ashes from tabletops, put everything back into opening time order. In an hour he was finished and back at the bar, staring at the dance floor again. There must be more he could do.

There was the room where Renoult kept the extra cases of liquor. The owner had talked a few times about cleaning it out, but never made it a priority. The spaces behind the stacks were so well hidden anything might be growing there. He took a mop and pail from the closet and went to it. He wouldn't even tell Renoult. Let him find out for himself and wonder how it had been done. If the owner asked Albert or Aimée, each would deny it, and it would be a hoot to pretend he knew nothing of it either. Let him think one of the drunken customers had slept off his stupor, then felt guilty enough the next morning to repay his host with a jag of cleaning.

Gus reorganized everything in the room. He got on his knees and scoured the floor, cleaned the dust and dirt from the cases and scraped off the mold. He even washed the musty bricks behind the boxes. By the time he was done he had worked up a sweat and needed to bathe again, but it had been worth it. Everything was purged and cleaned, and he looked at the room, proud of how he had reformed it. Renoult would be pleased as well. He headed back to the lav for another rinsing, but as he got to the door he heard steps in the hallway above. The footfalls were light, like a woman's. She paused at the top of the stairs and then started down, tentatively. If it was Aimée, why would she be so slow? He went out and set himself against the bar, and watched a pair of white buttoned boots lead a lacy, lemon-colored hem as it sashayed down the steps. This finery couldn't be Aimée. Gus saw the tip of a matching parasol swing into view as its owner descended.

When Kera alighted from the last step, she stopped in a model's pose, setting the point of her umbrella on the floor and resting her palms on the handle. She raised her chin, and the brim of her enormous white hat framed her face in its halo. In all that yellow she seemed to Gus like the sun having broken through the clouds. The simple blouse and skirt he remembered had been replaced by clothing he'd only seen advertised in magazines and the windows of expensive dress shops, and the woman he'd sat next to in the dressing room of the theater was now from a world that flaunted that kind of extravagance. The Frenchman had done this for her—no, he had done this *to* her—changed her seriousness, her compassion into something frivolous, a plaything to satisfy his whims. In less than a week he'd turned her from the woman Gus had known into a stranger. But she had to have gone along with the transformation willingly to alter so fast. She was the Parisienne Nightingale now, around the clock, and Gus could barely bring himself to call her Kera.

She spoke first. "Oh Gus. I hoped I'd find you here. When Maurice said he'd seen you in Le Secret I could hardly believe it. I was so happy he found you."

"I've been looking for you, too. When your Frenchman came in I…"

"I know," she said. "He told me what happened." Kera put out her hand and he took it in a handshake. "It's so good to see you."

He hoped she didn't think he would kiss it. That kind of thing was for her boyfriend. Could he have changed her that much in so short a time? "You certainly got all dressed up to come see me," he said. "Or is there someplace else you have to go?"

"No," she said. "I only came to see you. I hope you don't mind my getting here so early. I just couldn't wait for you to come find me. I had to see if you were all right."

"This place isn't much, but the people are friendly. We help each other get by." He went behind the bar and took out the Scotch again. He pulled a shot glass from underneath and slapped it on the counter. "And I see you've been doing okay for yourself, too."

"Maurice was…is very generous. He took me to Brussels! We went with Monsieur Jaurès to hear his speech. Oh, it was quite a time."

"That's great. Just great." He held up the bottle to offer her a drink, but she shook her head, no.

"Gus, I've seen so many things in the last few days. Things I never dreamed I would have seen. And oh, that Monsieur Jaurès! He is simply brilliant."

"You know," Gus said, "we're supposed to get on the ship in a couple of days. I have the money for the train fare."

"What of Jack? Have you found him? I'm very worried about what might have happened."

Gus put his drink on the counter and stared at Kera—at this woman who used to be Kera. "I haven't seen him. Not since he left here that night."

"We should notify the police. I can have Maurice contact them…"

"Do you want to go home, or don't you?"

"What do you mean?"

"The ship back to New York. We're supposed to meet it in a few days."

"The ship…I'd almost forgotten. With everything that's been happening… You can understand."

Maybe he shouldn't have mentioned the money. If she needed a ride to Le Havre her Frenchman would provide it—in a private train car no doubt. It sounded like he'd been showing her the town—the continent—every night since they'd gotten together. Why would she want to leave that? Bertré's money could take her away from the city when the war came as well.

She took a breath and reached into her sleeve for a handkerchief, raised it to her neck to dab at the first perspiration of the day, but stopped. Instead she waved the lace in front of her face, and slid it along her wrist until it was tucked away again. Gus perused the abrupt curves of her outfit—she must be wearing a corset again. These same angles, in the guise of the Nightingale, had once aroused him. Now they were a charade.

Kera hesitated. "I want to go with you Gus. I know I belong back in the states. I just need you to tell me…"

Gus looked deeper into her face and saw a dark shadow on her cheek, under her eye, diffused by her makeup. She didn't know what she wanted. She'd wanted him, it had been obvious. But when he'd softened and thought he might give them a chance together, she reversed and set off with Bertré, as though she'd never given him a second thought, and the dandy had encouraged her to become silly and vain. As the Nightingale it was no surprise she might act that way. But Gus knew who she really was, and that the looks and the attitude were just a façade. Now she wore that mask all the time, and hid away the person he could have appreciated. He and Kera had never been synchronized, and it was just as well, the way things worked out. He looked at her in the expensive clothes, draped with rings and a necklace, dressed to please her rich boyfriend's whims, and stopped caring whether she went back to New York. "I don't know what you should do about that," he said.

He saw her gaze lower to his ragged pants and bare feet. In her high-heeled boots she was a few inches taller than him, and Gus felt awkward over the difference.

Someone else was coming down the stairs. Gus recognized the slap of Aimée's flat shoes against the boards. She moved fast, and when she reached the bottom she ran towards him for a few feet, then stopped, seeing him not alone. She looked different. She'd fixed her hair with pins and a bow, and wore a fresh white blouse and dark skirt. She looked prettier to him than yesterday. She spoke—it sounded like surprise. Kera understood, and responded in French, and the two women continued to talk, without emotion as far he could tell, exchanging information as though they were acquaintances at a party. He expected Aimée would be angry, or jealous—that Kera would be fearful of the tiny woman. But they merely talked. He listened for any clue to the topic—a name or an English-sounding word. Finally he sensed a change in Aimée's tone. She gestured towards him with an open palm. Kera crossed her arms over her bosom. Aimée had to be describing their night together. "Kera," he said, but before he could continue, Aimée raised her voice and began speaking in an unbroken stream of squeaks and exclamations. Gus knew she was swearing too. Kera, for once, didn't allow herself to be berated and shot back. He should step in between them. Aimée was the kind of woman who might make her point physically. They began talking simultaneously, each trying to speak over the other. "Stop," he said, but they ignored him. "Stop," again. They were consumed by their argument. Gus reached out and took Aimée by the forearm and pulled her into him. He kissed her—a long, full kiss between lovers, and she threw her arms around his neck to embrace him. He held her like that for half a minute, turning them just enough so he could see Kera out of the corner of his eye. When they parted he stared at Kera. Aimée hung an arm off his shoulder and he slipped his hand around her waist. "Does that answer your questions?" he said.

Kera started walking towards the stairwell, and Gus had already begun to regret the display. What else could he have done?

She stopped before the first step and looked at him. "Maurice was right," she said.

"What do you mean?"

"Never mind."

"Tell me."

Kera took a breath. "He kept asking me what I felt for you. He's so kind and giving. Ever since I met him he's taken care of everything for me, and he's shown me a world I never would have had a chance to know. He gave me every opportunity to be a part of that world, yet he knew that I was still thinking of you."

"So what did he say?"

"I don't remember."

"I want to hear it."

"All right. He said you were an urchin, a little schoolboy, all dirty and stupid, and that I was the foolish girl who always believed she could rescue him, make him change and grow up."

Gus tensed and Aimée gripped his shoulder tighter.

"He said that what I felt for you was pity, Gus. I said, no. I thought it was love."

Gus opened his mouth, but couldn't speak. Kera waited. Finally, he said, "And was it?"

"He was right, Gus. It was pity, all along."

"I'm sorry. I didn't want your pity, you know. I didn't really want anything." Why was he apologizing? The misperception had been hers. He thought to take it back but instead stared at her, knowing she considered his situation stupid and pathetic, inferior, which only proved how much she had changed. If he could conjure a song to play in his head he would leave the discomfort of this conversation. But his mind turned up nothing and Kera spoke again.

"I only came here today to tell you that Maurice has asked me to stay in Paris," she said.

"I thought you were afraid about the war."

"Maurice says I'll be safe with him," she said. "And I believe him."

Kera looked at Aimée, but spoke in English. "Do you know what it is like, my dear, to look out from the balcony of a beautiful apartment and see all of Paris in a single glance? To have a wonderful man bring you gifts every day? A wonderful man who knows how to make love to a woman? Who is an expert in the field?"

Aimée turned to Gus and said, "Que est elle disant?"

"Of course you don't," Kera said.

Kera spoke again to Aimée, this time in French, and when she was done she smiled. Whatever she'd said incensed Aimée, who responded with epithets that Gus assumed might even embarrass some of the men who frequented Le Secret.

"Just as I thought," Kera said. She went up the stairs. Aimée started after her, but Gus held her back. Aimée kicked the air where Kera had been. She hollered a few more phrases up the stairwell.

He put a finger to his lips, and when she came next to him, transferred it to hers. She kissed it, slipped her lips over it and began nibbling, tiny bites until he pulled it away and replaced it with his mouth, and they welded themselves together, as much in passion as against the city that existed up the stairs from the bar. When they parted she pulled a glass from under the counter and joined him in his libation with a sherry. "Salut," she said, holding it aloft. He answered with, "Cheers."

"I guess we're going to have to figure out how this works," he said. She cocked her head to look at him. "I know. Neither one of us knows a word…"

He held his glass out. "Glass."

She held hers up. "Xérès."

"Yes," he said. "Zher…Zheray."

"Oui, oui." She poured herself another drink and held up the bottle. "Xérès."

"No. Bottle."

Aimée looked confused and asked him a question he didn't understand. With the bottle in one hand and the glass in the other, she nodded at each with certainty. "Xérès…y xérès."

"But they're not the same." He looked around for a different object, but Aimée was already bored with the game. Now the music started—a song from the act—and he could hear the banjo and Jack's guitar as though they were in the room. But he didn't want to be taken away from reality, not this time. "Wait," he said, and ran back into his room. He brought the banjo out and took a chair. The latches on the case popped like corks and he pulled the instrument out for display, sitting it on his lap and strumming a few simple chords. "Banjo," he said.

"Oui, banjo."

Gus smiled. "Oui. Banjo," he repeated. "Now you try." He got up and steered her into the seat. She took the instrument from him, surprised at its weight, and he maneuvered behind her to place her hands on the strings. He couldn't think of anyone else whom he'd allowed to hold it. Her hands were too small to fit over the strings in the proper position, but it didn't matter. He transferred the pick from his hand to hers, and guided her wrist to where it should begin. Together they pulled through a flat-sounding twang, but it was good enough to make her stop and applaud. She got up with eyes that told him to take over, and he sat down with the instrument. "Tu jeu la musique," she said, and he knew what it meant. He would play her something happy—to celebrate their new-found affection, and he chose the melody from Silver Bell—it had been part of the act a few years ago. It was always one of Jack's favorites. Gus started tentatively, and Aimée began to dance—twirling in pixie steps to the rhythm. When he saw this he slowed the tempo. She eased her timing into his, described the slow circles of a dream with her body, and closed her eyes while she moved around the dance floor. Gus hung on every movement of her simple ballet. He knew she could not see him, and he let tears fill to the rims of his eyes—a sadness had been welling in him, despite the happy song, and now it had pushed its way to the surface, ready to release.

At the end of the song she stopped in front of him and leaned in, ran her finger along the planes of his eyes, and wiped away the moisture that poised to spill over. She began to sing in French—a simple tune like a nursery rhyme—in a young mother's expression. He looked down, knew he could interpret the song, and began to accompany her in as soft a tone as the banjo would allow, notes as quiet as her voice. Her music seemed to be telling a story, and he sensed it was about someone like him. As she sang she touched him during certain words—on the arm, on the top of the head. She lowered her voice in a faux baritone and he knew the character was in trouble. But this was momentary, and soon she resolved the song into a happier sound that she maintained until the final measure. When she finished, she bowed, and this time he applauded. He began to play again—another lively tune—but Aimée put her hands on his and stopped him. "Renoult," she said, and then something else, and then, "et Albert," and he knew she was telling him the others would be here soon.

Gus put the banjo into its case and took it to the back. When he stashed it into its dark corner he paused, registering the must and gloom. He imagined himself lying on the floor of this cell, his head propped against a hill of old blankets, staring at the ceiling as though frozen in time. The look on his face melded the future and present into a single gray eternity. He ran back out to the cabaret. Aimée was sweeping the floor at the far corner of the club, facing the stairs, and he watched her body move back and forth in sync with the broom. How simple it would be to go to her, take her in his arms again and tell her that he loved her. She would understand it, even in English.

Gus crept towards her like a burglar, hopeful the surprise would work to his advantage. She still hadn't turned around. He reached out his hand. But as he placed his fingers on her shoulder, a loud burst reverberated down the stairs. Aimée dropped the broom.

Another report, and they both looked up the passageway. Could those have been gunshots? Gus motioned for Aimée to remain behind and he started up towards the ground floor. But he could hear her following him. He turned and again waved at her to stay, but she kept climbing the stairs.

Gus halted at the doorway to the building and listened. Aimée pressed into him, and the warmth of her calmed him. He stepped into the alley, she right behind, and they scanned the area without finding the source of the shots. They walked out to the street. Gus expected to see a crowd of people, or at least a policeman or two investigating the noise, but there was nothing—only what seemed to be a typical morning parade of people on their way to work or meals or whatever it was that those who weren't trapped by circumstances were able to do with their lives. "It must have been something else, a taxi backfiring, maybe," he said. Aimée answered in French and Gus smiled, as if he could understand her. He looked down the street for a glimpse of yellow, to see Kera walking away, but that was foolish. Of course she would have had a taxi waiting to take her. She was gone, enveloped by the city, captured by its ways. It must have been what she'd wanted all along. Jack was somewhere in that maze of buildings too, having surrendered to his own wants. It was clear he didn't want to go back to the way things used to be either.

Gus noticed how much the temperature had risen in just a couple of hours. The early breath of cooler air had been a mirage, a trick to convince the unsuspecting that the days of hellish weather were over, and he ran the back of his hand across his moistened brow.

Chapter 13
Friday afternoon – Gus

WHAT HAD he seen in the back room? The dark had played tricks on him, but it scared him anyway, to see himself like a ghost, as though he had died there and no one cared to look for him.

It haunted him while he and Aimée investigated the noises outside. But the vision receded when they came back down and she let the white blouse slide again from her shoulder. She undid her top buttons, and slipped off the other shoulder, her skin like pearl in the dim cabaret light. Gus took her shoulders in his hands and kissed her; led her to a table and sat her on the edge, slowly working his mouth down her neck and onto the remaining buttons, plucking them loose like berries from a shrub. They made love—what else could they do without the bond of language? But this was a noisier, hungrier love, replacing the shyness, the tenderness of last night, an act of need that cemented them as a couple on a different level as they rocked the wobbly table. Even in this Gus heard music— the rhythm of an uneven leg tapping against the floor—and it helped him drive the haunting image from his mind. What if someone came down the stairs and caught them in the middle of it? Let them. He wouldn't stop until his spirit was purged.

When they had dressed and slumped into chairs, Aimée stretched her leg over and rested it on his, and Gus had an impulse to push it away. He wanted to get out of the cabaret for a while and think everything over, but with Aimée here, hanging on him, he could not leave without explaining, and he had no way to explain it without a translator. He could walk up the stairs, but what if she tried to go with him? If he walked to the telegraph office would she go there as well? If he went further, say to the Seine for a few moments of contemplation, would she do that too? Why not all the way back to the states?

Why not? If he left for New York in a few days as planned, would she feel so attached already that she would want to come with him? Would he be disappointed if she didn't? He paced the floor in front of the bar and she stared at him. What if she did want to go? Kera had made it clear she didn't need her ticket. If he found a way to apologize to her she might let Aimée have it. He looked at her, still draped over the chair, completely and unashamedly relaxed, and considered options. She stared back and smiled, said something that sounded sweet, a compliment for his performance, perhaps.

There was another ticket too—it had to be in with Jack's belongings, which Gus was sure were still somewhere in the Fromentin's keeping. Gus could make up a story and wheedle the passage from the hotel staff… But he'd probably have to apologize for his behavior there, too.

But he was thinking too far ahead; too fast. What made him think that after one day a woman with whom he couldn't converse would want to sail across the Atlantic, to start a new life where she could communicate with virtually no one? He shook his head. She must think him strange. He hoisted himself onto the bar. But he couldn't nudge the possibility out of his head. If there were more time—a month or two—they might get to know enough about each other so the idea wouldn't be as ridiculous. But it *was* ridiculous—both the thought of Aimée accompanying him and the wish for more time. His ticket was stamped for August 2, and Gus knew from his previous encounters with shipping clerks about the impossibility of making a change under wartime circumstances. He was going away.

Albert bounded down the stairs and went over to the bar to begin his preparations for the day. Even during the morning hours there would be someone who wanted, who needed a drink, and Renoult's philosophy said that no one in such a state should be denied. It made for a long day, but the staff had time for personal business before the main throb of customers. What intrigued Gus most about his coworker was how energetic and buoyant he always seemed to be, even after working until past midnight the evening before. But then, Albert didn't have to sleep on a concrete floor.

The big man patted Gus on the shoulder as he went past. When he got to the counter he noticed the Scotch, still uncorked, and the wet glass beside it. "I needed it," Gus said. "There was a bit of a scene here this morning."

Albert raised his eyebrows to pose the question.

"That woman I was telling you about," Gus said. "She came here to see me. It wasn't...not what I thought it would be."

"I see," Albert said. "Too bad. I could tell you were interested in her."

"No. Not really."

Aimée joined them. She moved right into Gus and hooked her hand over his shoulder, as though they had been together for years, and said something in French to Albert. Gus let her keep it there, and reached around to place his hand on the small of her back. He glanced down to make sure she had buttoned her blouse all the way up.

"I understand now, I think," Albert said. "I will ask no

questions of you...but you have my compliments. A French woman is always the better choice."

"I do need a favor, though," Gus said. "Would you explain to Aimée there is something I need to take care of, and that I have to leave for an hour or so? Tell her it's an errand for Renoult."

"As you wish."

Albert spoke to Aimée, and Gus backed away, holding his thumb and forefinger out for her to see that the interval would be brief. He went back to his room, slipped on a shirt and shoes, and pulled the banjo from its case. He might think more clearly if he had it with him. As he headed up the stairs he heard Aimée ask something, and was sure it included the word "banjo," but he kept on without looking back. Albert would think of some way to explain it.

The temperature had reached the nineties again, and it took only a few steps before he could feel sweat building under the instrument on his back. The telegraph office was a few blocks away down the main street. He might stop by there. Although he had enough money to get to Le Havre now, he was curious to know if Max had ever responded to his message, even to say he couldn't help. It would be nice to know at least one American cared about him.

But first he detoured onto a side street—if it didn't bring him back around he could always retrace his steps. A longer walk would yield more time to think. The Rue des Deux Frères was less than a street than a cobblestone walkway hemmed tight by apartments, most of which had their red or blue shutters thrown open in a futile attempt to gain relief from the heat. He noticed a small café, and a tree nearby with a table just barely in the shade. Gus took the banjo out. He strummed a few chords from Silver Bell until a black apron and a pair of thin, wrinkled hands holding a notepad and pencil caught his attention. The waitress had white hair and too much lipstick and rouge. She smiled, revealing two rows of nicotine-stained teeth. "Café?" she asked.

Despite her appearance, she gave the impression she had been beautiful when she was younger. "Yes…oui," he said, and patted the coins in his pocket to make sure he'd brought enough. The woman asked him another question. Gus heard "mange"—what his mother used to say to him to get him to finish his food. He looked around and saw a man at another table with a pastry. He pointed. "That."

"Croissant. Bon."

He played a few chords from a song about New York. Home. But he wasn't really going home. After twelve years on the road with Jack and the wandering time before, he didn't have the right to call anyplace home. That was somewhere a person stayed for more than a week or two, and he hadn't done that often enough. He'd been more correct the first time, at the bar—he was simply going away. He was always going away, making exits, leaving stages and venues. It was a far less demanding thing to do than going home, where one had to be accountable, be part of something with rules and expectations and attachments. Going away took only a wave or a tip of the hat—pick up the paycheck on the way out and head for the station—maybe we'll see each other again in a year or so. For a time, going away had fulfilled his need for escape—each trip to another city took him farther from himself, farther from the man who had lived in stairwells, from the man he refused to try to understand. But even that was a trap. Going away usually meant a new kind of boredom—holed up in a crummy hotel room, sometimes with Jack, until it was time for the next show, dealing with the stage crew, learning the idiosyncrasies of audiences in different parts of the country. Going away meant each week trying to remember where he was and where he was going, feeling the eyes of the crowd when he was on stage and Jack's stares when they were alone, and wishing he could go even farther away.

The waitress came out with the coffee and croissant just as Gus finished his tune. She placed them on the table and stood back to applaud. The man at the other table turned and added his appreciation too. Gus nodded at them. The customer asked him a question and Gus shrugged. "Sorry. No French," he said. The man looked confused, and Gus tried again. "No Francais." This brought a chuckle and a smile.

He'd probably asked him where he'd learned to play, or if he was a performer. People didn't ask him that often in the states. It would be wonderful to be able to answer him, to talk about the instrument, perhaps suggest the man come to a show and bring his wife—tell him he could get them in free if they met at the side entrance. He would invite the waitress and her husband as well. After, they could all meet back here at the café for coffee—and Aimée would join them to converse until the morning hours.

It was a silly dream. Learning the language would take months, maybe years. In the meantime every conversation would turn out like this one—a comedy of gestures. Gus saw himself as one of the clowns in the theater, miming his way through a scene, bringing out a sack to bop the other person over the head if he didn't understand. But he had learned to play the banjo—music was a language and he had mastered it. Couldn't he eventually do the same with French?

Aimée could help him. Their first attempt at communication hadn't been successful, but he looked forward to the next. Surely Albert would help. He picked up his coffee cup and took a sip. Oh, of course! Gus tapped his forehead—sherry! She had been describing the drink, not the containers. He laughed to himself. He would have to go back and have Albert explain it to her. She would get a laugh out of it.

The woman brought the check. Although she'd written the amount at the bottom, Gus still couldn't determine the correct denominations, so he took a few coins from his pocket and placed them on the table, indicating to her to take what she needed. Once she did, he placed a finger on a large, silver-colored piece and slid it towards her. "For you."

"Oh, no, no, no," the woman replied, with a bit more explanation he couldn't understand. She moved the coin back to him and chose another, smaller size. She held it up and spoke, as if to say this was more suitable for the tip, before dropping it into the pocket of her apron.

Gus walked back to Boulevard de Clichy and down to the telegraph. As he arrived he heard what sounded like shouting, coming from behind the buildings on the next street. The clerk recognized him from his earlier trips and shook his head, no, as soon as he came through the door. Though it didn't matter at this point, Gus was flummoxed that Max had continued to ignore his cable. "Would you like to send another message?" the clerk asked.

"No. I really don't need help anymore."

The noise around the corner became louder, more than just an argument. Several others on the street went over to look, one of them waving at friends to come and view the spectacle. Gus wandered over as well—for once he would enjoy being the audience.

A group of ten or so stood behind a banner on a narrow patch of grass—a tiny park among the buildings giving them a venue for their political statement. Crude letters dappled their canvas: Les travailleurs s'unissent contre la guerre. There was that word again—war. It must be close now. At least now more people were concerned, but in favor or against? A ragged fellow with a damp mop of hair had faced off with them and seemed to be lecturing. They shouted and waved at him to leave, but he only went on, pounding on a book and barking his philosophy. Even in French he seemed not to make sense.

The confrontation would escalate, Gus could see it. The rules of the street applied. Someone in the group would size up the stranger, looking for a weakness, and decide he could handle him. With a subtle look he'd make sure one or two of his comrades picked up on the idea. Then all he needed was a word that could be taken as an insult. It was important to a man's sense of honor to be properly provoked, not to engage until a threshold, even a farcical one, was crossed. To do otherwise would suggest bad form; even hooligans had a protocol. This was how it had always started when Gus was alone, except it was never about politics or philosophy. On the street simple greed motivated men, and it made two or three against his one acceptable. For him, though, the incentive had been survival. Gus's hands balled into fists. The instinct was still strong.

The interloper continued his hectoring; he uttered whatever word the assembly deemed necessary. One of the men in the group had enough. He pushed the man's shoulder.

Instantly the intruder grabbed the protester from the group and hauled him towards the street. Two others caught up to them and tried to pry them apart, but they had misjudged their foe. Although thin, he controlled the bigger men like children, flinging them off and pulling the first man away. He held his miserable rival in a headlock and threw him to the ground. The thin one jumped in the air and came down on his opponent's neck, smashing the man's face in the gutter as they landed. His victim lay motionless, blood oozing into the cracks between the cobblestones.

Three more jumped the stranger and pinned him to the ground, and still he kicked them off to continue the brawl. Someone was bound to get the police now, but they wouldn't arrive for several minutes. The rest of the group and some of the onlookers rushed to the fallen man's aid.

The attacker became obsessed with violence. He began going after the rest of the group, even the women. Gus had to be involved now—to drive this madman off, to memorize his face for when the police arrived. As he moved towards the fight he recognized the scarecrow shoulders and mangy hair; the dark, hollow eyes—could it be the one who left with Jack that first night at Le Secret? He'd only seen him then for a few seconds, but Gus felt sure. He was called Raoul.

The madman pulled a straight razor from his coat. He went after anyone he thought he could reach, slashing at the air in front of him as though it too were an enemy. Gus took the banjo from his shoulder. In the street, no resource can be overlooked. He needed a weapon that would scare the man off and held the banjo by the neck as he began to stalk. Still Raoul did not run. He turned to face the threat and licked his lips, relishing the combat. Gus let the banjo sway in front of him like a pendulum, and pulled the upswing into position to strike. If only this fool would get the message and run, but his insanity only drew him closer.

Gus sensed the crowd surround them, a circle enclosing their Apache dance, eyes on his performance. But this was not a song he could allow to carry him from the stage; there was no place for euphoria. He had to focus on the man in front of him now flicking his razor open and closed.

He swung at Raoul with every memory of the street he could muster. But Raoul ducked, parried the blow with his forearm, and Gus lost control. The instrument landed ten feet away in the grass, its strings jabbering in distress.

Gus raised his hands to fight off the blade, but Raoul did not charge. Instead he stared at the banjo. He started moving towards it and Gus knew what he had in mind. They reached it at the same time, but Raoul still had his razor and swiped at Gus. He had to back away. But he could not let this maniac run off with his livelihood, his life, and he inched closer as Raoul toyed with the strings. He had always fought because he'd been attacked; if he were to save the banjo he would have to be the aggressor. The thief raked his scarecrow's fingers below the bridge and the banjo shrieked—a noise from hell, as though the instrument was possessed—Gus hadn't known it could make such a sound.

Raoul liked it. He abused the strings again. Gus leaped. He tackled Raoul and the banjo fell free. Raoul hurled a knee into Gus's midsection. Another man from the group came to help, but Raoul kicked him in the chest, hard, and he fell back. There would be no more help; who would dare?

Raoul had the banjo by the neck. Gus had one more chance, and he lunged, catching the strap and wrapping his hand around it. A police whistle sang in the distance. As they wrestled, Gus looked into the eyes of the thief—Raoul peered back from behind his mask of hair. His face was blank, emotionless, like that of a gargoyle. His eyes did not blink. Gus wrapped the strap around his forearm and brought his free hand up to help, but it was not enough against a man who had no conscience to hold him back. Raoul jerked the neck, sending Gus to the grass. He hung from the strap, kicking in vain at Raoul's legs.

Raoul began to drag him across the pitch, then gave the banjo a jolt that felt like the buck of a wild horse. The strap broke off and the burn of leather against his arm made Gus finally release, and he lay at the gargoyle's feet.

Raoul let the banjo drop behind him and took out the blade again. He slashed as Gus recoiled, slicing through his pants and piercing the back of his leg as he tried to roll away. He swiped again as Gus crawled, catching him where he had been scarred long ago. He scrambled away, clutched at the wound. He felt weak. The sounds around him merged into a din from some faraway place. Over it Gus heard a hollow, angry voice: "I teach. I teach you good."

No, Papa! I didn't know what he wanted.

"You no touch a boy again. You no touch nobody!"

The boy had been so friendly. He was from the high school, where Gus longed to go. He had something to show, something fun. If Gus would just come behind the building with him. Come with me.

"I make you sorry!"

No, Papa.

The hand with the blade poised to strike. Gus folded into himself and accepted his sentence.

And then there were hands on him, helping him sit up, dabbing handkerchiefs at the blood trickling from his leg. Raoul was gone and the banjo with him. Gus pushed himself up, ignoring the pain and the comforts of the crowd. He walked slowly, making his way through the chaos like a spectre in a graveyard, silent, until he reached the edge of the park and collapsed at the feet of a policeman.

Once the police determined Gus was an American and not involved in the politics of the dispute, they let him go. The only one at the station who spoke English—and badly at that—was a sergeant who told him to forget about recovering the banjo. The police were too busy quelling anti-war agitators to try to find it. When Gus told him he would locate it himself, the cop laughed. "Monsieur…Paris, you cannot know." In the mangled statement Gus recognized that he was right.

He went back to Le Secret, fingering the tear in his trousers as he walked. His wounds had become numb. The weight he'd never noticed, removed now from his back, felt strange in its absence, like a missing limb. He felt almost as if he didn't know how to walk in a coordinated manner without the banjo pulling against his shoulder, holding him erect, and as he crossed a street he reached, unconsciously, to adjust the strap. He could buy another when he got back to New York, but it wouldn't be the same. A new instrument would never have that feel. It might take years to get used to the difference.

Outside the cabaret he paused, not wanting to go down the stairs and have to explain to everyone what had happened. Without the banjo Bertré would be proven right—he was nothing but a janitor. But where else could he go? He would have to endure it all for two more days. Perhaps everyone would be busy and he could hide in the back until he felt ready to face them. If not, let them ask their questions and offer their sympathies. He didn't have to listen.

At the bottom of the stairs he sensed something had changed since he'd gone. Albert worked behind the bar and Renoult sat at a table going over figures. A customer leaned over the counter, half drunk already, but none of that was unusual. It was a sound. The gurgle of a child. Aimée came out from a back room holding a baby, wrapped in a gray blanket. She brought the child to Gus. "Il s'appelle Henri," she said, and held it up for his approval.

The baby was like a ball of dough to Gus. He didn't remember ever being this close to one. It smelled of powder. Its arms and legs pumped continually, as though powered by a little steam engine. Aimée moved it closer and held it out for him to take, but Gus backed up a step. He thought he heard her say "papa." He didn't want the responsibility. But she persisted, placing Henri into his chest. When he took it she gasped, noticing the tear and the dried blood. She shouted at him. The baby began to cry. Instantly he offered it back. Aimée rocked it in her arms, still asking questions. Gus shot a glance at Albert.

"She wants to know where did you get the hole...and the blood."

"I fell. It was stupid."

"You are all right?"

Gus nodded. "What is it...the baby...doing here?"

"Not the best place for a baby, eh, but today we'll make an exception," Renoult said. "She wanted to bring it."

"To show you," Albert said.

"Me?"

"I think maybe to see if you liked it." He laughed. "Or if it liked you."

"Yes," Gus said, and turned to Aimée. "Oui. Henri...bon."

Aimée smiled. "Beautiful, oui?" she said.

Renoult interrupted. "You know, Albert and I, we have never seen her like this with any man. She is, for the first time, like a...a wife." Albert laughed again and Renoult joined him. Aimée, despite not knowing what had been said, began to giggle along with the mood, making the men laugh harder. Gus stood there and took it, too miserable to join in the humor.

"Don't be mad at us," Albert said. "We are happy for you…that is, if you are happy for yourself."

"It's not that," Gus said. "It's the banjo."

"Yes, you took it with you," Albert said. He stuck his nose into the air as though sniffing for it. "Did you leave it someplace?"

"It's gone."

Albert furrowed his brow. "Sold?"

Gus stared at him. "Not sold. Stolen."

"Que?"

Renoult asked, "Did you go to the police?"

They did not understand; how could they? He'd had this banjo since his grandfather died. He'd played it in the bars and stairwells of two dozen cities and on the railroad tracks in between. He held it in his hands when he wasn't playing; he made sure to touch it when he slept. He made it his life and knew enough not to trust anyone near it. But since he'd been in Paris he'd exposed it to all kinds of dangers. He'd allowed it to be damaged in the fight outside the theater. He was loose and blatant with it. The theft was inevitable. He wanted to curse them all for being so insensitive.

They were waiting for an answer. "The police did nothing," he said. "They wanted to arrest me."

Aimée heard the frustration in his voice and moved next to him. She held the baby with one hand put the other around his waist. This time Gus pulled away. The questions, the probing made him uncomfortable. He craved the cool feel of the banjo in his hands. She made a move to follow, but Gus's eyes warned her off. Aimée asked Albert to explain. He told her what had happened, then added in English, "What can we do to help?"

"I don't expect anything from you…" He stopped, and

they waited for him to finish. Gus looked down at the bar he had cleaned this morning. Dozens of customers would come in throughout the day to defile his labor and he would have to clean it again tomorrow. He looked away from them.

"Tell us what happened," Renoult said.

The four of them sat at one of the tables, leaving the drunk at the bar to fend for himself. When the man called over to Albert to get him another drink, Renoult waved back and said something that seemed to be permission to go behind the bar and pour his own, as the man helped himself to a cognac. Renoult watched as though making a note to add it to the man's bill. Gus recounted what he could remember about the fight. Albert translated for Aimée as he spoke. When Gus mentioned Raoul, Albert sat up straighter.

"That one!" he said.

"I thought we were going to ban him from the club," Renoult said. "I knew he was going to be trouble for someone."

"He is crazy," Albert said. "And he is the one who took it?"

"Yes. I guess I'll never see it now."

"If we find him, we find the banjo...yes?"

"You know where he lives?"

"No. But I know who does—that little poof who bleaches his hair. The one who smokes the women's cigarettes. He's a maggot. I've seen them leave together."

"Another one who will be banned," Renoult said.

"And I know where *he* lives! Eighteenth arrondissement. It's practically around the corner."

Aimée tugged at Albert's sleeve to get in on the information. He translated the exchange, and she tapped Gus's shoulder with her free hand in support.

"Tell me where I can find him," Gus said.

"It won't help. He speaks no English." Albert looked at Renoult. "Can you spare me for an hour?"

"Go!" the owner said. "But come back right away. I can't nursemaid a baby and the drunks at the same time."

Gus and Albert climbed two flights in the stinking tenement and stood outside the door of the one Albert had said knew Raoul. They'd walked only a few blocks from Le Secret, into a warren of buildings well off the boulevard, and Gus was no longer surprised that such squalor existed so close to the main street. There were places like that in New York. The same smell of grease that lingered in Le Secret's alley wafted through this gray hallway. The door to the apartment looked like cardboard, as though they could knock it down with a single blow.

"Will he be here?" Gus asked.

"He'd better be. I have no wish to wait."

Albert pounded on the thin wood and the door quivered for a few seconds after he stopped. "L'ouvrir, Valentin!"

Nothing.

Albert repeated his command and raised his foot, ready to kick it in.

A twitter came from within, like a bird in its nest. Albert put his foot down and crossed his arms to wait. His fingers drummed against his biceps.

When the door finally opened a crack, Gus saw chopped white hair that seemed to have been cut with a knife instead of scissors, and the top of a badly sunburned face. The eyes were bloodshot and dark. The nose had been particularly fried, and bits of pinkish, parchment-like skin hung, waiting to finish peeling. Its owner raised his head to look into Albert's eyes, and pressed a smile between cracked lips.

"I see he has been getting out in the sun," Albert said.

The man said, "Albert," in surprise, and stepped back to swing the door open. He threw his arms wide as if expecting an embrace, but Albert stood his ground and shook his head like a bull ready to charge. If he had the man would have been gored into oblivion by the big bartender. He was a rag doll, held together by a striped shirt made for a boy. A length of rope secured his pants. Gus hadn't thought Valentin's head especially large when he'd poked it around the door, but seeing it teetering on that emaciated body made it look enormous.

Valentin dropped his hands into a pose that suggested he somehow knew Albert as a friend, and was puzzled by the big man's reluctance to hug him. He reached out to take Albert's hand. "No." Albert said, and then went on, explaining their presence. He made it clear the visit was all business.

But Valentin appeared to be a man who was never about business. He sidled up to Gus and ran his hand from the shoulder down the arm, stopping to squeeze the muscle of the triceps on the way. Gus froze, and Albert pushed the little man away from him.

Albert spoke again, accusingly, and Valentin swiveled his head side to side. Then he said something in response.

"He says he never heard of Raoul," Albert said.

"Is he lying?"

"I'll get it out of him."

Albert pushed Valentin into the middle of the room. Gus followed them in and Albert instructed him to close the door. It was less a room than a closet. There was no furniture he could see in the bad light, and no door in the wall from which a Murphy bed might swing out. All he could see was a pile of blankets and scraps in a corner of the room, and a piece of half-eaten fruit on the floor, already brown where the skin had been pierced. Valentin coughed.

Albert took the little man's wrist. He fell to his knees and let out a squeal of pain.

"Do you have to hurt him?" Gus asked.

"It's necessary."

Albert yelled at Valentin again in French. Another high-pitched reply. "Ha!" Albert said. "He says if he tells us where Raoul lives, Raoul will beat him up. Now we're getting somewhere."

The barman slapped Valentin with the back of his hand,

and he fell into the wall. "It looks like he's going to get a beating, one way or the other."

Valentin tried to fight back, but it was like a fly trying to take on the swatter. Albert pulled his victim up and twirled him to face Gus, then held him in a vise-like grip. Gus could see a trickle of blood from the man's already damaged nose. Albert said, "Want to take a punch? I'd say you've earned it."

Albert stretched Valentin in front of him, pulling his torso upwards so hard the man's shirt popped out from his pants to reveal the ashen belly of a starving prisoner. Gus clenched his fist. What had this man done to him? So many others had lied and cheated him, but this man had done nothing. His only offense was to know the address of someone who had committed a crime.

Valentin tried to clasp his hands, to pray for mercy, but Albert held him by the arms and he couldn't. He began to plead—the whine of a child. Gus had never abused someone so helpless, but they needed the information. To get it he would have to become as threatening, as dangerous as Raoul, as dangerous as the rest of the world.

He could see Albert becoming bored with the game. In a second he might let their captive go and head back to Le Secret. Gus pulled back and slammed an uppercut into the pallor of Valentin's abdomen. The little man's head jerked forward then back. Gus hit him again. Albert released and let him fall to the floor, holding his stomach and making gagging noises, as though choking on his own vomit.

Gus shouted at him, even though he knew he couldn't understand, "Where is the banjo?"

Chapter 14

Friday, late afternoon – Jack

NO MAN'S land. A place halfway between the wall and the door, which Jack had reached after more than an hour of pulling against his restraints and the weight of the bed, a place where the air pulsed like an impending storm, as Jack didn't know when Raoul might return and was terrified of what would happen if he did.

When Raoul had left, Jack put the little strength he'd regained into freeing himself. His hands, though, were too tightly bound, and the bed was heavier than he'd imagined. The gag, however, felt pliable. He had to lift his torso onto the mattress, high enough so he could use the tips of his fingers to pry the cloth away. That alone took what must have been half an hour and left him spent. But he had freed his mouth—his voice—and could at last call for help. At first, because he was so drained, his cry was not much louder than a whisper. He would have to do better, send his voice out to the balcony.

Jack rested. When he felt ready he began to take deep breaths. He held the last one for a moment and then sang his plea, pressing the air out from his depths, to the closed door and shuttered window and beyond.

No response.

He called again. And again. An hour of entreaty. At the beginning, each cry for help was a command, an imperative: come for me. But when no one noticed it turned into a statement: I am here. It lessened into a request: please find me. Finally, Jack begged, for acknowledgment as much as rescue, for someone to at least admit he was still alive and still mattered. It was as if Raoul had known there would be no reaction to his calls, and had gagged him merely as an insult, rather than a precaution. What kind of place was this, in which no one responded to distress?

When his voice went hoarse, and he could call out no longer, Jack began pulling again. But by then he didn't have the strength to move the bed more than a few millimeters at a time. Each tug drained him so that he had to rest for increasingly longer periods. By evening he'd managed perhaps two feet. Then fear consumed him. Raoul usually showed up at dusk, in preparation for his evening prowls, and Jack realized he'd never make it to the door before his tormentor reappeared. Each time he heard steps in the hallway or a noise outside the window he froze. When a pair of shoes sounded close he shifted the process into reverse. But the effort in that direction was as futile, and soon he was unable to move at all.

The sweat he'd spent in his trials was not replenished by drink all that day, and Jack lay unconscious until well into the night. But when he awoke, the hour unknown, he saw that nothing had been disturbed. Raoul had not come back.

He'd been too weak to try again and slept, tormented by dreams of being pursued, dehydrated by the heat in the flat, until the next day. He had no idea of the time. In this purgatory, without food or water, he was barely able to hold his head up, let alone cry out again. And so, like a man in the desert, he decided to wait for nightfall.

*

Again the echo of heavy shoes in the hallway. This time they didn't fade and Jack braced, knowing he was stranded where he should not be. A cough, and the key in the lock. Raoul shuffled in clutching a large, black thing—it took Jack a few moments of squinting to recognize it as a banjo. Raoul dumped it in a corner and the instrument sounded a note of despair. The beast took off his jacket. His shirt was soaked through and had rust-colored stains and spots, from the armpit to the waist on the left side. He dabbed at them with his opposite hand and fell into a chair. Raoul had difficulty breathing, and when he peeled shirt from skin, Jack saw a gash along his ribs that covered his side in blood.

Jack watched Raoul close his eyes and try to will his pain away. He realized he would receive no punishment for the bed-moving indiscretion—at least, not yet. His captor was too focused on his own agony to notice. The man was hurt, perhaps badly, but any sympathy Jack might have towards him subordinated to his own desperate needs, and he let his hand drop to the floor, in hopes the noise would rouse his captor. When Raoul opened one eye to look, Jack spoke as clearly as he could, a croak that begged, "Water."

Raoul reached for a bottle on the shelf above the table, and the motion made him wince. He pulled the top off with his teeth, an act that contorted his face in pain, took a swig and brought it over. Jack opened his mouth. Raoul jammed the bottle between his lips, knocking the rim against his front teeth. Jack couldn't even tell what he was drinking, but sucked until there was nothing left. "More," he rasped.

"You fix me," Raoul said.

Jack spoke in whimpers, like a child. "Please. More drink. Water."

Raoul put his hand over the gaping wound and stared at Jack, as though analyzing options. Finally he brought down another bottle and a nugget of stale bread.

"I'll help you," Jack said when he was finished drinking. "Untie me?"

"Oui," Raoul said, but then he turned and went out of the apartment, leaving the door open, and Jack could hear him walk towards the lav. If only he could find enough voice to scream out into the hallway. Raoul must be in considerable discomfort, since he'd left him this opportunity.

He brought back a basin of water and long strips of cloth that could be used as bandages. He kneeled next to Jack and began, with one hand, to undo the leather straps. Jack could hear him grunting with every exertion, saw him clamp his mouth shut each time he pulled at the knots. When he finished, Raoul sat on the floor, panting in the heavy air. Jack leaned forward, put his hands between his knees and his head down on top of them. He massaged his wrists against each other and pressed his legs together. The skin where he had been bound was proof of the leather, aching bright red. It throbbed, and probably would for some time, but at least he could feel the blood returning to his fingers. "Give me just a minute," he said, sleepily, but Raoul did not respond. His eyes had closed, his shaggy head drooped back between his shoulders. He was perhaps asleep—maybe, miraculously, unconscious. How long would this last?

Jack planted a foot against the floor, braced his elbow on the edge of the bed and pushed. But he still didn't have the strength to get up. At last he was free—Raoul had passed out and the door was unlocked—yet he couldn't move to save himself. He knew it would be some time before he could walk.

Raoul opened his eyes. "You are doing something," he said.

Jack had no idea what that meant, but to be safe he changed the topic. "Do you have medicine?"

Raoul snorted. "Use water. Is enough." He slid over. The liquor on his breath worked like smelling salts, and Jack twisted his head away.

"What happened?" Jack asked, as he dipped the first

cloth into the basin. "What happened to you?" He picked up the strip and cupped his free hand underneath to catch the water as it dripped off, then slurped the excess into his mouth. He held the cloth near the wound and stopped. "This is deep," he said, still having trouble speaking clearly. "And dirty. I should clean it first."

"No medicine!" Raoul breathed.

"We can use that." The alcohol on Raoul's breath reminded Jack of the rye still sitting on the shelf, and he trembled a finger at it. "To kill the germs."

Raoul struggled up to get the whiskey, and brought it back. Jack needed both hands to turn the bottle over and soak the rag. "This will hurt," he said, and jabbed it into Raoul's open skin.

When the alcohol took effect, Raoul jerked backwards and said something in French that was surely an epithet. He grabbed Jack's hand and pulled it away, and Jack could tell there was still plenty of strength in him. He'd have to be careful how he proceeded. But he had hurt him. After the days of abuse and neglect it was wonderful to be able to return some of the pain that had been inflicted, and despite his weakened state and the threat of retaliation, Jack leaned forward again to deliver the sting. "Medicine," he said. "You must let me."

Raoul bit his lip while Jack played doctor, soaking the cloth again and again and applying fresh revenge to the wound. If only there were some way to incapacitate Raoul completely.

"Tell me, Raoul," Jack said. "Was it a fight?"

"Socialist pigs. I fight them all."

Jack remembered Raoul's original mission. "That man. Did you…"

Raoul swiveled his head and looked at him from an angle. "He lives still."

"Then you couldn't find him."

"I find him. Too many were near."

Jack dipped a strip in the water and held one end against Raoul's torso. He rose to his knees and began to wrap the fabric over the gash and around the body. To reach around back he had to press in close, and rest his chin on Raoul's shoulder. Raoul began to stroke Jack's hair, and Jack relaxed for a few seconds and let him do it before bringing the end of the strip around. He took Raoul's hand from his head and brought it gently to the ends of the cloth, instructing him to hold them until he could place the next layer. The delight of their first night together tried to nudge its way into Jack's consciousness. That rough hand had been so exciting against his skin, smoothing the way for the pleasures that came next. Now it rested limp in his palm—not demanding or strangling, but soft, the way Jack had once imagined the future might be.

He had to block that thought. Could he be so stupid and despicable as to let his only chance at freedom pass by in some ridiculous fantasy? He focused on the far corner of the room, where the banjo laid. It looked like Gus's, but of course, they all looked like that. "Where did you get that?" he asked.

"I take."

"You found it?"

"Oui."

It had to be a lie. "Where did you find it?"

Raoul grunted. He put his hand into Jack's face and pushed him away, and Jack sprawled back on the floor.

He must have stolen it. "Why?" Jack asked.

"To sell."

That was the obvious answer. But after so long in this torture chamber, Jack didn't know whether the explanation meant the truth, or just a trick his brain played on him to conjure more memories of Gus. Why not bring Gus into it? It was just the reminder Jack needed to send his mind tumbling from the last ledge of sanity. That stupid instrument brought it all back at once—the whole history of

None of this is Jack's fault!

them together, right up to last week. By now Gus had probably made good on his word to collect the back pay, and now he was working the Vaudeville by himself, no doubt pocketing both of their shares. He'd leave for America ...maybe he'd already left. Jack stopped his ministrations for a second to realize that Gus, in his own way, was as evil as ? Raoul. Just waiting for a chance to take advantage. And as always, he had let him. For twelve years Jack had put Gus's happiness ahead of his own. He'd made performing...everything...easy for him. For that, Jack had always been rewarded with avoidance, sometimes condescension, and an ever-deepening spiral of animosity that had eventually led him here—the pit of self-hatred.

He shook his head to throw off the thoughts, but knew he couldn't. The images of Gus flowed freely, filling the room and Jack's swirling consciousness. Now, sitting in front of him, where Raoul had been, was Gus, his dispassionate face staring through him—vapid and unfeeling as a mannequin, selfish, uncomprehending. Lost, as always, in the fortress of his solipsism, and Jack chastised himself for failing to recognize it for all these years.

He spoke again to Raoul. "You have to get rid of it."
"Que?"
"The banjo. I can't bear to see it."
"Is money to me. I sell."
"Put it away somewhere. Out of sight."

Jack knew as soon as he said it there was nowhere Raoul could move the banjo that he wouldn't see, and he became agitated. As he reached for another bandage, he threw his hand into the basin, splashing water on the floor and onto Raoul's leg. He stopped in panic.

But Raoul took up the wet hand, brought it to his lips. He sighed, an indication the pain in his ribs was subsiding. "You good to me, puppet," he said. "You heal me well."

Jack felt a calmness trickle through him. This simple compliment was turning him around...and that was the problem. Everyone knew this about him. They fed off it. They didn't have to plan a strategy to outsmart him, because Jack's flaw was so stupidly obvious anyone could work it to his advantage—Raoul, Gus, even Kera in her way could find a kind word that turned Jack from outcast into friend, and secured his loyalty. He *was* a puppet. He knew that as soon as he wrapped Raoul in bandages, he would push him back to the bed and tie him again, and then leave and forget everything until his appetites drove him back here. This time, though, amid the imbalance raging in his head, in the heat and hunger of his captivity, the message he had always denied himself made it through. Perhaps fear had opened the path—the desperation of this situation at last great enough to defeat his rationalizations. He went cold inside—but deliciously cold. Cold like them. And as he stared into the blank eyes of that stone face, and saw both Raoul and Gus at once, Jack knew he could do what he must.

He took another cloth from the pile, the longest one he could find, ran it through the basin, held it up and wrung the excess out. In the hot air, the fabric released a musty smell that reminded him of the beach at Coney Island, and the memory helped subdue his anxiety. He imagined that just outside the apartment was sand and ocean, and that when he walked out of here he would stop for a while and run his toes through the grains, face into the gritty breeze and let it rouse him from this nightmare. He slipped the bandage over the others and brought the two ends together, tying them in a loose knot and letting them hang down over Raoul's waist. "This is too long," he said. "It will show through your clothes."

"So?"

"Do you have scissors? I can cut the ends."

"No."

Jack thought for a moment. "The razor," he said.

Raoul went to the shelf again and retrieved the blade. He snapped it open and tried to cut the loose ends himself.

But his damaged side reduced him to one hand, and he couldn't keep the fabric taught enough to slice. Jack put his hand out.

"Here," Raoul said. "Finish."

"Sit on the bed."

Raoul sat and turned sideways to offer the bandages for trimming. Jack kneeled in front of him, pushed his shoulder gently to get him to turn more. Blood started to ooze into the cloth, spreading sideways along the warp. He let the straight razor rest in his palm and examined it before curling his fingers around its bulk. The white horn of the handle felt smooth and cool against Jack's withered skin, the color almost matching from where the blood had been drained from him over the last day. Jack looked up, at the side of Raoul's face, at the day-old stubble sprouting from that red cheek, at the hawk-like nose flaring for breath in the heat. It was a face of ignorance, filled with hatred everywhere he looked. Why hadn't he seen it that first night?

Jack took one of the ends of the cloth in his free hand and pulled to tense it. He drew it harder until he could feel Raoul resist, and set the edge of the blade against the fabric, an inch from Raoul's wound. He slid the razor's edge across the threads and watched them pop apart, a few at a time. His hands began to tremor and he looked up. Raoul was looking away, at the little window, at the streams of light that passed through the cracks in the wood shutters. Jack turned the edge towards Raoul's body. He took a deep breath—his hands shook terribly now. He pushed the point into the layers of cloth that swaddled Raoul and dragged it—hard, harder, through the bandages and into the skin, into the open cut until Raoul felt the steel in his side and shot backwards, into the wall, and Jack pressed in, keeping the razor against the wound. But his hands! His hands so weak from being bound, so unsure of violence. He couldn't stop them from shaking, couldn't keep his grip on the handle, his finger on the spine of the blade, and as Raoul squirmed away the weapon dropped to the floor, the thud on the wood a gunshot in Jack's ears, and he sat, frozen, like an animal caught in the sights.

Raoul swung his arm and struck Jack on the side of the face. He hit again and Jack fell back on the bed. The gash in Raoul's side bled even more than when he had come in, through the makeshift bandages, and blood ran onto his pants. "I'm sorry!" Jack said.

The butcher held one hand against the re-opened wound, and with the other swept down and picked up the razor. He closed the blade into its sheath and pointed the blunt end at Jack. Then he turned it around and snapped it open again with a graceful, practiced flick of the wrist, as though he held a switchblade, the metal glinting with malice. With his forefinger he levered it closed. Then flicked open again. Then closed. Raoul spoke in French—a long, rambling sentence, punctuated with slurs and spits. Then, "Enough of you," he said. He gave the razor one last flick—nonchalant, as though snapping his fingers, and stalked closer.

Jack did not close his eyes. He thought he should have—he had when Raoul shaved him in adoration, and again when he'd done it in anger. But now he couldn't. He looked straight into the black eyes, watched the steel as it flashed in front of his face. He saw Raoul's arm swipe in front of him, and felt warmth along the width of his abdomen—liquid, trickling down onto his union suit, seeping under the garment and onto his leg. Raoul struck again, higher, across the chest. Jack panted from fear, but felt no pain. He was entranced by Raoul's every movement—the sinews of his arms and neck tensing and relaxing as he slashed back and forth, a scythe of brutality; the eyes focused on his target; the scowl daring him to cry out. Raoul stayed at arm's length. He never lunged in or thrust the razor forward. Instead he kept a rhythm, each pass piercing the skin just enough to draw blood, but not deep enough by itself to inflict a deadly blow. Jack realized Raoul wanted this to last. He was enjoying the cutting too much to be satisfied with a single, deep slice. And Raoul wanted him to be the witness of his own demise, to take in every detail, just as he was doing—to let his terror build until he succumbed from fright as much as injury.

Where Jack could not bring himself to close his eyes to the torture, Raoul did. He placed his hand on Jack's shoulder, pinning him to the mattress, and shut them, and then lifted his head in ecstasy as he continued the assault, painting slashes and Xs onto Jack's torso. He went higher with each stroke and in a minute was just below the shoulders. A few more cuts and he would reach the throat, and Jack knew that even with this lessened pressure, one well-placed swipe would mean the end. Let it come. He stretched his neck tight and lifted his chin as much as he could, offering the taut surface to Raoul. Still he kept his eyes open. Raoul opened his and stared down at the carnage he had wrought. He lifted his free hand from Jack's shoulder and let the blood that had splashed onto it drip down onto the bed and floor, before wiping it across his face.

Now the pain began for Jack, as the shock of the attack diminished and air sucked into every ragged slice in his skin—pain beyond what he had known at Raoul's hand two days ago. Jack's nerves messaged agony into his brain, enveloping him like an electrical storm and holding him, their piercing song detaching him from reality and all its sensations. He could not move, or hear. He sensed his mouth hanging open, but could not make a sound. He watched as Raoul backed away from him slowly, looking as though he were in shock himself over what he had done. The razor rested in his hand, poised and ready to strike again, a drop of blood on its tip. But instead of coming forward again he carefully closed the blade back into its shell and let it fall to the floor. Raoul stared at Jack a little longer, and then finally tore himself away from the sight.

Jack's vision began spinning, taking in details from every corner of the room: Raoul pouring what was left of the water in the basin over his head as though cleansing himself of this sin; the banjo leaned against the wall where some paint was peeling; a book on the table; Raoul to the closet to take out a shirt; Gus with the banjo in his lap; now a gun on the table. Jack's hearing returned. The banjo was playing a song. Raoul had the book in his hand and was reading aloud. His French sounded like chanting, echoes, like a man standing at the altar of a cathedral, but off-key.

The banjo music stopped. Raoul put on his jacket, checked the gun, and shoved it into a pocket. Jack heard him say the name Jaurès. He tore some pages out of the book and slid them into the breast pocket of the coat. Jack saw Raoul open the door of the flat and disappear. He heard the door close and the sound of shoes diminishing into the hallway.

Jack finally closed his eyes, but the world did not stop spinning. He prayed that he would pass out, but the pain from each of the cuts kept him awake—together the dozens of assaults on his body created a cacophony of sensation that made him imagine being burned alive. The smell of his own blood and sweat mingled, convulsing his stomach, and while he lay there the drink and bit of food he'd consumed came back up. He turned his head and spewed it onto the mattress, then turned away from the sight.

His breathing slowed. Through the searing pain he noticed that the vomiting had broken the sweat, and Jack wondered if this last reaction meant his body was still working, clinging to its existence. He thought then that he might not die, that Raoul had deliberately cut only deep enough to bleed him into a state of incapacity. Restraints were no longer necessary—the razor had done the work of the leather this time. Jack would lie here until Raoul came back, and the butcher would do this to him again.

But what if he were wrong? What if he died? Or what…yes…perhaps he had already died—days ago when

Raoul first used the razor. That would explain this hell he had been cast into, obscured because no angel had appeared to pronounce damnation. He was not only to be tortured in this underworld, but left ignorant, to wonder through eternity whether this was his end, or if other, even more horrible afflictions awaited.

Maybe he had died weeks ago, or even years. Then this would all have been hell—no fires and pitchforks, just miserable shows in stinking theaters, tagging along behind Gus, waiting for the future to connect with his hopes and change it all. It had fooled him, kept him thinking things would get better by offering a few minutes of pleasure here and there, then snatching the promises away and dangling them just out of reach, where he could only see but not partake. If this moment was real, if this torment still part of the world, then there had to be a future. But for Jack, every moment had always been about the present—trying merely to get by, to make it through to the next show without despairing, then starting the cycle again the next day, the very act of participating in the charade keeping it going, keeping him from realizing the nature of his punishment. Yes, if this were real, something would have changed by now. It would have had to, if only from pure chance. But nothing ever changed—nothing. If he could stand up and walk out of the flat, back to the Vaudeville to climb on the stage with Gus, still nothing would have changed. He would again wait until the end of the show and run out the back door of the theater, into the claws of the monster, with full knowledge of what would happen, and he wouldn't try to change a thing. He knew he could not help that. What was the difference between a hell on earth and the one below? There was no way to know, really.

Jack touched his bleeding chest and brought his hand to his lips. He licked his fingers and felt the liquid ease onto his tongue, trickle back into the dryness of his throat. The blood was tasteless. He felt that his tongue had swollen. He opened his mouth and thrust it out, then bit down—hard, like biting into an apple. No difference. The pain he floated on was the same—no more, no less, but unrelenting.

With his last spark of strength he curled his left arm over his torso and took hold of the side of the bed. He pulled, rolling his face through the bloodstained mattress until his body fell off and flopped to the floor. He landed on his back, with his head to the side. Slowly, over the course of a few minutes, he pushed himself back into the bedframe so that he wound up half sitting, with the mattress serving as a cushion for his head. From there he could reach it. It was an arm's length away, and he stretched, like a ghoul clutching at the shoulder of its intended. He picked up the razor and dragged it into his lap. The handle was smooth and cold in the hot air. It felt real—more real than anything he could recall.

He didn't have the energy to flick it open as Raoul had, so he placed his fingers alongside the spine, and with some effort, pried it apart. He would make sure of things now. The red marks on his wrist made a perfect guide. Jack stretched his fingers back to tense the tendon below the heel of his hand, and touched the blade's edge to the rosy skin. It felt like the razor had that first night with Raoul—full of sinful promise. He pressed down a little to test the sharpness, and eased off to compare the sensation to the inferno raging on his savaged chest. This wouldn't hurt a bit. He lifted the razor and sketched three furrows into the skin, and placed the point at the start of the first line. Through his shallow breathing he managed a deep breath. His forefinger went to the spine, and then he added pressure until the skin split open and his blood appeared. Firm now, he told himself. Cut deep along the lines. He watched as the blood pumped free, first in little swells, then surges, matching the beat of his heart. There was a noise in the hall—footsteps. No matter. Then Jack turned his head away and closed his eyes.

Chapter 15
Friday evening – Gus

EACH STREET he encountered offered an opportunity to disappear, to recede from his troubled world to where no one could find him. They were not really streets, but alleys—alleys with names to distinguish them from the anonymous and even narrower passages off the boulevards, like the one that led to Le Secret—titled to afford their residents the small dignity of a place on a map. But they tempted Gus, sparked his memory, and taxed his resistance to taking refuge once more in a doorway or a stairwell. It was so hot. And it would be easy to settle in for an afternoon that would turn into a night that would turn into another day. Perhaps the banjo wasn't so important after all.

He stood at the end of a sunbaked corridor with crooked apartments on either side that jutted out almost to the gutter. The path forked, each direction meandering into medieval curves that made it impossible to see an outcome. Albert's directions were useless now. The bartender had written them out in French, thinking it best that if Gus became lost he could show the paper to passersby who knew the neighborhood and could point him, if not lead him, to the next street on the list. But there was no one in sight. Gus stood and listened for the approach of a samaritan, but heard no footsteps, no chattering cart wheels, only the imperceptible sound of heat ricocheting off stone. The occupants of this slum were not so foolish as to brave the infernal evening, especially during this week of unrelenting temperatures. He stared again at the crumpled sheet in his hand, at the ink that had smeared and would soon become illegible in any language. He rested his other hand on the handle of the knife Albert had given him and he'd sheathed under his coat.

    He saw a strip of shade against the buildings on his right, and nestled into a notch between two structures. It was not appreciably cooler there, but at least he didn't have to contend with the searing rays. From there he examined the street's architecture—a clutter of styles from centuries past, more compressed even than the tenements of Manhattan, people packed into living quarters so close they mocked any attempt at privacy. And yet, among the stifling flats he noticed specks of color: yellow curtains in a window, pots of red geraniums on a ledge. Someone had hung a tiny French flag from a shutter. Modest gestures, but they made these places something more than the gray hovels of his New York. As cramped as they must have been, they hinted at the individuality, even pride, of their tenants. Like Aimée. She would live in a building like one of these. Her apartment would have just enough room for her, her baby and her mother. Her bed would be in one corner, a crib next to it. A closet for the few clothes they needed and a cupboard for food. A chair where she would sit, holding the boy in the mornings before she had to leave him and head for the club. Aimée would choose a flat that faced the morning sun, and he knew she would have something on display—flowers or a picture she had painted. He thought of her peering into a mirror, the sun illuminating the room and serving as her makeup light. Her fingers would wiggle as she added the bow to her hair, as though she were playing an instrument. At the cabaret she had been the first person he had ever allowed to caress the banjo.

When the sun encroached on his space he pushed himself from the space and decided to choose the left fork, the better to keep the sun at his back. Still the sweltering air, reflected off every surface, made his search dreamlike, and he floated around the bends of Rue Saint-Rustique. If Albert had been able to come with him they would be at Raoul's by now. Instead he was hopelessly lost.

From around the next curve he heard an argument. A man screamed, incensed at someone too intimidated to respond. Gus slowed and maneuvered to peek around a building. The screamer looked old and covered in filth. He shouted and gestured, but the object of his tirade had run off. Whoever offended him must have committed a serious breech to incur this much anger in the deadening heat. And surely the man roasted under a heavy, tattered coat better suited for winter, which he wore over a black sweater and a shirt. Even his head sweltered under a mossy thatch of hair that came to his neck, and a beard that covered everything except his nose and eyes. The only outlet for the heat within this man was through his mouth, and he kept spewing his anger to the empty street in front of him until he saw Gus.

"Qui êtes-vous? Êtes-vous avec eux?"

Gus moved into the street. The man seemed to stare directly into the sun, but did not avert his eyes or blink. He was not old, in fact seemed not much older than him. Gus held out the paper and the man shuffled forward and snatched it away.

"Do you know...?

The vagrant glanced at the paper, then stuffed it into a pocket inside his coat, and they stared at each other for a few seconds. The man made a face that Gus read as recognition, but he knew he'd never seen him before.

"Can you take me there?"

The man rushed forward, but Gus didn't fear him, and

let him grasp him by the shoulders and draw him close. He had the stink of soil and grease. When he at last backed away he said, "Vous devez me payer." He shook his coat and Gus heard the jingle of coins from deep within the shroud.

Gus fished in his pockets for some money and came up with two silver bits. He held them out. "Pour vous," he said. His hand was almost ripped away along with the coins, and the man took off into the space between two apartment houses.

When he got to the crevice and looked, the man had gone in sideways, squeezing between the bricks, and was waiting for him. "Suivez," he said. The way was tight, even for Gus, and he sidestepped to keep pace with his guide, although he couldn't see the other end of the passage. It was fittingly dark—in these cracks of civilization the sun loitered for only a few minutes before moving on behind the tops of the buildings. They maneuvered through turns and around corners—centuries of people snaking through here had made the stones smooth, and more than once Gus had to fight the urge to slide down and curl himself into a ball in the dark. The man kept rambling at him. Stopping might be lunacy, but so was going forward. He would have to trust his lunatic guide.

A shaft of light, shaped like an edge of steel, flashed at the end of the corridor. They emerged into another narrow road, this one lined with dilapidated tenements. Gus's escort pointed to a teetering pile of bricks and said, "Là!"

"This?"

"Là!"

Gus dug in his pocket and managed to find another coin, which he dropped in the man's palm. His guide turned and shuffled down the road, shrugging his coat higher over his shoulders.

This building didn't have the touches of individuality he'd seen on the other streets. Its bricks mimicked the color and texture of rust, and were painted over in soot and grime, and seemed impervious to a wash or cleansing rain. The shutters here lay bare and broken against the façade. Some hung from a single hinge, others were missing. He smelled garbage nearby. It was in worse shape than the building in which they'd found Valentin.

What he and Albert had done to the little man. If only he'd cooperated. Gus couldn't erase the image of how they'd left him lying on the floor in a heap. But there was no other way. Albert had been particularly brutal, resorting to abuse at the outset. He seemed to have his own reasons for pummeling Valentin, apart from locating Raoul, and Gus didn't question them—Albert had been too good a friend these past few days. Gus found another slice of shade and sat—he'd have to rest for a while before going inside and confronting Raoul. He remembered well how strong the man was—a strength unfettered by conscience and which made his violence irresistible. To survive, Gus would have to turn the tables on Raoul. In his years alone in New York he had always been the victim, the defender; he could not recall making an unprovoked assault. That changed today.

The entry to the flats had no door. Gus went inside and paused at the stairs to review his strategy. He would be quick and forceful. It was important that he surprise Raoul—rush him as soon as he opened the door to his room, get the advantage and find the banjo as quickly as possible. He fingered the Laguiole tucked into his belt, wrapped his hand around the slender, curved hilt and drew it out. He let it rest lightly against his palm and imagined a quick thrust into Raoul's midsection.

The hallway smelled like soiled laundry, and Gus covered his nose and mouth with his sleeve to avoid the stench. Valentin had told them Raoul lived on the second floor, number twenty-nine. Enough of the doors nearby had numbers that he could figure out the rest.

Try as he did to step lightly, every stair groaned under his weight. If Raoul were in his apartment, he would hear someone coming. Gus drew the knife and held it behind his hip.

Raoul's place was at the end of the hall. Stealth proved impossible as the floorboards continued to shriek out his location. He envisioned how Raoul had abused those people in the park this morning, and how they seemed unable to stop him. He replayed the man's evil—what he had done to him and how he'd stolen the only possession that had meaning. It should make him angry; wild with rage so that when he saw the gargoyle's face he could lash out at it without hesitation. But Gus's anger had dissipated at Valentin's. He could not bring the fury back. He knew that made this task twice as dangerous. Why not quit then?

He stopped at the door and pinned himself against the wall adjacent to it. It was partially open, and he could hear breathing inside. He turned the knife over in his hand. A drop of sweat fell from his forehead onto the hand holding the weapon. He rubbed it against his pant leg, then wiped his brow with the sleeve of his jacket, and watched the silver blade glide past his eyes. Aimeé was waiting for him at the cabaret. Gus had said he would go after Raoul alone and Albert called him a brave soul. They would want the details. They had him in their thoughts as they worked. Maybe even Renoult as well. He took a deep breath and held it.

Enough.

Gus eased the door open until it shuddered against the apartment wall. He scanned the room, knife hand tensed, expecting Raoul to leap out of some corner. Instead he saw a body on the floor, bloodied and rolled onto its side, in a fetal pose, unclothed except for an undergarment, and looking beaten and bruised. Blood flowed from around the hands.

Raoul? Had another victim of his malice come here first and done Gus's work for him?

No, the skin was too light, the hair too short. It was someone else. He knelt beside the man and put his knife down, turned him onto his back, and saw that it was Jack.

"You," he said, and struggled for something else to say.

Jack opened his eyes.

There were strips of cloth littered about, as though Jack had been trying to make his own bandages. Gus picked one up and looped it around Jack's forearm several times, covering the open wound. He pressed it down into the wrist, and pulled the ends tight to staunch the blood flow. He tied another strip over the first, even tighter. Jack's chest had been butchered, and each of the two dozen or so cuts still oozed as well. How could it be? The slashes in Jack's wrist were the marks of suicide, but then, how did he get the wounds on his chest? Raoul. He wanted it to look that way. The only question was which he had done first.

There wasn't enough cloth to cover all the damage. There was no sheet on the bed and no curtains to slice, so Gus took off his jacket and placed it over his partner. He looked around—an open razor laid on the floor next to Jack. A washbasin lay upside down a few feet away. The contents had been poured out, and the water mingled with Jack's blood as it pooled in a depression and seeped through cracks in the floor. There was the banjo, against the wall near the door. Gus would have to get help, somehow.

"No," Jack whispered.

Gus turned back.

"We have to get you to a hospital."

"No," Jack said. "Raoul. He's going to kill…"

Gus could barely hear him. He knelt next to his partner, took the unbandaged hand and held it. "Kill who?" Jack managed to wrap his fingers around Gus's. He seemed to be fading, hallucinating. When he opened his eyes again they did not fix on Gus, but circled the room. "Jaurès," he said.

The strange man in the club yesterday. Everyone loved him. Gus put his other hand on Jack's shoulder. He let it lay there for a few seconds, and could not remember the last time he had deliberately touched his partner—even during their rehearsals and shows they had rarely brushed, even accidentally. Jack managed to raise his uninjured hand to his shoulder, and let it rest on Gus's fingers. He spoke as if from a dream. "I watched you. I always watched you."

Gus squeezed Jack's hand and looked into the beautiful face, now pallid and bruised from the ordeal. "I know," he said. "I was afraid to admit that I knew."

"It doesn't matter now."

Gus let go of the hand. He dabbed his handkerchief against Jack's forehead. "I'm going to get you some help."

"No. He has a gun. He'll kill them all."

"You need a doctor. Right away."

Jack breathed in little gasps. He closed his eyes and did not move for a minute, and Gus watched. This might be his last memory of him. As Gus rose, Jack came to for another moment. "Leave me," he said. "Jaurès."

The people in the bar had fallen over themselves trying to please Jaurès, even Renoult. Albert had explained how valuable he was to the nation, but he had another connection to the crowd besides his position. Gus had felt it too, even though he'd met him only briefly. Some kind of intuition, as though he knew what others felt and was able to share their emotions. And the way he'd put down that dandy in front of everyone.

Jack had lost so much blood. He was barely breathing. Even if he could somehow find help it might not be in time. And Jaurès was far more important than his friend.

And *them*...Jack said *them.* Jaurès was with other people, probably his aides—probably Bertré. And if Bertré was with him then Kera might be too. Raoul was going to kill them all.

Gus went to the door and looked back. Jack had closed his eyes again. The bandages he had wrapped around his wrist seemed to have stopped the bleeding. He ran the length of the hallway, pounding on each door as he passed in the hope that someone was at home. But no one answered. He went to the stairs and raced down—into the street, into the inquisition of the sun, but it was as deserted as before. He began running, with no direction or goal in mind. Just running. Panting for air but not stopping. He would run until he saw someone and make him help. He needed a cop. He needed a way to make whomever it was understand.

If only he could find a main street there would be shops and people. He could persuade a taxi driver to transport Jack to a hospital. But here there was no one, and no way a vehicle could fit into the tight passages that served as roads. Or he could find a doctor. But for all he knew he could be running away from all that. And if he went too far he might not remember how to get back to Raoul's building. He stopped and began to shout.

Back and forth on the avenue he called, "Help! Come out! Please!" Someone had to be in these buildings. Even if the people didn't speak English they would surely recognize the panic in his voice.

Finally, a few shutters and windows opened and heads poked out. A man with no shirt yelled at him, gestured and went back inside. A woman looked at him from her upper floor, and turned her palms up in confusion before retreating. A young girl stared.

"Little girl," Gus called to her. "I need your help. I know you can't understand me…"

She replied to him in French. It sounded like she was asking a question; trying to find out what was wrong.

"Please. My friend is hurt." Gus pointed back towards the window to where Jack lay. "He needs to go to the hospital."

The girl stared for a few more seconds, then ducked away. What was the matter with these people? But they were only doing what he had done so many times himself. There was always someone else who could act first. He began shouting again. Perhaps on the next street he would find compassion.

Before he could make it to the corner, however, the girl

at the window came running from a doorway. She pulled a woman by the hand and pointed at Gus. The girl spoke and he recognized the word "hôpital." But the mother held her daughter back, and asked him questions he did not understand. "Please," he said. "My friend. He's hurt. He has to go to the hospital. Hospital." He waved for them to follow. The girl pulled against her mother's restraint, and they came slowly, keeping a distance, and he waited at the stairway landing. He saw the girl's dress was torn and hanging from her shoulder. She was shoeless. But her face was clean and pretty. The mother looked older—perhaps this was the girl's grandmother, but like the tramp who'd led him here, it could have been the life she'd lived that had aged her.

Gus started up the stairs, but the woman stopped. "No, no," she said to the girl, adding what sounded like an admonition. Her fear would keep them from becoming involved. He couldn't blame her—what did she know of him? Why should she believe him—and in this neighborhood as well? But the girl twisted her arm free and ran inside. Gus saw her from the stairs and motioned for her.

The mother shrieked, "Emmanuelle!" and ran in after her. She would learn in a moment. Then, if she turned away, there would be nothing else he could do.

He ran to the room and the girl followed to the doorway. Her mother caught up, and when she saw Jack she pushed her daughter back into the hallway. "Qu'est il arrive?" she asked, and put her hand against Jack's forehead. She began to ask more questions, until she realized Gus couldn't answer. He drew the jacket away from Jack's body so she could see the extent of the assault. She gasped and turned her head.

"Emmanuelle!" The girl poked her head into the flat. The mother gave instructions. She said, "Vite, vite!" and the girl bolted.

They sat together with Jack in the sweltering apartment. The woman fanned Jack's face with her hand. She looked at the Laguiole and razor on the floor, and glanced at Gus before looking away. Did she think they had fought and Gus did this to him? If he retrieved his knife now it would look even more incriminating. He had blood on his hands, as well, from where he'd applied the tourniquet. He had assumed she'd sent the daughter to get a doctor. What if it had been to the police? He touched his hand to his chest. "I didn't…"

The woman nodded. He had to trust them. He couldn't know where the girl was going. And if she did bring help, would it be of any use? The woman repositioned herself so she was sitting on the floor, next to Jack, and took his hand in hers. She patted it and began to sing—a whisper of a song that seemed to rise on the thermals blanketing the room. Gus sat against the wall. He picked up the melody and hummed along for a few seconds, until they let the music fade away. After today he would probably never see these people again. "Thank you," he said. "Merci."

It may have been a few minutes or a few hours—time had melted in the heat. Emmanuelle called from down the hallway, "Mama! Mama," her little feet slapping the floorboards as she ran to the room. She was so light the wood did not to creak as it had when Gus walked there. She looked in the door for her mother and spoke—a breathless torrent—then ran away again, back down the stairs. The woman rose and tapped Gus on the shoulder, and he followed her into the street, where a man waited with a horse and cart. Another man was walking quickly up the cobblestones towards them, carrying a black bag. How had Emmanuelle done it? He looked at her, now exhausted, sitting on the bottom step to catch her breath. He went to kneel in front of her, to thank her, but the driver pulled at his shoulder, grunting at him to come upstairs. They waited for the doctor and went up.

Gus stayed in the hallway with the driver, and looked through the doorway while the doctor attended to Jack. He wiped more sweat from his brow. His white shirt had soaked through from the day's exertion and was transparent. The others must be able to see through the fabric as it stuck to him, and he pulled it away from his body to let it air out.

The doctor spoke in French to the woman as he worked, no doubt going on about Jack's condition. The man's tone was deliberate and serious—the quality reserved to prepare loved ones for the worst. It would be the same in any language, and it was enough. Maybe Jack had been right—he should have run out to find a policeman to save the politician. Jaurès's life was paramount.

The physician motioned that he and the driver would have to carry Jack down to the cart. He adjusted his pince-nez and spoke—trying to explain his prognosis, probably. Gus tried to indicate he already knew, but the doctor went on as though his medical opinion was too important to be kept to himself.

The driver was a small man too—a weed in overalls, skin desiccated from years in the sun, crisp and hard like an insect's. He picked up Jack's feet the way he might grapple with a sack of flour, and Gus said, "Easy!" The doctor cautioned them to go slow. Gus had Jack's torso in his hands, his pale, wet head against his shirt, and he could see blood seeping out from under the coat, dripping onto the floor as he carried him. Jack's skin felt cool to the touch despite the hot air—clammy, softer and more pliable than skin should be. He was so light, it was as though he had already ceased to exist, and Gus transported only his memory.

The mother had gone ahead of them. She and Emmanuelle cleared the cart and spread some straw around to cushion the ride. A dozen or so of the neighbors had heard the commotion and came down to investigate, and two of the men helped Gus and the driver put Jack in the cart. One of them adjusted Gus's coat on top of him. In the piercing light Jack's face looked white, as though he had applied too much stage makeup again. The doctor squeezed into the back with his patient. Gus would have to jog alongside if he wanted to go with them.

Then he remembered the banjo, still leaning on the wall in the apartment. It was stupid now, selfish, but he would have to go back and get it—he would never come back to this street. Gus waved at them to start, noting their surprise at what they must have thought was abandonment of his friend. But he signaled them once more to go, and ran up the stairs to the room. He brought the banjo into the hallway to examine it—there was a dent in the resonator and the tailpiece looked as though it had been dragged along the sidewalk. The fingerboard looked cracked as well. It was unplayable now, maybe irreparable. He ran his fingers along the strings and listened as they hummed and squeaked their story of what had happened.

The strap had come apart in the scuffle with Raoul, so he had to carry it in front of him instead of on his back. He cradled it like a child, and gazed at it as he went down the stairs, focused as though reading the story of his life, not watching his step and nearly tripping halfway down. He ran into the street to catch up to the cart, but it had already turned a corner and was out of sight. A few more steps and he stopped. Most of the neighbors had left. Gus sat down on the curb, and let the banjo slide through his grip onto the hot cobblestones.

Emmanuelle and her mother came over, and Gus put out his hand to thank them. The mother slipped a note into it—the doctor had written the name of the hospital. The woman offered what sounded like consolation. She put her hands together in prayer. Gus did the same and hung his head. The next time he looked up, he saw the mother and daughter walking and holding hands, heading back to their apartment building. They looked as though they could have been walking through a park, or along a beach.

There had been no sense in trying to go all the way back on foot. Gus ran with the banjo for several streets, listening for the sounds of the city, moving towards them, finding wider avenues, which at last led into a boulevard. It was unfamiliar, but it was civilization. Cars and buggies rolled past. People trod along the sidewalk, glaring at the man in the dripping wet shirt, with bloody hands, struggling with a battered instrument. "English?" he asked some of them. If he could communicate with someone, he might still be able to warn Jaurès. But they avoided him. At last he found a policeman, and mentioned Jaurès by name, but the cop still shooed him away. There was nothing to do but go to Le Secret.

He hailed a taxi. The trip back to the cabaret took twenty minutes and throughout it Gus wondered about Jaurès and Kera. It was surely too late to stop Raoul. He felt his fingers go numb. Jaurès would be dead, and the French would blame him. Kera's family, too, once they found out. Abandoning her to save a man who was already dead. Gus saw crowds of people lining the streets to pay tribute to their leader. He saw himself, alone with a priest, while the man mumbled over Kera's coffin in some empty French cemetery.

As he took the banjo out of the taxi around the alley from Le Secret, Gus noticed the sky reddening, and realized he had been gone most of the day. It would be dark in another hour. He went down the stairs quickly, and had to push through a group of customers standing near the opening to get to the bar. The size and energy of the crowd reminded him it was Friday. Patrons surrounded Aimée and Albert. One of them knelt on the floor and put his hand on her ankle. She picked up her other foot, set the shoe on the man's shoulder, and sent him tumbling backwards to the delight of the people in his party. Then Renoult was in his ear, from behind. "Why is it that I should not fire you?" His displeasure must have been building throughout the afternoon.

"At least you recovered your banjo. Find a chair and get to playing," Renoult said.

"No. Wait."

"You are saying no to me?"

"We have to find Jaurès," Gus said. "He's in danger."

"What do you mean?"

"It may be too late. I wanted to tell someone," Gus said. "I couldn't find anyone who speaks English."

Renoult had him come behind the bar, and called Albert to huddle with them. Gus told them about Jack and the warning he had given, and lamented again the time that had lapsed. "This Raoul," Renoult asked Albert, "is he capable of murder?"

"I wouldn't be surprised."

"He's like an animal," Gus said.

Aimée rapped on the bar to let Albert know she had more drink orders. Gus looked over and she smiled, her tough working façade instantly softened. He reached over the counter to take her hands. She saw the blood and began to ask questions, but when she saw it wasn't him bleeding, her tone changed from shock to scolding. He wanted to jump over and embrace her, but Albert put a hand on his shoulder and spoke to Aimée, and she understood.

The big man turned back to his work and started pouring drinks again, but kept an ear to the conversation. "What do you think we should do, boss?" he asked Renoult.

"Maybe Raoul is crazy, but maybe he is serious too. Who knows? But if something had happened we might have heard by now. Let's try to get to Jaurès."

"How can we find him?" Gus asked.

"We telephone that newspaper where he works. If he is not there, they may know where he went."

"Telephone him how?"

"Go to the telegraph office."

Gus took a step and stopped. "Albert has to come with me."

"What?"

"To speak French."

"I can't spare him now," Renoult said. "Look at this crowd."

Albert, still listening, faced his boss. "Daniel," he said. "If it's true…this is Jaurès."

Renoult stared at him. "I'm sorry," he said. "I am not thinking. Go with him. I will take care of the drunks for a few minutes."

They moved around the bar to leave. Gus hesitated and looked at the banjo, propped against the bar. He couldn't leave it there, not after everything that had happened. But as he moved to retrieve it, Aimée went over and put her hands on it. She spoke to him, and her eyes said it would be safe with her.

In the street he started running and passed Albert, who went into a trot to catch up. The big man still wore his bartender's apron, and it billowed out to the side as he ran. "You know," he said as he clopped along the sidewalk, "I've never called Renoult by his first name before. I wonder if he will let me back into the club after such an affront."

The telegraph operator let them contact *L'Humanite*, but charged Gus thirty sou to do it. Albert stayed on the line for only a few seconds. He set the heavy receiver into its cradle and drummed the counter. "They say he is at dinner. He went with friends just a few minutes ago. They're at Café du Croissant."

"Is there still time?"

"It's not far from here—just a few streets. You can make it in two minutes if you run."

"You're not coming?"

"What can I do now that you can't? If you get to him in time he will be safe. And Renoult needs me."

"Tell me how to get there," Gus said. "And keep it simple this time." He reached into his pocket and brought out one last coin. He dropped it on the counter. "Better ring up the police too."

Gus took off at a jog. His only rest since morning had

been the taxi ride back from Raoul's building, and the heat of the day and the exertion slowed him considerably now. He hadn't had a chance to clean up or eat since before he and Albert left for Valentin's. But Jaurès had been at Le Secret yesterday—holding that little glass in his hand, holding the attention of just about everyone in the place. He had treated Gus like a man instead of a janitor, even without speaking to him—he had made Bertré show him respect as well. All of them—Jaurès and Bertré, and Kera with them, would be sitting in the restaurant, relaxing, having drinks. He took a deep breath of the balmy evening air, looked to where the sun had just gone down behind some buildings, and ran faster.

Chapter 16
Friday night – Kera

"WELL THEN, we shall need room for eight, at least," Bertré told the waiter. "Put us near the open window so we can have some relief from this unbearable heat." The outdoor seating at Café du Croissant was already filled with Parisians weary of the high temperatures, and cranky that the weather had lasted a full week. They lingered under arcs of taut, striped umbrellas teetering above the tables, even though the sun was near the horizon and shade was superfluous. Most of the diners looked as though they had entrenched themselves for the evening—languid, leaning back in their chairs, cigarettes or glasses of port in hand—and would never finish their meals, no matter how many others waited to be accommodated. That left only the café's stagnant interior, and despite the yawn of the open window, the breeze it invited proved negligible. Kera could tell he was upset about it.

The waiter moved as though leaden. Bertré would assume he was yet another indolent, but Kera saw the young man's latent rebelliousness—he would comply, but not concede. The waiter's eyes were mocking, challenging Bertré's authority, daring him to make something of this nothing, and if he did, it would expose his false and ostensible superiority. Bertré took the bait. He folded his arms and watched the man drag two tables together and spread linen over them. When the waiter returned with extra chairs, Bertré made him realign the tables—made a show of it—forcing him to leave the chairs in the aisle where they bothered another group of diners. Such was her man's world, that even in the pointlessness of table arrangement there had to be a protocol, a reinforcement of his place in this society. Kera laughed to herself, because it wouldn't matter soon. She had packed her bags while he was at *L'Humanite*. She didn't want to spend another minute in that apartment. All she had to do now was tell him.

The way Bertré had acted when they came back to the apartment last night! She had not seen him like that before. After Café du Croissant he sat silently, as though waiting for her to speak first. But she was not in the mood for talk, not with everything that had happened, not with the fool he'd made of himself. She sequestered herself in the bedroom, but he came to her, put his hands around her waist, still without words, and tried to kiss her. Kera backed away, but he persisted, shyly, forlornly, minus the usual leering and torrent of compliments that accompanied his seductions—he'd become a beggar instead of the confident man she'd known, rejected by his leader and desperate now for attention. Eventually, she relented, took him by the hand and led him to the bed.

He slipped her lingerie away from under her dress, and as he mounted her, she closed her eyes. She felt herself sliding towards the head of the bed, felt him push on top of her, but just as she began to accept the moment, he stopped. Perhaps it was too much drink, or the draining emotions he had been through during dinner, but he couldn't consummate the act. He slithered off the bed and went into the next room.

And just when she thought that was all there was to it,

when she closed the bedroom door to him, he threw it open and grabbed her by the shoulders. He shook her, hard, pushed her down on the bed, and tore the neckline of the dress she wore. This was not the playfulness of that first time. He did not allow her to fight back. "It's you," he shouted. "Because of you Jaurès has turned against me." He slapped her and she cowered at the head of the bed. "You and that bastard Longuet, conspiring to destroy Jaurès's trust in me. You think I don't know, eh? You think I'm too stupid to figure it out?"

He hit her again and her cheek throbbed, and he pulled back for another blow. She put her arms in front of her face and began to cry. Between sobs she tried to reason with him. "It's not true, Maurice. You know it's not true."

He could no longer reach her face, and began slapping her shoulders and the top of her head. "You ruin my position, but you have no problem spending my money!" he said as he tried to slip blows around her defense.

Kera went limp and stopped trying to block his hands. She curled into a ball on the mattress. Bertré backed away. He picked up a statuette and held it over his head as though he might fling it at her. He took a deep breath, then slammed it to the floor and broke it in two. "What you have done to me," he said. "What you have made me become." He turned and shuffled out of the room. She could see him sitting in a chair in the corner, staring, like a child being punished.

She waited all morning for Bertré to leave, put on her most pleasant mask and strained to keep it there through his coffee and egg, enduring his windy pronouncements about stories in the competing newspapers and his disagreements with their editorials, his ridiculous attempt to act as though nothing had happened last night. She even handed him his hat at the door and told him she looked forward to meeting him later for dinner. And as soon as the door closed and she heard him in the elevator, she readied herself for Gus, hoping he was all right, excited to see him, believing the glamour she wore was what he'd always wanted from her. Instead, seeing Gus with that little French tramp was the final blow. They were both tramps she'd decided, perfect for each other, and to save face, she lied to them about Bertré's asking her to stay in Paris. But there was nothing to keep her here, and her embarrassment intensified as she realized that there never had been.

When she returned from Le Secret, Kera emptied the bureau of jewelry, her toiletries and lingerie, surprised at how much Bertré had purchased for her in just the last week. She laid each piece carefully in a bag and went to work on a closet, covering the bed with her clothes. She held the yellow dress against her and looked in the mirror, turned sideways, fingered the sash at the waist and toyed with the silk ruffles at the bottom. Maurice had bought it for her when they returned from Brussels. Or, to be more exact, he had the portier run to a shop and purchase it. But it was beautiful, and she would take it with her. If necessary she would leave some of the worn and uninspiring clothing she'd brought from the states to make room. As she sifted through the closet she pulled out more of what he'd given her—a scarf, a hat, the matching parasol and gloves. And here was the lovely persimmon bonnet she'd picked out on her own and about which he'd said nothing—stuffed into the back on the top shelf. She would find a way to take them all with her. At least then he'd have to purchase new gifts for his next affair.

And now that she had watched Bertré play the buffoon before the other diners again—watched him clash with the help because they were the only ones he could be sure would subordinate themselves to him—she confirmed her decision to leave. She saw no future in this man. He was a sad clown, like Gus. They should become partners on stage, and the audience could debate which of them was more pathetic. His performance tonight would be like all the others—for

Curtain Calls

Jaurès's enjoyment, even if Jaurès hadn't yet arrived. Kera knew already that when he did, Bertré would make a point of informing him of how he had saved the dinner by belittling the waiter. How he shamed himself with his behavior; shamed her. Her momentary descents into affection for him were really her own loneliness. And she understood now that he cared far less for her than for his own strutting persona, less for her than his hero, Jaurès.

Kera fostered her anger. It was necessary if she were to end this relationship tonight. She would demand he give her cash for her welfare, and see to it she had a hotel room and enough money for the train to Le Havre. It was because of him that she had moved out of the Fromentin, therefore he was responsible. She worked on maintaining her ire until she had a chance to explain all this to him.

When the staff finally set tables and chairs, Kera sat down and expected Bertré to join her as they waited for the others. Jaurès was to bring them from the newspaper office. Bertré, however, remained standing and analyzed the arrangements. She realized what he was trying to anticipate where Jaurès would sit and plant himself alongside to be in the center of the conversation.

Kera rapped on the table and tried to stare him into a seat. If she were going to speak to him, it had to be now, and not in front of the group. It was bad enough to do it in a public place, but she feared what might happen if she waited until later, back at the apartment. But now Bertré left to chase the waiter down again. He insisted they had better wine than was served last evening, and he would pay—pay whatever the owner wanted—to have it brought out for Jaurès. The waiter told him no, and Bertré followed the man into the kitchen. Despicable. Perhaps she should go in there with him and tell him in front of the cooks.

Bertré came out with something like a smile on his lips. He carried a bottle of red wine. "I knew it," he said. "I knew they were holding back on us. This is from the owner's personal collection—he told me so. I've instructed them to keep us supplied, no matter the expense." He set the bottle in the middle of the table, and himself next to Kera. He was central, and could converse with the occupant of any seat. He cast his hand out like a fisherman, and snapped his fingers at the waiter to perform the corkage. "And the timing couldn't be better," he said. "Jaurès and the others are just arriving."

She saw the cane first as Jaurès came into view. Longuet was at his shoulder. The Sembats and Vaillant were with him this time as well, but the young staffers from *L'Humanite* had been left behind. She assumed this would be a serious discussion of the political situation. Kera looked at Bertré, who appeared eager as a puppy to have them come in. He told the waiter to hurry opening the bottle, and tapped his glass with a nervous, immaculate fingernail. Perhaps she still had a moment to talk. But Jaurès stood at the door. He placed his bowler on his walking stick and rested them against the table, and when he sat across from her and Bertré, the opportunity vanished. Chairs scraped against the tiled floor. Longuet smiled a hello. Vaillant, as always, ignored her. He and the Sembats were already into their own discussion.

Bertré tried to have the waiter pour a glass of wine for Jaurès. "This is an excellent vintage. Quite surprising for this little place. But it shows the value of perseverance."

Jaurès declined. "Bring us some sherry," he told the waiter. "I want to say something to the group. About our friend Longuet here."

"But Jean," Bertré said. "I've gone to a great deal of trouble to acquire this wine. The staff here—they haven't cooperated at all. I had to go into the kitchen and seek out the owner, and I can tell you they are quite upset with me."

"I'm sure of that," Longuet said.

Jaurès gave Longuet a look. He was already playing peacemaker between the two of them. "We will have some with dinner. It will be better with the food." Kera looked across the table at his tired face. In the few days she'd known him he seemed to have developed more lines, darker circles under his eyes. Wherever he went he was forced to negotiate—even in this petty spat.

The waiter brought the sherry and poured. Jaurès raised his glass. "We have been working for the past day to discover whether the strange notice from the draft board is legitimate or not, and I have to confess, we have been unable to prove otherwise. So as it stands, Monsieur Longuet must report for duty on Monday." Jaurès placed his thick hand on Longuet's shoulder, and the younger man looked down at the table, embarrassed at being the center of attention. Jaurès went on: "In his honor, I propose we use this evening to celebrate, to toast our friend and associate before he leaves. For once, let's relax and enjoy each other's company, like the good citizens who surround us. Let's be the simple French men and women we often desire to be. No politics tonight."

Vaillant and the Sembats raised their heads in surprise, and Jaurès chuckled to himself, and then said, "Well, perhaps a little."

Bertré began to applaud, and the others joined in. "You must be quite anxious to begin your new career," he said to Longuet.

Longuet raised his head until he was staring into Bertré's eyes. "Not at all. We haven't given up fighting this thing. Jaurès has promised. And wherever they send me, I will continue to look for ways to speak out against war."

"You do that and you'll find yourself in a cell, locked up as a traitor."

"I would be more of a traitor to France if I stayed quiet."

Again Kera sensed the two might escalate their discussion, and again Jaurès knew to come between them. He spoke to Longuet. "You'll do as I told you and keep your mouth closed. You'll train and march, and give me some time to solve this dilemma after you have to leave." He moved quickly to change the topic. "And what of you, my dear?" he said to her. "You too will be leaving us soon, yes?"

She turned to look at Bertré, and Jaurès guessed at her intent. "Unless Maurice has something to tell us," he said.

"Well, if he does, he'd better tell me first!" Kera said, and the entire party laughed, even the stuffy Sembats at the far end. Kera detected, for the first time, a hint of friendship in the smile from Mrs. Sembat. She would have to find a moment to sit with her and talk—after a week she didn't even know her first name. But Bertré did not laugh—instead he drank the remainder of his sherry and stared off to the kitchen, as though impatient for the rest of the meal to begin. It was all Kera needed to confirm her decision. He had never intended to ask her to stay, even from the beginning. The gifts, the promises—they were all merely means to introduce her to his bedroom. And of course he would never have been able to bring her there without those enticements. Knowing that he had turned immediately to coercion.

Gus had been right all along—he was a cad, and she had allowed her naiveté to keep her from seeing it. Well, then, she would tell him here, right now, that it had always been her intention to sail back to the states when the time came. She had enjoyed her time in Paris, especially getting to know everyone in the party, but her life was back in America. That is what she must say.

But before she could do it Bertré leaned across the table, asking Jaurès about developments at the Chamber. "Now I'm serious, Maurice," Jaurès said. "No business tonight. We haven't had a moment's rest for a long time. Those things will still be there for us to deal with in the morning."

Mrs. Sembat called to Jaurès. "Sir," she said. "I've just received some photographs of my little niece from the chemist's. She's such a beautiful child. Would you care to take a look?"

Jaurès looked relieved to have an excuse to get away from

Bertré, and he pushed himself from the table. Bertré turned to Longuet.

"Don't look at me, you old fool," Longuet said. Kera saw that despite Jaurès's admonition, he had become agitated over the reminder of his impending service. He looked as if fighting himself to keep from saying more.

Bertré asked him, "Why is Jaurès avoiding me? The last few days…"

"Listen." Longuet lowered his voice so those at the other end of the table wouldn't hear. Kera leaned closer. "We haven't found out where this phony draft notice came from, but I'm willing to bet you had something to do with it."

Bertré sat up straighter in his seat.

"He thinks so too," Longuet said, nodding towards Jaurès. "And because we can't prove it, I'm probably going to get my fool head shot off."

"You're insane," Bertré said. "I really think you've gone insane."

"At least Jaurès is trying to keep me from being sent to the front lines when this thing starts. But I'll tell you this—if they give me a gun, maybe I'll desert and come looking for you." With that, Longuet threw back the last of his drink, got up and stood by the door.

They sat alone at their end of the table. Kera knew she had to speak now. How could she begin? Everyone who had spoken to him in the last twenty-four hours seemed determined to insult him. She didn't want to add to that, but this had to be done. There had to be a way to broach the subject without being blatant and risking a harsh reaction.

Jaurès went around behind Mrs. Sembat to look at the photographs. Kera watched him as she considered her words. How jovial he always tried to be. Every day he carried the burden of France on his shoulders. Only he could keep the country out of the European conflict, and if he didn't, thousands of young men—men like Longuet—would be killed, and who knew what would happen to the nation? He carried that knowledge with him always, eating away inside him like a cancer. And yet at every opportunity he presented the world with his positive side. Here he was, spending the urgent hours before the war looking at a proud aunt's pictures of a little girl and acting as though it was important. Yet to him, she knew, it was.

"Lovely," Jaurès said. "She'll be a beauty." He took the empty chair between Mrs. Sembat and Bertré as the woman took a few more photos from her bag.

Then Kera thought she had it—she would ease into her escape from him by talking about the inevitable trip. "Maurice," she said. "I want to talk about my train to Le Havre. I have to make arrangements, and as you know, I no longer have means of my own…"

But Bertré was staring towards the patrons outside under the darkening sky, as though envious of their advantage. "Who is that man in the street?" he asked, although more to himself than to her. "He looks quite ragged. They shouldn't let him loiter by the diners."

"Maurice, I am trying to speak with you." Kera glanced and saw the one from Le Secret, the one who'd followed them last night. She'd lost his attention to this vagrant.

"He's a nasty looking one, isn't he? The streets seem to be full of pests like him these days," Bertré said.

She looked again. The man paced at the edge of the tables near the street, and appeared bothered by something. He ran his hand through the mess of his hair, and then pulled some papers from his coat. Perhaps this time he would stay and she could ask him about Jack. But in a minute. This was more important. "Will you listen to me, please?"

"I think I'll speak to the owner about this."

"If I were Jaurès you would listen to me!"

He finally turned to her, as did the others at the table. Jaurès leaned back in his chair, and looked puzzled. With some effort he produced for her a tired smile. Even Longuet, still standing a few feet away, was curious. "Fine, then," Bertré said. "What is it that must be addressed immediately?"

But Kera could not speak. The man outside had snaked his way though the tables and stood by the big window. He produced a pistol from his coat and pointed it at Jaurès. He began to recite something from the papers he held. It sounded like lines from a play. Longuet began moving towards the window. Bertré started to rise.

A shot penetrated the din of voices. Then the ice of shocked silence. Kera turned to look at Jaurès, who was bleeding from the forehead. Another shot. She saw blood blooming from his shirt, as though someone had placed a carnation. Jaurès fell back in the chair at an angle. His girth took him sideways and he tumbled to the floor at her feet. Mrs. Sembat screamed. The crowd came to life again, shouting, scrambling. Jaurès's face turned up, his eyes wide, looking directly at Kera. Blood followed the lines of his face, and trickled to the floor. His mouth came open as if to deliver a pronouncement. She could not tear her gaze from him. Someone pushed her to get to Jaurès.

Kera began to feel sick. She could sense the color draining from her face. She tried to get up, but was too weak. Her fingers trembled as she tried to steady herself against the table, and she reached for Bertré's arm. She needed to hold him, for him to hold her, but he was already on the floor with his hero's head cradled in his palms.

Longuet vaulted the window ledge and took off after the assailant, joined by several of the other men in the restaurant. She heard the pain in his heart like a crescendo, listened to it build into rage as he sped down the street. She prayed that the murderer did not stop and shoot at him, but she knew he wouldn't care. He might be happier dead with Jaurès than to face the future without him.

The others gathered around Jaurès. They wiped the blood from his face, but it continued to flow. It was on the back of the chair, on his beard and shirt, seeking itself in little pools on the uneven floor. Bertré leaned in to see if he was breathing. Was Jaurès merely sleeping, as he had been on the train from Brussels? A voice from behind pulled her back into the present: "He can't survive that. No one could." She looked around. The waiter was crying. She was the only person in the café still in her seat. The rest had crowded the window to look inside. Kera struggled up, embarrassed to have been sitting. Were they watching her? She heard someone call for a doctor. Someone else said it was too late.

Bertré laid Jaurès's head gently to the floor and rose to face Kera. She thought he would be looking for consolation now. He was even more of a child than she had come to expect. But he contorted with anger. "I could have saved him! And you stopped me! I saw that man outside. I was going to confront him. I was going to get the owner and have him removed. But you had to talk to me about some nonsense. A woman's problem, I'm sure. Something ridiculous."

"But Maurice…"

"And now Jaurès is murdered. Who will lead us?"

Quietly, she said, "You blame me for this?"

"I should have never become involved with you. I knew nothing good would come of it."

Vaillant closed Jaurès's eyes, turned away and put his face into his hands. Kera sensed her knees beginning to give. She had an overpowering urge to go down to the floor and touch Jaurès and tell him nothing would be the same with him gone. She wanted to hide from the onlookers who were watching Bertré rebuke her, but when she tried to push past him, he blocked her path. "Leave him," he said. "Let him rest in peace."

"Let her see him, Maurice. She is blameless. Let her pay her respects." It was Mrs. Sembat. She was crying but composed, and led Bertré away. Kera knelt by the body. Jaurès's open mouth—she knew what he meant to say, and through the cacophony of voices she now heard it clearly: the war has come. The war the nation had denied, had avoided, had craved—had arrived in France the moment the pistol fired. No one would try to stop it now. She picked up his hand, already swollen in death, and held it to her lips. Then she felt a tap on her shoulder to ask her to make way for the doctor. Bertré was still with Mrs. Sembat, and Kera made sure to go in the other direction, outside with the crowd.

A few of the people turned their attention away from the window and were trying to see down the avenue. "They've caught him," someone said. "Now they'll beat him to death." Kera and a few others raced towards the fight. She raised a hand to her forehead as she bounced along to get a view. The other hand held her skirts off the cobblestones. Five or six men had the killer on the street and were kicking him. One man had a shaft of wood, and the others moved back while he rhythmically hammered it into the assailant's torso and legs. As she got closer, Kera could hear Longuet imploring the mob not to kill him. "He must stand trial," he said. "The rule of law. Jaurès would insist!"

With the murderer unconscious in the gutter, the men stood back except for one. A short man in a white shirt had not had enough, she saw. He pulled back and kicked the killer in the face—did so again, and would have continued, but for two of the others finally restraining him and pushing him against a building. Kera lagged behind the rest of the group who had run there, and they obscured her view until she was able to push through. It was Gus, his clothing ripped and stained with grime. He thrashed to try to free himself. She ran to him and convinced the men who had him pinned to let him go. She saw that his face had been clawed in the fight, and he was bleeding there and on his knuckles.

He reached his hand to her, but it was not enough. She surrounded him, pulled him tight against her and buried his head in her bosom. Tighter and tighter she clung to him. She closed her eyes and he became immense in her arms, as though she were holding a giant, and she kept them closed as the fear she felt vibrated through her. And when, after a minute, he tried to break the embrace, she refused and kept him there until the energy had drained from her body and she went limp, allowing him to slip from her grasp. He staggered away and put his hands on his knees.

She was panting. "He killed Jaurès."

Gus hung his head. He mumbled something. Kera thought she heard him blaming himself.

"You knew he was here?" she asked.

Gus straightened and caught his breath. "He tried to kill Jack too."

"My God! Is Jack all right?"

"He's in the hospital. It was bad. I don't know the whole story yet, but this Raoul cut him up…"

"I knew he was in danger," Kera said. "I felt it. I wanted to help him. Why did he go away Gus?"

He didn't answer.

"Why didn't he tell me? Why didn't he let me help?"

"Jaurès," Gus said. "I tried to get here faster."

"How did you know, Gus?"

"Jack," he said. "He told me. He knew."

Longuet had waited for the police to arrive and take control of the prisoner. Now he faced Gus. "Thank you, sir," he said. Kera saw he was on the verge of tears. He appeared uncomfortable with his English, but thought of him as fulfilling a responsibility. "You have helped us and we are grateful," he said.

Kera spoke to him in French. "What did he do?"

"He caught him. Tackled him in the middle of the street. The bastard took a shot, but your friend didn't even slow down. Then he tried to run, but your friend jumped on top and held him until the rest of us could arrive."

Gus had started walking away, and Kera called to him, "I'm sorry." He stopped and turned to look at her. "I just wanted you to know that."

A policeman ran after Gus. He commanded him to stop, but it was in French, and Gus ignored him. The cop caught up and tried to turn him around, uttering something he couldn't understand, and Gus twisted out of his grasp.

"He needs to take your statement," Kera called to him.

"They all saw what happened. Let them tell it."

The officer mumbled about procedure, how Gus couldn't leave the scene until he had been cleared. "They won't let you go until you give them your version," Kera said.

The officer asked Kera if she would translate.

"No," she told him. "Find someone else."

"I beg your pardon, Madame, but you must. I will have to hold you as well."

"I don't want to. I can't. Please," she said, and began waving at Longuet. "This man can translate, and he was involved in the capture as well."

"Were you not at the scene?"

"No," she said. "I was out…taking a walk. I didn't see anything until they already had the man down on the street." Longuet arrived and the cop let her go. As she started away Gus held out a piece of paper for her. She looked at an address. "I will go see him," she said, and continued walking from the café.

Gus called to her, "What were you sorry about?" But she didn't stop. When she turned a corner she thought she heard Longuet calling her as well. Best to ignore it. She had to get back to the apartment and get the rest of her things together. Bertré wouldn't be there for a while, at least as long as it took for him and the others to console each other and talk to the police. That was if he came back at all. Either way she wouldn't stay the night there.

She hired a taxi to take her to the flat, and instructed the portier to alert her if Bertré showed. She went upstairs and finished stuffing the last suitcase, no longer bothering to fold the clothes. It would be a mass of wrinkles when she opened it again, but it couldn't be helped. She looked around for *such melodrama*

money—perhaps he had left a wallet or a few bills lying around. There was the pearl necklace—she could sell it or pawn it for the cash she'd need for the next few days. And through it all she endured a creeping nausea, a sense that she was committing a crime. But also she felt guilty of some greater wrong, an offense that made her stop from time to time and clutch her abdomen. What if Maurice had been right? She began to perspire, and at one point felt so faint she had to sit. All she had wanted was to be with someone— first Gus, then Maurice—to be a part of something more than masquerading as the Parisienne Nightingale twice a day. What was so horrible about anything she had done?

When she finished packing she lugged two bags to the elevator and sent them down, and returned to the room for the others. She stood at the doorway and looked back at the hard faces of the Greeks, pensive in alabaster, they too now judging her.

The portier summoned another taxi and loaded the bags for Kera. He asked if he could tell the gentleman where she had gone when he returned. "Home," she said. He held the door of the car for her. She began to duck into the back seat, but paused, took the portier by the shoulders and hugged him. He was surprised, but remained professional, and did not pull from the embrace until she let him go.

Finally she sat down, next to one of her bags that hadn't fit into the trunk.

The driver asked, "Destination, Mademoiselle?"

She fingered the necklace for a few seconds. "Hôpital Bretonneau," she said.

Chapter 17

Monday morning, August 3 – Gus

THE CUP was chipped, the coffee cold. Gus had to curl his hand inwards to hold a smooth surface to his lips and keep from spilling when he drank. The old waitress splashed through rain like a motorcar on a puddled street, spraying water over her shoes and hose as she went, ignoring the shower that drenched her hair and blouse. She ducked her head under the table umbrella that kept Gus relatively dry, a raised eyebrow framing surprise that he would take his breakfast in the elements. She pointed through a window at the empty tables in the café, and indicated he might prefer to sit inside. A man in a white shirt with rolled up sleeves, probably her husband, leaned his palms on the counter and angled forward as though in search of more customers.

"I'm okay here," Gus said. "I don't mind a little rain."

She stared at him until he remembered she didn't speak English, and he said, "No. Merci." She went inside and he watched her shake out her hair with her hands, go behind the counter and light a cigarette. Her husband didn't move.

The heat had broken, suddenly, in the middle of the night. Gus lay awake in his room and heard the first drops tap on the cobblestones outside. It had rained until morning, and when it stopped for a half hour or so, he made the walk here. A downpour started again almost as soon as he'd sat, but it didn't matter—he could stay as long as he liked. Le Secret was closed today—the first time, Albert said, he could remember Renoult swinging the loose-hinged door away from the wall to barricade the stairs. And on a Saturday, no less. The cabaret would be closed tomorrow too, and for a few days after that, at least. Not that anyone would be coming by.

Gus had left the banjo in the back room. It was battered and unplayable, but saved. He would have to see about repairs. It would have been nice to bring it along and play a song for Jack at the hospital, something to cheer him in his convalescence, but he wouldn't mind just sitting and talking to his partner either. They had so much to talk about now. As he placed the banjo amid some boxes, Gus was caught by its odd shape in the gray light—it was an orphan, unwanted and yet beautiful in its exile. He closed the cover and slid the case into a corner.

Renoult had sent the crowd away when the news of the assassination made it to the club. By the time Gus walked back in, only Aimée and Albert remained, straightening up. Aimée wrapped herself around him, her tears wetting his shoulder. The same reaction as Kera's, but not the same—Kera trembled and pulled at him, desperately, like a woman trying to keep from drowning; Aimée's embrace was for both of them. She would have stayed with him, but the baby, she said, and he kissed her to let her know he would be all right.

Albert said the crowd would have gone home anyway, out of respect, but that Renoult had made a scene, casting them out like sinners from the temple. Maybe he'd felt guilty over being more concerned about profits than Jaurès's safety. "He said he shouldn't have made me come back from the telegraph," Albert said. "I could have run faster than you. I could perhaps have gotten there sooner."

Maybe so. Would it have mattered?

    Renoult had left instructions that the door to Le Secret was to remain shut until he told them to reopen. Gus found the hand-lettered sign on the stair side in the morning. "Fermé." Closed. He was learning new words all the time. Halfway up the steps he paused. What if Aimée came back to see him? He should wait. He wanted to see her, but of course, he had no way to know. He couldn't contact her, and Albert wouldn't be coming in to help him. If he knew where she lived, he could go there. If he could write a few words in French, he could leave a note to tell her where he'd gone…that is, if he knew the address of the café. He took another contorted sip. But she would be at the club when he went back—he felt that.

    Gus turned his chair to face the street. There were fewer people out than usual, and those who were seemed not to notice the weather. They moved slowly, without cover, their eyes fixed on the pavement. There were no demonstrations that he could see or hear. There was no need for the factions to debate the war any longer. It would come now. He took a last drink of the chill, bitter coffee—this was what the future would taste like for the Parisians.

    When the rain reduced to a drizzle Gus put a few coins on the table and left. Albert had told him how to get to the hospital—it was on the other side of the Boulevard de Clichy. He started to cross and noticed the telegraph office a few doors down. Why bother? He knew what the answer would be. He'd wasted enough effort on the place—on Max. But halfway into the road he heard someone calling, "Monsieur! Monsieur!" He kept moving to the other side, but looked over his shoulder to see who had been hailed. The telegraph operator stood on the opposite curb, signaling him in a frantic semaphore. "Pour vous!" he said. He had a paper in his hand, and gestured that it was a message for him. Gus dodged traffic back to the south side. It was from Max:

SORRY FOR DELAY STOP   100 IN BANK FRANCE FOR YOU STOP   WILL DEDUCT FROM NEXT GIG

"He always finds a way to be a bum," Gus said, and the clerk hunched his shoulders.

Gus pointed at the word "bank." "Where?" The clerk aimed him down the boulevard.

A half hour later he retraced his path towards the hospital with an envelope holding what he assumed was one hundred dollars worth of French notes—enough to get them to the port with plenty left over, probably sent to cover any outstanding expenses. His cable to Max had described a bleak predicament for all three of them, and he felt glad he hadn't updated the message since or the amount would surely be less. At least the man had finally come through. They'd have to talk about the money coming out of the next job, though.

The rain had stopped again, but the sky remained in mourning. Kera had been lucky to know Jaurès, to talk to him. All Gus had was a few moments, a nod of recognition, a small service in defense of a stranger, and yet there was something spiritual about the man, as though he were unconcerned with the trivialities of daily life. The customers, sober or drunk, had paid homage to Jaurès when he came into the club—respect for sacrificing the little indulgences they enjoyed. The memory seized him, and his chest contracted with a sensation like the grip of a powerful hand—accelerating his heartbeat, rendering him anxious, on edge, aware of every sound like an animal out of its habitat. And what did the French feel? This loss was beyond anger, beyond grief, the absence of a thing too great to be fully appreciated or replaced.

He shivered from the cold, despite the coat he had found among the crates. It must have been an old one of Renoult's, since it was too large for him and had sleeves that reached to his fingertips. When he'd put it on it made him look like a child playing in his father's clothes, so he draped it over his shoulders the way he had seen Renoult wear his the night he and Kera stumbled into Le Secret. In the bar's mirror the black cape made him a true citizen of the city at last. Gus grabbed at the lapels and pulled them together as he walked into the wind.

Hôpital Bretonneau squatted before him. It sat long and low, laid out in a V down two streets with the point facing the intersection, the entrance set in shadow under a triad of arches, hinting at the witchcraft practiced within. Gus had been in a hospital only once before, when his mother died, but the memory of the smells jumped at him as soon as he walked through the doorway. Odors of blood, of ointments and disinfectants mingled with a hundred mysterious potions for doctors to experiment with. Which of them were they using on Jack?

He waited in a queue at the front desk, behind two nuns in their black habits dangling rosary beads that rattled like the rain against the windows. Both were so tiny they could barely see over the edge of the high counter. They spoke to a woman as stout as the two of them put together, no doubt chosen for the job to keep visitors in line. Gus listened as they entreated in muffled French, as though still in church. He looked around—at the clock on the wall behind the concierge, at the rows of square compartments where files were stored. Now, instead of the nuns, he heard Aimée's voice. She whispered something that sounded very serious in his ear, and then, without a pause, began laughing. How light and poetic it sounded, and he had to shake off the fantasy to keep ready for his turn.

There had to be someone who spoke English, who could tell him about Jack's condition, maybe let him go in and see him. The woman at the desk didn't seem promising, however. She shook her head at the nuns, as though telling them they would have to leave, or wait. They moved away and sat on a bench along the wall by the door.

The big woman stared at him. "Oui?"

So many awkward moments since he'd arrived. How to begin this one? "American?" he said. "You have an American here?"

"Que Américain?"

"Jack Sullivan. He is here?"

The woman turned up her palms and made a face. "No Anglais," she said, and began prattling off what sounded like a list of demands. He had been through this enough times and put up his hand and said, "Sorry." There were several women behind the counter and he would ask each one if she could help. Someone had to know at least a few words.

Before he could speak again, he heard a voice behind him, wet-sounding, as though the person were ill or had been crying. "Gus." Kera had come to see Jack too. She was dressed in clothes she had brought from America, a black skirt and plain white blouse, instead of the costumes her boyfriend bought for her. She wore no makeup today and the bruise under her eye had blossomed.

"I'm glad you came, Kera. It will do Jack good to see you…"

"He's gone, Gus."

"No."

"He died in the night. He lost too much blood, the doctor said." She covered her eyes with her handkerchief. The lace edges seemed to irritate her as she dabbed.

The hand gripping his chest tightened. "I should have come last night. I thought he might pull through."

"They said he called for you."

The link that held Gus to his world slipped a little, and his consciousness spiraled away from the waiting room, to the cauldron that was Raoul's flat, to Jack's shoulders in his hands, to the death mask of his face before they carried him down to the cart. He staggered away to a window next to the nuns, one of whom fingered the beads of her rosary, mumbling a prayer. He looked out at a few visitors coming out of the overcast into the hospital. "I did nothing," he said to himself. And he looked up into the iron sky.

There was crying behind him and he turned, composing himself. Kera had sunk into a wooden chair near a few other visitors waiting to be summoned. He went to her and knelt on one knee. "Jack didn't deserve this. You were great to come and be with him." His voice tailed off. "I wish I had."

"I'm scared, Gus."

"It's all right. The fighting is still far away. And you'll be safe with Bertré."

"I won't. I left Maurice. He's not…not the man I thought he was."

"I'm glad you figured it out," he said. He could say more, to get in one more insult against the man and mock her for not recognizing what a fake he was from the start. But it wasn't important.

Kera began to weep more deeply. She caught herself and tried to control it, but couldn't restrain one last, loud sob, and the others in the waiting area looked over. She turned away from them, towards the wall. "I lied, Gus. He never asked me to stay in Paris. Now I'm alone. I took my things last night and went back to the hotel."

"Good," he said. "That was smart."

"You don't understand. I have no money. I won't be able to pay for the room. I have no way to get to the ship." She started speaking faster. "I have some things I can sell but I don't know where, and I'm afraid to go to those kind of places by myself…"

He rested his hand on her shoulder and she quieted. "I heard from Max today, at last," he said. He reached into the coat pocket and took out the envelope. "He's helping us, if you can believe it." Gus took out a few bills and put them in his shirt, and gave the envelope to Kera. "I want to make sure Jack doesn't end up in some potter's field. My mother…" He looked away for a moment. "I want to make sure he gets a decent burial. The rest is for you. It should be enough to take care of the hotel and the train." She reached to hold him again and he drew back, remembering her suffocating grip from last night. "You don't have to thank me," he said.

"But wait. How are you going to get to the ship? Don't you need more of this? Oh, Gus! I can sneak out of the hotel and we can take the train together…"

"I'm not going back."

"What?"

"I'm staying here. In Paris." He stood up and took a step away from her.

"But Gus, that's crazy. Your whole life is back in New York."

"Maybe. And that's where it's going to stay. I have a new life here."

"You don't even speak French. How are you going to get by?"

"I'll figure something out," he said.

Kera paused. "It's *her*, isn't it?"

"Yes. And it's a lot of things. I have a few wrongs to make right."

"You'll sleep in that cellar, in the grime and garbage."

"Things will improve. They're bound to."

"And the war is coming…It's practically here. You haven't forgotten about that." She put the handkerchief to her nose to hold back a sniffle. "What happens if the fighting comes to the city?"

He raised his palm to silence her and reminded himself of a French traffic cop. He smiled. "I know I should go with you…"

"Then why don't you? I don't want to make that trip alone."

"I wish I could explain it better."

"Gus," she said. "You don't want to be here."

"I didn't," he said.

He coaxed her into accompanying him back to the administration desk and had her get information about a mortuary nearby. Then he gave her a light hug and said goodbye. He told her he knew she would be able to handle her trip back. She had done so much on her own in France—a simple boat ride would be nothing compared to that. Then he excused himself, and left her under the arches.

He would find the funeral home this afternoon. He didn't know what they could do with the money he had, but it had to be better than the alternative. If necessary, he'd pay for the rest on time. Then he walked. The clouds were beginning to break, and a patch of silvery blue appeared over the heart of the city. He walked towards it, registering the shops and apartments along the curving streets. It all seemed very new, as if he'd had his eyes closed before. French flags hung lifelessly from eaves and windowsills. Most of the businesses stayed closed, in honor of Jaurès. The great man would have a lavish funeral, with hundreds or thousands of mourners in attendance. Gus would go to that one as well, if he could.

He lost track of time, and in a while turned a corner and came upon the Theatre du Vaudeville. The monolith was still closed, and several other handbills had been pasted over the doors and walls. He looked up at the intricate carvings above the second floor glass, at the statues of muses higher up, at the row of close-quartered windows at the top, and wondered how long it had taken to build all that. He remembered the café under one of the awnings at the theater's side—it didn't look busy. He would try to find out what kind of sandwiches they offered for lunch. An older man, dressed in a blue serge, was making his way to a table. He went slowly, leaning most of his weight on a cane. He sported a gray mustache that ran the length of his jowls and met up with his sideburns, and from this expanse of bristles Gus knew him—the one who had translated the sign when the Vaudeville shut its doors. He was having trouble pulling the chair from the table and keeping his balance on the cane at the same time.

"Please," Gus said, "let me help you."

"Very kind of you. Sometimes it's difficult for me to get around these days."

"I was wondering, sir, if you wouldn't mind translating a few items from the menu for me. I don't speak French, as you can see."

"Of course." The man paused. "Seems as though I've translated something for you before."

"I don't know if I even thanked you for helping me."

"Quite all right. I knew you were in a spot."

They sat and waited for an employee to bring menus. "Did you ever find out what happened to the theater?" the old man asked.

"No. Never got paid either."

"It's difficult to be a performer, especially now. No one seems interested in art and entertainment. It's all talk of war."

"You sound like you'd rather talk about the stage."

"I'm a big fan of the shows." The man stroked one side of his mustache, his fingers following its curve around his jaw. He smoothed it as he went, and then worked on the opposite side. "Now," he said, "you're an American, yes?"

Gus thought for a second. "I'm from there."

"I'll wager you didn't know that vaudeville began here in France."

"I'd heard something about that."

"In Normandy, to be exact."

Gus squinted at the old man, who looked as though he was preparing a long story about the origin of the genre. But let him have his moment.

The man went on, "It pains me to see the doors closed. And for what? A lunacy that grips all of Europe."

There was a rumble from behind the theater, coming closer. As if to illustrate the old man's point, a line of taxis turned onto the street and continued down the boulevard.

Each carried a group of officers, five or six apiece. The men inside were packed close, their blue tunics pressed together to appear as a single garment. In one of the passing cabs a man draped a red trouser leg over the door, dangling his boot like a schoolyard delinquent. They watched the taxis weave down the road. A traffic cop ordered civilians to the side to let them pass. "On the way to the front," the old man said. "The declaration can't be too far off."

A few minutes later a battalion of foot soldiers followed the trail the autos had blazed. The men carried elongated rifles with bayonets fixed that towered over them and swayed like glinting stalks. They marched woefully out of step, their blue caps appearing to Gus like a cacophony of notes spilled onto a musical score. Their formation bulged at the sides and straggled at the rear, so that the massed units resembled a cattle drive more than an army off to battle. If this were the kind of discipline the French maintained, the war would be a very short one—they'd be routed at the first engagement. Gus could see their faces now, mustached but young, pale with inexperience. These would be the first to die.

"It's a dangerous time," the old man said. "I fear everything we love is about to change."

"It's a sad time," Gus said. "So much to regret."

"True. And that is why we must do our best to see it through." The old man looked at him. "May I say I am glad you are here to talk about it with me."

Gus thanked him. He took a menu from the waiter. As he listened to the soldiers continue to trudge past, he peered down at the words on the page and did his best to make sense of them.

Curtain Calls

Notes and Acknowledgements

THE DEATH of Jean Jaurès removed the last political obstacle to France's entering The Great War, and in fact Germany and France both declared war only three days after his assassination. The system of alliances in Europe at the time—pitting England, France and Russia on one side, and Germany and Austria-Hungary on the other—had maintained a balance that kept an uneasy peace for more than forty years. But by 1912 tensions among the nations were strained and the governments began arming for war. Only Jaurès's impassioned speech at the First Internationale kept the conflict from breaking out two years sooner than it did.

I've long been fascinated by the political events of that time. World War II, of course, is the better remembered war, but it's World War I, known then as The Great War, that shaped the course of the 20th century and the world we live in today. In fact, the Second World War was an extension of the first—after four brutal years of fighting and stalemate the tensions among the nations were exacerbated, rather than relaxed. The Treaty of Versailles, written by the Allies, ignored traditional cultural boundaries in order to redraw the map of Europe, and it placed economic conditions on defeated Germany that virtually insured a future conflict.

When The Great War ended in 1918, more than 20

million people had died—half of them from disease, as Jaurès predicted. Politically, the last great monarchies of the continent were replaced by popular governments, often via bloody civil wars. Germany, Austria-Hungary and Russia all saw their ruling families deposed. Spain and Italy also saw internal struggles. The Ottoman Empire collapsed. Virtually every nation in the western hemisphere was affected. The war also served as both metaphor and reality for the vast technological changes—an extension of the industrial revolution—that transitioned western civilization from still largely agrarian societies to ones in which mechanization dominated.

I had the original idea for *Curtain Calls* back in my twenties, when I was a college student. I knew my grandfather had been a vaudeville performer, and that he and his partner toured the Americas in the 1900s and teens, and it seemed a great setting for a novel. But Grandpa Gus was old and forgetful—he stayed in show business and didn't marry until he was in his forties, so by the time I became interested in his career, he was afflicted with Alzheimer's and didn't remember accurately. What our family did have, though, was a scrapbook, filled with photos and playbills and a few newspaper articles from that time. That was a good resource to help me envision the times and places in which my grandfather lived, but for the story and characters I turned to my imagination. As a result, Gus, Jack, and Kera are fictions. The French characters, except for Jaurès, are as well, although I did borrow the names of some of Jaurès's contemporaries.

I believed it would work best if the novel were tied to a historical event, something obscure enough to permit literary license, but real enough to give the story a solid foundation in the events of the day. The start of The Great War was the major event of those times, and my thinking centered on incorporating some aspect of the conflict. After a few unsuccessful scenarios I remembered a PBS series I had seen a few years earlier, called *The Great War and the Shaping of the 20th Century,* in which the French politician Jaurès was briefly portrayed. His life and assassination made a fascinating story and seemed open to adaptation. I had my historical hook, and I am indebted to historians Jay Winter and Blaine Baggett for bringing his story to light.

The major events of the last week of Jaurès's life have been rendered accurately, thanks to a marvelous biography, *The Life of Jean Jaurès* by Harvey Goldberg, which is the definitive work in English on the statesman's life. This may shed some light on a few plot developments, such as Jaurès's apparent demise in a train car returning from Brussels, and the newspaper party's switching restaurants in the middle of dinner. These and many others are true events, and it was both a thrill and a challenge to create rationales to explain such episodes.

Of course the dialogue and minor incidents were inventions, as were the roles of his entourage. Their names are real, but the information I found on them, apart from most of them being journalists, was sketchy, and I made the decision to cast them in roles that fit the story.

The assassin Raoul was also a real person. His full name was Raoul Villain (too corny even for a novel) and almost nothing is known about him apart from his affinity for Maeterlinck and his unbalanced mental state, which gave me great leeway in developing his character. Rather amazingly, Villain was incarcerated for the duration of the war, brought to trial in 1919, and then acquitted by a jury.

Jaurès is not well known in the U.S. (He is still considered a national hero in France, and there is a major street in Paris named for him.) A century of history, and the fact that he was a leader of the Socialist party in France may have much to do with his obscurity in this country. That is a shame. One may not agree with his politics, but there is no arguing with his vision and courage. His accomplishments, and his commitment to peace and workers rights (he lived during the time of some of the greatest abuses of labor), make him worthy of remembrance.

To create a feel for the city of Paris during those times I consulted many sources, which are listed in the bibliography, and I am indebted to those many authors and historians for their devotion to the past.

The credit for the opportunity to even write this book goes to my dear wife, Dona. Her support, both emotional and financial, gave me the time to spend countless hours in research and writing.

Many others helped. My sincere thanks to mentors Bruce Holland Rogers and Wayne Ude, and in particular Kathleen Alcalá, who provided expert advice throughout the early drafts. Many of my writing and editing colleagues deserve credit for their honest and thorough critiques that helped me see critical character flaws in the text. Among them are Kelly Davio, Tanya Chernov, Christine Purcell, Stewart Sternberg, Dora Badger, and the late Jon Zech.

Curtain Calls has been a labor of love and respect spanning many years. It's also been an object of literary faith for the last eight years of my writing life—faith in my creative abilities, and faith in the face of scores of rejections at the hands of agents and publishers, who in their literary wisdom continue to flood the reading market with childish fantasies and similarly tired tales. They always tell me how well I write, but that this is not a story the public wants to read. I hope to prove them wrong. Your interest in this book is a part of that effort, and I thank you, sincerely, for your support.

Curtain Calls

About the Author

JOE PONEPINTO is Publisher and Fiction Editor of the *Tahoma Literary Review*. His short stories and criticism have been published in dozens of literary journals. A collection of his stories, titled *The Face Maker and other stories of obsession*, is available through online retailers. He teaches creative writing and associated subjects at Tacoma Community College in Washington.

Bibliography

BOOKS

Cronin, Vincent. *Paris on the Eve, 1900-1914.* New York: St. Martin's Press, 1990.

Franck, Dan. *Bohemian Paris: Picasso, Modigliani, Matisse and the Birth of Modern Art.* Paris: Calmann-Levy, 1998.

Goldberg, Harvey. *The Life of Jean Jaurès.* Madison, Milwaukee and London: The University of Wisconsin Press, 1968.

Haine, W. Scott. *The World of the Paris Café: Sociability Among the French Working Class, 1789-1914.* Baltimore and London: The Johns Hopkins University Press, 1996.

Jones, Colin. *Paris: The Biography of a City.* New York: Penguin Books, 2004.

Seigel, Jerrold. *Bohemian Paris: Culture, Politics and the Boundaries of Bourgeois Life, 1830-1930.* Baltimore: The Johns Hopkins University Press, 1999.

Shattuck, Roger. *The Banquet Years: The Origins of the Avant-Garde in France, 1885 to World War I.* New York: Vintage Books, 1968.

WEB SITES

Note: Some of the web sites consulted in the research of this book have either moved pages, or hosts, or are no longer operating. I've done my best to list the sources used. –JP.

Culin, Stewart. "Street Games of Boys in Brooklyn, New York." *Elliott Avedon Virtual Museum of Games.* 2010.

Duffy, Michael, site editor. *Firstworldwar.com: a multimedia history of world war one.* "Vaudeville: About Vaudeville." *American Masters.* PBS.org, October 8, 1999.

Jaurès, Jean. "Our Goal, 1904: the first editorial in the first issue of *L'Humanité*." *Marxists Internet Archive.* marxists.org/archive/jaures/1904/04/18.htm

Kenrick, John. "New York Theatres: Past and Present." Musicals101.com, 2003.

Kenrick, John. "Researching Vaudeville Performers." Musicals101.com, 2004.

Ladnier, Penny E. Dunlap. "A Year in Fashion, 1910-1918." *The Costume Gallery.* 2004

Mentzer, Ray, site administrator. "Photos of The Great War: World War I Image Archive." *The World War I Document Archive.* The World War I Military History discussion group. gwpda.org/photos/greatwar.htm

Pitt-Payne, James. "James Pitt-Payne's Midi Website." pitt-payne.com/.

Ross, Kelley L. Ph.D. "British Coins before the Florin, Compared to French Coins of the *Ancien Régime*." *The Friesian School.* 2000, 2007, 2011. friesian.com/coins.htm.

Ross, Nelson E. "How to Write Telegrams Properly." *The Telegraph Office.* telegraph-office.com.

Urton, Robin. "The Northern Renaissance." *EyeconArt: Art History Pages.* robinurton.com/history/Renaissance/northrenaiss.htm

"1895 -1914 La Belle Époque." *Fashion-Era.* fashion-era.com.

"Anarcho-syndicalism faces a change in epoch: the CGT up to 1914." *International Communist Current.* January 1, 2005.

"American Beauties: Drawings from the Age of Illustration." *American Beauties.* The Cabinet of American Illustration, Prints and Photographs Division of the Library of Congress. loc.gov/rr/print/swann/ beauties/beauties-object.html

"American Variety Stage." *American Memory.* The Library of Congress. October 19, 1998.

American Vaudeville Museum. vaudeville.org/.

"French Line - CGT - Page 4, (1910-1914 ships)." *Simplon Postcards: The Passenger Ship Website.* simplonpc.co.uk/CGT_PCs_04.html.

Hotel Royal Fromentin. hotelroyalfromentin.com/#

"Slang." *History by Decades.* Writer's Dreamtools. writers-dreamtools.com/view/decades/default.asp?Decade=1910

The Economic History Association. http://eh.net/eha/.

"The History of the American Hospital of Paris." The American Hospital of Paris.

"Vaudeville: A Dazzling Display of Heterogeneous Splendor." *American Studies at the University of Virginia.* University of Virginia.

Made in the USA
Columbia, SC
13 June 2017